THE CRUELTY
OF MORNING

A couple of hours or more passed routinely.
The sun, not quite so burning hot now, had
moved around in the sky and shone on Johnny
again. He basked in its gentler warmth. He
felt drowsy.

But suddenly he was startled out of his
pleasant half-wakefulness by a piercing scream
which rose above the holiday clamour and
shattered his fleeting sense of peace for ever.
It was unnaturally high, a scream of almost
inhuman shock and fear.

Johnny jumped to his feet, no laziness about
him now, and like all holidaymakers around
him, ran to the sea wall and peered in the
direction of the screaming.

It was Jenny Stone he could hear. Jenny
Stone overcome with shock, yelling her heart
out.

Hilary Bonner has been a journalist for twenty years.
She is a former Showbusiness Editor of the *Mail on
Sunday* and the *Daily Mirror*, and has written several
non-fiction books on showbusiness. She now works
as a freelance, covering film, television and theatre.
She lives in Somerset. *The Cruelty of Morning* is her
first novel.

Also by Hilary Bonner

Benny: a biography of Benny Hill
   (with Dennis Kirkland)
Rene and Me: the story of *'Allo 'Allo*
   star Gorden Kaye
Heartbeat – The Real Life Story
Journeyman (with Clive Gunnell)

HILARY BONNER

The
CRUELTY
of
MORNING

Mandarin

Published in the United Kingdom in 1997 by
Mandarin Paperbacks

5 7 9 10 8 6

Copyright © Hilary Bonner 1995

The right of Hilary Bonner to be identified as the author
of this work has been asserted by her in accordance
with the Copyright, Designs and Patents Act, 1988

First published in the United Kingdom in 1995 by Mandarin Books

Mandarin Paperbacks
Random House UK Limited
20 Vauxhall Bridge Road, London SW1V 2SA

Random House Australia (Pty) Limited
20 Alfred Street, Milsons Point, Sydney
New South Wales 2061, Australia

Random House New Zealand Limited
18 Poland Road, Glenfield, Auckland 10, New Zealand

Random House South Africa (Pty) Limited
Endulini, 5a Jubilee Road, Parktown 2193, South Africa

Random House UK Limited Reg. No. 954009

A CIP catalogue record for this book
is available from the British Library

Papers used by Random House UK Limited
are natural, recyclable products made from wood grown in
sustainable forests. The manufacturing processes conform to
the environmental regulations of the country of origin

Printed and bound in the United Kingdom by
Cox & Wyman Ltd, Reading, Berkshire

ISBN 0 7493 1972 0

FOR MY MOTHER, with love and gratitude.
FOR MY FATHER, in memory always.
AND FOR CLIVE, for never doubting . . .

PART ONE

The Cruelty of Morning

It is just before dawn
and the street
beneath my feet
is colder
than the air.

I have left you behind
darling
Left you in the night
where you belong
In the warm sticky darkness
of my bed
In the raging sweet madness
of my head.

I have left you behind
darling
Bathed in the glory
moonlight creates
Cursed eternally
when daylight breaks.

There is no place for you
darling
in the chill of dawning
No room for you
darling
in the cruelty of morning.

Prologue

Jenny Stone was away with the fishes. Her powerful crawl had taken her right out to sea beyond the last of the rocks that stretched jaggedly away from the cliffs to the south of Pelham Bay. She paused for a while in her strenuous swimming, and floated, arms outstretched, eyes shut, basking in the hot sunshine like a contented whale. It was the first Sunday in August 1970, another gorgeous day in an unusually hot summer. A day Jenny, then only seventeen, would never forget.

A piece of seaweed brushed against her face and she flicked it idly away. A large lump of wood bumped her right shoulder, and Jenny, eyes still closed, reached out with the finger tips of her right hand.

She touched something very cold and clammy. Suddenly her sense of smell was overcome with a stench she had never experienced before – yet she recognised it. And before her eyes were properly open, Jenny knew what she was going to see.

Next to her in the water was the body of a young woman. She was naked to the waist. Her bright red skirt, torn and ragged, billowed with the rhythmic roll of the ocean. It was this material, hanging on the body in shreds, that Jenny had mistaken for seaweed. The dead woman's legs and arms floated stiff and angular as wood. Her face was turned to one side, eyes open and bulging, looking at Jenny in sightless horror. For a brief terrible instant the two faces, one full of life and vitality and hope for the future, the other distorted by violent death, were pressed together by the currents.

One

It had been just another row in a newspaper office. Her reaction had been way over the top and she already knew it. She had very nearly broken down and wept.

The tears pricked persistently against the back of her eyes. She just succeeded in keeping them back. Only once before, in twenty years, had Fleet Street made her cry.

Then she had been a young reporter of twenty-four, and following a particularly virulent, although not that unusual, attack from the news editor, had fled from the newsroom to the ladies' loo, desperately biting her bottom lip until, with relief, she could thrust shut the door of a cubicle. And there, alone with a lavatory pan, the floods of despair had overcome her. She had been two years into her first job on a national daily at the time, and already hardened enough to be angry at her own weakness. She had indulged in a good cry and then gone back to work. What else?

On her return to the newsroom, tear damage repaired as much as possible, the old hand reporter whom she sat alongside had not looked up from his typewriter.

'I'm surprised at you Jen,' he said quietly. 'Letting the old bugger get to you. Thought you knew better.'

Now she was forty-two. Of course she knew

better. She had coped with the toughest of jobs for twenty years, she had travelled around the world on the biggest and best stories, she had loved almost every minute of it, and she had finally made it to assistant editor of one of the top tabloid papers, the *Globe*. Well – until a few minutes previously she had been. So perhaps she didn't know better, after all.

It was May 1995. Early afternoon on an unseasonably hot day. She realised suddenly that she had been almost running through the streets. The silk shirt beneath the jacket of her linen suit was damp with sweat. The sleeves had started to wrinkle seriously under the arms and around the elbows. In the middle of everything else some small distant part of her brain sent a sharp reminder that she really must never buy linen again, however attractive the stuff looked on a hanger in a shop window.

She put a hand up to flick ineffectively at the fringe of her thick brown hair – it was stuck to her forehead. Her hand, she noticed in a detached sort of way, was shaking.

She paused and stepped to one side of the throng of people hurrying along the pavement. Typical London. Everyone rushing about trance-like. You could strip naked and stand screaming and nobody would notice. If they did they would quickly look away.

She stepped into the welcome shadow of a towering office block and leaned heavily against the wall. She was breathing in quick gasps, like a panting dog. Ridiculous.

'Come on Jen, pull yourself together,' she told herself.

Two passing young girls in micro skirts fleetingly

caught her eye and quickly looked away. True to London form.

What was left of her beleaguered brain shot off at a tangent again. 'I dressed like that once, several million years ago,' she thought to herself. This time her lips did not move. Definitely no more talking to herself in the street. Whatever next?

She fished in her shoulder bag for her mobile phone and dialled a number.

'Yo,' said a voice at the other end of the phone. She felt immediately more cheerful. A little light relief beckoned.

'Yo? What the hell does that mean? Have you joined the American marines?'

The man's voice became weary. 'Jennifer, how lovely to hear from you.'

'You're a liar, Dominic. What are you doing at home in the middle of a Wednesday afternoon anyway?'

'I'm resting.'

'You're what?'

'I'm resting. I have been suffering from exhaustion. Miles and I discussed it sensibly and now I take two afternoons' rest a week.'

'God, Dominic, you are a wimp.'

'No doubt by your Amazonian standards I am, Jennifer. But we can't all be that butch, can we? Would you like to speak to my wife?'

'Yes, I would like to speak to Anna. But you know, try as I do, I still can't think of her as your wife, Dominic. I just can't.'

Anna McDonald, her oldest and best friend, came on the line.

'Have you really got nothing better to do with your day than bait poor Dominic?'

'Not entirely one-sided, Anna. He's improving. And, actually, from now on I may indeed have nothing better to do with my day.'

'What?'

'Come to Joe Allen's for supper and I'll tell you all about it.'

'Tell me now. I can't come to supper. It's Dommie's half day.'

'No supper, no story. All will be told only over many large margueritas. Incidentally, how does Dominic get to fix himself two afternoons off a week?'

'Because he's brilliant. He's the best computer scientist in Britain. At least, he's convinced his bosses he is. And that's real brilliance.'

'It's obscene.'

'And you're jealous.'

'True. I'll pick you up seven-thirty.'

'If you are driving I'm definitely not coming. I remember the last time . . . just. And you insisted you were on the wagon . . .'

'OK. I'll get a taxi . . . Christ, you've reminded me! Brain death is setting in. I stormed off like a half-wit and left the car in the office car park. I'd better get it out of there before somebody else does that for me.'

'Jennifer, what have you done?'

'I'll tell you at Joe's. Seven-thirty?'

'Oh, all right. When I'm divorced can I bring Pandora and come and live at your place?'

'Only if you change the poor innocent's name . . .'

She pushed the 'end' button and noticed her hand

had stopped shaking. Thank God for Anna. Through two marriages, twenty-five years and countless ups and downs, Anna had always been there. Of course she would come to supper, and not just to pick up on the latest drama. She knew she was needed. And there was never anyone better than Anna in a crisis.

The memory of how she had first met Anna remained quite vivid to Jennifer and never failed to make her smile. Barely into her twenties then, Anna had already managed to appear totally sophisticated, Jennifer recalled.

The two women had both been hired on the same newspaper training scheme. Booked into a hostel on her first night away from home, eighteen-year-old Jennifer had found a nearby cafe and settled down for supper alone.

'Would you mind if I joined you?' asked a cool and round-vowelled voice. Anna, a doctor's daughter, had been brought up in Wimbledon and was conspicuously English middle-class in those days.

'I do so hate eating alone, don't you?' she continued.

Jennifer looked up for the first time into what she came to regard as arguably the most deceptively gentle grey eyes in the world and stammered her agreement.

Later, when they came to share a flat, Anna had arrived with one neat suitcase of extraordinary design which, after a seemingly effortless flick, had sprung miraculously open to reveal Anna's clothes, uncreased, immaculate, and sporting several designer labels, suspended in perfect order from their own hangers.

Jennifer, surrounded at the time by crumpled

debris and a selection of tatty carrier bags, had been impressed ever since. And thinking back to those early days with her friend had indeed made her smile.

The original shock reaction to her own behaviour had faded now. Jennifer had a game plan for the rest of the day, and possibly for the rest of her life, and she wanted to get on with it. First a quick dash back to the office car park, then home for a short course in revival – a long bath and several cups of tea. She hailed a taxi.

Back at the *Globe*, the key card still operated the doors to the car park. That was something. The Porsche continued to give her a fleeting sense of self satisfaction, although lessened somewhat by the dents and bruises on both sides. She told herself that driving a battered Porsche was a status symbol. The car was as smooth, as tight, and as quick as ever, but it was more than six years old and she had known that next time around she would not get another company motor like it. The days when she had swung the deal which included that car were long gone. Next time around it would be a small family saloon and be thankful. Yuk.

Oh well, she'd probably solved that problem. It was unlikely that the *Globe* would ever again be providing her with any kind of company car.

She slotted herself behind the wheel, thrust the gear lever forward and roared up the ramp, bouncing over the sleeping policemen. The tyres squealed as she jerked to a stop and prepared to use her key card again.

She looked at her watch. A ladies' Rolex. She had stormed out of the office at around one-thirty. At least nobody could accuse her of throwing a terminal tantrum after lunch. She was just in time to miss the late afternoon build up of traffic; she should make it back to her house in Richmond soon after three-thirty. Plenty of time to recharge the batteries before going around to Anna's. That bath, a knock your socks off shower, a pot of English breakfast tea, a bit of a sleep, an early evening gin and tonic, and a little pre-dinner sparring with Dominic. Things were looking up.

Unlike Dominic she was not used to being at home in the middle of a weekday afternoon. As she lay back in a bubbly bath clutching a steaming mug of tea and listening to a play on Radio Four, she thought she could get to like it. The rest of the afternoon passed peacefully. The phone rang several times. She did not answer it. The word was undoubtedly already getting around and she did not want to talk to anybody yet – except Anna.

She ordered a minicab for seven that evening.

'You're early, this must be serious,' said Anna.

She and Jennifer had always been an odd couple, the one appearing to be everything the other was not, both physically and in personality. Jennifer, striking looking but nothing more, was exceptionally tall and confidently forceful, bordering on brash on a bad day, inclined to toss her mane of thick dark hair when things didn't suit her. Anna was barely five foot one, petite in build, neat of manner, seemingly diffident in behaviour, and quite devastatingly pretty. Her wispy white-blonde hair, falling straight to her shoulders from a central parting, framed a perfectly even-featured elfin face almost always composed into the most pleasant of expressions.

She had an air of fragility about her. Confronted

by adversity, Anna would smile in apparent deference and flutter her eyelashes. She really did flutter them. Jennifer thought Anna was the only woman she had ever actually seen do so. Anna was acutely aware of her femininity and had always used it ruthlessly. Even now, well into her forties, she was the kind of woman men referred to as a 'sweet girl'.

The very thought always made Jennifer smile. Appearances could indeed be deceptive. Anna had handled Fleet Street better than anyone Jennifer knew. One of the secrets of her success was that she was invariably underestimated. Jennifer could not remember her ever failing in anything she had set out to achieve, and joked that she had chosen Anna to be her closest friend because she knew she could never survive with her as an enemy. Anna invariably got her own way without those around her even noticing. Jennifer had always been open-mouthed in admiration of her and quite green with envy. You couldn't even attempt to play the game the way Anna did when you were near six feet tall with the shoulders of a lock forward.

In fact Anna had a brain to die for, plus total confidence in her abilities, and was always quite certain of the various directions in which she wished to take her life. She had been a senior executive in the Murdoch organisation, widely tipped to be the first woman editor of a national daily, when she'd decided she would rather be a mother instead.

She had been almost forty when she met Dominic McDonald, fell wildly in love for probably the first time – in the past it had not been Anna's role to fall in love with the men in her life, they all fell desperately in love with her while she graciously accepted it – married him and became pregnant within a few months.

When their child was born she announced with her usual certainty that she was going to give her daughter the attention she had previously only given to her career, that she would be quitting The Street at least until Pandora came of school age, and that from now on she would be using her married name only.

Astonished pleas from friends and colleagues, and even, quite remarkably, from Murdoch himself, did nothing to shake her from her intentions.

At the time Jennifer thought Anna had gone stark staring mad. Now she wasn't so sure. But the events had always given an edge to her relationship with her friend's husband. Jennifer was honest enough to admit to herself that she did not like the power she felt Dominic had over Anna. Meanwhile her friend, sharp and cool as ever, merely accepted that her best friend and her husband were each jealous of the other's place in her affections, and that was, after all, quite as it should be.

It was no accident that while Jennifer waited for Anna to gather up coat and handbag, Dominic remained upstairs, resolutely engrossed in the task of putting Pandora to bed. Long, lanky, bespectacled, clever-faced, academic Dominic – a cliché on legs.

'I told him you were in crisis and he said that would doubtless make you more obnoxious than ever and went into hiding,' Anna remarked.

Over the first marguerita in Joe Allen's, Jennifer related her news. 'I walked out. Jack told me next week's features were crap just one time too many. So I resigned.'

'Good God, is *that* all?'

Anna was totally unsympathetic.

'You've had a row with the editor. Send in the bloody cavalry. That's what editors are for, isn't it? He won't even mention your so-called resignation in the morning, as well you know.'

'I'm not going to work in the morning.'

'Don't be so childish. Of course you're going to work in the morning. You always do. You're a survivor.'

'Not any more. After I'd screamed obscene abuse at the bugger, I put my resignation in writing.'

'So? He'll tear it up, won't he? He adores you, you know he does.'

'Hmph. He's got a bloody fine way of showing it. And I've had enough. I'm off.'

'Don't be ridiculous.'

'Ridiculous or not, I'm going home to North Devon tomorrow and I have every intention of staying there.'

'Really?'

Anna giggled.

'I'd love to hear what Marcus would have to say about that,' she said.

Jennifer raised her eyebrows and tried to look disdainful. Marcus was her ex-husband. The remarkable Sir Marcus Piddell, newspaper tycoon and government minister. He had begun life as a local paper reporter in North Devon and risen relentlessly to the top. His ambition and his singleness of purpose had always been breathtaking.

With explicit and colourful use of language, Jennifer told Anna exactly how little she cared about Marcus's opinion on any damn thing.

'Have you been at the gin already?' asked her friend. Yes, Jennifer admitted, ordering another round of double margueritas. But that did not alter her judgement about either her ex-husband or her future. She knew with dazzling clarity that Fleet Street was over for her. It was, in any case, a world that had changed almost beyond recognition. To survive, as indeed she was more than able, you had to change with it. She did not want to do that any more.

Anna, of angel looks and tiger tongue, was unrelenting. 'I don't believe a word of it. All you need is a night on the piss, which I assume is why I was dragged out to play. So let's change the subject, shall we? Let's talk about something else apart from bloody newspapers.'

'I used to think there was nothing else,' began Jennifer.

Anna sighed in exaggerated weariness. Jennifer promised temporary obedience and picked up the menu. The two women ordered a hefty selection of Joe Allen's upmarket comfort food and by the time they reached the Sticky Toffee Pudding stage Jennifer had begun to feel better.

'Have you noticed, those two guys over there can't keep their eyes off us,' she remarked.

Anna peered across the room. Sitting at a corner table was a PR man she vaguely recognised and another young man.

'Bent as ninepenny bits,' she announced.

'Rubbish, they've both fallen instantly in love with me,' said Jennifer. 'Take me home before I disgrace myself.'

They shared a cab, dropping off Anna first. She crept upstairs and eased herself into her side of the king-sized double bed, trying desperately and unsuccessfully not to wake Dominic. He mumbled something uncharitable about drunken women, and within seconds she had sunk into a deep alcohol-induced sleep.

It seemed like just five minutes later that the telephone rang.

Dominic drowsily picked up the receiver, cursed, and passed the phone to Anna. It was Jennifer.

'Christ, what time is it?'

'It's a quarter to seven, and I'm on the M4 heading west and I feel great.'

Anna hauled herself into some kind of wakefulness.

'You're still pissed, you maniac. Drive slowly for once, will you? Where on earth are you going, anyway?'

Giggles wafted across the airwaves. 'I'm going home to mummy of course. I told you I was going to. And I wanted you to be the first to know that I haven't changed my mind . . .'

'Jennifer, with the hangover will come remorse, I promise you. Remember Butch Cassidy and the Sundance Kid.'

Fifteen years ago, a Fleet Street legend had been created and two young journalists earned their cowboy nicknames when, after a drunken party, they took themselves off to Heathrow Airport and boarded the first plane to Los Angeles. They were half way across the Atlantic before they became sober enough to realise what they had done.

'Yeah, I remember. They both stayed in the States and made good lives for themselves. I remember that too.'

'Yes. Well, if you are really going home to mummy, Pelham Bay is hardly Hollywood, is it?'

'Annie, I have a house in Richmond worth half a million even in a slump. I am going to buy a cottage by the sea and eat lotuses for ever. I don't need all the props any more . . .'

'Oh yeah? When are you giving the Porsche back?'

The cellnet airwaves quavered slightly as Jennifer's blasphemous description of what Jack and the *Globe* would have to do to reclaim their car shot through the skies. Unadorned with four-letter words, the message was simply that if 'they' wanted the Porsche, first 'they' had to find it and then 'they' had to take it from her.

Anna began to laugh. Dominic grumpily got out of bed muttering that he might just as well now.

'I've got to go. Take care, you daft old bat. Ring me when you get to mummy's.'

With the last remark Anna found herself in convulsions of laughter. The giggles were infectious that morning.

'Mummy's! Poor bloody mummy, I say. She's really done it, you know, she's really chucked it all in,' she spluttered to Dominic, who was trying to look bored.

It would not be long before he would give in to his curiosity. That was one thing about Jennifer Stone, she had never been boring. Just about every other darned thing, but boring? Never!

As she approached the M5 turn-off at Bristol, Jennifer began to feel a relentless drowsiness.

'Sobriety, hate it,' she muttered to herself. And she wondered if her extraordinary sense of cheerfulness and adventure would wear off with the remains of last night's excesses.

She pulled in to the Bristol service station, parked, wound down the passenger window a couple of inches, fully reclined her driver's seat and fell soundly asleep.

It was a couple of hours later before she was fully awake. She fished her toilet bag from the untidy jumble which in the early hours she had flung into the front of the Porsche, and headed for the ladies' loo. There were smudges of old make-up around her eyes. Ugh. Her mouth felt like somebody's old socks and she suspected that her breath smelt much the same. After a haphazard clean-up, a quick rub of expensive moisturiser and a good scrub of her teeth, she was more or less ready for the day ahead.

She threw her toilet bag back into the car, checked her cash situation, picked up her laptop computer, and headed for the self-service cafeteria where she ordered a large pot of black coffee.

From the pocket of her black designer jeans she fished out the letter from a London estate agent that she had – with amazing clarity – thrust there just before leaving home. It was a round-robin expressing interest in her big detached Richmond Hill property. She expertly tapped into the computer a brief letter authorising them to put the house on the market. She had that to thank Marcus Piddell for, if nothing else. They had bought the house together when they married. She her share with all she possessed in the world, he his with just a portion of the astonishing amount of wealth he had acquired over the years. He had offered to buy the whole house himself and put it in both their names. She, as ever, had been too fiercely independent to agree.

She had, to some degree or other, loved Marcus probably throughout her adult life. When she'd said she could no longer live with him, she thought Marcus had ultimately been relieved, in spite of putting up his usual fight to keep her – out of habit more than likely; Marcus never expected to lose anything.

He had eventually offered Jennifer a lump sum of £200,000 and their Richmond house with mortgage paid up as full settlement. A clean severance of all their mutual ties. She had agreed with equal relief. Her lawyer had pointed out that she could have taken her husband for far more, but Jennifer just wanted out. If there had been children she would probably have taken a different attitude. But there were none. And even as things were and having quit her job, as long as she could sell the house all right she was a fairly wealthy woman. She still had the two hundred grand in the bank plus a few quid she had saved herself. It wouldn't last her long the way she had so far lived her life, but starvation was not just around the corner.

She ordered more coffee and a large Danish pastry. Fully fortified, she strolled back to the Porsche and plugged the lap-top into her portable bubble-jet printer. She signed the letter, fed it into the car fax, and watched it obediently wing its way back to the London estate agent.

It was ten-thirty. At the *Globe*, the morning would just be getting going, the senior executives putting together their story lists for the eleven-fifteen conference. It would be around then that she would be missed, that it might occur to Jack for undoubtedly the first time that her resignation had been serious. Arrogant bastard.

She unplugged the fax, switched the phone back to normal and dialled Pelham Bay 534536. Her mother sounded wonderfully reassuringly normal. She couldn't stop because she was going to Safeways with Auntie Pat. Jenny was on her way down? Oh, that was lovely. But what did she want for her dinner? How long was she staying, anyway, and to what did her mother owe the pleasure?

Old habits die hard. Accustomed always to protecting her mother from anything that might worry her, Jennifer heard herself reply that she had taken a couple of weeks' holiday. Any chance of a bed? It'll cost you, said her mother.

Jennifer smiled as she pushed the end button on the phone and then switched it off. From now on she would be using the mobile only for outgoing calls. She was on the loose. A rolling Stone.

Mrs Margaret Stone, widow of respected local builder Reg Stone, had never understood one jot about her daughter's life. And Jennifer neither imagined nor desired that it could ever be otherwise. There was warmth and security and a whole different world back at number sixteen, Seaview Road, Pelham Bay. And her mother's ageing had not changed that. Mrs Stone was almost eighty now, but she kept a fine home. All that should gleam, gleamed. The store cupboard was never bare. The patch of grass in the little back garden looked as if someone had trimmed it with a pair of scissors. There was always fruit in the bowl on the old sideboard and in summer flowers filled the vase standing before the fireplace.

Jennifer arrived there just before one o'clock. She

found the key – on the ledge as always – and let herself in. She switched the kettle on to boil and opened the cake tin she found in its usual place in the pantry. Inside were a pile of her mother's currant buns. She took one and bit deep into the crumbly sweetness. She'd never found better baking anywhere in the world.

The front door opened with a familiar rattle. In walked her mother and aunt.

'You'll not eat your dinner now, my girl,' said her mother.

Her smile was broad and ever-welcoming. She put down her shopping bags and opened her arms. Like a little girl Jennifer went to her and hugged her.

'Hello, my darling,' she said.

In the bags were hot pasties.

'No time to do you a proper dinner,' grumbled her mother amiably. 'There's tinned fruit and clotted cream for afters. You'll stay, Pat, won't you?'

They sat around the kitchen table. The local paper, still folded, lay on the worktop. And it was then the headline caught Jennifer's eye. 'Murder Inquiry Reopened After 25 Years. Did they lock up the wrong man?'

Jennifer felt her mother watching her. Margaret Stone's mind had yet to be affected by age. She was pin-sharp.

'All right, maid?' she asked gently.

'Yes, of course,' said Jennifer.

'Brings back a few memories, aye?'

Jennifer switched the conversation, asking about old schoolfriends, the welfare of other relatives living nearby, how the pebble ridge had held up to the early spring storms, and why the dickens had the council built a car park right over the river estuary by the new motorway bridge, as if that wasn't bad enough already.

All the while she could feel her mind slipping back in time. As soon as she could politely leave the table and the room, she used weariness as an excuse and retreated to her old bedroom, the familiar chintzy one at the back of the house.

Mrs Stone noticed that her daughter had quietly picked up the local paper and folded it under her arm.

Two

Jenny Stone had come face to face with death that long ago August Sunday in Pelham Bay. Twenty-five years later, everything remained quite vivid. That headline in the local paper was devastating. 'Did they lock up the wrong man?', she read. 'Police yesterday reopened inquiries into the murder of a woman strangled in Pelham Bay in 1970, and the disappearance of another young woman. The move follows the death of retired local businessman Bill Turpin. It is believed that vital new evidence has been discovered in his remote cliffside home which could also link Turpin with the murder of the Earl of Lynmouth twenty-five years previously.'

Jenny, now Jennifer Stone, well-known journalist and former wife of a Government minister, needed only to glance at that local paper story to find herself overwhelmed by a sense of panic.

She stood uncertainly by the window of her comfortable old bedroom in the little terraced house just a few hundred yards from the sea at Pelham Bay. The sea in which she had found the body. The village where so many demons had been unleashed.

She wrapped herself in the ugly old candlewick dressing gown still hanging behind the pink-painted door. It smelt of mothballs and felt wonderful. Rough and warm and reassuring. She lay down on the big wood-framed bed and shut her eyes, but it was no good. She reached out for the paper which she had folded on the bedside table and read that story again. Carefully. Slowly. What did it mean? Did the police think Bill Turpin had committed the murder? If he had, then there had been a terrible injustice all those years ago. But then, perhaps she had always secretly suspected that. A certain sense of guilt had been with her from the start.

And that other disappearance? She skimmed the print once more. No, no new details, not yet.

Her head ached dully now. It was more than last night's booze. This was the pain of an old wound. It was as if it were yesterday. So clear the picture. That day when one part of her existence had ended and another begun, the day Marcus entered her life for the second time, never properly to leave it again.

He had been plain Mark Piddle then, a silly name for a young man who was all sorts of things but never silly.

Twenty-five years later she could still hear the clamour of Pelham Bay at play on that busy summer Sunday. She could smell the tang of the salt in the air and taste the very vinegar of the sea. And once more she heard and smelt and tasted all else that came later.

Jennifer Stone was not the only one who read that local paper story with special interest.

In his penthouse flat overlooking the River Thames, Sir Marcus Piddell was enjoying his breakfast. There was freshly squeezed orange juice, expresso coffee and that morning's croissants from the best baker in town, brought to him as usual by his daily who was presently engaged in making his bed. It was unseasonably warm and he was sitting on the terrace in a Victorian rocking chair, his Gucci-clad feet resting on the rail. God, he was feeling good. Last night they had sent around a couple of girls from his favourite Soho sex club again. He always felt more awake and alive than ever after a night of strenuous, imaginative sex. It recharged his batteries. There was a warm feeling in the pit of his stomach and his genitals were still tingling inside his jockey shorts. He shut his eyes and began to relive last night's pleasures. It was almost as if he were touching the warm tender flesh again. A sudden sense of the tastes and the smells he had experienced overwhelmed him. He felt himself growing. When he was an adolescent the size of his sexual organs had actually embarrassed him. But not for long. He smiled at the memory, and reached down to his crotch to adjust slightly the bulge there. That was better. He could still think himself into an erection without even meaning to. Not bad for a man of forty-eight. The Soho joint was so much easier than a relationship – and they knew what he liked. He supposed he was taking a risk. But, what the hell! He was an unmarried man again, a free agent. Anyway he couldn't help it. He never had been able to. He had always taken risks.

He stretched. Self-satisfied. Super-successful. He loved the mornings, especially bright mornings like this. Always had done. He had never needed much sleep, and he was grateful for that. There were two things he believed all successful people had in common. An ability to manage with very little sleep and a relentless sex drive. Well, he *would* think that. Marcus Piddell could not imagine anyone sleeping their life away, and he could not survive without regular and exciting sex tailored to his special desires.

He resisted the temptation to unzip his flies and

reach in there to play with himself a little. He must stop thinking about last night's excesses or he would never get any work done.

He had already listened to the early news bulletins on the radio and read all the national papers. He retained the journalist's obsession with being well informed. He started to open the bundle of local papers from his Devon constituency. He had easily won the nomination as parliamentary candidate for his old stamping ground when the seat became vacant. Everybody knew how they like local-born men and women to represent them in Devon. He had walked the election – even though the story of his name change became a running joke in the press. They had a field day relating how plain Mark had suddenly become classier Marcus, and, most amusing to them of all, how Piddell had once been spelt P-I-D-D-L-E and pronounced accordingly – but only the papers he didn't control, of course, and it had not seemed to do him any harm. He was still a local boy made good. His rise to fame and fortune had been fast, and the new name – with emphasis firmly on the second syllable – merely something he picked up along the way. A flashier by-line, better sounding on the phone – and above all, no longer a name people laughed at.

When he stood for election, he was the chairman of Recorder Group Newspapers, a multi-millionaire businessman with enormous influence. Many of his contemporaries had been surprised that he should want to enter parliament. Marcus simply saw it as the next step. He'd had to resign the Recorder chairmanship when he became a government minister, of course, but that had made little practical difference. He still owned by far the majority shareholding in the group, and there was nobody at R.G.N. who doubted that he remained the only real boss.

He quite fancied being Prime Minister. That was his true motivation and, always brashly confident, he saw no reason why he should not be P.M., certainly well before he was fifty-five, which was still seven years away. That would give him at least ten years before his energy started to go. It would go, he supposed, although he could not really imagine that.

He glanced at his watch. Still only eight o'clock. Plenty of time to scan the constituency news sheets before his car arrived at eight-thirty to take him to the House. He liked to be at his office there before nine, even when he had stayed in the chamber till two or three that same morning. It unnerved the others a bit. They hadn't cut their teeth on daily newspapers like him. As an editor for almost ten years, he had developed the stamina to guide the last editions onto the presses in the early hours of the morning and then be back in the office before half the day shift had arrived. Kept 'em on the alert that way.

He opened the *Durraton Gazette* first. He always did. Extraordinary to think that he virtually owned it now. He chuckled to himself. It wasn't a bad old rag. It never had been. Then he spotted the second story on the front. Not even the lead. Old Bill Turpin was dead and the police were going to reopen inquiries into the Pelham Bay murder and the disappearance of a second young woman at the same time. He was just five hours ahead of his ex-wife in North Devon, reading that same insignificant local paper article.

It shook him to the toes of his Yves St Laurent silk socks.

Like Jennifer he scanned the story with professional speed. Like Jennifer he was looking for mention of something more. His eyes flicked down the page. Nothing to worry about. Not yet. He realised he had been holding his breath. He let it out with a rush. He could breathe again. At least for now.

Marcus made himself stay calm. He resolutely carried on reading through the other newspapers in his pile. At this stage in his career he could do without the reappearance of any ghosts from his past, however loose the link with him might appear to be and from however long ago. But he was a true survivor, and the story had not even made the nationals yet. It would do so, though, he was sure of that.

He picked up the draft of the speech he was to give in the House that afternoon. He put it down again.

His mind slipped back over the years – to the very beginning of his obsession with Jennifer Stone. He could see his white Mini Cooper parked outside the big Victorian house on the hill in which he rented a tiny flat, high above Pelham Bay. He could still see his girlfriend, Irene Nichols, so willing and compliant, lying, eternally grateful for almost any kind of attention, in his bed; and in his head, twenty-five years on, he heard the ring of the old black telephone calling him out on the murder inquiry. Down to the beach to see Bill Turpin.

Marcus could not help himself. He was right there in Pelham Bay with Jennifer, poor little Irene, and all the rest of them, on that hot August Sunday in 1970.

In his new bungalow overlooking the sea above Pelham, proud father Johnny Cooke was also doing battle with the past. There were many who could not understand how Johnny had felt able to return to

Pelham Bay after all that had happened. But where else could he have gone?

Johnny hugged his sleeping son so tightly the little boy started awake and began to whimper.

A couple of days earlier, Johnny Cooke had been checking the week's accounts when the phone rang. It was the new Detective Inspector in Durraton. Johnny immediately felt the familiar sweaty palm sensation, and that blankness camè over him again. Could he pop down to the station, the inspector wanted to know.

Johnny was suddenly very cold. Sweating, but cold. He was an established local businessman now. True, he was struggling to keep everything afloat as the recession took its toll on the holiday trade, but he was pretty sure he could hold it together.

The D.I. had been surprisingly sensitive and quick to reassure.

'It's all right Mr Cooke,' he said. 'We just want to let you know that Bill Turpin's died. The postman found him. You seem to be the nearest he has to family, and there are one or two bits and pieces we'd like you to help us clear up.'

Johnny felt the relief wash over him. He had spent seventeen years of his life in jail. He could not stand the smell of disinfectant. He could not sleep in a room with the door shut. Every morning he woke to the fear that he was still locked in a cell. And only after he had opened his eyes did any peace return. The normality of his life was a fragile thing.

Now having been to the police station and learned of the finds that had been made in Bill's cottage and what they might indicate, Johnny just could not think straight. He had suffered so much. He closed his eyes to try to shut off the memories. But it was no good. It never was.

Detective Inspector Todd Mallett, Durraton's new detective inspector, had been just a lad with nothing much on his mind except how to get his way with the temperamental girlfriend who lay beside him in the hot sunshine that August Sunday. Now, twenty-five years later, he was having a drink in the bar of The Shipwright's Arms with his father, retired Chief Superintendent Phil Mallett, who had been the detective chief inspector in charge of the murder inquiry – an inquiry about to be reopened.

Throughout his boyhood, Todd Mallett had been aware of his father's unease over this one case, the case which had blighted his career. Phil Mallett was a decent old-fashioned copper who always did everything strictly by the book. He would never cut corners. He would never bend the rules to gain a conviction. During his entire working life it had not once occurred to him to take a corrupt course of action in order to further his career. And so the Pelham Bay murder case had caused him sleepless night after sleepless night.

After it was all over he had been so unsettled by the result of the case that he had asked to be transferred out of the C.I.D. back to the uniformed branch.

Now a pint of best bitter stood untouched on the table before him and Phil Mallett sat with his hands clasped in his lap, eyes cast downwards. He felt that his worst fears were about to be realised.

His son took a swig of his own pint. It really wasn't fair. His father was one of the few top cops he had ever known who really gave a damn for anything except their own skins and their pensions. He placed a hand on the older man's shoulder. 'Look, nobody is ever going to blame you, dad, you did all you could,' he said. 'And anyway, we don't know anything for sure yet . . .'

Phil Mallett continued to study his big hands, calloused from years of working in the garden of his beloved moorland home. He didn't much care what people thought. He still blamed himself. He had not been strong enough back then. He had put his suspicions to one side. He had given in to the pressures around him. It was possible that a young man had lost his youth unjustly because of him.

Ironically it was his son who had called him to the newly set-up operations centre following the discoveries in Bill Turpin's cottage. And Phil Mallett wasn't sure he could live with them. The beer was still untouched in front of him.

'Thanks for the pint, Todd,' he said.

He rose to his feet and strode to the door, a big man, ramrod straight, a typical old-fashioned copper. His son followed, as tall but slimmer around the waist. Todd was a thoroughly modern policeman, a computer expert, sharper than his father, a bit of a wheeler dealer, yet decent enough – still a chip off the old block.

Phil Mallett was proud of his son. Much prouder than he was of himself.

In the street outside the village hall, where the special murder inquiry operations room had been set up, he could smell the sea clearly, hear the waves beating against the rocks. Strange. It was as if it were yesterday.

Three

At the far end of the seafront down in Pelham Bay, there is a seawater swimming pool that was originally called The Lido, and always will be by the locals – even though during the boom time of the 1980s they heated the water and renamed it Pool Riviera. Next to it, opposite the beach huts, is a public lavatory with a flat roof. And there, on the first Sunday in August, 1970, the young Jennifer Stone was sunbathing with the gang, Liz Butler, the Mallett boys, Angela Smith, and Janet Farrell. A funny place to sunbathe – but it caught the sun perfectly all day long and a low wall kept off the wind from the sea.

Jenny, they all called her then. She was seventeen years old. Just. Her birthday had been celebrated only a few days earlier. She lay with her long skinny legs outstretched, back comfortably supported by an upturned kitchen chair from Angela Smith's parents' beach hut across the footpath leading to the cliffs. A copy of *Cobbett's Rural Rides* was in her left hand, propped in the saucer hollow where her tummy would have been if she were not beanpole thin. Beanpole. They called her that sometimes. Jenny peered against the dazzling bright sun, no longer pretending to read, and kidded herself that if she hadn't forgotten her sunglasses she would have finished several chapters by now. But the A level syllabus had run half its course, and Jenny had first looked at her copy of Cobbett a year ago. Since then she had done little more than flick through the first couple of chapters and dismiss them as slow and tedious. Well aware of her lack of application, Jenny was resigned to having to rely on what she picked up in lectures – between day dreams.

The book finally fell from her grasp. Eyes closed and smiling just a little, Jenny dreamed happily of her one heavy sexual encounter to date – with that young reporter on the *Durraton Gazette*. Deep within the magic world inside her head, she lay outstretched against his hard bony chest and ran her fingers through the fuzz of hair that she knew sprouted there. Mills and Boon by the seaside. She felt his strong fingers stroke her body, his lips pressed hard on her lips and anywhere else he cared to press them.

She was five feet eleven inches tall, and convinced that there was at least six inches too much of her. She moved with gawky awkwardness, she was painfully self-conscious, she longed to be five foot nothing and shapely.

Boys just did not seem to notice her. She was too young to realise that they noticed all right but were too nervous and self-conscious themselves to pick on somebody who probably loomed several inches above them.

Then, two years earlier at an end of term school dance, that *Durraton Gazette* reporter, Mark Piddle, had taken her for a walk outside. Some walk. The dance had been arranged by staff at Jenny's school and the local boys' grammar school. Mark and his elder sister were there with their father, the vicar and school chaplain. The only drink provided was fruit punch.

Mark spent the evening lacing his glass with illicit rum. Jenny, captivated by Mark since she'd first met him at Sunday school when she was eight – he was six years older and seemed very grown up – grasped the opportunity to renew an old acquaintance. As soon as she saw him again she realised how much she fancied him.

Mark was exceptionally tall, almost six-four, with broad shoulders and great rangy limbs, and one of the very few men Jennifer would ever meet who could tower over her. It was not just his size that made that possible. Marcus was a towering personality in every sense. The power of his physical presence was always remarkable, even when he was a very young man. And the strength of his will was such that it seemed to reach out and bend you towards it. Jennifer always felt that with him. She suspected that she experienced it from those earliest Sunday school days. At the school dance it seemed, to the now fifteen-year-old Jenny, more tangible than ever. She felt as if a spell had been cast over her. Mark was a stunning looking young man, but his effect on her went far beyond the near perfect beauty of his appearance, although that in itself was devastating enough.

Mark was blonde and blue-eyed and drop-dead gorgeous. When he was a small boy he had been known in the neighbourhood as 'vicar's little cherub' – not a description he ever appreciated. The hair on his head was like a baby's, fly away and nearly white. It framed his face in a curly halo and made him look cherubic and innocent. Ironically he was to retain those guileless, fresh-faced, boyish good looks well into middle age. Looks that completely belied the kind of man he was.

Back then, Jennifer could not keep her eyes off him.

'Hallo, remember me?' she trilled in a break between the Gay Gordons and the Valeta.

Mark had poured a couple of healthy slugs of the rum into her glass of punch and when her eyes started to sparkle and her cheeks to burn had cheerily dragged her onto the dance floor. He knew a good thing when he saw one, and behaved as usual with the natural arrogance of the exceptionally beautiful.

He was always sexually precocious, Mark, and he was twenty-one years old by then. The age gap between them was a big one in teenage terms. As they danced, Mark developed an erection, and when he pushed himself against her she seemed to respond eagerly enough. He was vaguely aware that one or two of the teachers were looking on with some concern and that his father was glaring at him. The girl was obviously very young, but oh, how he liked them young. And so, after the briefest courtesy of only a couple of dances, he had just one intention – to get her outside. The opportunity came with the regulation speeches. With a bit of luck it would be ten or fifteen minutes before they were missed. Plenty of time for Mark. He had taken Jenny quickly by the arm and with her protesting in only the mildest of ways led her out through the kitchens to the dustbin yard. Here, in an unlikely setting for romance, Jenny received her first kiss and very nearly lost her virginity.

She found, as she had rather expected, that she thoroughly enjoyed the encounter, and made no attempt to stop Mark's wandering hands. She was only fifteen and Mark had deliberately poured rum into her, but it was not all one-sided. Not at all. There was a chemistry between them from the start. He excited her to distraction in that very first sexual encounter – something that would never change in all the years to come. Mark had always made her want things she felt she shouldn't want, do things she did not really want to do, sometimes did not even know were possible. That night his body was rubbing close and hard against hers, and he thrust his tongue between her teeth and deep into her mouth. He was balanced on one leg, pelvis pushed against her, the other leg bent upwards so that the knee forced her legs apart through the silky material of her skirt. His left hand was underneath her blouse, fingering an already erect nipple through the uplifting nylon lace of her obligatory Gossard Wonderbra.

With his right hand he deftly unclipped the fastening at the back, freeing her breasts so that he could take the whole of them in his hands.

Mark had had little finesse in those days, he had never felt the inclination to develop any, and anyway, on this occasion he knew he did not have the time. As usual he was ruled entirely by his own appetites. But, as he was already aware, that in itself could turn women on.

Before Jenny really knew what was happening, he had moved on from her breasts. With his mouth still clamped over hers, he had swept her skirt up around her waist and his fingers were inside her knickers playing with her. To his surprise she was already wet, and his fingers slipped easily into her. Jenny couldn't believe what was going on. It felt so good from the beginning. Shouldn't she be protesting?

She was vaguely aware that with his other hand

36

Mark was undoing his flies. He took her hand and put it around him. He was big and hard and throbbing.

Jenny felt the excitement she had yet fully to understand begin to overwhelm her. Mark was pushing her pants down now and she realised she was helping him. She mustn't. She mustn't get pregnant.

'I'll look after you,' he hissed. She knew better. But she was out of control. She stepped out of one leg of her knickers and with the new freedom he was able to thrust his fingers deeper inside her and move his hand over her crotch. He was instinctive about sex. Pure animal in his desire. What was she doing? There was such a buzz inside her. She knew she was moving with him like a wild thing. His thumb was rubbing her, clever, accurate, making her swell, driving her mad.

He had his other arm up under her skirt now and he began to lift her up so that he could plunge himself into her. He couldn't remember ever being with a girl who was so ready. Vaguely the thought occurred to him that she was the kind of kid he would expect to be still a virgin – but if she was, by God, she was ripe. This was going to be sensational.

As he lifted her, his fingers dug into her bare bottom and he was able to play with her there a little. Oh how he loved that. It was damp from her juices, flowing so freely now. She was wriggling with pleasure. She loved it too. She was just a kid, but, God, she was sexy. She was amazing. They were two of a kind. Two young healthy animals desperate for it. He felt her weaken even more.

She was moaning gently. She had forgotten everything in life except her own sex. He began to take his other hand out of her, moving and spreading his fingers as he did so, easing her as wide as he could. He put his hand briefly over hers and together they rubbed his cock in the warm wetness. He didn't think he had ever been so big.

Now he had both arms around her, clutching her bottom and lifting her towards him. He felt her long legs wrap around him. She had both hands on his bum now. She knew what to do, all right. It was as if she had always known. He didn't need a hand to guide himself into her.

His breath was coming in short gasps, he took his lips off hers, panting for it, tensing every muscle for the thrust.

She almost growled at him: 'Do it to me, now, now. Please. Please.'

He pulled back from her. He was going to go into her hard and strong and long . . .

And it was at that moment an anxious prowling teacher saw shapes in the dark and called out.

Mark swore and fell clumsily away from her. Jenny dropped to the ground, almost falling. He didn't try to pick her up. He was too busy attempting to shove his cock back inside his trousers. God what was he going to do with it now.

To her astonishment he ran off, leaving her there on the ground. She just managed to scramble to her feet and escape with her knickers in her hand.

Mark made no attempt to contact her again, and gave no signs of recognition when she saw him at the school sports day later that year. She was not to know the reason why until two years later. Several times she had phoned his paper. Each time she was told he was out. Since then there had been nothing like that encounter for Jenny. No other boys Jenny had met had even tried anything like it. Ineffectual fumbles yes. But there was nothing ineffectual about Mark Piddle. She had never known anyone else so overtly sexual – or so dangerous. She never would.

And so, lying there on the roof of the lav that hot summer's day, Jenny reflected on what might have been. She was never quite sure if she was secretly glad that teacher had turned up or not. She had been only fifteen. It was all a bit of a scramble and the consequences could have been disastrous. But sometimes she wondered if she was now going to stay a virgin for the rest of her life. Equally, sometimes she was afraid of her own sexuality. She had gone quite mad with Mark Piddle that night. Crazy for sex. Only she knew how much her body wanted and needed a man, a man who was all sex, like Mark. It thrilled her – and it frightened her.

Most of her friends were virgins too. The sexual revolution might have wreaked rampant havoc everywhere else in the world by 1970, but in Pelham Bay and nearby Durraton married men still had 'fancy women', the contraceptive pill had yet to become freely available, young girls who got pregnant had their bottoms smacked by hysterical fathers, and books with a high sexual content, from *Fanny Hill* to *Lady Chatterley's Lover*, were known simply as 'dirty' and you had to cover them in plain brown paper.

Jenny and her friends had been 'brought up proper'. It might not make much difference in the long run, but the rigours of doing their homework and not staying out late, added to more than their share of parental brainwashing, was inclined to protect their virginity for longer than usual.

So long, lanky Jenny lay dreaming about what she had never quite had, and of being five foot nothing and shaped like an egg timer. Angela Smith was five foot nothing and shaped like an egg timer.

A blow fly buzzed noisily in Jenny's ear. She flicked at it instinctively and her eyes opened in an involuntary blink. There was Angela, looking smugly angelic like her name, leaning against Todd Mallett instead of a chair. Todd was totally captivated by Angela in those days. His arm was around her shoulders. His hand rested on her left breast, pretending its position was an accident. He stirred and kissed the top of Angela's head.

That was quite enough for Jenny. She dumped Cobbett on the lavatory roof where she felt he belonged, and jumped to her feet shouting that she was going for a swim.

The concrete was burning hot beneath her bare toes. Jenny ran as fast as she could along the parade to the steps, down over the pebble ridge to where the sea hit the flat rocks at the bottom of the cliffs. There are places there where the Atlantic is deep and green and the rocks form natural diving boards stretching out to sea. When the tide is high and the surf is low, it is safe to dive in and down to the sand and pebbles and weed twenty feet and more below. Jenny knew every natural diving board that Pelham Bay had to offer. Nimble-footed she ran from pebble to pebble across the ridge. Years of practice made sure that she never stumbled. Speed and fleetness of foot were the secret. She headed for the farmost of the flat rocks and sprinted into a dive. Down, down into the cold water, then, floating slowly upwards into the sun again, Jenny rolled onto her back and lazily crawled seawards, looking back towards the holidaymakers splashing around in the shallows. She was a competition swimmer, powerful and confident.

It was four o'clock in the afternoon when Mark Piddle got the call. 'Your patch, old boy,' said his editor.

Mark was twenty-three years old now, a trainee reporter in the last year of his apprenticeship. He had first been to university and gained a degree. He often wondered how, because he had been an idle, although able, student, just waiting to do what he had always known was the only thing he could ever do – join the staff of a newspaper. He was spending the afternoon in bed with his girlfriend, Irene Nichols. He had moved her into his small one-bedroomed flat just two months before, and she was the first girl he had ever lived with. It was a whole new scene for Mark; he had found something he had needed for a long time, and everything else came second to the suddenly freely available sex which dominated his life. Everything, that is, except the job that he had dreamed of since he was a small boy.

He replaced the receiver on the phone in the living room, thinking briefly as always of the days when he would be able to afford a bedside extension. Standing there for a moment, naked, still half-erect, scratching his head, his beard and his balls, he wondered if he could manage any serious work that day. But the thought of a body found in Pelham Bay – a murder, his boss Jim Sykes had said – was almost as exciting to Mark as sex. It was just that the timing of the call had not been good. He hadn't finished yet. Through

41

the open door of the bedroom he could see Irene still lying on the bed, her little girl breasts pointing towards him, and he could feel his erection hardening again.

For just a couple of seconds he hesitated. Then he walked towards the waiting girl. It wouldn't take long now. He was nearly there.

'Who was it?' asked Irene, in the ringing tones of the commonest area of Durraton, which Mark always pretended he did not notice. In fact it grated badly, in spite of his loudly proclaimed socialist ideals. As the son of Durraton's vicar, Mark had been educated at a minor public school, populated mostly by farmers' sons, which had given him an average education, an above-average arrogance and sense of his own importance, an even more above average obsession with sex and all its possible variations, and a distinctive accent which he was just beginning to learn to tone down to a universally acceptable level.

'Jim,' he said, deciding on a show of totally false indifference. 'Still thinks he is working for a national daily, silly old bugger. Our rag doesn't come out until Thursday . . . but he just has to ring me up in the middle of a Sunday afternoon, doesn't he? My patch indeed.'

Irene wanted to know what the story was. Mark was too busy to answer. His hand had slipped down between her legs. Typically he thrust three fingers into her without warning. She instinctively flinched, but he pushed all the harder. She was willing enough even when he hurt her. That is why he had moved her in, to the dismay of her parents, who thought, quite correctly, that he was using her. His own parents pretended that they did not know Mark was living with anyone – let alone a girl from the lowliest council estate for miles around.

Mark was still at an age and way of thinking when all he required from a girl was a good time in bed. Actually, for him it was an attitude that was never to change much.

He never hit Irene – he was not violent in that way – but the sexual act was an act of aggression much more than of love for Mark. Their frequent protracted sessions left Irene more or less constantly slightly bruised and battered inside and out. But Mark excited her. He was someone from outside her limited horizons. And she doted on him, more like a puppy dog and its master than a young woman and her lover.

Mark was chewing on her breasts now. Her nipples were hard as buttons. She began to fidget obligingly. She had got used to the fingers so harshly pushed inside her, and they were not hurting so much. With his other hand Mark shoved her legs upwards, spread them wide apart, and began to play with her bottom. She flinched again. He reached for some of the cream on the bedside table. It was not so bad then. Soothing almost.

Anxious as ever, she spoke to him in drawling throaty tones dedicatedly copied from bad American movies. 'You're not going are you?'

'Certainly not,' lied Mark. He rolled over between her legs, startlingly aware of his own desperate horniness again and sure in the knowledge that Irene would demand no further arousal. He drove himself into her. She was ready at any time for anything he wanted to do to her with little or no preparation. Anything at all in exchange for the certainty that he would let her be there that night and the next morning and the next night. Ashamed of his thoughts he hammered into her, bigger and harder and more selfishly than ever.

He thrust inside her so forcefully she slipped towards the side of the bed, so that her head and shoulders were over the edge. He had his hands on her shoulders, forcing her downwards. This made her pelvis swing up towards him, and seemed to force her open even more. He was a long way inside her and it was sensational. He knew he must be hurting her back, but he couldn't stop. His mouth was on hers, his teeth bruising her lips. His tongue down her throat made it impossible for her to protest. Ultimately the top part of her body slipped off the bed, so that she was balanced on her head and shoulders, wedged on the floor against the side of the bed with her legs flailing helplessly in the air while he was still in there hammering away, relentlessly pressing her into the floor. The top of his body weighed a ton on her chest and shoulders, and he had his hands on her wrists now, pinning her down. His legs were still on the bed, and by kneeling slightly he was able to force himself into her even more powerfully. He liked the feeling of her total helplessness. He was so far in he thought he was going to touch his penis with his tongue as he thrust it into her throat. God, he liked it this way.

Irene could not move any part of her body except her legs. Ineffectively she tapped her feet against his back. He seemed to like that too. He was literally grinding her into the carpet. She could feel her back beginning to give with the strain when finally, with one last triumphant push, he reached orgasm. For her it was near agony. For him it was ecstasy. He took his tongue out of her throat and shouted out to her what he was doing to her and what was happening to him. As he lifted himself off her and fell back, she hauled herself onto the bed alongside him and clung to him tightly the way she always did. She got very little from him sexually and even less emotionally, and she always followed their brutal apology for love-making with the same embarrassing plea.

'You do love me, Mark, don't you?'

'Yeah, yeah.'

It was barely a minute since he had thrust himself into that knee-trembling gut-weakening climax, but Mark was young and strong, bursting with unspent energy, eager to get on with his life. He swung his long legs over the bed, ran his fingers through his curly fair hair and, turning slightly, looked down at the girl who would let him take any pleasure he asked for. He knew he should feel something more than he did for her. He actually wanted to feel more. But the harsh truth was that once she had satisfied his intense sexual appetites he didn't feel anything. Nothing at all.

'Gotta go,' he said.

'But I thought you weren't going.'

'Oh come on Irene. Get real. This is work.'

She pulled the sheets and blankets around her neck and watched him dress. His towering height and the spread of his shoulders seemed to fill the room. Sometimes it was as if that baby face and its halo of curls must really belong to somebody else. Sheer power surged from every inch of Mark. His limbs were thick and big-boned, but his body was lean and sinewy and totally masculine. It was covered by a

45

film of fine down, soft and shiny. A faint, almost transparent fuzz coated his legs, belly, chest and arms. There was even some of this fuzz on his shoulders and back. Around his penis the hair was longer and silkier but still curiously soft.

He coaxed his genitals into a pair of stretch under-pants and pulled on his faded blue jeans. He fastened his flies carefully and adjusted his balls as he did so. The mirror reflected a satisfying bulge and he knew that Irene was watching him as she always did. Amazingly he felt a slight stirring again. He ignored it but he was tinglingly aware that the bulge had grown larger. He put on a checked Levi shirt, leaving several buttons undone to show his suntanned chest. Strange that a man so fair did not burn in the sun. But Mark tanned easily. His skin was a gleaming pale gold. He shoved a notebook into a rear pocket of his jeans and a handful of loose change from the dressing table into one of the side pockets.

For the last time he approached the bed. He slipped his right hand under the bedclothes, widened Irene's legs, quickly felt the wet stickiness there, squeezed his fingers together, and with his usual roughness, plunged them into her.

Abruptly he left her. As he strode through the living room he glanced casually over his shoulder and called out 'Bye.'

Irene was swiftly out of bed. She had wrapped his towelling dressing gown around her and stood peering nervously around the bedroom door.

'Will you be late?' she called.

The answer came through the already closed front door. 'Dunno.'

Mark bounced down the stairs, wondering about

46

the lineage possibilities from the nationals, and whether, if he put his mind to it, he could find something that would last the week for the splash – front page lead – in the *Durraton Gazette*, and give him a bit of an edge on the big boys. He unbuttoned the breast pocket of his shirt where he always kept his car keys, and gave the balding tyres of his ancient battered Mini Cooper a vaguely anxious glance as he unlocked the door and stepped into the driver's seat.

'Crazy,' he muttered to himself. 'Only a bloody reporter would be expected to go and ferret out cops when he can't even afford to keep his car legal.'

He knew he could still live at home with his parents and save himself a fortune, he had done so for his first year or so on the paper after university, but there was no way he could conduct the kind of sex life he wanted and needed from Durraton Vicarage. The back seat of the mini did not lend itself to the games he liked to play.

He firmly dismissed all further thoughts of sex. The prospect of getting to grips with a major story had already wiped out any initial feelings of irritation at being disturbed. The girl he had left in his bed was now a million miles from his mind. She no longer mattered – anyway she would still be there for him when he returned, whenever that was. The violent private joy which had so recently engulfed his whole being had happened to another man. Now Mark was on the real job.

Mark lived at the top of Pelham Bay – on the edge of the woodland leading down to the cliffs and less than a mile from the beach. Born, bred, and schooled locally, he had many friends and contacts in the area. He knew his way around, and as he wound along the coast road had already decided which of his contacts he would visit first. Bill Turpin. Who else?

Four

Down by the beach it had been business as usual. Just up from the slipway, Bill Turpin's lads – bare-chested and belligerently beautiful – were handing out the deckchairs.

In Pelham Bay things had been the same for as long as anyone could remember. Bill Turpin, getting older, but still raking in the holidaymakers' cash just like shovelling sand off the beach. And a succession of young bloods, meaningless St Christophers nestling among newly sprouting body hair, showing off their bronzed torsos to the straw hat brigade.

On this hot August Sunday, the deckchair boys leaned luxuriously sullen against the sea wall. Theirs was the summer job for the budding Romeos of Pelham Bay, and has always remained so. Some things never change. An ideally idle way for students and professional loafers to make some beer money and eye up the imported talent. A job calling for little or no mental effort.

Old Bill Turpin habitually wore baggy grey flannels and grubby gym shoes without laces, so he shuffled when he walked. He was shirtless and weathered ebony by years of sun, salt, and wind – mostly salt and wind as he lived in Pelham Bay. Against his dark, gnarled body, even the deckchair lads seemed pale, plump and baby-like.

Bill had been born sixty-six years earlier in a

fisherman's cottage just back from the harbour in the fishing village of Brinton, set on the river estuary just a few miles up the coast from Pelham Bay. He was a man fashioned by the cruelty of the times in which he had grown to manhood and then to middle age, his life blighted for ever by forces and quarrels of which he had little knowledge and over which he had no control.

He came from a long line of fishermen. Men who knew from some deep instinct inside them where the fish would be that night. In season they caught salmon in the River Brin, stretching their nets across the river to trap the shoals of big rich fish swimming up stream to spawn. More often they sailed out to sea at night to catch herring and mackerel and whiting, and came back the next day or sometimes several days later with holds full of fish that they sold at the quayside.

It was a way of life the young Bill Turpin was naturally expected to follow, and did as surely as day followed night.

Bill was born just late enough to escape service in the first world war, but two of his elder brothers died in the trenches. Bill could still remember the day his family learned that his brother Edgar had died.

His father, a quiet, undemonstrative Devonian, had wrapped his strong brown arms around his sole surviving son and held him tight.

'They'll take you away over my dead body, son,' he had muttered. 'I'll swing before I lose another lad in the trenches.'

That war ended in time to save Bill Turpin. But it seemed he was destined to suffer at the hands of warring nations. In 1933 he married. He was twenty-nine years old. By local standards then he had taken his time in settling down. When he did wed he was sure as eggs were eggs that curly-haired Dorothy, twenty-year-old daughter of the village butcher, was the girl for him. Life seemed straightforward. It did not occur to Bill or his father, growing old now, but still fishing, that the world would be crazy enough to launch itself into another mighty blood-bath.

Bill's only sadness at that time was that he and Dorothy had no children. Then just as once again a world war was looming, the miracle happened. Dorothy found she was pregnant and gave birth to twin girls. The fisherman's happiness was complete. When his call-up finally came – he was pushing forty but the navy needed his seamen's knowledge and his boat – he was so convinced of his own strength and powers of survival that he saw the war as just a brief interval in his domestic contentment.

And he felt that in many ways he was a lucky man. The Government commandeered his solid wooden fishing boat to use as a minesweeper to detect the German acoustic mines which were operated only by metal-hulled ships. Bill was trained as a naval officer to skipper his own vessel. There was security for him in that. He was fighting on his own territory, after all.

Then came the telegram telling him his wife and daughters were dead. A crippled German bomber had emptied its load over Brinton before crashing into the sea. A freak accident. The pilot had ditched the bombs to lighten his aircraft. He scored a direct random hit on the cottage where Bill had been born and where he and his wife had made their home with his widowed father. The whole family were asleep in

51

bed when the bomb dropped. Grandfather, mother, and baby daughters died instantly.

Bill Turpin's heart also died that day. He signed his fishing boat over to the navy and volunteered for all the toughest jobs going, anywhere and everywhere his increasingly grateful chiefs wanted to send him. They assigned him to a special operations unit. Bill behaved as if he had a death wish, and it was against the odds that he survived. In the years to come he never spoke of his war days, but he returned in 1945 a different man to the gentle good-humoured Bill of pre-war days.

He soon surprised his old North Devon friends by buying, outright, a little house just out of Pelham Bay, an isolated stone-built cottage carved into the cliffside and with sweeping views out to sea. Bill explained that business ventures during the war had made him a few bob, and now he wanted to invest it in a new life. But how an impecunious fisherman had come to make the kind of money he now seemed to have was the subject of much speculation in the area.

Soon after the war there had been a huge robbery at the grand old Exmoor house owned by the then Earl of Lynmouth. Art treasures worth millions had allegedly been stolen, and Lord Lynmouth killed. Few could remember the details, but Bill had been some kind of a suspect for a bit. Nothing came of it, of course, and the police had apparently investigated only briefly, yet the rumours stuck around for generations and grew with the passage of time – as rumours are wont to do. Whenever there was a major crime anywhere in Britain, people in North Devon were inclined to mention the name of Bill Turpin. If you kept your ear to the ground in the pubs of Pelham Bay or Durraton you would hear whispers about old Bill being the brains, the muscle, or even the getaway driver – something never believed by anybody who had ever seen him drive – for everything from The Great Train Robbery to the famous escape of Mad Axeman Frank Mitchell from Dartmoor prison.

Mark Piddle and a generation of keen young reporters before him had all heard the gossip, and attempted with varying degrees of enthusiasm to unearth the hidden truth – assuming there was one. But far from being revealed as a closet master criminal, if Bill Turpin had anything at all to hide his tracks were superbly well covered. Consistent lack of success inevitably led to loss of interest for Mark, as it had to the other would be Carl Bernsteins before him. None of them were ever known to have found out anything worth a line anywhere.

Bill became regarded as a kind of mystery man, which he seemed almost to encourage and enjoy. Yet there appeared to be no mystery about his love life. Dorothy had indeed been the girl for him. The only girl. There was to be no other woman ever for Bill Turpin. He lived quietly for a while in his little house, and then gradually started to capitalise on the holiday trade which was on the up and up in Pelham Bay.

He would never fish again – that was part of his other life – but he seemed to have the knack of spotting what holidaymakers wanted and making cash from it. He had brought money back from the war all right, and he knew how to invest it in a way of life he understood. He remained a shadowy figure to the rest of Pelham Bay, a man nursing a terminally broken heart, asking for help from nobody, and accepting none. He appeared to have no friends and sought none. He was the sole survivor of his immediate family. A cousin had sought him out soon after the war and been sent packing. Bill Turpin wanted nobody close to him, nobody knowing his business – and nobody did.

He had come back from the war looking twenty years older than when he had left – yet the twenty-five years since then had barely altered him. Perhaps his back was a little more bent, but in 1970 Bill was still fit and strong in a slow sort of way. His eyes were a clear piercing blue and looked right through you. His head was bald, but so it had been when he came home in 1946, the crown of his head rubbed smooth by his tin helmet. The little hair left had whitened with the years, and his face appeared more leathery. That was all. Bill's early life as a fisherman had already engraved his skin with deeply etched creases.

He had become a landmark in Pelham Bay as the boss of a selection of seaside tourist-traps: he did not care how he looked or what people thought of him.

Jip, his black labrador-colly cross, followed Bill everywhere, walking at the same ponderous pace just a foot or so from her master's heels. Occasionally Bill would look down at the devoted dog and curse her in a mumbled growl.

Winter and summer he wore a grimy trilby hat, the brim turned down all the way round, and it was his habit to wear the hat indoors and out. In the summer the trilby protected his bald head from the sun. Once or twice Bill had suffered a sunburned head. Nowadays the trilby was never removed. The deckchair boys would joke about how Bill must look standing naked. His face and body weathered ebony. The top of his head and his legs startling white.

In winter he wore shirts with frayed collars beneath heavy cardigans and a big tweed overcoat with the collar turned up. The temperature of the day made little difference. He would don his thick winter layers and his heavy lace-up boots in early October, and stick to the overcoat and cardigans, however mild the climate, until shortly after the spring bank holiday. Then he would strip down to his baggy grey flannels, and, no matter how cold it might be, was rarely seen to put on a shirt, never mind a coat, until October.

Occasionally when it rained he would unearth the ageing military riding mac which he had picked up somewhere on his travels during the war.

'They don't make coats like this any more,' he would sigh, struggling into the stiff raincoat without bothering with a shirt beneath. The buckles were corroded and jammed almost solid, but Bill battled with them relentlessly. Then he would turn up the high collar and happily face any deluge, although, in reality, the old coat's waterproofing power must have been long worn out.

Bill's life appeared to be devoted to the making of money, and spending was no real part of it. He had one good suit, although it did smell of mothballs, and a fairly respectable car, a five-year-old Morris 1300. And once a week in the winter he would spruce himself up in the dark grey suit, dress in the only shirt he possessed without a frayed collar, select one of half a dozen unexciting ties in dark blues and reds, and drive to market in Durraton.

That was Bill's big outing. He would buy all the meat and vegetables he needed for the following week, chat to the few tradesmen he knew, and spend the lunchtime in one of the market pubs playing Euchre with dominoes. He enjoyed his market day outing every Tuesday, and would regularly down five or six pints of strong bitter. Then, as Tuesday was the only day of the week he ever had a drink, he would drive sedately but rather unsteadily home. You could get away with it in those days.

In the summer, of course, there was no market day excursion. Bill stayed steadily at his post, raking in the tourists' cash, wandering contentedly among his money traps. There was the giant slide in the fairground. The rate was two shillings for as many goes as you like, and in half a season the huge, ugly, scaffolding-like contraption would have already paid for itself many times over.

Then there was the bob-a-ride plastic elephant outside the public lavatory by the south-side putting green, and the belly boards and malibu boards which Bill rented out from the deckchair stand. The slot machine paradise of Penny Parade, where nothing cost a penny any more, remained probably the most successful money spinner of them all.

Bill Turpin could afford his deceptively lazy air. The seaside life brought him in a small fortune every summer. In the winter he could put his feet up while inventing new ways of emptying the tourist purse. Not so long ago, visitors to the Penny Arcade would have been happy with a few fruit machines, a couple of penny rollers, an automatic shooting range, what the butler saw, and an elderly football table. By 1970 they were already demanding electronic bingo and elaborate light-flashing sensation instead of those simple golden-oldie games of carefully-rigged chance. Whatever the customers called for, Bill Turpin gave them. And they paid for it over and over again.

So the cash flowed on this particular Sunday in drought-hit Britain. It was a magical day of bright blue skies and wispy white clouds and the crowds swarmed to the seaside in the hope of finding a Spanish sun beating down on English sand. But dear old Pelham Bay did not have a reputation for being the bleakest beach in North Devon for nothing. The wind was sending a sandstorm along the beach and whistling up the slipway which separates the pebble ridge stretching untidily northwards from the grand old sea wall to the south.

By midday the crowds were streaming landward of the iron-grey pebble ridge to shelter from the tornado that in other seaside towns would have been a gentle breeze. They dug hollows in the pebbles on the burrows side of the ridge and stretched their bodies agonisingly over the stones. Ultimately the discomfort of their angular beds beneath, and the burning of the sun above given a knife edge by the wind from which there was never a true hiding place, drove them to seek other amusement. And when they surfaced from their pebble pits, the holiday hordes, skins reddened and blotchy now, strolled up and down the seafront determined to enjoy themselves regardless.

With the true resolution of the British holiday-maker, they tucked into the local gastronomic delicacies, some not so delicate. The menu was varied: homemade ice cream, the artificial looking whip kings and pink and green rainbow-striped concoctions of the mass-produced sort, synthetic hot dogs, take away chow mein and chop suey, Wimpyburgers, fish and chips in cardboard cartons, bottled cockles and mussels pretending to be fresh, toffee apples, lukewarm tea in paper cups, fizzy pop, candy floss, and drinks on a stick.

Bill leaned with apparent idleness on the wall gazing at something floating in the sea. Or was there anything, right out across the bay beyond the rocks? There was just a speck in the distance. Bill's eyes might be tired but when he stared out to sea he could spot what others missed: the way the tip of a wave curled, a patch of dark water maybe, or the whirl of a current. All clues of some kind to a true seaman.

His face was screwed up tight against the bright light of midday glare.

'Could be nought,' he muttered.

He swung slowly away from the wall and the sea beyond and strolled across the promenade to his deckchair stand.

Johnny Cooke was over by the deckchairs watching old Bill through narrowed eyes. You could see his brain turning over, Johnny reckoned. What was he thinking, what was he plotting, what was he remembering as he stood there? Was he just counting his money in his head? That was what they all said, in Pelham Bay, and as one of Bill Turpin's deckchair lads Johnny had plenty of opportunity to indulge in the fruitless pursuit of trying to read his boss's mind. He could sense Bill's ice cool gaze swinging toward him. Boring into him. Johnny smartly turned his back and returned to his other favourite pastime of looking the grockles up and down. Grockles, the holidaymakers who annually invaded his beautiful county, responsible for turning lovely seaside spots like Pelham Bay into glorified shanty towns. Them and the greed they inspired.

A short, fat man wearing the kind of Bermuda shorts that had been in fashion five years earlier was struggling up the slipway. Behind him three small children were squabbling noisily, one in tears.

'Go on, go on, here's the money. Get yourself an ice cream and shut up, for Gawd's sake,' the man shouted.

It was just a typical Sunday in Pelham Bay. The smell of fish and chips and hot-dog onions drowned the tang of the sea. The rattle of the fruit machines, the clamour of the fairground, the ever-lasting hubbub of family quarrels and playing children, could all be heard loud and clear above the roar of the waves.

A couple of hours or more passed routinely. The sun, not quite so burning hot now, had moved around in the sky and shone on Johnny again. He basked in its gentler warmth. He felt drowsy.

But suddenly he was startled out of his pleasant half-wakefulness by a piercing scream which rose above the holiday clamour and shattered his fleeting sense of peace for ever. It was unnaturally high, a scream of almost inhuman shock and fear.

Johnny jumped to his feet, no laziness about him now, and like all the holidaymakers around him, ran to the sea wall and peered in the direction of the screaming.

It was Jenny Stone he could hear. Jenny Stone overcome with shock, yelling her heart out.

Five

Mark Piddle had arrived at the murder scene little more than a couple of hours after Jenny's shock discovery. Jim Sykes had got the word long before the news had been officially released. You had to hand it to the old goat, thought Mark grudgingly. And he would have been even quicker if he hadn't stayed at home after the phone call to give Irene one final seeing to. Mind you, that hadn't taken long. He roared the Cooper into the heart of Pelham Bay, and grinned to himself. Not a bad life . . .

He swung the Cooper, naked tyres squealing, into the sharp corner of the road down to the beach. It reached a dead end at the slipway, and to the right was a public carpark. Mark was a keen surfer and a member of the surfing club based in those days in the little wooden hut at the rear of the carpark. He waved cheerily at the carpark attendant. There was a kind of unofficial agreement that the surfers parked for free, but you had to keep the grumpy white-coated attendant sweet. A group of the lads were sitting forlornly outside the hut enjoying the sun, but despondent because that day, even in windy Pelham Bay, there was little or no surf.

Mark parked and briskly walked the hundred yards or so to the deckchair stand in search of Bill Turpin. There was not much happened in Pelham Bay that Bill Turpin didn't know about. Bill was not a gossip, and it was partly that which made his value as a contact so much greater to a reporter. If you could get the non-talkers to talk to you, then you were always on the verge of cracking the 'big one' – or so the Jim Sykeses of the newspaper world always promised.

Mark picked himself a chair, set it up, and sat down next to Johnny Cooke.

'Wotcher Casanova,' he said.

Johnny whistled a few unrecognisable notes and grinned at him. Mark was the only person who ever referred to Johnny's court case of the previous year. Everyone else pretended it had never happened. Johnny would have preferred it to be out in the open, so that he could explain to anyone he cared enough about that it hadn't been the way it seemed. It really hadn't. He found the direct approach a welcome change. It made him feel comfortable with Mark. He knew Mark's amusement was genuine. The reporter really couldn't give a damn.

He held out his hand. 'That'll be a bob for the deckchair, thank you,' he said.

'You have to be joking,' replied Mark. 'Where's the Walt Disney of the West of England?'

'On the prowl as usual. And if you don't get out of that chair smartish he'll make the pair of us into sausage meat for his hot dogs.'

Mark produced a packet of Gauloises and lit one – it was more of an affectation than a habit.

He puffed a cloud of smoke into the blue sky. 'Your boss and me, we're like that, mate.' He held up his hand with two fingers crossed. 'I'm telling you.'

Johnny was saved from answering by the arrival

of Bill Turpin who, chewing his foul-smelling pipe, seemed to materialise from nowhere. He had an uncanny knack of doing that.

'Doing all right on that paper of yours, then, boy.' A statement rather than a question.

Mark started. 'Yeah. Oh yeah.'

'Well then, price of a deckchair won't worry you. Johnny, give him a ticket.'

Mark fished around in his pocket for change. There was no point in arguing with Bill Turpin. The old man chewed his pipe some more. 'Discount for locals,' he said. 'That'll be a tanner.'

'Right,' said Mark. 'You've taken my last penny as usual, so what about some help? What do you know about this body, Bill. Is it on?'

''Tis on, lad, like I told the police . . .' he began. That made sense, thought Mark. Bill would be first stop for the cops too.

'I don't know much worth telling . . . I was standing there by the ice cream van, just looking out over the sea wall and I could see something floating in the water . . .'

Bill's voice trailed off. 'Anyway, next thing I knew Reg Stone's maid is screaming her poor little heart out right across the bay.'

'Reg Stone's maid? The councillor?'

'Yep. That maid of his is down here all summer with them mazed lot who lie around on the lavatory roof over by the lido.'

'Oh I know that lot. Don't think I know the girl though.'

Mark had never even asked her name that night at the school dance. Unusually for him he could still remember every detail of his encounter with Jennifer

Stone by the dustbins, although he had no idea who she was. He had been turned on by her to distraction, and it had been days before his excitement had died down.

But the school had threatened Mark with the police if he ever went near one of their young pupils again, and he was left in no doubt that if he tried to pursue the girl who had so aroused him, he would end up in jail. It was only because his father was the school chaplain that the police had not been called this time, he was told. He had shortly afterwards found Irene and had been using her ever since as a poor but willing substitute. Nothing that he did to Irene ever seemed really to satisfy him. Yet the young body that had clung to him so eagerly in the dustbin yard had left a lasting impression.

Mark had his notebook out now.

'How does she fit into it all then?'

'Found the body, poor maid. Out swimming.'

'Hey, what a great line. I'd better have words with young Miss Stone..'

'You'll be bleddy lucky. Took her straight off to 'ospital. In a terrible state. Terrible.'

'Shock, huh?' Mark turned to a clean page in his notebook, jotted down Stone and began to doodle the letter S into an elaborate snake. He picked Bill's brains about the time the body was found and any other details he could think of, but the older man was reticent, even for him.

'No way it could have been an accident, I don't suppose?' Mark looked at Bill thoughtfully.

'Not the way I heard it,' said the old man. 'Strangled. That don't happen by accident, do it?'

'Ah. Cops tell you that?'

'Mebbe. Cops! Pah. Don't know what they think I do all day apart from sticking my nose into other folk's business.'

Mark laughed. 'Trouble is, you usually do know other folk's business, don't you?'

'Too sharp by 'alf, boy, that's your trouble. You lads today need a couple of years in the army. That'd wipe the smirk off your smug young faces. Put on a bit of muscle too.' He shook Mark by the shoulder.

Mark tried to wrench away the old man's hand, but he could not force the bony fingers apart.

'Jesus Christ, Bill. Let go, will you?'

Bill obliged and Mark rubbed his sore shoulder. Bill looked pleased with himself, he was almost grinning. He secretly enjoyed his encounters with Mark when the young reporter came looking for information. They had had each other's measure from the beginning, these two. None the less Mark had no idea that Bill was even remotely aware of his attempts to uncover the secrets of the old man's past. Mark should have expected that, because he knew that Bill always found out about anything and everything happening in Pelham Bay. But with the brash confidence of youth, it had not occurred to Mark that Bill would have been aware of his futile investigations. In fact Bill had watched, untroubled, as Mark fruitlessly questioned distant relatives, business contacts, and anyone even vaguely connected with the old man. In a way Bill accepted this kind of attention as his right – more of an accolade than an intrusive insult, and he was quite certain that no local paper hack was going to make any discoveries likely to cause him concern. The older man would amuse himself giving Mark a bit of a hard time, but even so he always seemed to have some little gem that he would pass on – just as he had on this occasion. There was a lot in Mark which Bill Turpin recognised and which Mark Piddle had yet to learn about himself.

Bill thrust his right hand deep into the pocket of his old grey flannels, and with his left removed the pipe which all the time had been clasped between his teeth.

'Load of nancy boys you youngsters today . . .'

He paused, looking as if he might say more, then shoved the pipe back between his teeth and stomped off towards the Penny Parade. The faithful dog, which had been dozing in the shade of the deckchair pile, climbed creakily to her feet and followed.

Mark shouted after him. Bill glanced over his shoulder, still walking forwards. 'Do they know who the dead girl is yet?' called Mark.

Bill Turpin stopped walking. Mark was by his side again now. Bill blew a cloud of foul smoke into his face. Mark recoiled, coughing, and was sure he spotted a look of some satisfaction on Bill's face.

The old man turned on his heel and strode off without replying, upsetting the plans of his dog which was already looking for another place to settle for a sleep.

'Thank you so much,' Mark muttered to himself.

He set off along the seafront towards the lido. Police were mingling with the crowds asking questions, but Mark did not see any that he knew. He paused by the lavatory roof, raised a couple of feet above the upper path. The lavatory itself was entered from the lower path, almost at sea level. A girl and a boy were still there, squatting close together, talking intently.

'Hi. Mark Piddle. *Durraton Gazette.*'

The girl, shapely and sure of herself, stood up. She was wearing the briefest of bikinis. Mark found his eyes almost directly in line with her crotch and tried not to stare.

'If it's Jenny you want, she's in hospital,' said the girl.

'So I heard. Did you see anything?'

'We heard Jenny screaming and went to help her out of the water. A couple of policemen clambered out across the rocks to try to bring the body in. But we never saw it . . .'

The girl sniffed and the corners of her lips curled downwards. Mark thought how unpleasant her facial expression was. He preferred to look at her ripe young body.

'You don't know who the dead girl was, then?'

'No,' the girl caught hold of the boy's hand.

'What's your name?' asked Mark.

'Pussy Galore,' said the girl, simpering.

Mark was suddenly irritated.

'You wouldn't know what to do with it, darling, and nor would your boyfriend, I reckon,' he snapped at her, glaring at the boy and daring him to retaliate. The boy flushed and fumbled for words. It was a long time before Todd Mallett would grow into the kind of man who was not easily intimidated by anyone.

'Clear off,' he said lamely.

'Yeah, clear off,' echoed the girl, no longer quite so sure of herself.

Mark gazed steadily at the pair of them. They were embarrassed now. He was suddenly sure they were both virgins.

'If you want any more lessons you know where to find me,' he said.

The girl looked pleadingly at the boy. He tugged at her arm. 'Come on, let's go. Ignore him.'

Mark felt better now. He turned and jogged back along the sea front to his car. There was nothing left to see. The body was long gone. The only police in sight were junior officers asking routine questions. Mark supposed the County C.I.D. had been called in, but he would probably do best on the phone to the cops that evening.

Jenny Stone. The girl who had bumped into a body while out swimming. That was the obvious story. He climbed into the driver's seat of the battered Cooper.

'A nice new open sports job, that's what you should be driving, Mark boy.'

The mini started at the third attempt.

'Come on, heap,' Mark coaxed.

He grated the little car into reverse gear, kicked up a cloud of dust as he turned sharply and roared out of the carpark. He passed a couple of the boys from the nationals just arriving, and started to make his plans. He would stop off at home, make his police calls, see if anyone could name the body and quickly file a few pars of early lineage. If he could get some sort of story together before the staff men, it could be worth a few bob. Then he would drive to Reg Stone's house and wait for Jenny to be brought home. With a bit of luck, everybody else would go to the hospital. The national pack, area men up from Plymouth and down from Bristol, wouldn't know where Reg Stone lived, just back from the burrows in Pelham Bay – but Mark did, because Reg Stone was a councillor. The others would find out fast enough, but Mark would have the edge. If Jenny came out of hospital tonight, he might just be alone on the doorstep. He smelt an exclusive. He glanced at his watch. Jenny Stone would not be released from hospital for a bit, he was sure. If he got home quickly now there would be time for more than just filing some lineage. That sexual banter with those two good looking kids really had made him randy. The girl was sixteen or seventeen, Mark supposed. Irene was twenty-one, but she still had almost the body of a child.

By now he was driving so fast he almost lost the Cooper on the hairpin bend at the bottom of the hill leading to his flat. He regained control by the skin of his teeth, screeched to a halt and ran up the stairs three at a time. The front door was open, and he quickly bolted it behind him. Irene came into the living room from the kitchen to greet him. She was wearing a tight cotton dress. He could see her nipples through the material. She started to speak to him. He unzipped his flies and his cock virtually jumped out through the gap. Even he sometimes wished it wouldn't do that.

Irene wasn't sure she could take any more that day. She took a step backwards. He didn't even notice. His arms were around her. He picked her up and bent her face downwards over the back of the sofa, pushing her dress up around her waist as he did so.

'Not there, Mark, please, I'm so sore,' she said.

'Open your legs wider then,' he hissed. She did so. He thrust into her and started to come almost at once. It was like that for him sometimes. Particularly after he had been working.

An hour later he was sitting in the Cooper outside the Stones' terraced house. Waiting in the dark. He had been joined by the *Durraton Gazette*'s only photographer. At eleven o'clock, just as he had given up hope, Mr and Mrs Stone arrived home with their only daughter.

The snapper had his instructions. Don't snatch. Naturally he disobeyed and immediately shoved camera and flash into Jenny Stone's face. Her father was not pleased.

'She's upset,' he said. 'Leave her alone, you buggers.'

In the mere split second of flashlight, Mark had been instantly sure he knew Jenny from somewhere. He cursed his snapper, but resolutely continued with his persuasive routine of logic and sweet-talk. One quick chat with him now and it would keep all the other reporters at bay, he would tell the story sensitively, etc. etc. Jenny stared at the young man. She was coming around from shock. Gradually she began to realise who he was.

'It's all right, dad, I may as well get it over with. They said at the hospital half the world's press wanted to talk to me.'

Reg Stone gave in reluctantly. 'Ten minutes,' he said to Mark. 'She needs sleep.'

Mark followed parents and daughter into the house and shook hands with all three of them. As he did so Jenny smiled a small half smile. They were in the brightly lit hallway by now, and Mark could see her clearly. In spite of herself and all that was happening, there was a direct challenging look in her eye.

Jesus. It was that kid he'd nearly had at the school dance. Jenny. Of course. He hadn't bothered to ask her name that night, he'd been so horny, but when she had phoned his office she told them to tell him Jenny had called, Jenny from the dance. She must be seventeen now. God, she'd been ripe then. He remembered the feel of her. She hadn't just complied. She had gone for it. Extraordinary. He had wanted to go back for her the next day. How he had wanted to, he just hadn't dared after what had happened. Strange how well he could remember the sensations of that night. Two years on and he could still smell and taste her.

He pulled himself together. Put all those thoughts out of his mind. Gently he began to question Jenny.

He was a good interviewer, a natural. She was very articulate. She spoke in quotes. She was badly shaken, but calm. It was a great talk, and Mark knew it would make first-class copy.

When Mark and the snapper left, Jenny followed him out of the door and called after him. He turned back to her. She was silhouetted against the light from the house and her head was tilted slightly to one side. He could not see her face – just the shape of her standing there – but her body language was eloquent. She looked indignant and purposeful.

'Why did you never contact me again after the dance?' she asked quietly.

He was astonished. He didn't know what to say.

She continued to interrogate him. 'Why were you always out when I called your office?'

He knew he was mumbling and stumbling. How could she throw him like this? She was just a girl.

Eventually he found some words, 'You were only fifteen, for Chrissake, you were jailbait,' he said. 'I was warned off. Heavily.'

'I'm seventeen now,' she replied.

The photographer had got into his car and switched on his headlights. As she spoke, Jennifer's face was suddenly illuminated – one eyebrow raised as if in contempt. She parted her lips very slightly in that half smile. It was a mocking smile – and yet so seductive. She made him nervous. It was ridiculous, she was only a kid. Mark heard himself giggle weakly. He almost ran to the Cooper, gunned the engine and shot off down the street. He could feel her eyes on the back of his neck as he drove away. It made his skin prickle with excitement.

Jennifer Stone made two decisions that night: firstly that she would have Mark Piddle. This time he wouldn't get away. He would be the one to take her virginity. He had already very nearly done so after all. Soon, very soon, they would make love together. But this time it would be on her terms. When she chose. And somehow watching him work as a newspaperman had made her want him even more. She sensed the thrill that he got from his job and she wanted that too – which took her to the second decision. She would start writing to local papers tomorrow. She would become a journalist like Mark.

Strange that she could think that way on such a night. But she did.

Exhausted she fell asleep. But in her dreams she found the body again, only this time it had no face. She woke screaming. It took her mother almost an hour and two more of the tranquillisers she had been given to calm her daughter down.

Six

Johnny Cooke's mother heard on the six o'clock local news that the body of a girl, believed to have been murdered, had been found in the sea at Pelham Bay. She shook her head sorrowfully. 'I don't know,' she said to herself. 'What is the world coming to?'

Mrs Mabel Cooke had been born and brought up in Durraton. She knew everyone, and everyone knew her. She had that smugness about her found among certain people who live in a small town and are overly sure of themselves and their social standing.

She busied herself in the kitchen preparing a high tea. Neither Johnny nor her husband would be home much before seven, but Mrs Cooke liked to be prepared. She sliced meat from the lunchtime joint of pork, put tomatoes in a dish, laid the table with a selection of homemade pickles, and put three apple dumplings in the oven to warm gently. There were cold boiled potatoes and wrapped sliced bread to eat with the meat, tomatoes and pickles. Mrs Cooke did most of her own baking, but saw nothing incongruous in providing tasteless sliced bread along with her homemade delicacies. The apple dumplings she had baked the day before, using big green cooking apples wrapped in a thick layer of shortcrust pastry.

Soon after seven, her husband and son arrived. They sat at the kitchen table and waited for Mrs Cooke to brew the tea before touching the food.

Then they ate quickly. After they had finished, Mr Cooke lit his pipe.

'Did you hear about that murdered girl?' he asked his wife.

'I did. I tell you, Charlie, I don't know what the world is coming to, that I don't. Do they know who she is yet?'

Charlie Cooke shook his head. 'Reg Stone's maid found the body. Johnny 'eard 'er screaming, didn't you boy?'

Johnny nodded.

Mrs Cooke rubbed her hands together mournfully. 'I hope and pray it's not a local girl, that's all,' she said.

'Why?' asked Johnny. 'If it's not a local girl, doesn't her life matter then, mother?'

'Don't be so cheeky, young man,' snapped Charlie Cooke. 'That's your trouble, son. Too quick on the draw when you shouldn't be and not quick enough when you should be. You know full well what your mother means . . .'

Johnny picked up his cup of tea and headed for the sitting room.

'And where do you think you're going now?' said his father.

'Television. There's a film . . .'

'You get worse, boy, 'stead of better. No chance of you helping your mother wash up is there?'

'Oh, leave the boy alone, Charlie. I'm happier doing it on my own. Let him be.'

Johnny slunk gratefully into the sitting room and buried his senses in the over-dramatic thriller just starting on ITV. It treated him to a car chase, a shoot-out, half a dozen killings and an armed robbery within the first few minutes.

Mr Cooke soon followed his son into the room and, lowering himself into his favourite chair, grumbled: 'As if there isn't enough bleddy violence in real life, you have to watch it on TV too.'

Johnny ignored him. His father grunted, picked up the *Sunday Express* and turned to the sports page. When she had finished the washing up, Mabel Cooke joined her husband and son in front of the TV. About half an hour later the phone rang. It was Mr Cooke's Rotary Club policeman friend, Chief Inspector Ted Robson. The two men were on committee together organising the annual fête, and as they discussed final arrangements, Ted Robson described how he had been called out that afternoon when the body was discovered in Pelham Bay.

When Mr Cooke returned to the living room he remarked conversationally: 'Ted says that dead woman worked out at the Royal Western Golf Club – behind the bar. Marjorie something or other, Ted said . . .'

Johnny stopped watching television. He looked blankly at his father.

'You've played a bit there with your Uncle Len, Johnny,' said his mother. 'Did you know her?'

'Know her?' Johnny repeated vacantly. 'Um. I'm not sure.'

Johnny's father reached sideways and shook his son by the shoulder.

'Wake up boy, will you? Your mother asked you a question. Did you bleddy know 'er or not?'

'I . . . I suppose so. I saw her about the place. Yes.'

74

Johnny was twiddling a piece of hair around his fingers now.

'Where was she from?' his mother continued. 'What was she like then?'

Johnny shook his head.

'What's that supposed to mean?' his father asked.

'I don't know. I don't know.' Johnny got up and walked quickly to the door. 'I've got to go out.'

'I thought you wanted to watch this bleddy film,' said his father.

'I did, but I forgot something . . .' Johnny was on his way out.

'Where are you going?' called his father.

Johnny had already slammed the front door shut behind him and was running down the road.

Seven

At the bottom of his street, Johnny stopped running, turned around and walked back up the alley leading to the rear of the house where he stealthily took his bicycle out of the garden shed. He cycled as fast as he could down to Pelham Bay, straight to the golf club. Two police cars stood in the carpark. Johnny recognised one of the caddies, a boy who used to be at his school. As casually as he could manage, he asked what was going on.

'They've found Marjorie Benson dead,' came the reply.

Johnny rode as fast as he could down to the slip-way, propped his bike against the deckchair stand and set off along the three miles of beach. He took off his battered desert boots and red nylon socks and walked barefoot, kicking the sand with his toes. As he walked his chin sank lower and lower into his chest, and he began to sob great heaving sobs which racked his body. The tears came freely, burning hot and pouring down his cheeks, soaking the front of his tee-shirt.

A couple taking a late stroll along the water's edge looked at him curiously as he passed. Johnny didn't even notice them. His grief was the grief of a very young man, too young to know that time can heal and despair does lift. His world had ended and Johnny made no attempt to wipe away the tears. It was the first time Johnny had wept since the death of his grandfather, and once again he felt that overwhelming sense of guilt. This time he was to blame.

He stooped to pick up a handful of pebbles and threw them angrily into the sea, tears still pouring down his face. He squatted in the sand sobbing for what seemed like hours. But in the end the tears did stop. Dusk had turned to pitch blackness and within its comforting cloak he relived the six months of his life since he had first met Marjorie Benson.

It had been the day of his eighteenth birthday. His uncle had invited him to play a round of golf with him in the morning. Johnny was a natural athlete, he had been given golf lessons at school, and although he had played very little he wasn't bad. He had the makings of a good golfer. At lunchtime Uncle Len had made a great show of buying him a pint in the clubhouse – it was his eighteenth birthday after all. Marjorie was behind the bar. He had been aware of her from the moment he walked into the place. He found her extraordinarily attractive, and to his delight she seemed to take every opportunity to chat to him. She didn't talk down to him, either, the way he suspected most women of her age would – he guessed she was in her early thirties. She looked stunning in a simple short black skirt and soft clingy white sweater which emphasised her sleek boyish figure. He couldn't keep his eyes off her body as she moved. She caught him looking, raised her eyebrows inquiringly and smiled. He blushed crimson and was glad to be asked to join his uncle for lunch in the dining room.

It was while Uncle Len was visiting the gents' that Marjorie strode through the room, barely pausing as she dropped a piece of paper into Johnny's lap. It was a scribbled note inviting him to her room in the clubhouse and telling him how to get there.

'Make sure nobody sees you,' he was instructed.

Johnny couldn't believe it. Could this possibly mean what he thought it meant? As his uncle returned to the table, Johnny was afraid that he was still blushing and would give himself away. After lunch he turned down the offered lift back to Durraton with a vague excuse. As soon as the coast was clear he nipped up the stairs behind the bar and found Marjorie's room as directed. Surreptitiously he tapped on the door. When she opened it he saw that she had changed into a shirt which reached almost to her knees. She was wearing nothing else. Several buttons were undone at the front and he could just glimpse the slight swell of her breasts. Her legs were bare and brown and so were her feet. He even found her toes attractive. She leaned forward and lightly touched his shoulder, drawing him into the room.

He was overwhelmed by the nearness of her. He thought that she smelt of spring flowers and cool clear water drawn straight from a well. She closed the door behind him and he stood quite still, his arms hanging limply by his sides. He was terribly nervous. He did not know what to do. She stepped towards him, placed her hands loosely behind his neck and kissed him very gently on the lips. Her touch was feather light. He thought he had not felt anything so lovely in the whole of his life. She tasted of honey. He thought he had never tasted anything so delicious. He did not move. He realised he was frightened. He had been ever since the court case.

Now here was a complete stranger who was making all the going. Whatever happened he supposed he would get the blame.

She was caressing the back of his neck, long fingers reaching inside his shirt.

'Your skin is like satin bathed in sunshine,' she whispered. 'Warm, smooth, soft.'

She spoke beautiful English, with a slight accent Johnny could not place.

She placed her lips against his ear, barely touching, her tongue flicked against him, wet, tantalising.

'Would you like to stay here with me a while?'

He felt himself nod.

She smiled. 'Do you like me?'

He nodded again.

'Would you like us to lie down together?'

This time he could not even nod. He felt the deep blush spread over his face again and realised sharply just how afraid he was. Crazily he imagined some kind of trap. He pulled himself abruptly away from her, and took several steps backwards in the direction of the door, until he was able to reach behind him for the handle.

'I can't,' he stumbled. 'You don't know about me . . . I just can't . . .'

She moved towards him again and touched his cheeks. 'It's all right. Everything is all right. Just stand where you are, perfectly still.'

Her eyes were locked onto his. There was something eerie about her. It was as if she was hypnotising him, willing him to put his trust in her. She spoke to him softly, reassuringly, resting her arms lightly on his shoulders, before eventually she kissed him again, and gradually he realised that this was going

79

to be different from anything he had previously experienced. And he became quite certain that he could indeed trust her.

He could sense the poetry in her. This was how it had always been meant to be. She began to undress him. She unbuttoned his shirt and slipped it off him. Johnny knew he had a fine, well-muscled body. She stepped back and admired him and then she started to stroke his shoulders, his chest, his back, his stomach. Oh, and she was so gentle, so loving, all the time looking deep into his eyes. He reached out for her, ready now to take her in his arms.

'No,' she whispered. 'No. Don't move, my love.'

She crouched before him and unlaced his shoes. Lifting each foot in turn she took off his shoes and socks. Incredibly, extraordinarily she brushed her lips over his feet, flicked her tongue between his toes. She reached up and undid his belt, unzipped his flies and then slid his trousers down over his long lean thighs. Again he reached for her. Again she told him no.

She pulled his trousers off him, first one leg, and then the other. He stood before her in white Marks & Spencer Y-fronts. This was unreal, he thought. It must be a dream.

'You are beautiful,' she told him. 'So beautiful. You have the body of an angel. My own angel.'

She reached up and felt him through the smooth cotton. Then her fingers tucked inside the waistband and she pulled his pants down. First off one leg and then the other. Now he was naked. He glanced down at himself with interest. He wasn't even erect. She was in charge of everything this first time they were to be together. Even that.

She took him in her hands and stroked him and he started to swell. Then she knelt up and took him in her mouth. He had not known what she was doing to him was even possible. He really hadn't. Her lips were so warm, her tongue was so gentle, he thought he was going to die of pleasure.

Eventually she coaxed him to the bed, sitting him on the edge. She stood in front of him and he saw that she was naked. He had not noticed her slip off the loose shirt. He gazed at her, loving every inch of her with his eyes. This time she stood still, enjoying the feel of his gaze, understanding him and his desires. Her breasts were perfect, standing up, pointing towards him. Her flat tummy led to the warm mound of her womanhood and crazily he noticed that her pubic hair was a different colour to the distinctly red hair of her head. She sat on the bed beside him, took his hand and kissed it.

'Do you want everything I have in me to give? Do you want to give me everything?'

'Oh yes,' he said. 'Yes please.'

Her lips were everywhere, all over him, driving him mad. Then she showed him what to do to send her crazy. He stroked her, he sucked her nipples, and his fingers played endlessly in the soft wetness between her legs. By the time she opened her legs wide and guided him into her he was so excited it was over almost at once.

'I'm sorry,' he stuttered.

'Don't be,' she said. 'You are so beautiful. You are going to give me so much pleasure.'

She began to stroke his body again, starting behind the ears, rubbing, teasing, gently prodding, using her hands and her lips. With her fingertips she traced a

81

path from the pit of his throat to the base of his belly, and by the time she got there he was erect again and dying to be inside her once more.

For the second time she took him in her mouth and ran her tongue around him, up and down, around and around his stiffness. Then she mounted him and rode him, rocking backwards and forwards until she reached a wonderful, extravagant climax. As it burst from her, so she tightened around him, almost hurting him, urging even more sensation from her body. He watched her face. Her eyes were closed tight and her lips were apart. Her tongue was moving inside her mouth and her glorious body was opening and closing even more deliciously around him and she made him climax again, squeezing every last drop out of him and into her. He really was in heaven.

But afterwards she sent him away.

'I was alone and I needed it,' was all she would tell him. That and: 'You looked so handsome, so nice.'

Her eyes were full of longing and despair. She clenched her fists tightly, almost as though she were in pain.

He had asked if he could see her again and she had said no. Only when, in desperation, he refused to leave until she agreed, did she give in.

'Can you get out at night?' she asked.

Yes, he had said recklessly.

'Next week then, after midnight. I'll meet you at the back door.'

And so for four wonderful months he had sneaked out of his house at midnight and ridden his bicycle to the golf club where he hid it in bushes before meeting her at the back door. At first they met once a week, then twice, then three, sometimes four times. No wonder Johnny was so sure he had flunked his A levels. They just could not get enough of each other. She always made him leave before it was light. But he began to live only for those stolen few hours. She taught him so much. He learned to enjoy licking and kissing her sexy wetness as much as she seemed to like to take him in her mouth. He learned where to push with his tongue, where to squeeze with his lips, where to nibble, oh so delicately, with his strong white teeth. He would never forget the first time he brought her to orgasm with his mouth. She bucked beneath him like an unbroken pony. It was so exciting he had come himself all over the bedclothes.

And he would never forget the first time he climaxed in her mouth. He was sitting naked on the edge of the bed and she was kneeling before him. She was so good at it and her tongue was so clever. She had begun to play with his scrotum with her hands when suddenly it happened. He hadn't meant to do that to her. He had tried to pull himself away. But she had her hands on his bottom and was dragging him further into her. And as he pumped himself into her sweet mouth he realised that her throat was moving. She was swallowing his come. He found the idea so exciting he thought his orgasm was never going to stop.

Afterwards, when they lay in each other's arms, warm and snug and satisfied, he had apologised. She had told him never to apologise for an act of love. And anyway, it made her feel that she was drinking his heart.

Drinking his heart! Oh, the glory of her.

He was so happy he wanted to tell the world about

their love. But she insisted their meetings be the most carefully guarded secret. And so he had to creep in and out of the clubhouse in the dark to reach the joyous haven of her bedroom.

One night she had asked him what he would most like in all the world to do with her. He had replied that he would like to take her into deep woodland in the sunshine and lie her among golden daffodils and gently tickle her entire body with a soft fern until she begged him to touch her with his hands and to enter her and give her all of his love. She was delighted with his answer. The use of language they shared was a great part of their pleasure.

Three days later, Marjorie told him to meet her at a remote crossroads early in the afternoon. She arrived in a borrowed car and they drove deep into the countryside. It was the only time they ever really went anywhere together, and the only time they met in daylight. She parked in an old disused quarry and they ran hand in hand like children deep into dense woodland. It was early May and the spring flowers were still blooming. With lovers' luck they found a small clearing surrounded by big old oak trees. It was carpeted with daffodils and bluebells.

He had cried out: 'It's my daffodil glen.'

And she had replied with pleasure: 'Blue and yellow, like a painting by Monet, only nature is an even greater artist. You are also an artist, my love, and I am your canvas.'

He undressed her the way she had undressed him that first time, gently, tenderly, deliberately. The sun dappled her lovely body as he laid her down, found a piece of fern and began to stroke her with it just the way he had told her he wanted to. She opened her legs and he brushed her there with it, just a tease of a touch. When she could endure it no longer she reached for his hands and placed them firmly on her body and he could feel the strength of her desire through his finger tips. When he rolled on top of her she was smiling at him, her lips parted in anticipation of shared joy. When they climaxed together under the big oak trees, she took him truly to heaven again. Only after they had finished and dressed each other did he think of the madness of what they had done. Other people did walk through woods on sunny days. But that day their dream had held.

Then one night he dared to tell her that he loved her. And he felt her whole being tense beside him.

'Nonsense,' she said. 'Nonsense.'

But he meant it, from the depths of his soul he meant it.

'It's my fault, I should not have let it go this far. We've got to stop,' she said.

At first he thought she must be joking. Then he started to beg her to tell him she did not mean it. Then he was just begging. There were tears in his eyes and he was trembling. She felt her heart melt. He had invaded her soul and she could not turn him away. But she told him they must be more careful. She was sure the bar steward was suspicious, and it was imperative for his safety that nobody knew about them. He neither knew nor cared what on earth she was talking about. All that mattered was that she had agreed that she would go on seeing him, although from now on they would meet less often and in the sand dunes. It was summer, she told him, it was warm enough.

Anywhere would have been warm enough for

Johnny as long as Marjorie Benson was there. In the beginning he had thought that she was embarrassed because he was so young, and that was the reason for her demands for total secrecy. But gradually he realised there was much more to it than that. Marjorie Benson was a mystery. He told her everything about himself, his grandfather, how he had lost his virginity along with a string of other boys with a young school matron, even the court case he tried so hard to forget. She told him next to nothing. He knew that she was thirty-one years old, and that she wrote poetry. Her past was never discussed, any questions he might ask were ignored or skilfully fielded. She was intelligent bordering on intellectual and he sensed that she had been highly educated. She was certainly not Johnny's idea of your average barmaid.

He saw her as the loveliest thing that had ever happened to him. He accepted that their relationship had begun simply because she needed sex. He also knew that, however much she protested, it was far more than that now for both of them. That was all he knew. But it was sufficient.

And so they began to meet on the sand dunes. Not as often as before – he had to accept her terms – but at least they were still lovers. Several times more she tried to end it. He couldn't understand why, and she would not explain. She merely told him there was a part of her life she could not share with him, that she should not really have started a relationship with anyone. But she could never quite manage to dismiss him for ever.

'Don't you know that I would die for you,' he told

her once. His eyes blazed his passion. He really did love her.

'You do not know what you are saying,' she replied. And there was a deep weariness in her voice.

The very first time they met in the dunes, cloaked in the safety of the night's pitch blackness, they had gathered handfuls of scrub grass for a makeshift bed, stripped naked, and spread their clothes on top of it. She had told him to lie on his back and look at the stars, and then she had started to work on his body with her lovely warm wet tongue and her soft fingers.

She was from a different planet. He had found a kindred spirit, another total romantic, and he loved her so much for that. All other girls that he had known would have laughed if he had tried to use the language he and Marjorie shared. Her poetry was so much better than anything he had ever managed, and she wrote for him. He thought it was the most beautiful poetry in the world. Eventually he stopped trying to find out more about her because he realised he must accept Marjorie Benson merely for what she was to him, the complete package, mystery and all.

His favourite poem had been the one in which she came as near she ever did to telling him that she loved him.

> Tomorrow the floods may come
> or the snow
> Tomorrow may not be the same
> our fire may lose its glow.
>
> Tomorrow the world may end
> or the heavens part
> Tomorrow I may drive you round the bend
> and then the pain will start.

Tomorrow is another century
and I am not sure if this is meant to be
What we have is only make believe
A passing joy to give and to receive.

How can I say I love you
when I know it must go away?
I cannot say I love you
And yet I do today.

She had handed him the poem, scribbled on a page torn from an exercise book, and he had showered her with kisses. Her face had been wet with tears. He could still taste the saltiness of her skin.

He loved her so much – and now she was dead.

At first his brain did not function at all. He could not think in the present – only relive the glorious past with the woman he worshipped.

Then he had an idea. The only person he could think of who might be able to help him was Mark Piddle. Johnny jogged back to his bicycle carrying his shoes and socks, damp now from lying on the wet sand, pulled them on, and cycled swiftly up the hill to the rundown Victorian house in Cliff Road in which Mark and Irene shared a flat. By the time he arrived it was just after midnight. He was sobbing uncontrollably as he propped his bike against the iron railings outside, and when it fell over as he climbed the steps to the front door, he did not bother to put it upright again. He flung open the door – which was never locked – and took the stairs to Mark's first-floor flat three at a time. Johnny had been there a couple of times to play chess with the reporter. This visit would be a bit different.

There was no bell so Johnny hammered loudly on the battered door.

Inside Mark was still on the phone. He had already filed copy to four national dailies that night – the *Daily Mirror*, the *Daily Mail*, the *Express* and *the Telegraph* – and had nearly finished dictating his story to the copy-takers of a fifth title, Fleet Street's newest tabloid, the *Sun*. He would have loved to keep his interview with Jenny Stone until next day when he would have been able to file it early enough for it to get the show he thought it deserved, and he could then have gone for an exclusive deal with one of the major papers, but he knew the nationals' own staffers would have caught up by then. So he was completing a ring-around aimed at catching as many of tomorrow's last editions as possible. It would work to his advantage locally, though, because only the first editions reached Devon and so, with a bit of luck, the interview would still be fresh around the Durraton area for Thursday's *Gazette*. The snapper, too, was back in the office, desperately trying to wire a picture quickly enough to catch the last editions of the nationals.

It seemed that Irene, although waiting up for Mark, had fallen asleep on the sofa. The hammering grew louder and louder. Wondering who the hell it could be at that time of night, Mark covered the mouthpiece of the telephone receiver with his hand and yelled at her to answer the door.

Irene, now wearing skin-tight jeans and one of Mark's shirts, took some time to stir, but obediently heaved herself awake and went to the front door. Johnny was leaning against the doorpost. His eyes were wet and rimmed with crimson, his face red and swollen from the tears, and the front of his tee-shirt still damp with them. His jeans were covered with sand and wet patches from squatting on the beach. His whole body seemed to be shaking, and his breath jerked in short sharp gasps, making it difficult for him to talk.

His voice, when it came, was high-pitched and hysterical. 'I killed her, Irene, I killed her. I murdered her . . .'

Mark heard the shouted words just as he completed reading over his piece to the *Sun*. He hung the phone up quickly and dashed to the door.

'For Christ's sake,' he said.

Irene, gentle as ever, took Johnny by the hand and led him to the sofa. He was weeping hysterically again now.

'For Christ's sake,' said Mark again. 'Get him a drink or something. Brandy. Have we got any brandy?'

Irene shook her head. 'Only some beer in the fridge.'

'Tea then,' instructed Mark. 'Hot sweet tea. Go on, Irene. Move yourself.'

He could just catch Johnny's incoherent mumblings through the boy's tears.

'I killed her. I did it. It was me.'

Mark was stunned into silence. He became aware that the boy was wet with sweat, yet shivering with cold.

'Irene, get my thick fisherman's sweater,' he called. 'And hurry up, will you? Where's that tea?'

Irene brought the sweater promptly and made Johnny peel off his damp tee-shirt. She had also taken a clean towel out of the airing cupboard and she rubbed Johnny dry with it before pushing his limp arms into the jumper.

'You get the tea, the kettle's boiling,' she told Mark, who was so surprised at being ordered around by Irene that he did so at once.

Although the night was warm, Irene switched on both bars of the electric fire and Johnny's shivering grew less violent. He took the mug of hot sweet tea when Mark offered it to him and obediently began to sip it. He had stopped sobbing too. The liquid was warming him, making him feel better in spite of everything. He struggled desperately to gain control of himself.

Mark perched on the arm of the only armchair, watching him, amazed and fascinated.

'OK then, Johnny me lad, what's this all about?'

'Marjorie. She's dead.'

Johnny looked as if he were about to cry again.

'Get a hold of yourself,' snapped Mark. 'What are you saying?'

'Marjorie Benson. They found her today . . .'

Mark interrupted. 'I know that, for Chrissake.'

Of course he did. It was his job. He had been told the identity of the body by a contact at about the same time that Johnny's father had learned who she was.

'So what are you telling me, Johnny?'

'It's my fault. I murdered her.'

'You?' Christ, thought Mark. Was this going to be the big one?'

'Yes. If I had done what I should have done she would still be alive. I left her to die.'

'Now hang on a minute. Are you really saying you killed her?'

91

'As near as makes no difference.' Johnny buried his head in his hands.

Mark stood up. 'What the hell does that mean? Are you telling me that you strangled that poor bloody girl?'

'Oh no, oh no, no.'

Johnny wailed in anguish. His eyes were wide with horror.

Mark shook him by the shoulders.

'Listen to me, Johnny. Did you strangle Marjorie Benson?' Mark was pleased by how calm his voice sounded.

Johnny gazed at him in amazement. 'Me? How could I? I loved her . . .'

'Loved her? She was nearly twice your age. Was she your bird then?'

'I suppose so. As much as she was anybody's.'

Mark asked how long Johnny had been seeing her and a host of other questions about the relationship. He was surprised that nobody knew about it. Johnny explained about Marjorie's demands for secrecy. How they had met every Saturday night and sometimes one or two other nights a week in the sand dunes behind the burrows, right over by the estuary, where hardly anybody went during the day, let alone at night.

'On Saturday nights?'

Mark was starting to think now. His reporter's brain turning the information over quickly in his head. 'So you saw her last night?'

'Yes, we met in the dunes and made love. The moon was out . . .'

'After you'd screwed her, then what?'

Johnny winced. Screwed her . . . that wasn't what it had been like.

'I just left her there. She always insisted. I had to go first and then she would walk back to the golf club on her own. She had a room there. She never wanted to be seen with me, you see.'

'Terrific,' said Mark.

Johnny looked at him pleadingly. 'I came to see you because I thought you would know what they're saying. Did she die on the dunes?'

'Yes. The last time anyone saw her alive was when she left the golf club yesterday evening at about nine o'clock. Except you, apparently.'

'So it is my fault. If I hadn't left her there she would still be alive.'

Mark raised his eyes skyward.

'Johnny, have you been to the police?'

'The police? Of course not. I can't tell them anything.'

'You can tell them what you've just told me.'

Johnny looked as if he were going to cry again.

'She was all right when I left her.'

'Was she Johnny?'

'What do you mean? Of course she was. Dear God, Mark. You don't think I did it, do you?'

'No, no, of course I don't.'

Mark spoke swiftly. The prospect of Johnny losing control again did not appeal to him.

'I'm just thinking of the way it will look to the cops. You were probably the last person to see her alive – apart from her killer. What time did you get home last night?'

'I don't know. About one o'clock, I suppose. It was eleven-thirty when I left Marjorie, I think. But I didn't go straight home. It was such a beautiful clear starry night. I had my bike and I stopped up the top of Uckleigh Hill for a smoke.'

'Jesus Christ,' Mark said. 'So you sat there for over an hour? How do you think that is going to sound? Anyone see you?'

'No, I don't think so.'

'Naturally not! What were you doing?'

'Writing in my notebook. You know, a poem. I've told you before.'

'How could you write in the dark?'

'The moon was so bright. I like writing things by moonlight.'

'Jesus Christ,' said Mark, for the umpteenth time.

'Is it important?' asked Johnny.

'It's all important, Johnny boy. The doctors reckon Marjorie died between elevenish and one a.m. If you'd had the sense to go straight home to your mum, things might be looking a bit better for you.'

Johnny put his head in his hands again.

'I wouldn't have hurt her, never. You believe me, don't you Mark?'

'Yes, I believe you. But you *must* go to the police, though, Johnny. If you leave them to find out from somebody else, it will look even worse.'

'But they couldn't find out from anyone else. Nobody else knows. Only you. You wouldn't, would you . . .?'

'Whether I would or not will probably make no difference. I just don't believe that in a village like Pelham Bay, you and Marjorie Benson kept your great affair a total secret. Anyway, you've told me and I'm a journo. What if I go and write a story about the last love in Marjorie Benson's life?'

'Oh please, Mark. I can't take any more.'

'All right. You came to me as a mate, so I'll respect that. And I won't go to the police, either. But you should. You really should. You can't keep this thing hidden. It's not scrumping apples.'

'Look Mark, the police aren't going to believe a word I say, are they? Not after last year. I'm down in their books as some kind of violent sex maniac, aren't I?'

'Rubbish. Anyway you've got no choice but to chance it.'

Johnny lost control again. He jumped to his feet.

'Thank you very much, friend,' he shouted. 'I'm not going near the bloody police. And if you do, I'll never forgive you, never.'

'Hey, Johnny, wait,' Mark called, as Johnny wrenched open the front door.

But by the time Mark had followed him outside, Johnny was already on his bike, careering down the hill. And he'd forgotten to switch his lights on.

'Bloody fool,' muttered Mark.

He went slowly back up the stairs to his flat, deep in thought. Irene was full of questions he couldn't answer.

'Oh shut up and come to bed for Chrissake,' he snapped. 'I'm bloody knackered.'

For once sex did not feature in his mind at all. Irene fell asleep but, in spite of his tiredness, Mark lay awake for hours beside her. He certainly wouldn't go to the police, but what a good tale it was. A toy-boy lover who had been with the woman on the night she was murdered. That was a story that would write itself – an absolute cracker.

'You came to me as a mate so I'll respect that,' he had told Johnny.

Frightfully noble, but it wasn't going to get him a job on a national, was it? Still, he liked Johnny Cooke. And if he did blow the gaffe on him the whole affair could get very messy and he would be in the middle of it. He thought he would probably let matters take their course. He would keep his promise.

It was just about the last decent thing Mark Piddle ever did.

Eight

Mark woke feeling pretty ropy after eventually falling into a fitful sleep. He had dreamed an almost wet dream about Jenny Stone. He had an erection but there was nothing unusual about that. More unusual was the fact that he did not want to roll over on top of Irene and hump himself selfishly to orgasm. Seeing Jenny last night had stirred up all those feelings from two years ago that he had previously not allowed himself to remember. He resolved to telephone her as soon as he got to his office – he just hoped he hadn't misread the signs, because he wanted her. God, how he wanted her. He got out of bed and walked with some difficulty to the bathroom. He wanted to pee, but he couldn't. It was no good. He was burning up inside. He sat on the lavatory and made himself come. All he had to do was close his eyes and imagine he was inside Jenny Stone and it wasn't difficult at all. But it brought little relief. This was ridiculous.

He left the house at seven-thirty, before Irene was up, and raced the Cooper into Durraton to the office. When he got there he made himself a cup of tea and scanned through all the papers reading up on the various versions of the murder until he thought it was a respectable enough hour to phone the Stones' house. He just hoped Jenny would answer, and he got lucky. She did. The sound of her voice made the hairs stand up on the back of his neck. He was afraid his voice sounded high pitched and strange. His cock was straining fit to burst against his trousers.

After waking screaming from her nightmare, Jenny had been afraid to sleep again. When the phone rang she was sitting, wearing her pink candlewick dressing gown over her pyjamas, in the bay window of the front room. She had probably never moved as fast in her life at that hour of the morning as she did then. She jerked out of her seat as if it were fitted with starting blocks, and sprinted into the hall where the only phone in the house sat in isolated splendour on its own wrought-iron table. She picked up the receiver before the end of the third ring. Her mother had not even emerged from the kitchen.

It was Mark Piddle. Unbelievable. She felt as if she had willed him to call. She glanced at her watch. It was just gone eight o'clock. And he would have been working late into the night. She smiled to herself. Oh yes, he was hers all right, and this time on her terms. He had called to see if she was OK, Mark said. Not really, she had replied, but she would be.

The reporter thanked her for the interview and told her he hoped she would get over the shock soon. He was very formal. Then he asked if he could see her, maybe buy her a drink. She could feel his tension down the phone line. Her stomach seemed to tighten in a knot. She heard herself say yes.

'What time?' he asked.

'What do you mean, what time? What about fixing a day first?' she replied.

'It's got to be today.'

'Why?' She knew she was teasing him.

'Because I can't wait any longer,' he said.

She giggled. 'Half past six in the pub by the cricket ground,' she said.

'No,' he replied. 'Let's make it lunchtime. Then I'll take you for a drive. Please.'

He didn't often say please.

'Haven't you got to work this afternoon?'

'Please,' he said again.

They met at one o'clock. She was wearing shorts, a skimpy lacy top, and no bra. He wanted to reach out right away and touch her nipples. He could see them clearly through the flimsy material: they were big and dark. She asked for a Cinzano and lemonade. Ghastly drink. He bought it for her and ordered a pint of bitter for himself. God, he didn't want to waste time in a pub. When could he get her out of here?

She asked him to tell her everything he knew about the murder. He supposed that was natural enough under the circumstances. He gave her the basic facts, then, swearing her to secrecy, he told her about Johnny Cooke's midnight visit. He was trying to impress her. He explained how Johnny had kept saying that it was his fault, how at first he had thought the boy was actually confessing to murder.

'And he wasn't?' asked Jenny.

'He just felt guilty, you know,' said Mark.

She asked him if he was quite sure Johnny was innocent.

'Soft as shit, that lad,' Mark had replied, and had explained vaguely about Johnny's past. About the court case.

'One drunken night he got out of his pram with

some bird he picked up. Now he reckons he's labelled a sex offender. He may be right.'

Eventually she allowed him to lead her from the pub. They hadn't been there half an hour. It seemed like an eternity to Mark. He drove like hell. He knew where he was going. He took the river road away from the coast and swung the Cooper into the old quarry a few miles up the valley. There were bushes there you could drive straight into and be totally private even in daylight.

Before the engine had died away he had her in his arms. He remembered the frenzy of the dustbin yard at the school dance. She had made it quite clear then exactly what she wanted. His tongue was down her throat and she was responding just like before. He had one hand on her breasts, squeezing those seductive nipples, and the other on her lower thigh. He thrust it up the leg of her shorts and pushed his fingers inside her knickers. At last he could feel her. He could feel all the delicious crevices of her. She was wet again. Could she really be a virgin still? He had one finger inside her. God, she was hot. Then he felt her start to struggle. She was trying to push his hand away. He thrust his tongue further down her throat. He couldn't stop, he just couldn't. She was strong and firm and quite cool. Not frightened at all. She put both hands under his chin and pushed his face backwards off her. Then she slapped him as hard as she could right across one cheek. He collapsed back into the driver's seat, stunned.

'I thought you wanted it,' he gasped.

'I do,' she replied. 'More than you can ever imagine. And I want my first time to be with you.'

So she was a virgin. It was probably just nerves. He touched her cheek with his hand.

'So do I,' he said. 'Will you let me now?'

She shook her head.

'No. It's got to be right. I'm not doing it in a car. And I don't want to get pregnant.'

'You won't,' he told her. 'I brought a packet of three with me.'

'I don't want to lose my virginity to somebody wearing a plastic bag over his thing.'

Mark laughed in spite of himself. 'OK, I'll take it out,' he told her.

'Don't be ridiculous,' she replied.

His frustration was almost too much to bear.

'I don't remember you being bothered before.'

'No,' she said. 'I think I must have gone mad. That teacher did me a good turn. This time I want everything to be right.'

'And how do you plan to arrange that?'

'For a start I want to go on the pill and I want you to get them for me. I can hardly go to our family doctor, can I? You can fix it, I'll bet. Get me some pills and I'm all yours.'

She smiled what she hoped was her most winning smile.

'Just like that. And meanwhile what do you suggest I do with this?'

To hell with it. He unzipped his trousers.

'Oh that's OK,' she told him casually. 'I'll deal with that. I've done that before.'

She had too. She took him in her hands and began to play with him. It was bliss. She told him he could touch her on the breasts but nowhere else. He did better than that. He undid her ridiculous blouse, lowered his lips to her nipples, and sucked them like there was no tomorrow. He felt her stiffen and thought for one moment that she was going to give in and let him have her. It did not occur to him to try and force her. He wanted her panting for it, crying out for it, the way he knew she could. She worked on him like crazy and it didn't take long. He came in great spurts all over his trousers, the car seat, and her hands. But his desire to be inside her was so overwhelming that once again it brought scant relief. Calmly she mopped him up with a handful of paper tissues taken from the box on the back seat.

He took her home, then went out and got very drunk. He slept on the sofa. In the morning he stole a packet of pills from Irene's stock of them, which she kept in the bathroom cabinet. He just hoped she wouldn't notice. Actually he didn't really care. He had arranged to see Jenny again that evening. He picked her up at seven and drove straight to the lay-by. She didn't protest. He gave her the pack of pills.

'I've got a rug, we can lie down outside if you don't want to do it in the car,' he told her. 'Nobody will see us here.'

She glanced at the pills.

'Don't be silly, I've got to start taking these after a period and they don't make you safe right away,' she said. 'It'll be at least a fortnight.'

His lower body was one big ache. 'I can't believe this,' he said.

'Don't worry, I'll bring you off again if you want,' she volunteered, and started to unzip his flies.

'No you won't,' he said. 'It makes me feel worse than not doing anything.'

He decided on a last try. With the forefinger of one

hand he lightly traced the hardness of her nipples. He brought his lips close to her ear and began whispering to her.

'I won't hurt you. I'll make you ready and I'll slip into you so gently. I won't hurt you.'

Strange, he meant that too. He would never hurt Jenny Stone. He was sure of it.

'I know you won't hurt me, that's not the point,' she said rather prissily and with supreme self-confidence.

How could she be prissy at a time like this? And how could she be so cool and confident and in charge? Virgins weren't supposed to behave like that.

He carried on trying.

'You know how much I want to be inside you,' he said. 'You want it. I know you do. I want to fill you up. I want to drive you wild. You can be wild, can't you, crazy . . .?'

She pushed him away again. Grumpily he started the motor and drove her home.

She went straight to her room. She sat on the edge of the bed and reached under her skirt, putting both hands on herself. She rocked backwards and forwards. Her act of willpower was extraordinary. But never again would Mark Piddle think he could have her and just walk away. He had to learn to do as she said.

She wanted Mark to lie in bed longing for her body, just as she had longed for his so many times. She shut her eyes and tried not to think about him. She had never had sex, and yet she could imagine so vividly what it would be like.

Mark turned the car and drove back to his flat.

This time he was going to have to give it to Irene, and how he was going to give it to her.

She had been asleep on the couch and was still only half awake when he made her kneel on the floor. He didn't want to look at her face. He didn't want to see her compliance. He didn't want to see her wince when he hurt her inside. Poor little Irene. He was quite detached. She was just satisfying his need now until he could do what he really wanted with the girl who was driving him mad. He pushed himself straight into her. It didn't take long. But the frustration still burnt in his belly. He made her suck him until he was hard again and then he took her into the bedroom, threw himself on top of her and hammered into her once more. This time she was on her back with her head over the edge of the bed and he manœuvred her like he had before so that her pelvis was pivoted upwards and he could get deeper into her than in any other position. It was his second erection. It was going to last a long time. And it was going to take some satisfying. He pushed into her with all his strength, with all his might.

The next day was a Wednesday. Three days after she had discovered Marjorie Benson's body, Jenny still could not sleep without having terrible nightmares. And her desire for Mark Piddle was driving her wild. She was determined to stick to her own terms, and to make sure that he would never just drift out of her life again. But all day Wednesday passed and Mark did not call. Had she teased him too much? Had he moved on to some other, easier girl? Every time the phone rang in the tiled hall of 16 Seaview

Road, Jenny rushed to pick up the receiver. It was never Mark.

Johnny was at the deckchair stand again. He had turned up as usual every day since Marjorie's death, sticking to his routine. But oh, how he missed her, and how afraid he was. He thought he wanted to die. He could not eat, he felt dull and listless.

Bill Turpin did nothing but prowl around all morning. Johnny had been acutely aware of the old man's thoughtful staring. The boy tried desperately to behave normally. But he knew he was not winning the struggle.

He felt that Marjorie had been everything to him, She alone had understood when he had told her all about himself, and he had shared everything with her, the secret thoughts he had never allowed anyone else near.

That morning's tourists seemed noisier and more mindless than ever. Johnny felt contempt for them. He knew it was hypocritical, wrong even, but he couldn't help himself. All his life he had watched their convoys arriving, clogging the roads with their caravans and their campers, crawling along in fear of sharp corners and high hedges, winding lanes and steep hills. They threw litter over the moors, at the roadside, and on the beach. They crowded out the pubs on Saturday nights and demanded discos where once there had been only joyous peace. They provided a ceaseless market for the rubbishy souvenirs that appeared in all the shops just before Whitsun, and were relentlessly replaced as fast as they sold until long after August bank holiday.

But take them to the small unspoilt beaches of

North Devon where the cliffs are carved out of marble and the rocks have been given muscle by Michelangelo, where the sea is deep green above drowned forests and the sand is the finest in the world, and most of them would feel nothing. Johnny was certain of his own superiority. He revelled in the mighty poetry of nature. It was in his head all the time.

He had explained all this to Marjorie and she had not laughed at him, nor criticised when he told her how in a moment of madness the previous summer, he and a couple of friends had toured the district scrawling 'Grockles Go Home' on posters and lavatory walls. Marjorie recognised the true Johnny Cooke, and Johnny had loved that in her. He was no vandal. Underneath his veneer of bravado he was a quiet introverted boy, eighteen years old and already resigned to having nowhere in particular to go, happy to hand out Bill Turpin's deckchairs and daydream in the sun. At least, until last Sunday he had been.

Brooding adolescent Johnny, sensitive but youthfully arrogant, with his long wavy dark brown hair, black eyes and perfect body, was handsome and he knew it. There had already been a selection of girls in his young life, most of them much older than him, but he had never had a regular girlfriend. Until Marjorie. He had never before been interested in making the effort to get to know somebody, to care, to learn to love. By and large he had lived in a world of his own, wandering off for long lonely walks, reading the books he had found he really loved and not bothering or remembering to read the books he needed to read in order to pass his exams at school.

When he was thirteen, Johnny had been taken ill

with meningitis, and, during the weeks of convalescence became even more of a loner. Boys of thirteen are not usually very interested in sitting quietly and talking, in putting the world to rights, and Johnny's friends soon became bored with visiting him while he was sick. It was a thoughtful time for him. His instinctive confidence in the health and strength of his young body had been shaken rigid. He had been brought close to death at an age when death is a lifetime away and a lifetime seems like eternity.

It was almost too much to bear: the sympathy, the understanding, the sense of near tragedy. When he started to regain his strength, he needed to get out of the house, to clear his head. So he fell into the habit of visiting his grandfather, a big quiet man, a retired farmer who never seemed to get excited about anything, good or bad. Before he met Marjorie, Johnny's grandfather had been the only true confidant in his life – but then his grandfather had died.

The old man had lived in a solid square house with a garden of vegetables and fruit and a garage in which he kept his bicycle and sacks of potatoes and boxes of sweet smelling apples. He and Johnny would go for long, long walks through the fields by the sea. And Johnny would ask him what he thought of God and the Prime Minister, and why the world was always on the edge of war. On these walks he would pour out all the crazy mixed-up ideas and worries of a thirteen-year-old who had had too much time to think. And the old man would produce boiled sweets from deep pockets, butterscotch and fruit drops, some without paper and covered in fluff. He would rub them on his shirt to clean them and then take out his false teeth so that he could suck the sweets more easily.

He would listen with the patience of his eighty years and a lifetime lived in the peace of the countryside.

'In my day us was only worried about filling us bellies and keeping warm in winter,' he told Johnny. 'Then there was war, two of the buggers. And us worried about keeping alive. There wadden time for nought else.

'I tell 'ee this, boy, I don't know if us be better off now or not. Buggered if I do.'

His words never amounted to anything clever or profound, but the old man had a natural wisdom about him, and wisest of all, he knew how much Johnny needed somebody to listen. And so the boy spent almost all his days with his grandfather, and his evenings scribbling poems in exercise books.

Most of it was not really true poetry, just outpourings of feelings, the things he said during the day put on paper in bad blank verse. All about knocking down the walls of ignorance, rushing through dark tunnels into vacuums of freedom, and trying to get back through the tunnel again because it was cosier on the other side.

But as Johnny grew strong once more, he went back to school and refound his friends. He began to forget the fear. He stopped writing poems, and he stopped seeing his grandfather.

When the old man died he hadn't visited him for months. Johnny was consumed with guilt and the thought that his grandfather had gone for ever was almost unbearable.

At the funeral everyone was glad the weather was

fine. The ham was sweet, the pickles held the tang of last summer, the tea was strong, and they talked about everything except dying.

The coffin, and the flowers, and the body of Johnny's grandfather, flabby and red and ugly with great age, had been burned. Johnny thought suddenly of flesh burning. Just for a moment he had a dreadful vision of flames licking through the rosewood and biting into the still body of his grandfather.

He left his ham and pickles, went to the lavatory, and was secretly sick. When he came back his face was white, but his hands were steady. And he sat down and ate his meal.

Twice now in his young life he had been confronted by death. Its shadow would never leave him. The third time was approaching – and that would finally destroy him.

On the night of his grandfather's funeral, he had slipped out of the house taking with him all the money that he had. He had spent the evening in pubs where his age was not known, drinking more beer than he had ever drunk before. In the third pub he visited he found himself chatting up a pretty red-haired girl wearing thick eye liner and the shortest possible mini skirt. Through the beery haze she looked very desirable to Johnny. He bought her whisky and coke and ordered a large whisky for himself.

The girl happily took up Johnny's offer to walk her home, and raised no objections when he suggested a detour along the unlit riverside path by the park. They sat together on a bench and began to kiss. So far so good. She responded eagerly. Johnny fondled her breasts through the flimsy material of her blouse and she barely protested. He could feel that her nipples were hard. He didn't know much – but he knew that was a good sign. He kissed her, gently at first, then a little more forcefully. He parted her lips with his tongue and began probing, exploring, inside her mouth. She was still responding, flicking her tongue against his, sucking his mouth. Very promising. He began to undo the buttons of her blouse. She pushed his hand away. Each time he tried to get a hand inside her blouse she pushed him away. Oh, how he wanted to feel those pert rounded breasts, to tweak those hard little nipples between his fingers.

He had an erection in spite of all the booze. Hopefully he placed her hand on the bulge in his trousers. She felt it for a few seconds, moving her fingers just a little, then took her hand away. He couldn't make her put it back.

He began stroking her legs above the knees. He was aware that her skirt had slid up nearly to her crotch. She was teasing him with her mouth but not letting him do any of the things he so wanted to do with his hands.

Finally, drunk and frustrated, he held his left arm across her body and shoved his right hand, hard and directly on target, up between her legs. The skirt did not offer much protection. He ripped at her underwear, tearing tights and knickers in his eagerness. It was not until the next morning that he realised how stupid he had been.

The girl had screamed, struggled ferociously, and with the strength of fear managed somehow to heave him off her. She had jumped to her feet, slipped on the grass, fallen over, further damaged her already laddered tights, and covered her clothing in mud and grass stains. She ran off, sobbing and shouting that her father would kill her when he saw the state she was in.

Johnny sat on the seat a bit longer. He was very drunk. His stomach, assaulted earlier by the emotion of the day, started to rebel against the beer and whisky to which it was unused. He was sick again, and finally staggered unsteadily home still feeling dreadfully ill. His father, who had waited up, took one look at him and gave him the lecture of his life. It was mostly wasted because Johnny could remember almost nothing when he woke the next morning.

His memory began to return all too vividly a little later when two policemen arrived on the Cooke door-step. Johnny's mother immediately telephoned his father, who came home from the greengrocer's shop he ran in the town. The girl, forced by her parents to explain her appearance, had blurted out that she had been attacked by Johnny Cooke.

Johnny, suffering from the first real hangover of his young life, said over and over again that he didn't do anything. The truth was that he couldn't really remember what he had done, the police were not convinced, and so Johnny faced the court proceedings which were to continue to haunt him. The girl, it transpired, was only fifteen years old, and Johnny was charged with indecently assaulting a girl under the age of consent. The landlord of the pub where both youngsters had been drinking also found himself in trouble – but that didn't help Johnny.

What did help him, in true small-town style, was the friendship of his father with the local police chief inspector – his Rotary Club friend Ted Robson. Only that prevented charges of attempted rape.

Johnny had appeared before the magistrates, pleaded guilty, and been put on probation for three years. His protests had not impressed his father who never felt quite the same about his son again. His mother just pretended the incident had not happened. But the publicity in the local press had, she told her closest friends, 'nearly killed her'.

'Just you behave yourself, my boy,' she would warn continually. 'Another do like the last affair and it would kill your father.'

Johnny knew what she really meant. The eleventh commandment ruled his family: don't get found out.

Suddenly Johnny was startled back to the present. Bill Turpin loomed at his side. He had crept up in that disconcerting way he had. Silent footsteps. Johnny felt the old man's breath before he heard a sound.

'Morning boy. All right this morning be 'ee?'

'Yeah.'

'Feeling better, then?'

Johnny's flesh started to crawl. Did Bill Turpin know something? Oh God. If it was going to be anybody it would be Bill, the nosy old bugger.

'What do you mean?' he asked.

'Well, I thought you seemed a bit off-colour the last day or two.'

'Uh yeah, tummy's a bit dicky.'

'Oh.' Long drawn out. Speculative. 'I thought you might be fretting over that poor maid.'

Johnny tried to keep cool.

'What are you talking about?'

'That poor murdered maid. You saw a bit of her, didn't you boy?'

'What are you saying?' Johnny's voice came out in a croak.

'Oh, I used to see you pair scuttling off together now and again. I often take old Jip for a stroll over the dunes of an evening.'

Johnny knew his face was now crimson.

'I haven't seen her for a long time,' he said quickly. 'Not a long time.'

He didn't realise that he was shouting.

'All right, boy, all right. Calm down.'

Bill had his eternal pipe in his hand. He sucked on the stem, still staring.

'I am calm,' Johnny snapped. 'Do you mind if I go for a quick swim?'

Bill shook his head.

Johnny peeled off his shirt and jeans. Underneath he was wearing a pair of brief red swimming shorts. Two girl tourists walking by turned their heads for a better look. All the girls fancied Johnny, Bill Turpin knew that. Not surprising, he thought, good-looking boy and a fine body he had on him too. What a shame.

Johnny sprinted down the slipway and across the stretch of beach to the sea. Bill leaned against the sea wall. The faithful Jip nuzzled affectionately against his leg. He pushed her lazily away with a foot.

'Lie down, dog, will you.'

The old man tapped his pipe against the wall and began the ritual of refilling and relighting it. He drew on the tobacco, blowing smoke through his mouth and nostrils. Johnny had swum a couple of hundred

113

yards out to sea. He was moving very fast, ploughing through the water with his powerful crawl.

Bill watched, squinting against the already bright sun; motionless, controlled, like an old tomcat waiting to pounce.

Throughout the morning, Johnny wondered if he should take Mark's advice and go to the police himself. When the blue Q car pulled up on the no-parking zone by the deckchair stand, he knew it was too late for that.

He glanced quickly at Bill Turpin, but the old man looked away.

Johnny ran his fingers through his long hair, still damp from swimming, as he watched Detective Chief Inspector Mallett heave his bulk out of the car. The policeman approached, trying to look reassuring. He could see the panic in Johnny at fifty paces, and it was not his style to frighten those he interviewed. He wanted the truth and he thought he knew the best way to get it. He was a softly, softly man. People talked to Phil Mallett as a rule, they trusted him. He looked like a picture-book illustration of a Devonian country policeman, his skin smooth and creamy with very little beard, his cheeks excessively plump and pink. He adopted his most sympathetic, friendly look, and strolled over to Johnny with an almost too casual walk. The young detective inspector accompanying him was a different kettle of fish: an ambitious career cop, a graduate, whom Mallett suspected had been hoisted on him by those who thought his methods were too old-fashioned and too soft.

'Just you keep quiet unless I say otherwise,' Mallett hissed at him out of the side of his mouth.

Johnny knew his hands were shaking. He twisted them behind his back. The deeper he got into this, the more certain it became that his parents would have to hear about it. That was the worst of all. The recriminations, the tears, the oppressive caring.

'Been swimming, have you?' asked the inspector conversationally, looking at Johnny's thick dark hair, wet and shiny from the sea.

Come on, come to the point, get on with it, Johnny willed.

The young inspector was kicking the ground with the toe of one shoe. He was just as impatient. The boy should have been picked up by a carload of uniformed bobbies and whisked straight off to the station in his opinion. No messing. Give him a scare.

'Wouldn't mind a dip myself.' The chief inspector smiled as if he had made a joke.

Johnny tried to smile, but was not sure if he succeeded. Mallett leaned against a pile of deckchairs adopting his best 'I'm on your side . . . but' manner.

And then he asked the question Johnny had been dreading.

'I understand you knew the young woman who was murdered on Saturday?'

Johnny took a deep breath.

'Yes, I did.'

'Well then, lad, you'd better tell me all about it.'

Johnny told him how he had met Marjorie at the golf club and they had become friends. Just friends? Just friends, Johnny heard himself say. He had a feeling he was acting stupidly. He was right.

Phil Mallett scratched his balding head.

'Now why would a woman like that be interested in a young lad like you, Johnny?' he asked wryly.

'She was lonely. We used to walk out over the dunes and talk.'

'Talk, eh?'

'Yes.'

'What, a healthy good-looking feller like you? Out with an attractive older woman and just talking?'

'Yes.'

The detective chief inspector shook his head sorrowfully. His eyes were very gentle. When he spoke again his voice was flat and expressionless.

'I am not satisfied with your story, Johnny. I have to ask you to come back to the station with me now, where I will take a formal statement from you. I suggest that along the way you think very carefully about what you are going to say.'

About bloody time too, thought the young inspector, as the two men led Johnny to the waiting car.

Johnny was taken to the station's only interview room where, sitting on a hard upright chair before a wooden table, he had stared resolutely down at his hands, clenched tightly in his lap, almost throughout the interrogation. His palms were sweaty and he was painfully aware of the tape recorder relentlessly putting on record the awful mess he knew he was making of it all. At last he raised his eyes and looked directly at Phil Mallett.

'I was in love with her,' he said. His chest felt tight.

The young inspector could contain himself no longer.

'Love?' he snapped. 'Is that what you call it? Is that what you called what you did to that girl on the river bank last year?'

Phil Mallett motioned sharply for the D.I. to be silent, but it was too late.

Johnny looked as if he had been hit.

'I knew it, I knew it, that's why I didn't want to tell you anything. I'm already branded by you lot, aren't I? But you're bloody wrong.'

'When did you last see Marjorie Benson, Johnny?'

Johnny hesitated, just for a second.

'Ages ago.'

Oh God. Another mistake? He didn't know which way to turn.

'I don't think you're telling the truth,' said the detective chief inspector.

Johnny felt the panic overwhelm him. Had Bill Turpin seen him with her the night she died? And had Bill talked to the police already?

God, pray that the policeman was bluffing. Johnny was sweating now. He couldn't admit that he had been with Marjorie just before she was killed, making love to her, pushing himself inside her. He just couldn't. He didn't even think about forensic evidence. About his semen in her. He was too muddled, not nearly clever enough for any kind of crime.

He tried desperately to clear his head. He'd call the bluff.

'All right, all right, I last saw her on the Tuesday before she died.'

'Not on Saturday? My spies tell me that you always saw her on Saturdays.'

Oh God, oh God, Johnny thought, he was tying himself in knots here.

'Not last Saturday,' he repeated. 'Not the night she died.'

Pray it was a bluff. Pray.

'I see,' said D.C.I. Mallett. 'Where were you on Saturday night then?'

'I went to the pictures.'

'Who with?'

'On my own.'

'Anyone see you?'

'I don't know.'

'What film did you see?'

Johnny felt the trap closing around him. What was on at the Palais last week? He passed the cinema often enough.

'James Bond . . . the new one . . . *On Her Majesty's Secret Service*,' he stammered.

Fortunately for Johnny, the policemen hadn't seen the film either. But he wasn't fooled.

'My advice to you is not to lie to me, boy,' he said quietly. 'If you do, things will only get worse for you . . .'

At that moment, Johnny could not imagine how things could get any worse. He did not know the half of it. And he was not yet aware that while he was being interviewed. Mark Piddle had arrived at the police station.

Mark had something to report. Quite a lot to report. He was not his usual cool self. Like Johnny on the previous Sunday night, he could not stop shaking, he was fighting for control. He knew how important it was to get things straight in his mind. He had every right to be upset. But he must not appear to be frightened.

He blurted out the short version of his story to the desk sergeant, and was immediately taken to a side office to wait for Phil Mallett to become available to interview him. They brought him a cup of tea. He drank it gratefully, spooning in the sugar. He didn't take sugar in his tea normally. But this was not a

118

normal day. He stirred so much sugar into his cup the tea was almost like syrup. It was good for shock, they said.

And he was shocked all right.

Nine

The following morning, Jenny learned why Mark had not called her. His girlfriend Irene had been reported missing. She had disappeared. Police feared a double murder, linked to the Marjorie Benson strangling.

Jenny rang Mark at the paper. He had not given her his home number. Because of Irene. He had never made a secret of Irene, but Jenny had not cared. Poor Irene had somehow always seemed irrelevant.

It took her until Friday to get hold of him, and when she did he sounded strained and distant, although she supposed that wasn't surprising. Still no word about Irene, he told her. She had not come home on Tuesday night, then he discovered she had not been at work all day on Tuesday. That was all he knew and it wasn't much. The police were worried. They feared the worst for Irene; that there was a nutter on the loose. Nobody seemed to give much for Irene's chances of being alive.

As he talked to Jenny, Mark began to experience the familiar stirring of his loins again. He fought for control. He couldn't see her. Not yet. But by God, even with all that had happened, he wanted to.

Jenny felt as if she was going quite mad. She was plagued by images of death. The body of Marjorie Benson floated determinedly in her head; there was no escape from the recurring nightmare of that face.

And now the disappearance of Irene seemed to draw her further into the horror story. She did not want to become any more involved, and she knew that if she saw Mark again then she would. Yet Mark was the other image that was plaguing her. Mark kissing her and touching her, Mark finally entering her. She could not walk away from him. Her body craved him. The stress and unease brought her period on early, and as it started her first thought was that this meant she could begin the course of birth control pills more than a week earlier than she had expected. Then she would be protected. Then she could go to Mark on *her* terms. And she would to go him, in spite of a nagging feeling that she shouldn't.

Mark had not gone to work on that Wednesday when Jenny had tried so hard to contact him. In fact he had spent most of Wednesday at the police station, reporting the disappearance of Irene and giving the details of his midnight visit from Johnny Cooke on the night Marjorie Benson's body was discovered. Looking strained and anxious, he explained that he had been worrying about Johnny's visit and all that he had said, had realised that he should have reported it earlier, but had been sure that the boy would see sense and go to the police himself. And he hadn't really believed that Johnny Cooke had killed Marjorie Benson. He thought Johnny was just hysterical. Then Irene had disappeared leaving no note, no word. This wasn't like her at all, but they'd had a bit of a row, and he thought she'd gone to spend the night with her parents. It wasn't until the hotel where Irene worked called to ask if she was all right because she hadn't been in the day before and yet again hadn't turned up, that he had started to worry and decided to go to the police. And it was then that he had begun to wonder if Irene's disappearance could possibly have anything to do with Johnny and with Marjorie Benson's murder.

'God, I hope I'm wrong,' he told D.I. Mallett.

Mark came across as a controlled and highly intelligent young man, with nothing to hide but under great stress, and aware that the police would have to check him out.

It is a fact of criminal record that most murders are committed by the relations or lovers of the victim. If Irene Nichols was dead Mark Piddle would, under normal circumstances, be the prime suspect. But these were patently not normal circumstances. There was the Marjorie Benson murder to consider and, in any case, there was no reason yet to suppose that Irene Nichols was not alive and well. People walk out of their homes all the time. Often they turn up again sooner or later. Sometimes not for years and years, and sometimes not at all. But even that doesn't necessarily mean they are dead, and it's certainly very difficult to try a case for murder without a body. There have only been a handful of such cases in history.

And so Phil Mallett, although thorough as ever in his inquiries, was reasonably satisfied by Mark's statement. The same could not be said about Johnny Cooke's muddled ramblings. There was not yet enough hard evidence, but the finger did seem to be pointing more and more at Johnny, who actually had a record of sexual assault. Johnny was kept inside for further questioning, and meanwhile the investigation proceeded with tests on Johnny's clothes, his hair and skin, and, of course, his body fluids.

The D.C.I. was coming under more and more pressure from his peers to find a way of successfully charging Johnny; the bright young detective inspector who was snapping at Phil Mallett's heels seemed to have no doubts whatsoever.

'It's always the lover,' he said sagely – as if he had the benefit of years of experience of such matters, instead of merely a college education and too fast a promotion in the opinion of his immediate superior.

As the evidence against Johnny Cooke accumulated, Phil Mallett felt himself being pushed further and further along what seemed to be an inevitable route. Nobody had time for what they called P.C. Plod tactics. D.C.I. Mallett had been brought up in the force to believe that good police work involved tying up all the loose ends, being absolutely sure of yourself. But nowadays nothing mattered except figures, the ratio of crimes to convictions. Nobody talked about justice any more. That was almost a dirty word, and Phil had come to accept that you could only fight for your idea of the right way of doing things up to a certain point. One man cannot turn the tide. Anyway, perhaps this time he was wrong because he could not even fully explain why he was so afraid that a terrible mistake was about to be made.

The forensic tests proved that Johnny had had sexual intercourse with Marjorie Benson shortly before she died, and when the results of a search of Johnny's home were reported to him, the D.C.I. knew that was it.

He could no longer hold out for more time. The tide had come roaring in right over his head.

With rare self-discipline, brought on by the shock he had experienced, Mark did not contact Jenny. By Sunday, exactly a week after she had floated into Marjorie Benson's body, Jenny was desperate to see him. Her period had lasted only three days as usual. She thought she would now be more-or-less protected by the pill course she was beginning. In any case, she could wait no longer. She caught the Durraton bus on Sunday morning, alighting at the top of the hill above Pelham Bay, and quickly walked the couple of hundred yards to the house where she knew Mark lived. She was praying he would be there. She needed him and she was going to have him. She was being quite calculated about it, and was rather surprising herself.

Downstairs in the hall there was a list of all the tenants and their flat numbers. It was another hot day, and Jenny knew she was sweating slightly by the time she climbed the stairs to his flat. Mark answered the door shirtless, wearing only a pair of loose shorts. His face lit up when he saw her, but then clouded over again, as if he wasn't sure whether he wanted to see her or not. Her eyes took in his bare torso, his broad shoulders, his narrow waist, and his strong, muscular legs. She was tall, but he towered above her. He was all that a young man of twenty-three should be and more – lean and hard and very fit-looking. Much the way she had imagined from the touches and glimpses of him she had previously experienced. Seeing him like that in reality after having dreamed about him for so long threw her a little.

'I – I was just passing,' she stammered.

'I was just going out,' he lied. He was hardly dressed for going out. She was aware that he looked nervous and unsure of himself. And she already knew that was most un-Marklike.

'I know you're upset, I reckoned I might be able to take your mind off things,' she said.

That sounded pathetic, she thought. Hardly surprising he didn't reply.

'Well, aren't you going to invite me in then?' she asked. Even more pathetic.

He stood back, letting her pass, and closed the door behind her.

To hell with it, she thought. 'You might like to know that I am now fully protected against unwanted pregnancy,' she announced.

She knew she was being quite shameless, particularly under the circumstances, but she just could not stop herself.

'What's the matter?' she asked. 'Don't you want me any more?'

He was still silent. She knew something was very wrong with him, and assumed it must be Irene's disappearance. He was just not reacting the way she had already grown to expect. Strangely, her confidence was returning now. She reckoned she could fix that – make him react exactly the way she wanted him to.

In one sudden movement she slipped her tee-shirt above her head. She was not wearing a bra. She unzipped her mini skirt and removed it and her knickers both at once, in one fluid movement. Now

125

she was standing naked before him. It had taken mere seconds.

Mark just stared at her. Her breasts were full and round. He had touched them, had his mouth round them already, and he knew how beautiful they were. But seeing her totally naked was something else. She was innocent – yet completely aware. There was nothing coy in the way she stood, she was a young woman waiting to make love for the first time. She was breathing deeply and her breasts were rising and falling in rhythm. The honesty of her desire gave her beauty. His breath caught in his throat. His eyes were fixed on her pubic mound. She caught the direction of his gaze and involuntarily her hand reached for herself, and she lightly fingered the hair there. She stared at him, unblinking, every inch of her an invitation. Yet he did not have an erection. Mark Piddle, superstud, was standing looking at a naked young girl, and he didn't have a hard-on. He was transfixed. Mesmerised.

'It'll be all right,' he heard her say softly.

She was reassuring him. Amazing. But he began to believe that this time it would be.

She stepped forward and took him in her arms and he buried his head in her neck. Then the smell of her engulfed him. The same body scent that had driven him wild two years earlier, that had excited him so much when they had been together in his car, when she had refused to let him take her, even though he knew she had wanted it as much as him. He was aware that she was sweating slightly and also that her juices must already be running. She smelt of earthy demanding sex. And it was delicious.

Now he was starting to swell at last. He felt her

126

slip her hands inside his shorts and her touch was electric. She undid the button of the waistband. They were old tennis shorts and their soft whiteness flattered his youthful brown skin. With the fingers of one hand she traced patterns through the fuzzy baby hair covering his chest, down over his flat stomach, down, down. He helped her remove the shorts. He was wearing no underpants. They stood naked, looking at each other. He was fully erect now. This time he took her in his arms.

'I won't hurt you, Jenny, I'd never hurt you,' he muttered urgently, unaware that it had never occurred to her that he would.

His cock dug into her belly, damp yet burning against her. He could feel her eagerness and began to realise that she had no fear of the size of him, nor of the power of his desire.

'I know you won't,' she said, clinging to him.

'I am going to make you so ready that when I put it into you it will just slip in as if it belongs there,' he told her.

'I think it does belong there,' she whispered.

He melted. He laid her on the bed then and opened her legs and buried his head between them. She had read about this, but what Mark was doing to her exceeded her wildest expectations. He licked and sucked and nibbled her to distraction, and she felt herself opening wide as he darted his tongue in and out of her. Mark was loving it too. Out of guilt he had occasionally done this to Irene – although only usually to get round her again after having served her roughly. But he knew the pleasure it could give. It was the only time he ever brought Irene to orgasm, because when he actually entered her he always did so with such force and selfishness that the poor girl didn't stand a chance.

This was the bed he had shared with Irene. He tried to put all thoughts of her out of his mind. With Jenny starting to writhe and moan beneath him, it was not difficult.

She was saying something. What was it? She was squeezing his head with her legs, blocking his ears.

'Can I taste you too? I'd like to know what you taste like.'

Could she? This was unbelievable. This was sensational. This was what he had been looking for all his life. She was just like him. She was pure animal, and the sex in her was taking control of her now. Her first time and she wanted to suck his cock!

With practised agility he swung round in the bed so that he was kneeling above her. He was careful not to push it at her – he didn't want to put her off. She teased the end of him with her tongue. She paused – and he was sure she was licking her lips. Then she lifted her head and took him in her mouth. He realised that she really had been licking her lips, deciding to herself whether she liked the taste and the smell of him. Obviously she did. Her tongue moved like a hot wet worm and she sucked him into her.

He couldn't stand any more of it. He was afraid he was going to come in her mouth – and that would be sure to put her off on her very first time. He hauled himself off her, turned around and lay on the bed beside her. She looked dreamy, eyes half closed, in another world.

'Do it to me, do it to me now, oh please, oh please.'
Those same words, that same husky voice, two

years on. He rolled over on top of her, held himself up on one arm and reached with his other hand to guide himself into her. She was there before him, her hands around him, steering him into her. Incredible. Her legs were bent up around him. She was ready. Gently, gently, firmly, firmly, he pushed himself slowly into her until the whole length of him was inside. Then he started to move. He saw the surprise flicker fleetingly in her eyes, then the lust darken her pupils. Suddenly she was moving with him, as if she had done this all her life. It had not hurt her at all. She had indeed been ready.

She heaved and rolled and tossed beneath him like a wave in the ocean on a wild stormy day. It was too much. He came like a steam engine, shooting into her deep sweetness. He had never felt such ecstasy. Such fulfilment. All his life he had been violently searching for this kind of satisfaction. Yet here was the satisfaction without violence at all. He rolled off her, breathing like a marathon runner, and felt a wonderful peace enveloping him. He thought he could sleep for a month, float away on a cloud of joy. But he wouldn't let himself do that. He wanted to take her to the heights of orgasm, to make her fly. He realised that he had never before given a damn whether any woman he was with came or not, but this was different. This was really different.

'I'm sorry it was so quick,' he whispered to her. 'The second time I'll last for ever, I promise. I want to make you come and come. You are going to have amazing orgasms, I just know it.'

She was lying beside him, panting still. Smiling. Eager for anything that might come next. He stretched out a hand and began to play with her.

'You are something else,' he said.

Her smile broadened. Then she threw back her head against the pillows and went for it, using his fingers. Just watching her made him hard again very fast. This time he would have the control to give her even greater pleasure. He lowered himself carefully on top of her again, and very gently eased the length of him into her. He thought he was bigger than he had ever been, but she didn't seem to mind. Mind, she loved it.

When he was completely inside and he knew she was comfortable with him in there, he started to move, to really move. He could feel her muscles opening and closing around him all the time as he sucked and stroked her breasts. After a while he rolled her over on top of him. He reached behind and played with her there with his fingers. Teasing, tantalising the glands she had not known existed. She loved that too. She was off in a trance. He kept thinking she was going to come at any moment, but he knew that she hadn't quite made it.

He lay beneath her, thanking God that he could always last so long the second time. Then he lifted her off him and bent her over the edge of the bed. He wanted her in every possible way, and he knew she wanted that too. She was strong and athletic, not a compliant cell in her body. At one point, face down and flat on the bed, she had somehow managed to lift her legs and wrap them around him backwards, making him go even deeper inside her. Then she reached back with her arms, stretching behind him, and probed and pushed and stroked with her long fingers. She must be double-bloody-jointed, he thought desperately as he was finally unable to last any longer. His second orgasm was better even than the first. Deep deep satisfaction once more. Oh yes, this was what he had been looking for. If only he had found her before. And if only he could make her come. God, he wanted her to come.

He lifted her up the bed and rested her head on the pillows. Then he cuddled her. He had never bothered to do that to anyone before, either.

'That was the best ever,' he told her.

'I bet you say that to all the girls,' she replied.

'No,' he said truthfully. He looked at her glistening with sweat, still panting. 'God I want to give you an orgasm.'

'Well maybe I've had one,' she replied. 'I don't know what it's supposed to feel like.'

He laughed and shook his head.

'No. You'll know when it happens. And it's going to be a sensation. I'm sure of that. Shall I try one more time?'

She smiled invitingly. This time he went down on her again. Irene had always come so obligingly quickly when he did that. But not this one. He sucked her for ever. He wouldn't let her suck him. He wanted her to concentrate on herself. She did. Giving in totally to all the lovely softness, the wet warmth of it. She was so close all the time, he knew that. But he couldn't quite send her over the edge.

Eventually she had to go home and he still hadn't brought her to orgasm.

'It was good for you, wasn't it?' he asked anxiously.

God, he had never given a damn before. Then he asked her if she could get away the next evening and be with him; he would make her come then – definitely. She just smiled.

The police called the next morning and asked Mark
to go to the station again, for the third and final time.
Several different officers went over every word of
Mark's statement, asking him the same questions
many times. Again and again they made him tell
them what had happened, with Johnny, with Irene,
checking and double-checking every fact. Always he
gave the same answers he had on the previous
occasions. All that he said made sense. Every so often
they left him alone in the interview room, except for
a constable standing silently just inside the door. And
every time he was left alone he found himself thinking about Jenny. In fact, apart from his actual sessions with the police, and in spite of all that was
going on, and all his unease and his fears, he spent
most of the twenty-four hours before he would be
with her again thinking about her.

By the time she arrived at his flat the next evening,
he had all kinds of plans for her. They melted into
each other's arms as she stepped through the door.

'God I want you,' he muttered.

'Me too,' she said eagerly.

No game playing with this one. Pure lust, pure
sex, pure need. He undressed her slowly and carefully and, when she stood naked before him, led her
into the bedroom. There was a big white towel on
the bed. She looked at him with just a hint of alarm
in her eyes. He whispered reassurance. Obediently
she lay down as he instructed and waited for him.
He could smell her already. He stripped to his under-
pants. His erection had started as soon as he heard
her knock on the door, but he was trying not to think

about it. He reached for the baby oil he had put on the bedside table.

For the rest of the afternoon, Mark used all the imaginative tricks he had ever learned to bring Jenny Stone to the heights of her considerable sexuality. She purred with pleasure, like a great big sexy kitten. A wild cat kitten, he thought, a puma, a panther. He used his fingers and his tongue and the touch of his body, feather-light and tantalising, but he would not enter her until she begged him to. Not until she seemed almost unconscious with pleasure, crying out again and again for him to fuck her, did he eventually do so.

And even his extraordinary sexual energy was waning by the time he finally saw her face change and knew what was beginning to happen to her.

Watching her writhing beneath him, listening to her animal cries, experiencing her contractions so acutely it was almost painful – he had known she was going to be wild, yes he had always known that, but Mark had not imagined anything like this. The feeling for him was sensational. Now he could let go at last, now he could think about his own pleasure. He relaxed his tense muscles and in one final, nerve-rending thrust he was coming too, coming with her, shouting his joy as loudly as she was screaming hers. In the last throes of her passion she kicked out so hard and with such strength that she smashed a hole in the sloping ceiling at one side of his bed and severely stubbed her toe.

She felt no pain. Only the greatest, most extreme, and inexplicable pleasure in the world.

Afterwards it took him a long time to calm her down. To bring her back to normality. She lay trembling in his arms, damp and warm and wonderful and stinking of it, her hair soaking wet with her own sweat, unable to speak at first.

When she did she grinned crookedly at him, raised her eyebrows quizzically, and said: 'So that's what all the fuss is about.'

He kissed her long and hard on the mouth.

'What do you think?' he asked.

'I don't know how I ever lived without it,' she replied.

And she meant it.

Ten

During the rest of that year, Jenny and Mark continued to explore the craziest heights of their sexuality. He didn't think any two people could be better matched, although she didn't know yet that they had anything special. He was quite sure that she thought it was always like this and that every woman was like her. She was still at school, for Christ's sake. Mark sometimes fantasised to himself about Jenny in a gymslip, but he instinctively knew never to ask her to play dressing-up games. To her, that would be silly and demeaning. She was an animal, a highly toned totally sexual animal, not a tart – and Mark knew the difference.

In the September, Jenny had gone back to school, the final year of her A level GCEs, and not even her closest schoolfriends knew she was sleeping with Mark. From the very beginning, sex to Jenny Stone was something you did, not something you talked about. She wasn't into giggly girly chat, and she was always suspicious of people who talked about sex all the time, wondering whether they actually did it at all. Anyway, she had to be careful – her parents thought Mark was too old for her. She overheard her father once telling her mother that he didn't like the look in the young feller's eye. Jenny knew exactly what he meant, and she loved that look in Mark Piddle's eye.

Their lust for each other did not diminish, instead it seemed to grow more intense. They were obsessed with each other's bodies.

Irene did not reappear. Sometimes Jenny tried to talk to Mark about it, but he would immediately pull down the shutters. He told her it was another life; whatever had happened to Irene, he did not want to know about it any more.

At the end of August, Johnny Cooke was charged with the murder of Marjorie Benson. The word was that the police suspected him of having killed Irene too, but, in spite of extensive searches, no body was found.

For the rest of her life, Jennifer Stone could never get over her own reaction to Johnny's arrest. At first she hardly noticed it, just as she had hardly noticed the disappearance of Irene. She had been trying to put the murder and her discovery of the body out of her mind, and it wasn't all that difficult because of her obsession with Mark Piddle. She was totally besotted by him as he was by her. All she could really think about, night and day, was their sex life together. That had become the sole reason for her existence, and it was desperately hard for her to concentrate on her schoolwork or to behave normally at home. Her excuses for the time spent in Mark's bed were always elaborate and well thought out, but, none the less, she knew her parents suspected that something very heavy was going on.

If she had thought about Johnny and the murder and the events surrounding it, she might have been concerned from the beginning – but, strange though it appeared in retrospect, she did not think about it at all.

The trial did confront her with some unpleasant realities. It started at Exeter Crown Court just before Christmas. Jenny, of course, was a witness because she had found the body, and so was Mark, to whom Johnny had made his confession. Twenty-five years later, Jenny remembered that as the start of her niggling worries. She was quite sure in her own mind that Mark had originally told her he believed Johnny to be innocent. When she confronted Mark he was as cool as ever. He must have confused her, he said. Johnny had confessed, right enough, and Mark reckoned he was guilty as hell.

He didn't look at her as he spoke. But she accepted what he said. She was, after all, quite besotted by him.

At the trial, Johnny continued to protest his innocence. There were three main pieces of evidence against him.

He had had sex with Marjorie Benson probably only minutes before her death. He eventually admitted that was so only after forensic tests showed that semen found inside her was his.

Secondly, when her body was discovered she was wearing a skirt but no blouse. She had obviously struggled with her assailant, and clumps of hair had been ripped from her head. The missing blouse, torn and crumpled, had been found screwed up beneath a pile of logs in the shed where Johnny kept his bicycle. There were hairs found on the blouse with the follicles of skin still attached to them. They came from Marjorie Benson's head. And the blouse had large imitation brass buttons, one of which bore a clear thumb print – it was Johnny Cooke's. Johnny's defence counsel had asked why on earth the boy should take such damning evidence to his own home. The prosecution counsel countered with a list of murderers who had collected bizarre and incriminating souvenirs from their victims. The jury was captivated, so much so that Johnny's barrister wished he had never queried the evidence in the first place.

Thirdly there was Johnny's confession to Mark Piddle. Mark gave his evidence with his usual cool lucidity. He told the court how Johnny had come to him within hours of the body being found, and, still in shock, had confessed everything and begged Mark not to go to the police. He had said: 'I killed her,' and: 'It is my fault she is dead.' Mark gave what he described as a more or less verbatim account of the midnight meeting. He was articulate and convincing.

Jenny had already given her evidence when he was called. As a material witness she was therefore able to sit in the public gallery if she wished. Upset again by the renewed vision of that grotesque body floating beside her, she had nearly left the court. But some morbid fascination led her to stay for the rest of the day, and as she watched Mark in the witness box, she began to feel more and more uneasy. He was so sure of himself, yet while he was talking she looked at Johnny Cooke, the accused. He was staring at Mark, shaking his head. At one point he started to stand up, as if he was going to protest, until his barrister put a firm hand on his shoulder, keeping him in his seat. Jenny listened very carefully, then she waited outside the court for Mark. She was more bewildered than anything else.

'Mark, you told me Johnny was innocent, that he didn't really confess to anything . . .'

The words came tumbling out. He interrupted her briskly.

'You misunderstood me. He told me he killed the woman. I wanted him to be innocent – that's different.'

Impatiently, he bundled her into his car and drove her home.

On the way she did not speak, but went over it all again and again in her mind. Question: Why would Mark lie? Answer: To get Johnny convicted. Question: Why would he want that if he didn't believe Johnny was guilty? Answer: Because he was involved in the Marjorie Benson murder himself.

He couldn't be, could he, not her Mark? And it didn't make sense anyway. Mark had never met Marjorie Benson, had he? Also he had been nowhere near the sand dunes that night. He had been working late and then went to a village dance miles away with his photographer. The police had checked that out – the police had checked everything. His alibi was cast-iron.

Jenny had never seriously considered the possibility that Mark could have murdered Marjorie Benson, but even when she made herself do so, it quickly became obvious that he could not have done it. So what was it all about? Why was he landing Johnny in it? Or was she just being silly? Was her memory playing tricks on her, after all?

She did not know Johnny Cooke – had maybe seen him by the deckchair stand but never spoken to him. She had no feelings for him either way, and if he was the murderer she hoped he rotted in jail. But if he was not? Jennifer Stone always had a reasonable sense of justice, yet she supposed she could be mistaken about a lot of things. She was still in a state of shock when Mark had described Johnny's midnight visit to her. That was true, although the doubts persisted.

Irene's disappearance was the most disturbing factor of all. Jenny had never met her, and knew very little of Mark's relationship with her. She had known Mark was living with someone when she had so blatantly decided that she was going to sleep with him, yet it had never seemed relevant to her desire for Mark. And when Irene had disappeared there had been a large element of convenience about it as far as Jenny was concerned. She certainly did not like to think about the more horrendous explanations for Irene's disappearance.

What if Mark had done something terrible to Irene? Jenny could not bring herself to allow the word 'kill' even to enter her head. But then what had he done with the body? Also the police had been over his flat and no doubt his car with a fine toothcomb. She'd been reading too many detective novels. Only professional hit men got away with murder – people like Mark left clues, as Johnny had done.

The trial ended two days later. Johnny Cooke was found guilty and sentenced to life imprisonment. He was led off to the cells still protesting his innocence. Mark was at court to hear sentence passed. Immediately afterwards he drove straight to Jenny's school and waited for her outside. She was muffled up in her thick woollen uniform coat and a big scarf, with her school beret down over her ears. She didn't look at all sexy, but appearances could be deceptive.

Couldn't they just? Whatever she was wearing, whatever she was doing, he could see only her face in the throes of orgasm and her body naked and wrapped around his. She spotted the Cooper at once and walked over to it, opened the door and climbed into the seat beside him. He didn't touch. He knew the rules. The procession of schoolgirls marching past the car were already bursting into giggles at the sight of them together. Jenny wasn't smiling. At once she asked him about the verdict. When he told her she looked away, out of the window.

'Do you think it's right? Do you really think he did it?'

She could feel his eyes all over her. She could always feel that.

'Yes,' he replied.

'I am so mixed up about everything, all the different things you told me,' she said.

He leaned forward a little, close to her ear. His breath was warm and damp and familiar.

'I can tell you three things with total certainty,' he said. 'Firstly, what I said in court is absolutely the way it happened with Johnny and yes, you are mixed up, but it's not surprising that your memory is playing tricks on you about a time when you had just found a body floating in the sea.

'Secondly, Johnny Cooke is as guilty as hell. Justice has been done. He deserved life and he got it.

'And thirdly, I am going to take you home with me now and I am going to remove all your clothes and I am going to put my tongue inside you and I am going to lick you and suck you until you come all over my face. And then I'm going to fuck you for a month – without stopping.'

She turned to him. His eyes burned into her. The corners of his mouth were just twitched into a smile. She felt herself beginning to want him. All the questions she had planned to ask were stuck in her throat. Oh God, if she had understood the full power of sex before she ever did it she might have remained a virgin always.

He parted his lips and ran his tongue along his teeth.

'If we stay here a second longer I shall take off your knickers and do it to you in front of all your little friends,' he said.

The idea rather appealed to him.

He started the engine, gunned the Cooper into gear and roared off towards his flat. He could hardly wait, he was aching for her again. And he knew full well that she was aching for him too – and that she always would be.

Johnny Cooke could not remember being taken from the courtroom to the cell below. Neither could he remember the drive several days later to one of the grimmest prisons in the country – Dartmoor.

He had lost weight during his months on remand in Exeter city jail, and the muscle seemed to have wasted on his strong young frame. The healthy tan had faded, his eyes dulled.

It seemed unreal to him. Loss of liberty was the ultimate punishment to a young man like Johnny, who loved open spaces and the beauty of nature and the freedom to enjoy and explore them more than life itself. The rugged splendour of the moors glimpsed through the barred window of his cell in the desolate old prison on the edge of the little town of Princetown merely added to his anguish. Dartmoor was built by and for prisoners captured during the Napoleonic wars – the very sight of the place from the outside is a chilling reminder of another age. Yet The Moor, as it has always been known to its inmates, remains a key part of the twentieth-century prison service. Behind its towering black walls in the early winter of 1971 lay a world about which Johnny Cooke had had no idea. A world of fear and misery stripped of all human dignity.

Johnny was whisked at speed through the forbidding granite archway which forms the prison entrance. There was no way he could have seen the words carved almost two centuries earlier on the archway's top three blocks by some long-forgotten craftsmen. *Parcere subjectis* – a line of Latin taken from Virgil's *Aeneid*. It means 'Spare The Vanquished'. But Dartmoor Prison has scant history of sparing anybody.

Because of the nature of his offence, which was regarded as a sex murder, Johnny was taken to the notorious D wing – at the time home to a selection of the most vicious criminals in the country.

Johnny's looks and youth caused him predictable torture. Johnny was not in any way streetwise or tough. He was bullied physically and sexually. From the start there were things that happened, things he felt unable to avoid or resist, which destroyed any vestige of self-esteem he had left.

Early on he considered suicide, and even deliberated over ways in which he could kill himself. He really did want to die, and he was so desperate that it was probably only lack of courage which prevented him from ever actually making an attempt on his own life.

Johnny could not stand pain, never had been able to. There was a weakness about him in spite of his imposing physique, and certainly he was never strong mentally, always muddled and unsure of himself.

In D Wing Johnny spent many hours a day locked in his cell. Unlike most city prisons, The Moor never had a space problem, and so almost always serious offenders serving long sentences were given cells to themselves. This could result in seemingly endless solitude spent in a small confined space. From the very first time the heavy door of his cell slammed shut, Johnny found himself in a cold sweat. He quickly discovered that confined spaces terrified him and could turn him into a gibbering wreck. He almost certainly suffered from claustrophobia, and the effect on his mental condition was devastating. None the less he came to prefer the hours spent trembling alone in his cell to those in the public areas of the prison where he was open to the unwelcome attentions of his fellow convicts. Visits to the latrines were particularly frightening. There were things that happened to Johnny in Dartmoor Prison which he found so horrible that his only defence was to shut his mind, to divorce his inner being from his body and its torment.

He retreated into an inner shell. Almost from the moment he was taken to The Moor, Johnny stopped protesting his innocence. He simply did not have the energy. He felt broken, like a tired old man. His hopes and expectations had slumped to the lowest level, to that of mere daily survival. He had only one desire left – to be left alone.

Johnny's barrister, unhappy throughout with the way the trial had gone, suggested an appeal. Johnny shrugged big bony shoulders. He could not even be bothered to speak. There was no longer any fight left in him. At the end of a second prison visit, throughout which Johnny remained almost totally uncommunicative, his barrister advised him that he felt obliged to abandon the planned appeal.

'I can't do it without you, Johnny,' he said. 'I need you to help me rebuild our case . . .'

Once again Johnny merely shrugged his shoulders.

Every month his mother dutifully made the trek across the moors to visit her son. His father never came, which was actually a relief to Johnny. Mrs Cooke brought cigarettes and food, homemade cakes and pies. She was always best at the practical side of things, but the way in which she so determinedly continued to do the right thing by her boy was almost painful. So was the hurt in her eyes. With resolute brightness she almost ritualistically related to him the goings on at home. Silence seemed to frighten her, and throughout each visit she talked ceaselessly. Johnny found solace in silence, he longed for it, having swiftly discovered that, in spite of enforced solitude and high walls, prisons are noisy echoing places. He no longer wanted to talk to anyone really, and he certainly had little to say to his mother. He might have been comforted by some slight display of physical warmth, some show of tenderness amid the cruel bleakness, and once he reached across the table in the visiting room to touch his mother's hand. She flushed and coughed and fussed a bit, leaning back in her chair away from him, still chattering about nothing. As quickly as she could she withdrew her hand, placing it firmly in her lap out of reach.

Not once did Mabel Cooke reach out to touch her

son, and from the moment he was convicted she never again mentioned the murder. From the very beginning she did not ask him to tell her whether or not he was guilty. Johnny assumed she had made up her mind that he was.

He did not know that he had the right to refuse her visits. If he had known he would probably have done so. They simply made him despair even more.

Jennifer didn't dwell long on Johnny Cooke's plight. Life was just too good for her. She did not want to think about anything that might spoil it. Quite deliberately she put Johnny's trial, Irene's disappearance and the whole rotten business out of her mind. Once she had done that, every day was a corker. She started to write to local papers asking for a job as a trainee reporter. The more she saw of Mark, and the more she learned of Mark's job, the more certain she became that journalism was the career for her.

It was nearly Easter when Mark gently broke the news that he had been offered a job in London, in Fleet Street. She surprised him yet again. She didn't mind a bit. You could hardly build a career for yourself in Pelham Bay, she said, and she wouldn't be far behind him anyway. She was heading for Fleet Street, she told him, definitely. He assured her that he would still try to be with her as much as possible. There were always weekends, he wanted her so badly. She had said cheerily that she wanted him too, but a man had to do what a man had to do – and so did a woman. She grinned at her own nonsense, completely unworried by his news.

Not for the first time he was struck by the equality of their relationship. In and out of bed they were on a par. She instinctively understood his desire for a wider canvas because she already had that desire herself. All that puzzled her was that she had not even known that he had been applying for jobs on the nationals. He mumbled something about it coming out of the blue. Was it her imagination or did he flush slightly?

Always there were things about him that made her uneasy on occasions, but the power of his personality and the intoxicating effect he had on her overcame any doubts she had about him, as would be the case through so much of her adult life.

It didn't occur to her that he would even try to be faithful to her, indeed, how could he be? He was young and strong and eternally randy. But there was no reason why his behaviour with other women should bother her in those heady pre-AIDs days. The young Jennifer was almost without sexual jealousy, frankly she didn't see the point, and once she became sure of Mark's need for her, sure that he was not going to leave her, she found she was totally unworried by whatever he might be doing when he was not with her. In any case she had absolutely no intention of being faithful to him should a suitable opportunity arise to experiment elsewhere. It hadn't yet, as it happened, but then that was hardly surprising in Pelham Bay.

And so, almost ten months after the death of Marjorie Benson and the disappearance of Irene Nichols, Mark Piddle left for London to join the *Daily Recorder* as an investigative reporter. Three months later, Jenny Stone landed a job as a trainee reporter on a local paper in Dorset. Just before she left North Devon she had sex with another man for the first time. It was an unlikely coupling. Smug Angela Smith's boyfriend Todd Mallett.

She went to bed with him mainly because she liked to fantasise about wiping the smugness off Angela's face by telling her in graphic detail exactly what she had done with Todd – she actually had no intention of so doing, but it was a delicious thought. The policeman's son, recently enrolled in the force himself, slept with her because Angela was driving him crazy. She still wouldn't let him have it, he would probably have to marry the old bag before she would do it, he had told Jenny. And Jenny was quite sure that was exactly what he would do in the end.

Todd was a much more hesitant lover than the man she was used to. He made love like the boy he was – he was just nineteen – but he was gentle, considerate and affectionate. Their lovemaking was warm and cuddly rather than erotic: unlike sex with Mark, it did not disturb her. She felt in control, and was absolutely sure that if she wanted Todd more permanently she could have him. She suspected he was falling in love with her and needed only a little encouragement to leave Angela for her, yet that was the last thing she wanted. She liked sleeping with Todd, but the experience served only to increase her desire for Mark and the level of sexual thrill only he had so far provided. Fortunately Mark proved to be as good as his word. He was doing his best to screw the whole of London, but throughout everything his singular need for Jennifer remained undiminished, and whenever he could get away he would visit her, as he had promised. First he would make the long trek back to North Devon, where he no longer had a flat and had to stay at the Durraton vicarage with his parents. So for a time they were reduced to using the back seat of his car for their sexual adventures, no longer the Cooper but an estate car chosen for the express purpose of those lovemaking weekends. Later he would travel to Dorset where, thankfully, Jenny had her own bedsit and later a flat shared with Anna McDonald who, with the television volume turned as loud as possible, stoically endured weekend after weekend of bedroom noise.

'You'll be worn out by the time you're twenty-five,' she told Jennifer – not actually believing a word of it.

Discovering sex had transformed Jenny Stone. At a glance she looked and behaved much the same. She remained something of a tomboy, but men usually became instinctively aware of the ferocious sexuality lurking just below the surface. There was something indefinable in her manner which suggested the level of sexual enjoyment she was capable of.

Gradually, as she sought out new partners, she began to realise how special the sex was between her and Mark. They were kindred spirits all right, and when they were together it was always sensational. She didn't give a damn what or who he was doing in London, and he asked her no questions. She knew he would always come back to her, as, she suspected, she would to him. There were no other anxieties worth mentioning.

She was starting to enjoy the only twenty odd years in history when, if they wished, women could indeed treat sex the way so many men did. The only twenty years in history when they could sleep with whom they liked, whenever they felt like it, without fear of either pregnancy or death. And Jenny Stone was going to make the most of every thrilling minute of it.

PART TWO

Diamond Day

It was in the golden sunshine
of an emerald studded morning
that you looked at me and said
a diamond day is dawning,
my love.
In the waking waterside glare
we were going to share
the beauty of a dove.
To seek the joy of light
the sheer ecstasy of flight
every sweet fantasy in sight.
Colours yellow, blue
and red,
Heart mellow, true
and disconnected from the head.

Your eyes were violet
Your lips were velvet
Your touch was sacred.
You too, my love
were like the dove.

If only I had understood
In even the craziest romantic mood
That dreams are as well as
And maybe as much as
But never ever instead.
And even lovers must get out of bed.

Eleven

It took around four years for Jennifer Stone to complete her weekly newspaper training, virtually exhaust Dorset's supply of male sex objects, and graduate to an evening paper, the hours of which were interfering with her sex life. She knew she was more than ready for a move to London. Mark suggested she apply for a job on his newspaper, the *Daily Recorder*. She was invited for an interview and swiftly hired as a reporter. It had been remarkably smooth and painless. Marcus, for so he had become, smiled benignly. Well, she thought, it couldn't possibly be anything to do with him. He might be the star foreign man already, but he was still only a reporter.

Together they found her a flat. He had half-heartedly suggested she move in with him.

'Certainly not,' she had told him curtly. 'I do not intend to live with any man unless I marry him.'

He had roared with laughter and asked what on earth had possessed the sexiest creature he had ever come across – more laughter – that she should suddenly display such morality.

'Nothing to do with morality, just practicality,' she had replied, mildly offended. 'If I ever move in with someone, I am going to be absolutely sure I am not going to want to move out the next week. I don't want my home to depend on my sex life, for Christ's sake, do I?'

He had agreed, with another outburst of mirth, that she most certainly did not.

'Look, we need to be free spirits, it works for us,' she had said.

He did not really need persuading. She was sure he was secretly relieved. But he did try, very occasionally, to do the right thing, did Mark.

'One thing you must remember,' he had instructed. 'Marcus, not Mark. When you come to London you must learn to call me Marcus.'

She giggled. She could understand why he wanted to change Piddle to Piddell, but Mark to Marcus? She remembered asking him about that and being told it was a much better by-line name. Typical of him, he rarely missed a trick.

He told her she should stop being Jenny – that was a name for schoolgirls and waitresses. Jennifer Stone was a good name, a strong name.

'A good by-line name?' she had queried with a smile.

'Damn right,' he had replied. And so it proved to be.

Jennifer too was successful from the start in Fleet Street. She was a general news reporter for four wild years. Away on stories she occasionally strayed, but back home in London there was only Marcus. She moved to a smart flat in the Barbican at about the same time that she was transferred into the features department as a senior writer. And in the four years after Jennifer had arrived in town, Marcus rose to be deputy editor. His promotion had been swift. He was thirty-two years old. The present editor was due for retirement the following year and Marcus was being groomed to take over. He had bought himself a mews house in Chelsea. He drove a Daimler provided by the *Recorder* – an editor's car a year or so in advance of the job becoming vacant, a clear statement of management's intent. When he became editor, there would be a chauffeur as well. He was Fleet Street's greatest golden boy, and it all seemed so effortless.

Together they were a much sought-after couple. They had youth and glamour, that aura of success about them which is inclined to make people so much more attractive then they would otherwise be. They still did not live together, but they were an established item in the media world.

Their sex life was even more extreme than their working life. Every time they made love it seemed to be a little wilder, a little crazier than the last. She told him all her fantasies. He would get her to tell him again and again how she would like to have two men at once, and sometimes, with his tricks and his sexual wizardry, he would almost make her believe that she had.

Some mornings when she woke she found herself wondering how far they would go together. How far would Mark go for a sexual thrill? How far would she go? Occasionally it bothered her, made her anxious. After yet another extraordinary all-night sex session she would not always experience quite the old glow, quite the old joyful fulfilment. Instead she would feel a bit jaded, uneasy. As she lay pondering the night's escapades, she would invariably hear Marcus cheerfully whistling as he splashed around in the bathroom. No crisis of conscience there. The thought made her grin. Marcus invariably bounced out of bed without a care in the world, as if he

155

had just enjoyed eight hours of deep, uninterrupted slumber. His powers of recovery never ceased to amaze her. Recovery, what was she thinking about? He never seemed to need to recover. His dressing room was entered through the bathroom. When he emerged he was always immaculate in Armani suits and Gucci shoes. The white blonde curls gleamed with well-being. He smelt slightly, never too much, of Paco Rabanne. He was handsome, successful, and on top of the world. He had the body and the stamina of an athlete, the looks of a Hollywood film star, the brain of an academic, the street wisdom of a barrow boy, and no morals to mention.

Often Jennifer could only groan and pull the sheet over her head.

Marcus was endlessly inventive. There was the time he and Jennifer were invited to a smart media dinner party. In Hampstead. Where else? They were very much on that circuit now, and their opinion about these evenings they felt obliged to endure was something else they had in common. They both despised them as pretentious pompous occasions. At this one, given by a top TV man, there was the usual careful mix of politicians, journalists and tycoons. The conversation was stilted and contrived and unbearably clever. During the pre-dinner drinks session, Jennifer noticed Marcus in deep conversation with the hostess, really turning on the charm, and she could see the woman responding to his blatant sexuality. She wondered how many women around the table he had had. She never allowed herself any illusions about his ability to be faithful, although, strangely enough, in the four years now since she had been living in

London, sharing his life if not entirely his home, she did not think there had been many other women. And certainly none that mattered. She had also strayed while away on trips – it never seemed important to either of them. She knew that Marcus was obsessed with her and her body. She couldn't help loving that, and the thought of it turned her on. She decided to think about something else. When the dozen or so guests came to sit down at the long narrow table, she was surprised to find that she and Marcus had been seated opposite each other – unusual at this kind of dinner party for couples to be placed that close together. She felt Marcus staring at her. She glanced at him and saw that he was looking triumphant. She knew the expression well. Could he have been fixing this with the hostess, she wondered, and why on earth would he bother?

A few minutes later she learned the answer. She was wearing a long silk skirt with a slit up the side almost to the top of her legs. She knew Marcus found it sexy. She was chatting with the guest on her left now, and she could hear Marcus talking too, but she knew his eyes were upon her, his gaze boring into her. Then she felt something stroking her leg. Good God, it was his foot. He had his shoe off and the touch was smooth. But then, he always wore silk socks. A second foot found its way inside her skirt and eased her knees apart. This was ridiculous. She felt herself flush. She shot Marcus an imploring glance, but he wasn't even looking in her direction. He was deeply in conversation with the politician's wife on his right who looked as if she would like to take him upstairs immediately. Typical bloody Marcus. He could always do about ten things at once and give nothing away. Nobody in a million years would suspect what he was doing with his feet. The second foot had reached its target now, he was using his toes expertly. On some kind of automatic pilot she felt herself widen her legs. Immediately the second foot joined the first and with much wiggling of toes he eased her flimsy knickers to one side and pushed a big toe inside her, playing with her. Valiantly she tried to compose herself and to carry on listening to the Sunday paper editor sitting next to her pontificate about privacy and the press. Fortunately he barely drew breath, so she didn't have to speak, and he was so carried away with his own self-importance that he didn't notice the curious expression on her face. She knew she had gone quite red now, and she was having difficulty controlling her breathing.

She was vaguely aware of Marcus making something of a show of dropping his napkin. When he bent down to pick it up he grabbed her right foot, slipped off her shoe, and placed her stockinged foot firmly on his crotch. He was still talking and had completed his task so smoothly she was sure nobody would have noticed a thing. Anyway, who except Marcus would get up to tricks like this in public with his own bloody woman, she thought to herself. Good Lord. Her foot was actually touching his naked cock, she realised with a slight start which she hurriedly tried to disguise as a hiccup. Marginally less embarrassing than revealing that you were involved in a mutual masturbation session at the dinner table. His flies were undone beneath his napkin. How on earth had he managed that? OK you bastard, she thought, now stay cool, Jennifer. She slipped off her other shoe and with her two stock-inged feet went to work on him like crazy. By the time dessert had been served she noticed with some satisfaction that his conversation had at last started to falter. His eyes were shining, and he had that tremble in his lip which always happened when he was terribly excited. It will serve the bastard right if I make him come right now, she thought. Then she realised he was speaking to her, and that her own breathing had quickened to short sharp gasps. This was terrible. She was losing control.

'Darling, I knew we shouldn't have come,' she heard him say sympathetically.

She looked at him in horror and realised that only she would be remotely aware of any possible double meaning as he explained to the assembled throng that poor Jennifer had been suffering from an asthma attack that day and it had been a little optimistic to attend this dinner but they had both so wanted to be here. It seemed to be coming on again. He paused and looked at her. She could cheerfully have throttled him. He must take her home, he continued, and so with apologies he was on his feet and around the table and helping her out of her chair. Her knees felt shaky. Asthma indeed! Still, at least it meant nobody expected her to speak. With some concern she looked down at his trousers. His flies were done up. How had he managed that so quickly and without even her noticing? He was a magician. She couldn't trust herself to attempt to say goodbye.

They left quickly. Marcus walked her down the driveway towards the main road, assuring his hosts that he could pick up a taxi there easily. As soon as the front door was shut he took her by the arm and dragged her into the shrubbery to the side of the house. He flung her against a tree trunk and pushed her skirt up around her waist.

'You bugger,' she said.

But she was referring to the sweet torture of the dinner table, not what he was doing now.

'Yes please,' he said.

She pulled his face towards her and clamped her mouth on his, forcing his lips apart with her tongue. Eagerly he sucked her tongue inward and their mouths became fused together. His hands tore at her and he crumpled her skirt carelessly with his urgent embrace. That would never be the same again. He clawed at her tights, reducing them to shreds as he ripped them apart. She fumbled urgently with his zip, she wanted to get at him every bit as much as he wanted to get at her. With one strong arm he lifted her slightly off the ground, her back wedged against the tree, and she wrapped her legs around him. He forced her pants to one side and thrust himself straight into her. He knew he wasn't going to last, he adored this kind of sex. Within a couple of minutes he exploded inside her and he was far too quick for her. He came out of her and she stood there before him with her legs apart, still gasping for it.

'Do you remember by the dustbins all those years ago?' she asked, her voice dry with desire. 'It was like that again, wasn't it?'

When he could speak he agreed that it was and said to her: 'Come on, let's go back to my place, and then I'll make it happen for you again and again, I promise.'

She could still barely breath. The itch inside her

was driving her mad and she told him she couldn't wait, he had to make her come where they were, he had to. Obediently he dropped to his knees, his fine dinner suit probably ruined for ever in the mulch of leaf mould on the ground, and sucked her into a climax. She shouted in triumph and it lasted a long time. When he raised his head for air he said he hoped nobody inside the house had heard and she told him graphically how little she cared about that.

'You started it, you sex-crazed beast.'

Laughing together, they adjusted their clothing as best they could, walked out into the road and hailed a taxi.

By the time they reached Marcus' house he was ready again, and they made love for hours on the big bed. He never seemed to tire of her. In the middle of the night when he was deep inside her he asked her to marry him. She was shocked; she had not expected that. She had never given a thought to marrying Marcus, and they had never before discussed marriage. To her surprise she heard herself say that she would, she cried that she would. When they had finished he reached under the bed and handed her a small package. It contained a beautiful diamond engagement ring.

'Good God, did you really mean it then?' she inquired.

'Would I joke about marriage?' he replied with another question.

She reached out and touched him casually.

'Are you sure it's not just that?' she asked.

He looked down.

'I want to marry you in spite of that,' he grinned.

'You're not built for monogamy, Marcus,' she told him.

'The only time I have been with another woman since you came to London is when you have been away for weeks on end,' he said.

She knew it was the truth. He had not lied. She would not have believed him if he had said that there had been no one else at all.

He went on: 'You're not away so much now and I believe I can control myself . . . if you can.'

He grinned at her. He had no illusions either.

'Touché,' she said.

He lightly kissed one of her breasts. The touch of his lips never failed to make her flesh tingle.

'When I can have you there is nothing and no one else. We have the best sex in the world.'

'Anything else?'

'What else is there?'

She wasn't even sure he was joking.

'Well, for example, do you love me?'

She looked inquiringly into his eyes. They were sparkling. They almost always were.

'To distraction,' he said.

In the morning he was ecstatic. Even more like Marcus than usual. Later in the office, a delivery boy arrived laden down with great boxes of lily of the valley. She had once told him they were her favourite flower. It was only years afterwards that she discovered that lily of the valley are lethally poisonous.

There was a note asking her to join him for lunch at Langans. She did so joyfully. The next couple of weeks were wonderful. They partied with their friends and they partied without them. They planned their future together. They started house-hunting.

They both wanted a big town house somewhere very central; they wanted children, too, but not yet. Marcus had convinced himself that he deeply desired a normal family life, and that he could have that in spite of all the things about him which might seem to conspire against it.

Jennifer and Marcus were the couple the whole of London envied. Years later, Jennifer could never remember whether she had had any suspicions about Marcus at that time. Had she really taken him so much at face value? Had she never suspected that he had an underlife? She wasn't sure. One occasion did stick in her head, however. Shortly after agreeing to marry him, she had decided to confront him again with some of her lurking doubts. Marcus often took phone calls behind closed doors, sometimes in the dead of night. He was always vague about his movements, going missing without explanation for hours on end, occasionally overnight.

She had blurted out her anxieties to him about his behaviour, the anxieties that had been with her ever since the early days in Pelham Bay, the way she often wondered how he could have made so much money in such a short time, how he seemed able to fix anything and everything so effortlessly, and how she still fretted about Irene and her disappearance and what it continued to mean to both of them.

'Nothing,' Marcus had replied shortly. 'Irene's disappearance means nothing to either of us any more. If I could ever have done anything about it, I would have done, but I am not going to let it ruin my life – or yours.

'And as for being successful, have you ever noticed how hard I work?'

It was true. He did work hard, and he was clever, but was there more to it than that?

'OK,' she said. 'But there is something going on in your life that's a secret and you won't let me know about and there always has been.'

She paused. Typically he said nothing to fill the pause.

'I want to know once and for all if it's another woman,' she said.

He chuckled then and told her not to be ridiculous, but she persisted in cross-examining him.

'All I can think of is that you have been having an affair all these years with someone who is unavailable, a married woman, and if it's not that, what the hell is it?' she asked.

He sighed. He had to tell her something because he knew she would not let him off the hook now, and he also knew, another born politician's skill, how to appear to give way while actually giving next to nothing.

'OK, you silly cow,' he said affectionately. 'I'm a Freemason, that's all.'

'You're a what?' Jennifer was stunned, she felt her head rock back on her shoulders.

'I'm a Freemason,' he repeated, with a small smile. 'You're supposed to keep things secret, that's half the idea of it.'

'Good God,' she said. This made sense of so much, but it was still curious. From the little she knew of the Masons and the great deal she felt she knew of Marcus, he was the last man in the world she would have expected to join.

'Why on earth didn't you tell me before?' she asked. 'Surely you could have told me that?'

'I thought you'd laugh,' he said. Clever as ever, he decided to play it lightly now.

'I don't know about that,' she said. 'All I know about the Masons is that my father would never join them – because he believed they were a cartel who look after their own at the expense of anything and anybody else inside and outside the law.'

She looked at him questioningly. He seemed more than a tiny bit sheepish. Well, he would be, wouldn't he? Apart from anything else, Marcus liked to give the impression he had carved his life and career singlehandedly with help from no one. Only he would know the degree of assistance he had had from Masons in high places, and, Heaven forbid – she thought back to that first job so readily offered her by Marcus' newspaper – the help she had unknowingly received.

Marcus was not rising to the bait. 'We all need a bit of a helping hand now and again,' he said casually. 'All you are talking about is a group of hard-working men who will support each other through thick and thin. What's wrong with that?'

She didn't understand enough about the Masons to know whether that was more or less the sum of it or not. She merely nodded and said: 'You've been a member since Pelham, haven't you?'

He shrugged his agreement.

'Fascinating,' she said, the journalist in her taking over now. 'How much help have they really given you, then?'

For a moment Marcus frowned and looked as if he might be about to say something in anger. Instead he decided to stick to the light approach.

'Oh, you'd never guess the half of it,' he said. 'I

mean, I'm so useless at the job I wouldn't have lasted five minutes as a hack, let alone anything else, without help, would I?'

She raised her hands in defeat. Marcus was a quite brilliant journalist who had always been destined for the top, and that was one of his many attractions to her. So he was a Freemason. That didn't really bother her much, although she would have preferred to have known all along. Mind you, she could see how he would be embarrassed by it. She asked some more questions. Some he would answer, some he wouldn't.

Yes, of course he went to regular lodge meetings, and that probably accounted for most of what she described as his mysterious disappearances. Yes, he had to admit that he had joined because he thought it would do his career good and he didn't see the need to apologise for that. No, he could not and would not tell her how he came to join. Masons had to be invited, they couldn't just apply; if he told her who had invited him he would be breaking his oath.

Marcus made it all seem quite normal, and Jennifer had no reason to believe that, behind the ritual rigmarole, the Masons were anything other than just that.

She was actually relieved and reassured by what she had learned. She thought it was all a bit silly and probably a bit reprehensible – jobs, perks and God knows what else for the boys – but she already knew that one way and another the world was riddled with that kind of thing. The Masons had no monopoly on nepotism, and alongside all kinds of unpleasant explanations for the more mysterious aspects of Marcus' behaviour which had flicked uninvited through her brain over the years, being a Mason seemed relatively innocent and straightforward. It was also quite amusing. She knew the Masons wore robes and used all kinds of regalia in their ceremonies, and there was a distinctly funny side to the thought of a man as stylish and sophisticated as Marcus indulging in such pursuits.

When she realised she was going to get no more hard information from him, she found herself teasing him about all of that.

'I've always wanted to know if Masons really roll their trouser-legs up,' she said, stifling a giggle. 'Go on, share with me the intimate secrets of your apron . . .'

Marcus went along with it good-humouredly enough. 'Mind your own business,' he said, only pretending to be stern.

He was actually relieved that Jennifer seemed so untroubled, and he thought he had handled things rather well. He hoped that would be the end of her niggling mistrust of him – and it seemed to be at the time. She could live happily enough with the knowledge that he was a Mason, and would, in fact, have no further wish to know anything much about it.

She certainly did not intend to let it interfere with the good times. More than anything else, what she remembered from those heady days in London was the sheer fun of it all, the stimulation, the excitement.

Then came the day a few weeks after they had become engaged, when Marcus asked Jennifer to join him at his flat as soon as she could get away. He had an engagement present for her, a surprise. She duly turned up straight from the office. She was wearing a black Paul Costello suit with very high heels. She looked about ten feet tall. The effect was dramatic. Marcus opened a bottle of good champagne – his favourite Krug, the price of which still rather shocked her – and gave her a glass, finest Waterford crystal, naturally. He kissed her fleetingly on the lips, and his tongue lightly traced a line across her mouth. He too had just arrived from the office. He had taken off his jacket and tie and was wearing only the trousers of his suit and his handmade Jermyn Street shirt open at the neck. He looked very attractive, and he looked dangerous, but then he frequently did. The fluffy blonde curls and the handsome, eternal boyishness were so deceptive. He reached out and touched her cheek, hardly a touch at all, and yet so suggestive.

'Undress for me,' he said huskily.

'Is that my surprise?' she asked, with a smile. 'That's no surprise.'

'Later,' he replied.

His eyes were very bright.

'Please. I want to look at you.'

Why did she find him so irresistible? Why did she always do what he asked? She undressed in front of him as he had told her to. When she had stripped down to her bra and pants, she turned around with her back to him and gestured to him to undo the catch. He did so barely touching her with his hands, but she could feel his hardness against her. She stepped forward, letting the bra fall away and her pants drop. Then she turned around and faced him. She was smiling at him, expectant now.

He took her into the bedroom and sat her on the edge of the bed. He knelt before her, opened her legs, and began. She lay back on the covers, spreading her legs wider, loving it, as always. He worked on her until she was crying out for him to be inside her. He stood up and undressed before her, naked, strong, beautiful. He came forward as if he was going to enter her, and then he eased himself up her body until he was sitting astride her face. He was going to tease her tonight. She didn't mind. It would be all the better finally. She started to suck him and she felt his hand stretched behind him playing with her. She was aching for it. His fingers were so clever. Then she became aware of something very strange.

She realised two things at once. One was that Marcus was now holding both her wrists above her head with his hands, forcing her arms back on the pillows. And the other was that there was something at work again on the most intimate part of her. It was a tongue, a hungry seeking tongue. Somebody else was in the room with them, and that somebody was sucking her. She couldn't see who it was. She didn't even know if it was a man or a woman. She started to struggle. Marcus was thrusting deep into her mouth. Relentless. She could not speak. She looked up into his eyes and saw the wicked enjoyment there. Marcus was telling her that this was her surprise, this was her fantasy. Two men. So it was a man, she thought obscurely, thank God at least for that. Marcus was still talking. He wanted her to live it out, to explore every remotest part of her sexuality, every extreme. He wanted to watch her do it. He wanted her to have it all the ways she had ever dreamed of. She was still struggling. Two strong arms had pinned her legs down, forcing them apart. The tongue was busy, darting in and out of her. She felt herself begin to weaken. Whoever it was was good, very good, and she was so ready there. It felt so sweet and so exciting, she couldn't struggle any more. God, what was happening to her? She didn't want to do this but she couldn't stop herself. Marcus had been clever.

She was starting to move with it now. The other man sensed the change in her immediately. He let go of her legs and she wrapped them around his head. He began to use his hands on her as well. She was going wild for it now, and when she looked up at Marcus she saw the triumph in his eyes. The bastard. When the sucking abruptly stopped, she knew what was going to happen next. The strong hands held her legs apart again and the stranger entered her, very powerfully, straight in. She was open and ready, but she felt herself stretching. This guy was gigantic. Marcus was big, this guy was a freak. She was completely filled up. It hurt a little at first, but he was good, moving only slightly inside her, gently to begin with, gradually building up the strokes until it felt as if he was hammering her right down into the feathered depths of the bed. This was pure sex. She had not even seen his face. This was the sexiest thing that had ever happened to her. She was living out all her wildest fantasies. She was crazy with excitement. She was going to explode. She came like fury, a wild, angry, gut orgasm, and as she did so Marcus could contain himself no longer. He shot into her mouth and he told her to swallow it as he pumped himself dry. Meekly she did so.

He rolled off her and for the first time she saw the man who was inside her. He was not letting up. The size of him was extraordinary, and his body was stunningly beautiful. He looked like a professional stud and undoubtedly was. He was probably shorter than Marcus but he was heavier, almost certainly a body builder. Every muscle was perfectly defined and his olive-brown skin was hairless and shiny, as if shaven and oiled. His hair was very black, and his eyes were black too. He was staggeringly handsome, almost too handsome, and he was definitely a pro. He had her bum right on the edge of the bed, his knees wedged against the side of the bed for extra purchase. Marcus, panting slightly, crouched on the bed watching.

'You bastard, Marcus,' she hissed.

His grin was devilish.

'Nooo,' he coaxed.

His voice was like molten silver, soft and liquid and burning.

'This is your fantasy, my darling, and we are going to do it to you every way you ever wanted and we are not going to stop until you are begging for mercy and you are going to adore it . . .'

She closed her eyes in anguish, because she knew it was true. She was going to love this. This really was her fantasy. He knew how to excite her with words and she felt herself moving like hell with the stud again. He had lifted her bum right off the bed now and was pushing his fingers inside her there. She came again, even more violently than the first time. She thought her whole body was going to burst. Marcus was beside himself. He pulled the stud off her and played with her with his fingers, asking her what it felt like in there now. Then he got the stud to lie down and made her climb on top of him and ride him. At first she didn't think she was going to be able to – he was so big. But she could, she could.

171

While she was doing it, Marcus began to work on her bum, and when he was hard again he climbed astride her and entered her there. He did so with greater ease than ever before. Her every orifice was crying out for it. When he was fully inside her, she had her complete fantasy. Her eyes opened wide and she screamed and screamed as she came. Marcus was glad his flat was soundproofed. This was too much for the stud, professional that he was, he shot into her, but Marcus was not going to be finished for a long time. All night long they kept this up. The stud was an expert masseuse. Halfway through the night he produced scented oils and massaged her whole body until she was crying out for his sex again.

Eventually she became vaguely aware that he had dressed and that Marcus was handing him money. Oh God, she thought. She felt disgusted. Then Marcus was in the bed with her again, holding her close, talking to her, asking her how she liked her surprise, asking her if there was anything she would not do, asking her if she would like three men the next time, or four. Had she ever done it with a woman? Would she do that for him? He'd hire a couple of studs as well, if she liked. Telling her how much she liked to see her do it, asking her if she would like to watch him. He was out of control, he was like a junkie for her, he was hard again. He could not lose his erection that night. She had almost passed out with exhaustion and the excess of sex, she was no longer able to respond or to protest. He rolled her over on her front, pushed three pillows underneath her, and went into her one last delicious time.

It seemed like only five minutes later that she heard the familiar splashing sounds and the whistling in the bathroom. After a while out bounced Marcus. He looked fresh as a mountain stream, flashed a toothy grin, and came and sat on the bed next to her. He smelt of toothpaste and soap. Somebody had recently told him aftershave wasn't stylish, so he had stopped using it at once. He tousled her hair, bent over and kissed her lightly on the lips.

'You are sensational,' he said. 'Fucking sensational . . .'

She stopped him. 'Marcus, I wish you hadn't . . .'

He grinned again.

'That's not what you said last night, my beauty.'

She rubbed her eyes. She thought they were probably red and puffy. She was half awake, only half conscious, perhaps. Her whole body felt trampled on and used. She wasn't going to be able to sit down comfortably for a week. God she felt tacky.

'That makes it worse . . .' she started to explain.

'Don't be daft, you're the sexiest creature in the universe and it's my mission to help you make the most of it,' he chuckled.

She desperately wanted to explain how she felt, but she couldn't, not in the state she was in – and probably never to Marcus. His sexuality was even more frightening than her own, and he never seemed to have any qualms.

'Marcus, I don't ever want to do anything like that again,' she managed to say.

'What?' he replied.

His smile was super-confident. He wasn't really listening to a word she said.

He reached under the bedclothes, he was really motoring now.

'You could take an army in there, you sexy bitch,'

173

he muttered. He pulled on his jacket and headed for the door, looking back suddenly over his shoulder.

'Listen, don't go to work today. I'll come back at lunchtime,' he said.

Jennifer groaned.

'OK, OK, I know you're a worn-out woman. No sex. Just champagne and smoked salmon, a cuddle, and a few reminiscences. All right?'

It was like talking to the wall. He really lived in a world of his own when it came to sex. He thought she was in the same world as him, and half the time she was – but not quite. For her there were limits. This morning she knew that for certain, and she was quite overcome with self-disgust. She got out of bed, staggered into the bathroom, stood under the shower, turned on the taps full-force and remained there for several minutes. Then she went back into the bedroom, dressed, and gathered together all the various items of clothing she had ever left in Marcus's apartment. Having packed everything that belonged to her in a couple of carrier bags, she took off her engagement ring and left it on the dining-room table.

Then she left.

She took a taxi to her flat and when she was inside dialled Marcus's number and left a message on his answer-phone.

'You went too far,' she said. 'This is the end because I am afraid of what might happen next. I will try to keep out of your way. I never want to see you again. Fantasies are just that, fantasies. I am disgusted with both of us. How could I marry a man who would do what you did last night?'

She hadn't meant to say so much. The message was supposed to be brief and dignified. Oh God, she was aching all over inside and out. Her lips were swollen and her breasts so tender she couldn't bear to put her bra on. Between them they had nearly chewed her nipples off – and at the time she had been encouraging them and begging for more. Oh God, Oh God.

She could not face work, she felt terrible, physically and mentally she was a wreck. From when she was a girl she had sometimes been in awe of her own sexuality. She hated Marcus for taking her to breaking point, and she hated herself for responding the way she had. The reality of her fantasy had exceeded her imagining of it. She had reached heights and depths that she had never even dreamed of, but it all seemed so unsavoury now. In the cool light of day she was filled with self-loathing. She never wanted to let go like that again, and she really did not want to know about the man who could calmly arrange something like that, a man who was supposed to love her, a man who had asked her to marry him. She had fallen into the sweet trap at the height of her sexual excitement. He had planned it in advance, hired some stud, paid for another man to fuck her. She shivered. What would Marcus think of next? She knew that for her own sanity she dare not hang around to find out. Worn out and thoroughly depressed, she crawled thankfully into her own bed and fell instantly asleep.

She was woken by the phone and glanced at her watch. One-thirty. She had slept for four hours. Marcus would be at his flat now and had obviously found both her message and his ring. She pulled the plug out of the phone on the bedside table. Her answering machine could do the work and she didn't even want to hear the bloody thing ringing.

Twelve

One thing Jennifer knew for certain was that she could not go on working on the same paper as Marcus. She made a few phone calls the following day and landed another job with more ease than she had expected. She had underestimated herself. She was young, talented, and energetic, and her reputation was growing.

She was hired by the *Globe* as chief feature writer, and immediately threw herself both into her work and into a new relationship. She was desperate to forget Marcus and have nothing more to do with him. Their sexual exploits had really shaken her that night. She couldn't quite elucidate it, but the feelings of sexual revulsion – as much with herself as with Marcus – which she was now experiencing had cleared her mind, so that her various worries and doubts about him had returned, in spite of the justification he had rather offhandedly offered her. She had to free herself completely.

'And I'm going to, have no doubts about that,' she told Anna. 'I never want to see Marcus Piddell again.'

'Really,' replied Anna. 'Bet you lunch at the Connaught you go back to him.'

'I just hope your expenses are up to it,' said Jennifer.

Marcus did not give up easily. He was used to getting what he wanted. At work she dodged his calls and at home she hid behind her answering-machine. A couple of times he even doorstepped her office, which surprised her a little because she thought he would have been concerned about his image. She remained resolute, refusing even to stop and talk to him, but knew that if she were to hold out against Marcus's persistence, she needed something to take her mind off him. And the only something which could possibly do that job for Jennifer Stone would be another man.

And so when nice Michael Appley had shown an interest in her when they met at a dinner party, she had readily embarked on a new affair. Michael was a college lecturer whose subject was history, and all Jennifer's friends, particularly Anna, believed that he himself would soon be history too. Jennifer found him quite charming, which he was. He was like a great bear, a big man in his mid-thirties, already spreading to fat but attractive enough. He had a beard because he couldn't be bothered to shave, and wore whatever clothes came first to hand in the mornings. Michael Appley was a complete change after Marcus, and that seemed like a jolly good idea to Jennifer. They went to bed together the first night they met. He was gentle and caring, just how she had imagined he would be. She found him delightful and enjoyed sleeping with him, but should have been warned off, because when they had finished her body invariably still ached for more.

Jennifer was totally on the rebound from Marcus, and quite incapable of a proper emotional commitment to anybody. None the less she convinced herself that she was in love with Michael, and he was definitely in love with her.

They were married within three months and divorced a year later.

Jennifer felt guilty about Michael for the rest of her life. It was only two months after they were married that she strayed for the first time. New sexual opportunity seemed to arise consistently, and Jennifer could rarely resist it. She never again wanted to go as far as she had with Marcus, but his influence on her had been overwhelming. She needed regular, challenging, exciting sex – she couldn't help it.

Michael tried not to notice. Ultimately she became more and more careless, until he could no longer pretend ignorance of her activities. Deeply hurt, he had asked for a divorce. Jennifer had not even bothered to try to explain. What could she say? She didn't argue. In fact Michael would probably have liked her to attempt to justify her behaviour, because he secretly wanted to try again with their marriage. He loved her, he just wanted her to behave like a wife.

She, on the other hand, knew that it was hopeless. She needed her own space again. She had been deeply scarred by Marcus and had felt that the love of another man could heal her scars – but in fact she should never have married Michael. It had just been a stupid romantic dream.

Marcus had married only weeks after her. He had wed his editor's secretary. By the time he became editor of the *Daily Recorder* the following year, that marriage too was over. He began to telephone Jennifer again, but, amazed at her own determination, she stuck to her resolution. Marcus was the one man who had control over her, their sex life still frightened her, and if she agreed even to meet she suspected she would succumb to him.

179

Fed up with London, she accepted the chance to go to New York as Features Editor of a paper there owned by the *Globe*'s parent company.

Eventually Marcus married for the second time. His new wife was nineteen years old, at seventeen years his junior she was little more than half his age, and had a title but no money. It seemed a fair trade.

Marcus sent Jennifer an invitation to the wedding which, in spite of being divorced, he had managed to arrange in a rather grand church on the outskirts of London. Never ceasing to wonder at his cheek, Jennifer declined even to reply.

A few weeks after Marcus's second set of nuptials, Anna McDonald flew to New York on a business trip and Jennifer took her to her favourite New York restaurant, a delightful but unfashionable establishment where she liked to relax with her real friends. It was tucked away off the beaten track and in no way a place for seeing or being seen, yet suddenly, just as she and Anna were about to order their dinner, Marcus turned up with his new wife.

Jennifer could hardly believe her eyes. She was stunned. It would surely have been stretching credibility even to consider that Marcus had deliberately sleuthed out her regular haunts, but New York was a big town, boasting several thousand restaurants, and he had not seemed inordinately surprised to see her already sitting at a table. Indeed, with his customary self-confidence, he strode purposefully across the restaurant with his new bride in tow and flamboyantly introduced her to the two women.

Her name, it transpired, as Jennifer vaguely recalled from the wedding invitation, was Pamela.

Lady Pamela, Marcus pointed out with obvious satisfaction, while explaining with a ridiculously rakish wink that they were on a delayed honeymoon. Pamela was tall, skinny, and horsily good-looking – the kind of looks that you know can only be English upper-class and yet you can't explain exactly why. Her hair was very dark and skin very pale. She had that assured air about her which so often comes with an obvious public-school education, and in some ways she seemed older than her nineteen years, while retaining the naivety of a young woman who has never had to fight for anything in her life and never expects to.

None the less she seemed quite untroubled at meeting her husband's ex-partner in such a manner. An immaculately manicured hand was produced for a firm handshake.

'How lovely to meet you,' she announced heartily. Unlike Marcus she had yet to bother to modulate her public-school accent, which was pure cut-glass.

'Good to meet you too,' muttered Jennifer. The words came out in some kind of dreadful mid-Atlantic drawl. God, this bloody man was the only person in the world who could throw her off balance like this. She felt extremely uncomfortable and very angry with herself. Marcus's new wife was just a kid and yet it was Jennifer who was behaving like one. She had stood up when the couple approached her table and now wished she hadn't. Sitting down again, rather clumsily, she groped for her napkin which she had dropped on the floor. With the swift agility she remembered only too well, Marcus picked it up and familiarly placed it on her lap. Jennifer felt herself beginning to blush. Marcus's gaze was upon her as he rested an arm on his wife's shoulder. Casually he brushed a finger against Lady Pamela's neck beneath the heavy dark hair. Jennifer could see that he was scratching her flesh lightly with his fingernail. The young woman shuddered, almost imperceptibly, but Jennifer noticed.

'So he does that to you, too,' she thought. And her blush deepened as she had a brief and unwelcome vision of their two bodies together in bed, Marcus with all his mighty sexuality, Marcus doing to this debbie young thing all that he had done to her . . .

She forced herself to look away, and became aware that Marcus was still staring at her. His eyes were smiling, almost mocking. He flashed a grin. Was it her imagination or did his tongue dart swiftly across those immaculate white teeth? The bastard. He was reading her mind. He knew full well what she was thinking about. She tried desperately to look at ease and knew she was failing. She could not trust herself to speak at all.

Anna came smartly to the rescue. Thank God, as ever, for Anna, who, of course, had not stumbled unnecessarily to her feet, but remained sitting, a picture of composure, throughout the somewhat awkward confrontation. Anna's eyelashes fluttered briefly. She looked up at Marcus from beneath their pale fringe. Anna McDonald had never particularly liked or trusted Marcus Piddell, and neither did she fear him.

'Don't let us keep you newlyweds,' she said sweetly. 'I am sure you would rather be alone . . .'

Mercifully Marcus led his young wife away to a table at the far end of the restaurant. They were elegance on legs, he all Armani and Gucci as usual, she dressed in a style which said, simply, *class*.

'Good God, what on earth was all that about?' asked Anna.

'I wish I knew,' said Jennifer. 'And I wish I hadn't fallen apart like I did. Without you I think I'd have died.'

'I doubt that,' replied Anna. 'You might have succumbed to his evil clutches again, though . . .'

'Don't be ridiculous. He was with his new wife for Heaven's sake.' Jennifer was trying very hard to behave like a successful independent woman again.

'Really?' said Anna. 'And what the hell was he doing in this restaurant? It's hardly New York's answer to The Ivy is it? I reckon the bugger found out it's one of your places. He's probably been dragging his child bride here every night since they've been in the city, just waiting to put the pair of you together.'

'That's absurd,' said Jennifer.

'Is it? I'd never put anything past that man. He wanted to see you wriggle. He's obsessed with you.'

'Well I'm certainly not obsessed with him any more.'

'I do hope that's true – for your sake.' The gentle grey eyes were momentarily serious. Then they started to twinkle.

'It's just occurred to me – that poor little cow has become blessed with the name of Pam Piddle,' said Anna, chuckling into her third martini.

'Piddell,' corrected Jennifer, smiling easily now. Anna was making her feel better again, as usual.

'Piddle to me,' said Anna 'And always will be . . .'

It was Anna who later told Jennifer that Marcus had bought a mansion in Kent – which in Anna's opinion gave the marriage half a chance of working because it meant that with all his city commitments, Marcus had to spend most of the week apart from his wife.

He had risen to become chairman and chief executive of his newspaper group. Jennifer heard about it in New York and wondered idly how he had managed that and also how much power Freemasonry really had in the world order of things. His reign was controversial, decisions were constantly being taken which hit the headlines in other newspapers. They seemed to have no pattern. The left-wing political stance of the newspaper was turned upside down – most of the time. With Marcus at the helm the *Recorder* appeared to have little or no direction. It did of course – it went unfailingly the way which suited the aims of Marcus and those who pulled his strings.

None the less the paper kept its circulation and its profitability, because Marcus was an excellent newspaperman who employed the best journalists and insisted on the best stories, both when he was editor and later – as long as they did not interfere with any of his masterplans. For the readers the *Recorder* was still the best popular paper going. Only the readers mattered – and how they mattered!

When the *Recorder* somersaulted right on to its head and backed the Conservatives at a crucial general election, Marcus and his newspaper were widely credited with having brought about what seemed unthinkable at the time – a Tory victory over the incumbent Labour government. Marcus was duly rewarded with a knighthood.

In New York, Jennifer chuckled to herself. Trust Marcus. He had a wife with a title so he would have to match it, and he had promptly done so. Everything that she read about him told her that he was becoming more and more powerful. His integrity was frequently questioned in the papers, but then, wasn't that the case for any super-successful man?

In New York, one sunny Sunday morning, the phone rang in Jennifer's apartment. Her mother was on the line. Her father had just suffered a major heart attack and been rushed to hospital.

Jennifer took Concorde out of John F. Kennedy Airport. She couldn't mess around. She dreaded that her father might die before she reached him. And when she arrived at Heathrow and immediately called Devon, her worst fears were realised. She tried to remember when she had last been home to Pelham Bay and couldn't quite. She hired a car at the airport, and could not stop crying throughout the three and a half-hour journey to North Devon – she shed tears of grief for the father she had truly adored, and tears of guilt too. As is so often the case, the guilt was probably hardest to bear.

The funeral was well attended and curiously comforting. Her brother Steve had flown back from his home in Australia. If Mrs Stone wished that just one of her two children lived near to her, she never said so.

As she stood by her mother's side in Pelham Bay's pretty little church, Jennifer was surrounded by familiar faces from her past. She spotted Bill Turpin sitting at the back. He hadn't changed a bit. Strange how he always stood out, that man. She had forgotten that her father even knew him, but then, her father knew everybody.

Todd Mallett was there, a sergeant now. More solid and dependable-looking than ever.

Outside the church he appeared quietly at her side and took her hand briefly.

'He was a good man, I'm sorry Jenny,' he said.

She held her tears back and thanked him for his sympathy.

'You're a good man, too, Todd,' she wanted to say, but she didn't. Instead she asked him about Angela and his family; three fine boys, she had heard.

Out of the corner of her eye she noticed Bill Turpin slipping quietly away, speaking to nobody. Typical of what she remembered of the strange old man.

Johnny Cooke's parents were also there. It was the first time Jennifer had seen them since the trial, how many years before? She had not recognised them at first, but they had attracted her attention, even through her distress at her father's death. Mr and Mrs Cooke had a weariness about them. Their son was still in jail. Mabel Cooke continued to make her monthly visits. Charlie Cooke just pretended Johnny had never existed. They barely raised their heads during or after the service. Jennifer's mother, kindly even in grief, had sought them out in the churchyard and invited them back to her home afterwards to join the family and other mourners.

Mrs Cooke looked grateful, but shook her head. 'No dear, thank you,' she said. 'We just came to pay our respects . . .'

'Who was that?' Jennifer asked.

186

'You know them – that Johnny Cooke's poor parents,' her mother replied. 'Thank God I've got you and Steve.'

Jennifer had held her close in the car as they were driven back to the little terraced house. She vowed to visit more often in future. But she didn't of course.

Thirteen

Jennifer didn't even tell Anna McDonald at first when she started to see Marcus again. All the half-told stories about him and his activities she'd seen over the years made her feel uneasy and slightly embarrassed. From the moment Marcus had started to rise to power she had suspected that she would find many of his business dealings shocking. Yet that would probably be so with most big businessmen. And Marcus had become one of the biggest. A genuine tycoon. Chairman of a giant publishing house with a property company and a chain of launderettes also under his wing. Launderettes? Trust Marcus. His very first business venture had been to buy a launderette soon after he first arrived in London in 1970. It was a boom time for that business and Marcus was always quick to spot the main chance. Most unlike a journalist. Jennifer remembered asking at the time how he had found the money for such a venture. A bank loan, he had replied shortly. It seemed reasonable, because although he had little or no collateral, if there was one man who could talk a bank into a loan for no good reason at all it would be Marcus Piddell. And nothing had changed.

His empire frequently brought him to New York, and for the last few months he had been determinedly wooing her. It had been the previous year that he had telephoned her out of the blue. Before that their break had been total and, apart from the bizarre restaurant meeting, she had not seen or heard from him since his marriage. He had explained on the phone that he was in town and was lunching with an American writer he knew Jennifer had always admired. He wondered if she would like to join them.

Her warning mechanism sparked into action. None the less she hesitated before replying. He was quick.

'Look Jennifer, I know it's long over for us and I am not going to try to start it again, I promise you. I just thought that after all this time we could be friends and I know you would like to meet this guy.'

It was a cliché, but it worked. Probably because she wanted it to. Jennifer met the two men at The Russian Tea Rooms as instructed. The American writer was delightful and brilliant and Jennifer did indeed enjoy meeting him. Marcus was charm itself. But then he would be, wouldn't he? He talked about his aristocratic young wife a lot, giving Jennifer just the odd sidelong glance to see how she was taking his remarks.

At the end of lunch he pecked her lightly on the cheek and said he would be back in New York soon and maybe they could go to the theatre or something. She walked alone back to her office, suddenly aware that she was vaguely disappointed that he hadn't made a pass at her. She shook herself angrily. She was not going to fall into the Marcus Piddell trap again. He would never change. She knew for certain that, one way or another, further involvement with him would mean the end of the last of her self esteem.

She was having an affair with a married lawyer at the time. The arrangement suited her perfectly. It

189

wasn't really an affair, certainly not a love affair, certainly not on her side. She wasn't so sure about him. She would have to watch that. But so far so good. After Marcus and then Michael, with the guilt of that still heavy on her shoulders, it was going to be a long time before she was ready for emotional involvement again. Sometimes she thought she never would be.

And she would not think about sex with Marcus. She would not. Only of that last degrading night after which she had never wanted to see him again. Well, perhaps he had changed, but no, she would not even consider it. He would never change, would never lose his extreme sexuality, his brinkmanship. Anyway he was married. And she pitied his wife, or, if the truth be told, half pitied and half envied her. Enough. It was over between her and Marcus and would remain so.

Three weeks later Marcus called again. He had two tickets for a Broadway show. Would she like to go along? For old times' sake, nothing more. He took her to supper afterwards at The River Cafe in Brooklyn, from which they could look across at the illuminated shape of Manhattan, then he took her home to her apartment in the chauffeur-driven limo which conveyed him around town nowadays. He was the perfect gentleman. From the foyer of her apartment block she watched his car leave, aware again of vague disappointment. This was ridiculous.

And so every two or three weeks Marcus would turn up and they would dine together or go to the theatre. They talked of his business empire. He appeared quite frank. Without embarrassment he discussed the suspicions voiced against him and dismissed it all as jealousy. He was convincing, as always.

Each time they met his manners were perfect. But there was no mistaking the longing in his eyes. She felt he was courting her, and she was right. Eventually one night he suddenly told her that he was divorcing his wife. Startled, she asked him why.

He shrugged his big shoulders. 'It was another mistake,' he said.

'Is that all?' she asked. 'Simple as that? You make it sound like ordering the wrong meal in a restaurant.'

He shook his head. 'Pamela wanted children. I thought I did too. Since seeing you again I have realised there is only one woman in the world I want to be the mother of my children.'

He looked at her directly. She did not want to meet his gaze.

'I have changed, Jennifer,' he said. 'Sex isn't everything any more. If I could relive one night of my life and do it differently it would be the night I lost you.'

She felt herself begin to melt. How was it that he could still do this to her?

'I have always wanted to marry you. I still want to marry you,' he continued.

Then he proposed to her. They were in his hotel suite. They were supposed to be going to the theatre. She bet he hadn't even bought the tickets. It wasn't going to be that easy, she thought, but she accepted that she was probably kidding herself.

'You are married already, Marcus,' she pointed out flatly.

'I told you, we are getting divorced,' he said.

'You will never change,' she said.

And her answer was no. No she would not marry

him, even if he was free. He didn't seem to listen. Typical Marcus. He was still staring at her, allowing his eyes to undress her.

'I want you Jennifer,' he said. 'And from now on it will be only you, I promise.'

She supposed it was inevitable. She allowed herself to be led into the bedroom. The sex was as extraordinary as ever; but he was more careful, more gentle, more affectionate. Maybe he had changed after all. Thankfully, he was just as exciting. He reduced her to a trembling wreck, unaware again of anything in the whole world except her own sexuality. Only he could drive her to those kind of extremes, only he could make her entire body shake with desire, only he could make her beg for more and more. It was just the same as it had always been, and she realised how much she had missed it.

The next night she went out with Marcus again. He said he had been on to his lawyers in London. They reckoned they could rush the divorce through in a couple of months, and that did not surprise her. His name pulled strings and he had the knack of getting his own way fast – she knew that. She was afraid and excited all over again. Damn Marcus Piddell. She feared she was going to have to give him one more chance. She wanted to believe so much that this time it would be all right, yet she tried very hard not to let him see how close she was to giving in.

Eventually she confessed to Anna that she was seeing Marcus again and even that he had asked her to marry him – but she insisted that she was determined to turn him down. Her best friend was not convinced. 'Poor bloody Lady Pamela,' Anna remarked caustically. 'Never stood a bloody chance.'

'Nonsense,' maintained Jennifer. 'If Marcus goes through with divorcing his wife it will be absolutely nothing to do with me. Seeing him occasionally is one thing, but I have no intention of ever making any kind of commitment to him again.'

Yet she was kidding herself, and she knew it, even though when Marcus returned to the UK she was still refusing to marry him, and continued to resist through two more of his flying visits.

Then, on one of her periodic trips to London, just weeks after his first proposal, he took her to dinner at The King's Head, a little pub by the river in Wapping. It was unlike him to want to dine anywhere that was not excessively trendy, but he knew how she liked cosy pub restaurants and perhaps he was hoping that the romance of a waterside setting might influence her. Maybe sensing that she was near to agreeing to share her life with him again, he asked her once more if she would marry him. She gazed out of the window wondering idly if Marcus had arranged the stunning full moon as well as everything else, and somewhere in the distance she heard her own voice saying yes.

'You win, Marcus. I'm probably insane. But yes, I will marry you.'

They had not started the main course. He said nothing in reply. With a wave of his hand he gestured for the bill and paid it. His eyes were inside her head again, inside her body, drilling deep into her. She knew what was going to happen. She felt the old crazy excitement mounting. He took her by the hand and led her from the restaurant. Just down the street there was an alleyway leading to the riverside and he half dragged her into it. 'We'll get mugged,' she protested.

'No,' he said. 'Not tonight.'

He led her down the alley until it turned abruptly to the left, into a dead end with the Thames on one side and a disused warehouse on the other. In a shadowed corner away from the startlingly bright glow of the moon, there was a boarded-up window with a wide stone ledge. He backed her against it and lifted her on to the ledge – it was just the right height. Vaguely she thought it was bound to be filthy and that would be the end of her Saint Laurent suit. His eyes did not leave her face as he plunged into her. No preamble. No need. Animal. Basic. He was urgent in her, still staring unblinking at her. Deadly serious.

'From now on this is for you. Only you. No more games. Just you and me and this. Because it can only be like this for us.'

His words were staccato. It was over very quickly. He was making a point, he was consummating their new engagement. It was like shaking hands on a deal. The thought made her giggle. He was the only man she had ever had sex like that with. In a daft sort of way it was special to them, had been since the scramble by the dustbins at her school all those years ago.

Fourteen

When they got back to his apartment Marcus apologised. Jennifer thought it was the first time she had ever heard him apologise for anything. And she had never seen him look so nervous. She realised how afraid he was of losing her again. He was afraid she had been offended by his alley antics. She had reassured him that she could never resist his gut sexiness – that had been his first appeal to her and it was not going to go away. They were two of a kind. It was just that this time there had to be limits or they would destroy themselves and their relationship. He knew what she meant.

The skirt of her Saint Laurent suit, which had started the day a pale lemon colour, was indeed ruined – its seat now covered in grime. 'Tomorrow we'll go shopping. I'll buy you the shop,' he said.

'Flash bugger,' she replied.

But for the first time the thought crossed her mind that he probably could buy the shop if he wished. Extraordinary.

She never did go back to New York. Marcus's divorce came through with the kind of smoothness Jennifer knew to expect from him. They were married in the West Indies in the winter of 1987.

'I told you Lady Pamela never stood a bloody chance,' said Anna McDonald. 'And you owe me two lunches at the Connaught. One to cancel out the one I bought you when you married poor old Michael, and the other to settle our bet. I always knew I'd win in the end . . .'

Uncomfortably aware that her mother deserved far better, Jennifer had told Margaret Stone of her marriage plans on the telephone. 'Yes, of course I understand you wanting to go away on your own to get married,' her mother had said, while quite clearly not understanding at all. 'I just hope you know what you're doing this time. It would make a change, I'm sure . . .'

The lawyer lover and the New York apartment were all dispensed with by remote control. Jack at the *Globe* agreed to have Jennifer back in London as Features Editor, creating a vacancy to do so and pretending not to notice that she had more or less walked out of New York. But then, she was known in Fleet Street for having an impetuous streak, and only a combination of considerable talent and her likeableness allowed her to get away with it. Also Anna was absolutely spot-on right – Jack did indeed adore her, and who knows what other forces were working for her, thanks to Marcus. Even then that thought did occur to her.

One way and another it was an extremely neat operation. It would be, of course: Marcus was a neat man both physically and mentally. His house, his office, even his desk, were always immaculate, and so, Jennifer suspected, was the order of his mind. He never liked mess or loose ends. But she had had enough of living in America anyway. London was home.

In the sunny splendour of Barbados' Sandy Lane Hotel they drank too many rum punches and planned their new life together. They would have a baby before it was too late, maybe more than one. They were both ready. On returning to England they bought the house on Richmond Hill. It had plenty of room for a family. Once again they were the media world's golden couple, only this time even more so.

Two years passed relatively uneventfully and things were still pretty good. But Marcus had changed in many ways. At first Jennifer was sure he was being faithful to her sexually, yet there was so much she did not know about his world. Just as before, he would sometimes disappear for hours on end, maybe a whole day, and nobody in his office ever knew where he was. She asked him about his Freemasonry and he admitted readily enough that, yes indeed, the Masons demanded a great deal of his time nowadays, especially since he was apparently now a member of several lodges and a grand master of more than one. But still she felt uneasy. A few times he said he was embarking on business trips abroad and she discovered by chance that his stories just did not add up. He told her that his business interests were so complex now he could not begin to explain, he could not stop to take anyone else on board. She accepted it more or less because she couldn't face a confrontation and, looking back, she realised that she had not wanted to rock the boat. She had not wanted there to be anything amiss, she had not wanted another broken marriage. But she was uneasy. His telephone had a scrambler on it, for God's sake, and he never failed to take most of his calls behind a firmly closed door as far away from her as possible – just as he had from the very beginning of their relationship. But perhaps all men at his level of success needed to be discreet about their work, she thought to herself. He remained as plausible as ever. You didn't discuss deals worth millions of pounds on open, unscrambled lines, he said, and there were some kinds of business so delicate and confidential that you did not allow anyone to overhear – not even your wife.

Frequently she would walk into a room when he was talking on the telephone and he would immediately hang up. Once or twice she picked up the phone when it rang and there would be no one at the other end. Classic signs of an affair. But she wanted desperately to trust him. She had thrown in her lot with him.

Their sex life remained as exceptional as it had always been. It was almost twenty years since they had first been together, and their desire for each other was as great as ever. Unusual, she thought. But in spite of the quality and frequency of their lovemaking, Jennifer did not become pregnant. Eventually she went to her gynaecologist for tests. Nothing indicated any reason why she should not have a child, but she was thirty-six years old and her body clock was ticking away.

'It'll happen sooner or later, darling, you'll see,' Marcus reassured her.

It didn't happen and eventually her doctors asked to test Marcus. He agreed easily enough; it did not seem to occur to him that the problem might really be his.

Jennifer came home late one night to find him slumped over the kitchen table with a nearly empty whisky bottle by his side. It was the first time she had ever seen him really drunk. Marcus did not like to lose control. Except in bed. He stirred when she entered the room.

'Wanna drink?'

She nodded and then sat down opposite him. He poured fine malt whisky into a crystal tumbler. Even in despair, Marcus would never allow his standards to drop. Not Marcus. She knew something was very wrong. She waited for him to speak.

'You're not gonna bloody believe this,' he said finally. 'I'm bloody sterile.'

His eyes were red and swollen. She realised he had been crying. She instinctively reached forward and held his hand.

'It doesn't matter,' she said.

They both knew it did. Probably more to him than to her, as it happened.

'Biggest, horniest bloody dick in bloody town and it's bloody useless,' he muttered angrily. 'Bang bloody bang. An' all I fire is bloody blanks.'

It was after that that things started to go wrong.

The matter was never discussed again. Nor were any alternatives like adoption. Marcus hardly ever seemed to want to talk to her about anything. He had a grimness about him that she had not been aware of before. For the first time ever the sexual chemistry between them began to let them down. Sometimes Marcus would come home very late and sleep in one of the spare rooms, saying that he had not wanted to wake her. She had determined that this time she would remain faithful within her marriage. There really was little point in remarrying in your mid thirties unless that was your intention. But she did stray once or twice. Not because she craved further sexual excitement, but because she felt so alone, so isolated. The emotional side of her relationship with Marcus had always been a little strange. There was no doubt of its strength. But it was all so closely entangled with the sexual magnetism between them. Love was not a word often mentioned. Jennifer had once told Anna that, when she had finally married Marcus, her strongest feeling had been one of inevitability. It was her destiny, and whether she loved him or not, and of course she supposed she did, was irrelevant.

When they ultimately parted she experienced the same feeling of inevitability. Probably the way in which it happened was inevitable too. She had become pretty sure that Marcus was indulging in sexual activities she would rather not know about. But nothing had prepared her for the revelations on that grey, chill October night in 1992.

She had to travel to Paris to negotiate the buy-up of a big Royal scoop with a French magazine, and she was booked on the last flight out of Heathrow. Minutes after the flight was called there was a bomb scare and the entire airport was cleared. She waited an hour or so in the nearby Hilton Hotel and finally decided she had had enough. She would catch the first flight the next day, and she would take a taxi home to sleep in her own bed.

As her key turned in the latch she sensed that things were not as they should be. The hall was dark but there was a dim light showing through the cracks around the closed door to the living room. It was what she could hear that had turned her blood cold. High-pitched squeals, sobbing, and rhythmic grunting. She threw open the door.

A startled Marcus turned around so that he was

looking straight at her. The expression on his face horrified her. His eyes looked crazed. His lips were pulled back over his teeth so that he seemed to be snarling, sweat was pouring from him, the muscles of his neck were bulging with his exertions. He was naked, and leaning over the sofa before him were two young Oriental girls, who were also naked. Marcus was still thrusting into the backside of one of them. Even as he looked into the horrified eyes of his wife, he could not stop his body carrying on with what it was doing. The girls also turned to look at Jennifer, and their faces showed pain and fear. They were weeping. Marcus had later claimed they were at least sixteen, but Jennifer remained sure that they were even younger. They were physically tiny and she knew how big Marcus was.

Jennifer took in the whole sordid scene in seconds. Still clutching her overnight bag for the Paris trip, she bolted for the front door, slammed it behind her, and ran to the Porsche parked in the driveway. Although she had used taxis for her original journey to the airport, she found to her relief that her car keys were in her pocket. Hastily she unlocked the car door, slid behind the wheel, tossing her bag onto the passenger seat, crashed the gears into reverse and roared out of the drive backwards and at speed. She was fortunate that for a brief moment there were no passing vehicles on the road behind the house. Had there been, she would have smashed straight into them, because she had not looked in any direction. As she gunned the car forwards with a clumsy lurch, she was vaguely aware of the front door to the house flying open and a frantic Marcus, clutching an unbuttoned overcoat tightly around his nakedness, tearing down the drive behind her. Too late. Much too late for everything.

She drove back to the Airport Hilton and arranged parking for her car for the duration of the two-day Paris trip. She booked a room for the night, plugged in to a house video and ordered a large meal and a bottle of good claret on room service. She refused to think about what she had just witnessed. All she knew was that this time it really was over between her and Marcus. She did not want to see him again as long as she lived. The man was depraved, and the terrible thing was that she had always suspected it. She had parted from him once before because she was afraid of what he could lead her into. Now she knew that Marcus Piddell could never have taken her halfway towards the depths he was capable of.

Marcus had just been elected a member of parliament in her beloved West Country. As usual he had sailed through it, and she had played her role of politician's wife pretty well too. Yuk. She thought back to the weeks of canvassing. Marcus had stayed in Durraton for the duration and she had travelled down from London every weekend, to stand smilingly alongside him in draughty village halls, even knocking on doors. He was good at the campaigning, and also he had a true knowledge of the West Country. She had hoped that he would turn out to be a good constituency MP. And certainly, along with his parents and her mother, she had been briefly very proud of Marcus. In spite of all his extraordinary success in the city, and his rise to becoming a newspaper tycoon, it still meant a great deal to him to be given this kind of recognition in the place where he grew up. Jennifer had found his undisguised joy quite disarming, and had shared every moment of his jubilation. Now she wondered what sort of man she had helped into a position of such potential power. Because the one thing she had been sure of from the moment he won the seat was that Marcus would not be content to stay on the back benches for long.

After she had eaten as much of the food as she wanted and drunk most of the claret, Jennifer reached for the phone to call Anna – it was a lifetime's habit. Then she replaced the receiver in its cradle. What was she going to tell her oldest friend? She had no wish to share even with Anna what she had witnessed that night.

She undressed, climbed into bed and pulled the covers over her head. Strangely she slept quite well, and in the morning, professional to the last, she flew to Paris and negotiated a tough deal. On her return, she found herself a smart service flat in Kensington, and wrote to Marcus telling him she would be paying for it with his credit card until they had sorted out their affairs. She wanted a divorce and she wanted it fast.

Marcus had prevaricated. He had pestered her much as before when she had left him. By his standards he positively grovelled. Certainly he made the same old promises, and told her how much he needed her. He would not discuss divorce.

Every feeling that she had ever had for him had finally been destroyed. She was quite simply disgusted by him and wanted him totally out of her life. She told Anna that much – but she never told her why. 'You were right, everything you ever thought about him, you were right,' she said.

'I didn't think I ever told you what I thought about him,' replied Anna.

'You didn't have to.' Jennifer managed a wry smile.

'I certainly didn't want to be right,' Anna continued. 'I just wanted you to be happy . . .'

And she questioned Jennifer no further. Anna was always such a good friend, ever-present when needed, to listen or not. Strangely undemanding. Constant.

The national press quickly picked up news of the Piddell's splitting up, but both Jennifer and Marcus stuck to their official line that they were amicably separated and had no further comment. There wasn't a lot of mileage in that – a kiss-and-tell was what the anti-Marcus tabloids needed. Half the press pack of Great Britain would have liked to get their hands on almost anything discrediting Marcus Piddell.

Eventually, not believing what she was doing, Jennifer agreed to meet Marcus for a drink one lunchtime on an old river barge that had been turned into a wine bar. It was moored by Waterloo Bridge. The day was sunny, so she suggested a walk along the Embankment and, as they strolled, she told him bluntly that if he did not agree to a divorce immediately and come up with a reasonable settlement in her favour, the story of his sordid sexual habits would suddenly be front-page news.

Marcus had been amazed.

'Good God, Jennifer, that's blackmail,' he had exclaimed.

'Yes,' she replied drily. 'Terrible thing, the collapse of morality, isn't it?'

The next day she received a letter delivered by messenger from Marcus's solicitor. It agreed to a divorce by the quickest possible means and Marcus offered the house in Richmond, mortgage fully paid-up, and £200,000 cash in full and final settlement. The only condition was that she should not discuss his affairs with any third party. Affairs . . . she had giggled in spite of herself. The choice of words was more appropriate than perhaps the lawyers were aware.

She agreed at once, knowing that Marcus was probably expecting and wanting her to prolong their association by sticking out for a better deal. After all, that kind of money was just a drop in the ocean to him. But the Richmond house was worth three quarters of a million at the time, and Jennifer just wanted as clean as possible an end to it all.

Soon afterwards Marcus was made a junior minister. A grateful government, in power largely because of the newspapers he still pretty well owned, was only just starting to reward Marcus Piddell. In North Devon they were all fiercely proud of him. Jennifer found it quite sickening.

Back in Pelham Bay, Johnny Cooke found the rise and rise of Mark Piddle even more sickening than Jennifer did. By 1992 Johnny had been a free man for four years. Or had he? Johnny's life sentence lasted seventeen years – it might have been less had it not been for recommendations of a long sentence given by the judge at his trial.

But for Johnny it really did feel like a lifetime. The years before his sentence now seemed just a dream. The years in prison felt as if they had happened to someone else. When he first went to Dartmoor it was the other way around. It was the prison which was unreal, a kind of grim fantasy place. By the time he left, prison had become dreadful reality, his complete and only world.

Gradually, over the long months and years, his condition of imprisonment had begun to change. He had wheedled his way into the more trusted jobs. Being allowed to work in the prison gardens, among plants and flowers, ultimately preserved his sanity. That and reading. He was finally allowed almost unlimited use of the prison library, and found great solace in books. Johnny had first learned the joy of losing himself in a book when he was still at school. Even back then he had always felt somehow awkward, out of place, different.

Now, the grim reality of his loss of liberty, even the oppressive way in which the walls of his cell seemed to close in on him, all disappeared when he was reading. Only his body remained within the granite of The Moor, his soul escaped to roam free as the wind whistling across the tors towards the ocean he so much yearned to see again.

Johnny was to remain grateful for the rest of his life for having been given the ability to bury his entire being inside the magic world of print on page.

Books saved his sanity. The physical labour in the garden, combined with almost daily work-outs in the prison gymnasium, saved his body from decline and restored much of the strength Johnny had lost in the early years. He almost wallowed in building up his body. He became obsessed with muscle development and with stretching his muscles at work in the garden. There was, after all, nothing else. When the time eventually came for him to leave jail, he was not sure that he wanted to go. He had become afraid of the world outside. He was completely institutionalised.

When he finally went home to his mother's house in Durraton in 1988 – his father had died while he was inside or he doubted he would have been welcome there – Johnny perversely experienced the same sort of near breakdown which he had gone through when he was sent to prison in the first place. The ability to come and go when he pleased, and do and be whatever he wanted on a whim, terrified the life out of him. His mother fussed dutifully.

'You're my boy, and there's always a place for you in this house,' she told him stoically.

He had no idea where else he could have gone – he had gone to prison a boy and emerged a man who had never experienced freedom. The attitudes of alleged friends, neighbours and people he met in the town numbed him. They nudged and stared and made no attempt at understanding, and certainly none of them wanted to employ him. Why should they, he thought? He was after all a convicted murderer. He did not feel free at all. He remained imprisoned within his heart every bit as much as he had ever been by the iron bars and granite walls of Dartmoor.

It was Bill Turpin who finally released him. Bill Turpin who gave Johnny the opportunity to start his life again, to regain his self-respect and at least to look for a reason for carrying on. It took a long time – but it was a beginning.

From the moment of his release from jail, Johnny was drawn to Pelham Bay. The might of the sea entranced him, as it had always done, and anyway, Pelham Bay was the only place which seemed to mean anything to him any more. This was where it had all happened . . .

Then one day, as he stood by the sea wall staring out at the ocean, just as Bill Turpin had all those years ago, the old man had appeared silently at his side and offered him a job. Right out of the blue. 'Nought much to start with, look after my fruit machines, keep an eye on the deckchair boys, nought much . . . but us'll see,' said Bill.

'Why?' asked Johnny. In his state of mind it was all he could think of to say.

Bill Turpin sucked on his old black pipe – the same one, Johnny reckoned. 'I never thought you was a bad lad . . .' Bill mused. And he ambled off along the promenade leaving Johnny standing, still bewildered.

Was it guilt, wondered Johnny. Was that it? He had learned at the trial that he had guessed right all those years ago and it had been old Bill who had tipped off the cops, told them about Johnny and Marjorie and seeing them together in the sand dunes. Johnny shook himself. What the Hell?

He trotted after the old man, catching him easily. 'I'll take it,' he said. 'I'll take the job, whatever it is.'

For Jennifer Stone, life went on much the same as it had before – but without Marcus. She returned to Pelham Bay only occasionally, but she did return to break the news of her divorce from Marcus – before it hit the local papers.

Marcus, who could charm for England when he wanted to, had always made a huge fuss of Jennifer's mother. And Mrs Stone could not help being impressed by him, particularly after he became the local MP. He was what was still referred to in Pelham

Bay as 'a good catch'. Among the many things she did not understand about her daughter and her daughter's life was why Jennifer had not married Marcus when she first had the chance. After all, the pair of them had been obsessed with each other since Jennifer's schooldays – and Mrs Stone knew and suspected more about that than anyone. And so this second divorce for Jennifer was a considerable shock as well as a disappointment.

'Not another one, dear. Whatever is your Aunty Pat going to say this time?' was Mrs Stone's first remark.

'Mother, really!' said Jennifer, exasperated. Nothing changed in Pelham Bay. For her mother, the biggest problem still of a broken marriage remained the reactions of family, friends and neighbours, and because Marcus was a public figure, the break-up would be all the more embarrassing.

Margaret Stone saw nothing strange in her own reactions. 'Thank goodness your father isn't alive to see this,' she continued. 'You know how upset he was the last time . . .'

Jennifer retreated thankfully to the anonymous sanctuary of London. She loved her mother dearly, but often came to the conclusion that they were on different planets.

Not long afterwards, Jennifer Stone was made an assistant editor at the *Globe* – number three in the hierarchy – although she suspected that was as far as she was going to go.

And so it all might have continued, had Jennifer not endured one office row too many and decided to walk out of the paper. She would have heard about

Bill Turpin, of course, and all that was discovered in his cottage. But whether or not she would have become personally involved if she had not physically been in North Devon at the time, she would never know . . .

To have actually arrived in Pelham Bay at the time of old Bill's death had seemed like another stroke of destiny. That summer Sunday, twenty-five years earlier, had in one way or another shaped the whole of her life. It had brought her and Mark together, forced her to grow up, introduced her to fear and the darker side of life. She had always known that it had played a part in shaping Mark's future too, and not just that part which included her.

She relived virtually the whole of her life that afternoon in May 1995 as she lay dozing on the big old bed in her mother's back bedroom. And by the time she went downstairs again, she had vowed that she would at last try to find the answers to some of those old nagging questions.

PART THREE

The Dream Is Over

The dream is over, lover
And there'll never be another.
You cast your spell on me
And I gave in quite willingly
To a lifetime's fantasy.

But it was not to you I gave my love
I saw what was not there to have.
I offered my heart
To a thing apart.
I offered my flesh
To so much less
Than the man I created
Inside my head.
I offered my mind
And I was blind.

We shared sweet madness
Cocooned within badness.
My whole being craved
To be possessed by you.
I was afraid
Yet remained obsessed by you.

Strange, now that I see you clear
How I cannot bear you near.
The dream is over, lover,
And there'll never be another.

Fifteen

The next day the urgency of the previous afternoon had mostly left Jennifer. She decided to go for a drive around all her old haunts and to take her mother with her. That would win a few bonus points. They drove to Pelham Bay, to the carpark by the cliffs, and her mother said she would be quite happy sitting in the car while Jennifer went for a bit of a walk.

She strode out along the cliff path for a while, and then sat herself on a big sandstone boulder almost at the cliff edge. It was a brilliantly clear day. You could see Lundy Island and across the water to Wales. The only sound was the whirl of the wind and the crash of the waves against the rocks below. There was hardly anyone about, just a lone couple in the distance walking their dogs, and one man out on the furthest point of the rocks down below, casting a fishing line. The sun was a flash of silver on the water, which was so darkly green and blue that in places it appeared almost black. The foaming crests of the waves curled and entwined and reared up into endless bucking shapes, demonstrating with extravagant clarity how they had come to be called white horses. From where she sat there was a sheer drop a couple of hundred feet down to the sea, and she felt suspended above it. The wiry heath grass was springy beneath her feet, and the boulder on which she perched felt warm from the sunshine, although the breeze had a bitter chill to it. And it was the strength of the wind that day which was keeping the sky so clear and free of clouds. The wild flowers were in their full blaze of late spring glory, the deep pink of campions mixing crazily with the vivid blue of bluebells. A backdrop of deep green fern lay at the foot of dense woodland lifting up from the flat ledge of the cliff top and stretching right back over the great hill beyond. It was a magical day. The air tasted of salt – how she missed that in London. The wind was like a massage of sharp needles against her upturned face. She closed her eyes and breathed in the wonder of the moment.

Some lines of T. S. Eliot, which she had discovered only recently and instantly known the truth of, flashed unheralded across her mind.

> 'We shall not cease from exploration.
> And the end of all our exploring,
> Will be to arrive where we started,
> And know the place for the first time.'

She had begun to walk back to the car and her patiently waiting mother. But instead, on autopilot, almost, she had taken the other track, the one she knew led past old Bill Turpin's cottage. If she was to unravel any of the mysteries of the past, this would be the key to open the first door. Instinctively she knew that, and although one half of her wanted to carry on with her life and have nothing more to do with the past, she could not do so.

She was not able to get very close to Bill's cottage because the police had cordoned off the area. She could not even follow the path which would have taken her past the cottage and along a circular route back to the carpark. A uniformed officer told her politely that she would have to return the way she had come. Over his shoulder she could just glimpse the activity at the cottage. There were a number of police there, many dressed in overalls, and they appeared to be digging up the garden.

Jennifer tried without a deal of success to talk to the young constable about what was happening. Just as she was ready to give up and reluctantly retrace her steps, she heard a familiar voice, a good strong solid Devonian voice issuing orders. She smiled. He always had that ring of authority about him, did Todd Mallett. People were inclined to do what he told them automatically, couldn't be a bad trait for a policeman. She turned to the constable again and asked if perhaps she could have a brief word with Sergeant Mallett, who was an old friend, she explained. Or maybe he was Inspector Mallett now?

The constable swiftly corrected her. 'Detective Inspector Mallett, madam,' he said.

He took her name and told her he would tell the detective inspector she would like to see him.

Minutes later, a beaming Todd Mallett strode across the grass towards her and held out his hand in greeting. A little formal, she thought, but he was, after all, a police inspector in front of all his men.

'Congratulations on your promotion,' she said, grinning.

'Not before time, some say,' he replied.

'Which is probably to your credit.'

'Glad something is,' he said.

He looked her up and down appreciatively. She was wearing the same tight black jeans she had worn

215

for the journey down the day before. She wore black leather boots and a heavy black leather jacket with a lot of shiny metallic bits and pieces on it. An expensive-looking silk scarf was just visible at her neck. Her thick brown hair had been blown all over the place by the wind and her skin, as clear as ever, appeared lightly tanned. He supposed she could afford to buy sunshine any time of the year she pleased. Her eyes were just as emerald green and sparkling with life as he had remembered them. She wore no make-up. He thought that, by and large, the years had been kind to her. The hand which he clasped in his returned his grip firmly. She had workmanlike hands, the nails on her long fingers, although immaculately manicured, were clipped short and unvarnished. Her body remained as slim and lithe as ever. She never seemed to put on weight, and remained athletic-looking even though she took little or no exercise – he remembered that, apart from her swimming at school, Jennifer had always been totally uninterested in any kind of sport or exercise routine. He thought she looked like a biker, which he assumed was the intention, and reflected briefly that she was about the only woman in her forties he knew who would not appear totally ridiculous in such an outfit.

'It's been a long time,' he said.

'Not since the funeral . . .' she responded.

'Must be almost ten years?' His voice a query. 'You look good.'

'So do you.'

It was the truth. Unlike his father, Todd Mallett had not thickened in girth with the years. He was a sportsman who still played cricket and had only recently given up rugby. His sporting activities had broadened his shoulders over the years, and given him plenty of muscle, while keeping in control any family tendency to fleshiness. The straight set of his mouth left no doubt as to his physical and mental toughness, but his grey eyes remained gentle and honest. He was just as she remembered him.

'Are you here for long?' he asked, trying to make conversation.

He was aware of the constable watching them with interest.

'Maybe for ever,' she replied.

Naturally he thought she was joking, but she wasn't.

'I'd like to talk to you,' she said. 'About all of this really . . .'

She gestured towards the activity around Bill's cottage.

'Is that why you came?' he asked.

'No. Sheer coincidence,' she replied truthfully. 'But I can't help wanting to ask some questions now, now that . . .'

Her voice trailed off. He understood though, one of the few that did.

'A pint tonight, at the Old Ship? Round eight o'clock?' he queried.

She nodded enthusiastically.

'Thank you, Todd,' she said.

She hurried back to the car then. She had kept her mother waiting far too long, selfish as ever, but meeting Todd like that, and with him apparently in charge of whatever inquiries were going on, was a stroke of luck. She'd always been a lucky reporter. She smiled at the memory of her first Fleet Street news editor, who had told her when she had once remarked on a piece of extraordinary good fortune that he only employed lucky reporters.

She took her mother out for lunch at the Waterside Hotel and then drove home. She was restless during the afternoon, just waiting to meet up with Todd.

Eventually eight o'clock arrived, and she pulled into the carpark of the Old Ship just as Todd arrived in a big Volvo estate car with a baby seat strapped in the back. It was a timely reminder of his marital status.

'Good God, you haven't got another one, have you?' she asked with singular lack of tact.

He smiled ruefully.

'Yup, the three boys almost grown and bingo, along comes Charlotte Anne. As far as I can recall, I haven't touched Angela much more than four times in the whole of our marriage, and every time a coconut.'

Jennifer laughed.

'Don't be ridiculous,' she said.

'Not as ridiculous as you might think,' he told her. 'Just a very small exaggeration. Still, I wouldn't be without the little one. I've always wanted a girl, and she's a cracker.'

Not for the first time, Jennifer reflected on what a good decent man Todd was, and wondered why she couldn't have grabbed him with both hands when she had the chance. No way, she thought. He was far too nice for her.

Inside they sampled some locally-brewed ale and she started to ask about Bill Turpin, his death, and the discoveries at his cottage.

It was then that Todd dropped his bombshell.

'Look, this is going to shake you,' he began. 'You

may as well know the biggest news first. We did a complete search of Bill's cottage, including digging the garden. You saw that today.'

She nodded. On edge now.

'This afternoon we found the remains of a young woman. She had been buried there for many years. That news is just about to be released.'

Jennifer looked at him as steadily as she could. She knew what he was going to say next. She just knew.

'All we know for certain so far is that she was extremely small, in her late teens or very early twenties, and the approximate year she died. We have to wait for forensic now to help us identify the body, and of course there is always a chance with a corpse of this age that it never gets identified at all. But I have a hunch.'

He glanced at her. She was gazing at him steadily. She looked pale. Vulnerable. Not like herself at all.

'Go on,' she said quietly.

'My hunch is that we've found Irene Nichols,' he said.

A cold sweat enveloped Jennifer. So Irene had been dead all these years. She supposed she must have known it really. She struggled to keep her composure, and when she spoke she realised that her voice sounded perfectly level, which was not what she had expected. Years of Fleet Street training, clearly.

'What else did you find?' she asked.

Todd looked uneasy.

'There's one thing I must ask you,' he said. 'This is private isn't it? Nothing to do with the paper?'

'What paper?' she replied.

'Oh, like that is it?'

'Yes. Very like that,' she said.

He had told her all of it then. Maybe he shouldn't, but he appreciated her urgent need to know.

Bill Turpin's body had been discovered by the postman. Twice he called and heard Bill's dogs howling. The house was shut up, so he had hammered on the back door to no avail. The door was bolted on the inside, but a kitchen window had not been properly fastened. The postman was a small man, slim and athletic. He clambered through the window and found the old man slumped across the kitchen table. He had used Bill's phone to call the police. Two local officers and an ambulance were on the scene within half an hour and were immediately confronted with their first surprise. Bill had been sitting at the table surrounded by papers and money. A great deal of money. Nearly a quarter of a million in used notes, and over a million quid's worth of share certificates. There were also statements and various papers referring to numbered Swiss bank accounts. Just a brief glance had showed Todd that Bill was worth four or five million. And probably much more. Everybody knew he had been successful in the holiday trade, but his local business ventures could not possibly have netted a fraction of the riches Bill Turpin had accumulated.

The papers had all been stacked in a tin box which had been taken from its hiding place by the inglenook fireplace. The door to the old bread oven was open when Bill's body was discovered, and careful examination revealed that at the back of the oven was an ingeniously fabricated hiding place. The stone construction of the oven seemed solid enough, but if pushed in the right places the back pivoted to one side. And beyond it was a cavity containing two more tin boxes. So cleverly concealed was this hiding place that, had old Bill not been actually dealing with his boxes at the time of his death, and had he not left the door of the oven open, it would probably never have been found.

One tin box contained jewellery and two watches – a lady's watch and a man's pocket watch, a beautiful antique half hunter. The other held a selection of yellowed newspaper cuttings and a scribbled notebook with what could be computer codes written in it.

Todd was watching her face.

'The pocket watch was inscribed, which was helpful,' the policeman went on. 'It belonged to the last Lord Lynmouth. He was murdered a couple of years after the war and his watch was taken the night he died. He disturbed burglars at his house on the edge of Exmoor and was strangled. There was a spate of big art thefts at the time – heavy stuff, priceless treasures disappeared that could only have gone to a certain kind of private collector, because goods like that could never have gone on display, too easily recognised. Quite an operation, it was, and nobody ever did get to the bottom of it.

'There was always some suspicion that Bill Turpin had been involved, though. Do you remember hearing about the robbery when you were a kid?'

Jennifer half nodded, half shook her head. She did remember something: there had always been gossip about Bill. And she vaguely recalled Marcus telling her in the early days how he had once tried to turn Bill Turpin over and what a waste of time it had been. But Jennifer did not want to interrupt. She waited for Todd to get on with it. She wanted to know everything he could possibly tell her.

Todd didn't push her. He took a long slow pull of his pint and eventually he continued.

'The Earl of Lynmouth had a housemaid, who came forward and claimed that she had been hiding in the pantry at the time and had seen the old Earl murdered, and that she recognised the man who did it. She named him as Bill Turpin from Brinton, the village where he lived before the war, but she would never tell the police how she knew him. The police investigated as best they could, and, according to my father, who remembers the talk about the case even though it was before his time, there were those who were quite sure the housemaid was telling the truth. I mean, how could she just conjure up a name like that anyway? But the whole thing was bizarre. Nothing and nobody could persuade her to say any more. Apparently she was tuppence short of a shilling, very much on the slow side. According to Lord Lynmouth's widow she had a history of fantasising, and there was no real evidence to link Bill to the crime – any more than there was with arms dealing out of Bristol and God knows what else folk said he was involved in in those days.

'Eventually the whole thing receded into local myth, as these thing do, and was dropped. More or less forgotten about until now. And Bill Turpin may have got away with one hell of a crime – although I doubt you could prove that, even now we've found the watch.'

'And the other watch?' asked Jennifer, suspecting she knew the answer.

'A dainty silver thing, inexpensive, tarnished with

the years. My guess is that it belonged to Irene Nichols. I shall be showing it to her parents, but I don't want to give them more misery for nothing, so I'm waiting till forensic have come up with the goods.

'The cuttings we found included stories on the Lord Lynmouth burglary, several of the other big art robberies of the period, the disappearance of Irene Nicholas, and the murder of Marjorie Benson – the girl whose body you found.'

He paused and took another long draught of his pint.

Jennifer felt she was being told too much to grasp in one sitting.

'So what are you saying, Bill Turpin was a mass murderer, he strangled the Earl of Lynmouth and then years later he killed Irene Nichols and Marjorie Benson?' she asked.

'I know,' Todd said. 'It does sound far fetched. But there's more. The Swiss bank statements indicated a regular annual income and several big one-off payments. Most came around the time of the murder of Lord Lynmouth in 1945 and during the following couple of years, and there was one for £100,000 in 1970 – dated not long after Irene Nichols and Marjorie Benson were killed.'

Jennifer gasped. 'You don't think Bill Turpin was some kind of paid hit man for goodness' sake, do you?'

'A pretty highly paid one, if he was,' Todd replied. 'That or a top of the league burglar, or both. I just don't know. It's going to take a bit of sorting, this one . . .'

'You're telling me,' Jennifer managed to mutter. 'I don't know about Lord Lynmouth and his treasures, but who would pay somebody a hundred grand to murder poor little Irene and some barmaid? Anyway, I don't see that you have anything concrete linking Bill Turpin to the Marjorie Benson murder.'

'Maybe not,' said Todd. 'But we have quite a coincidence, don't we?'

'The *Durraton Gazette* made it sound like more than that, as if you had hard evidence. OK, so he had stashed away cuttings about Marjorie Benson's murder. You could never have jailed him for that, could you?'

Todd shook his head. 'Of course not, but I'm sure they fit together somehow. There's always a pattern. And we haven't finished yet – the inquiry into the Marjorie Benson murder has been reopened just like the *Gazette* said.

'Two murders in a little place like Pelham Bay within a few days – there's not been another killing in Pelham since, you know. And nobody ever managed to find out who Marjorie was all those years ago. She remains a mystery. There was nothing at the golf club to give a clue as to her background, we couldn't find any medical or national insurance records, nothing, and nobody every reported her missing. And we still have no motive for her murder, let alone murderer.'

He leaned back in his chair, warming to his theme. He had already given a great deal of thought to the Lord Lynmouth connection, and it cleared his mind to explain his thinking to Jennifer.

'You have to remember that Lord Lynmouth was the richest man in Britain and one of the richest in the world in those days,' he continued. 'There has never been private wealth like his in this country since. He died worth eight billion even after half his most valuable treasures were nicked. You can't imagine it really. I don't believe his death was a hit-man job, I honestly do think he just got in the way of a massive burglary. He had next-to-no security. He didn't stand a chance really. And he was up against real pros.

'That network of fine-art burglaries was mightily organised all right, because even now I don't think any of the sculptures or paintings taken have ever surfaced. The word in the trade was that there were a small group of manic collectors with money to burn – probably gathered God knows where during the war – who were willing to pay a fortune for old masters and that kind of thing, and then quite content to keep the stuff behind locked doors; the kind of stuff money normally cannot buy because most of it is either in museums and galleries or going to end up in them.

'Several galleries were done at that time too – and nobody does that kind of thieving unless they have their market worked out. It's very big business indeed. Lord Lynmouth had a Leonardo de Vinci, you know. Can you imagine what that was worth even then? He'd left it to the National Gallery, but it walked the night he was murdered and has never been seen since.'

Jennifer was watching Todd, her jaw dropped. His face was tight with concentration. It had clearly become something of an obsession for him.

'Irene Nichols I agree with you about,' he went on. 'It's impossible to imagine anyone paying money to have that poor little kid knocked off. But there does appear to have been another motive.'

'And what was that?' Jennifer struggled to keep her voice calm.

'Well, we don't know yet. Forensic have a long way to go . . .' Todd was uneasy again.

'Oh come on, you've got this far, you have to tell me the end of it. I know damn well you'd have had a pathologist on the spot, and he probably already has a pretty good idea of exactly what happened to the girl.'

Todd smiled. 'Once a court reporter, always a pain in the arse,' he said.

Her eyes implored him. He continued.

'The soil in Bill Turpin's garden was of the kind which preserved the body in much better condition than might have been expected after twenty-five years – like some of the bodies found in the Fred West murder investigations in Gloucester last year,' he said.

'So we were able to deduce more than we would have thought. Almost certainly the girl died of a broken neck. And we think there was a sexual motive behind the murder.'

Jennifer heard herself ask another question, the obvious one.

'Not Bill Turpin, surely? He must have been well over sixty even back in 1970?'

Todd scratched his head. 'I know. It doesn't seem likely. But Bill was always a fit man, even in his sixties. And nobody ever knew anything about his sex life. He never appeared to have one after the war, according to my old man, and maybe that poor kid buried in his vegetable patch is the reason why. Maybe that's what he liked to do to his women.'

'What was what he liked to do to his women?'

Todd looked away. 'The girl we found was tiny. There is damage to her pelvis and her back. The pathologist believes that someone had sex with her with such force that it broke her neck . . .'

Jennifer stared at him. She had one last question.

'She has been buried for twenty-five years, surely you are talking theories. Even accepting that her body has been exceptionally well preserved, is there any way of actually proving that she was having sex when she died, and if there was, is there any way of scientifically proving who the man was?'

'I am not sure about the first question, but it's a definite no to the second,' said Todd, glumly.

Jennifer leaned back in her chair. He had not mentioned Marcus. There was no reason to, nothing to link Marcus with Bill Turpin and the body in the garden, nothing at all to link him, apparently, not even if it was Irene.

But Todd Mallett did not know what she knew about the man she had married. Todd did not know the doubts and fears she had lived with for twenty-five years.

Suddenly, as she sat in the lounge bar of the Old Ship, warm, beery and smoky, a comforting room, she could see again, clear as day, the image of her husband in the throes of his extreme sexual desire with those two young Oriental girls. There had been a crazed look in his eye which had frightened as well as disgusted her. A look she had never seen before. Unreal.

What if Bill Turpin hadn't killed Irene Nichols? What if Mark had done it? What if Mark, later to become Marcus, Sir Marcus Piddell, government minister, was a murderer?

227

She tried to put the thought out of her mind, just the way she always had. But she couldn't, not this time. Wasn't this what she had suspected from the beginning, a suspicion that had lurked throughout her adult life and which she had never allowed herself to face fully. She had to discover the truth once and for all, to discover if there was a missing link between Mark and old Bill Turpin. But what link could there possibly be? And if Mark was a murderer, why was Irene's body in Bill Turpin's garden? Why was her watch concealed in one of Bill's hidden tin boxes?

She didn't know the answers and she wasn't sure she had the strength to find out. Probably only she would ever suspect that Marcus was capable of murder, and she sincerely believed that only she had a hope of ever proving it if it was so. Yet if she set off on the path she was considering, she was already starkly aware of how her own life could be damn near destroyed by discoveries that she might make. For most of her adulthood she had been Mark Piddle's woman. She had slept with him for the first time only days after Irene's death. God, had she really been that unthinking, that callous? So much of what she was beginning to remember she would rather forget, but that was how it had always been.

She had drifted off into a kind of stunned reverie. Vaguely in the distance she heard Todd Mallett's voice, kind, concerned, asking her if she was all right.

'It was all a long time ago,' she heard Todd say, and with a supreme effort of will she lurched back into the present.

Todd looked boyish. She knew that he cared about her, suspected he still carried a torch for her. He was an attractive man whose strength and kindness shone

228

from his gentle grey eyes. She felt that if she could be close to him he would, if only for a short time, keep the nightmare at bay. She needed that.

'Do you still have the beach hut?' she asked coolly. The hut, belonging rather tackily to Angela's parents, was the place they had used to make love all those years ago.

He was startled. He had genuinely not expected this, not after so long.

'Y-yes.' He actually stammered. There was a query in his voice.

'I'm sorry,' she said quickly. She felt a fool. 'I didn't mean to suggest . . . well I did. But forget I did. Please.'

He shook his head. 'Jenny, I can think of nothing I would like more. I was just surprised . . . and flattered.'

He emptied his glass. 'Let's go,' he said.

She followed him meekly. He and her mother were the only people left in the world who called her Jenny. It made her feel like a schoolgirl again, if only very fleetingly.

'We'll leave your car here,' he said, and escorted her to the Volvo.

He opened the passenger door for her. All she could see was the baby seat in the back, and she realised suddenly that she could not deal with any more guilt.

She turned to him and kissed him softly on the lips.

'I'm sorry,' she said. 'I want to, but I really shouldn't have said anything. I just can't . . .'

As ever he was understanding.

'It's OK, you're probably right,' he said.

He kissed her forehead and closed the door of the Volvo.

Together they walked slowly across the carpark to the Porsche. For once in her life she wasn't sure she could cope with sleeping with anybody. Her brain was still in turmoil. She was not going to be able to stop now. She had to see this thing through, and she might as well get on with it.

Trying to sound very casual, she asked: 'Will you be speaking to Marcus?'

'Of course,' Todd said. 'Somebody will be, anyway. If it is Irene, that is. He was living with her at the time, after all. But it'll just be a formality.'

'I see. There's nothing to link him, is there?'

'No.'

He was puzzled. He had never liked Marcus Piddell. Todd thought he was an arrogant twister who had wheeled and dealed his way to the top, not caring whom he had trampled on along the way. It probably went right back to the time Mark had ridiculed him and Angela on that long-ago Sunday in Pelham Bay, and Todd had always resented the hold Mark had over Jennifer. He was by and large a decent cop, he would never allow his personal feelings to colour his professional judgement. But even if he had wanted to think that Mark might be in some way involved, there was absolutely no indication of this.

Jennifer interrupted his musings.

'I forgot to ask you about the notebook?'

'Oh yeah – another bit of a mystery that. The notebook is indecipherable at a glance. If it does contain computer codes and we could break into them, we might find some answers – Bill had a sophisticated computer in the cottage – but we've been unable so far to jack into the files on the hard drive, and there appears to be no additional software for it.'

'Could I see it, and the watches and the other stuff you've collected?' Jennifer asked.

He wanted to know why. She decided to tell him this much of the truth.

'I know it's crazy, I just feel they might mean something to me that they don't to anyone else,' she said.

'It's evidence, Jennifer.'

'So? I wasn't planning to steal the stuff.'

She opened her car door and started to climb in. He caught her by the arm.

'Ten o'clock tomorrow morning at the operations centre in Pelham Bay village hall,' he said.

With his other hand he gently touched her face. He smiled at her. 'I suppose it could never have worked for us, could it?' he asked.

'No chance,' she said. 'We might have had fun trying though.'

He shook his head. 'I don't think I was ever supposed to have fun,' he said.

She laughed. That was the trouble, he thought, she had never taken him seriously for a moment. And he had never been able to take her lightly enough.

As soon as she got home to Seaview Road she phoned Anna.

'Come to your senses yet, have you?' asked her friend.

'Shut up,' said Jennifer. 'Listen. I need some help. In total confidence. You and me only.'

231

'Oh God,' said Anna helpfully. 'What have you done now?'

Jennifer took a deep breath.

'Nothing. I need some cuttings. Are you still able to use the library at the *Chronicle*?'

'Yes. In return for copious quantities of malt whisky every Christmas. But why do you need me and the *Chronicle* library, for Christ's sake? Can't Caroline help you? She keeps phoning me, incidentally.'

Caroline was Jennifer's secretary at the *Globe*. Or used to be – Jennifer wasn't quite sure any more. In either case, Caroline would help willingly. She would also talk. She couldn't help it, and Jennifer had always accepted it as congenital.

'Anna, you know Caroline can never keep her mouth shut, and this is serious. I want cuts on Marcus.'

'Bloody Hell, Jen, I thought you didn't want to hear his name again. You'll never get him out of your system, will you?'

Jennifer was getting impatient.

'Will you listen for once? It's nothing to do with that. I have discovered something I would rather not have done, and I need to do some digging. I want copies of all the scandalous stuff about Marcus, all the speculation pieces about his money, the row over that devaluation story in the *Recorder*. Anything like that, anything at all.'

'What's going on?'

'Anna, I can't tell you, not even you yet – I may have got it wrong. Will you fax the stuff to me?'

'I suppose so. When do you want it? As if I couldn't guess.'

'Tomorrow?'

'Jennifer, it means going in to town and I wasn't planning to. And that means rearranging everything for Pandora . . .'

'Please, Anna. I wouldn't ask if it weren't vital.'

'Oh all right,' said Anna. 'Whatever it is that's getting at you, I expect you should leave well alone, but I don't suppose you will listen. You never do.'

'Said the pot.'

Jennifer was already feeling more cheerful, more positive. She had known Anna would do it for her. She had never let her down yet. Jennifer held the phone away from her ear and smiled as Anna launched into a reassuring grumble concerning 'being taken for granted', and 'hare-brained ideas'. The most wonderful thing about her oldest friend remained the way even the briefest and least consequential conversation with her could lift the deepest depression. Even when the world was closing in totally, the familiarity of a really good friendship could make you think that there was something in life worth carrying on for. Perhaps because she had never had children, she valued her one or two true friendships more than the friends concerned would probably ever know.

She had been away barely two days, and so much had happened in North Devon that she had almost completely forgotten her other life. She did not want any further dealings with Jack and the paper until she had things a little clearer in her mind, which looked like being not for some time now. She had resigned, and when it dawned on them all that she really meant it, she assumed they would stop paying her. There wasn't really a lot more to it, except the car, which was no longer worth a great deal. She just couldn't be bothered with sorting it out, so it was easier to be an ostrich for a while and carry on driving the damn thing around.

'Thanks Anna,' she said.

'Again,' said Anna.

'Thanks Anna again,' Jennifer repeated obediently.

'Too bloody right,' said Anna.

But as she replaced the receiver, Anna McDonald felt deeply uneasy.

'I don't know what's going on,' she told Dominic. 'But something has happened to throw Jen completely. She's just not herself.'

'Well, that's good news at least,' said Dominic.

Anna couldn't even be bothered to register that she had heard what he had said. She was talking to herself really, thinking aloud.

'She's in a right state about something.'

The phone call had interrupted her lugubrious husband's enjoyment of a late-night movie on TV.

'Jennifer bloody Stone is always in a right state if you ask me,' he grumbled.

The next morning gave Anna her first inkling of what might lie behind Jennifer's call. The reopening of the old murder inquiry in Pelham Bay and the discovery of a body in Bill Turpin's garden was a front-page lead in the one tabloid paper the McDonalds still had delivered along with the *Times* and the *Telegraph*.

Anna studied the piece thoughtfully, then contemplated calling Jennifer back and giving her the third degree. She decided against it. If the old bat wasn't telling, then she wasn't telling.

She would get the cuttings organised and have another go at Jen that night.

Sixteen

Jennifer slept fitfully – still unsure that she really wanted to dig up the past, but at the same time quite certain that she was going to. She could feel her anger and disgust at Marcus welling up inside her. She knew that if she tried to destroy him she would probably end up destroying a large part of her own life. She had shut her eyes quite determinedly and refused to examine her eternal doubts about his business dealings. She had walked away from the more unpleasant aspects of his sex life. To her shame she had done nothing about the youthful sex for sale trade that she knew he must be involved in. But murder? Now that her eyes had been involuntarily opened, her journalistic antennae were operating at full power. She wanted to know exactly what had been going on, what exactly the undercurrent she had felt for so long in Marcus's life was really about. She was sure that everything was linked in some complex way to the goings on in Pelham Bay so long ago.

She was still fretting in the morning as she sat in her mother's kitchen drinking tea. It was always tea for her in the mornings. There was nothing like a strong cup of English Breakfast to cut through a hangover, not that she had one that morning, it just felt as if she did. Her mother was already up and about. It was a treat for her to have her daughter at home, although, as usual, she wasn't seeing much of her. Jennifer had always been rushing around doing something. Ever since her teens. Maybe even before. Over tea and toast they chatted about family. Her brother had married for the first time relatively late in life, and had had twin boys and then a daughter in short order. Mrs Stone was delighted. She had more or less given up any hope of being a grandmother. The bad news was that Jennifer's brother had been disillusioned with the Britain he had found waiting for him when he left the airforce, and had emigrated to Australia where he worked for a small charter aircraft company. It was mostly *Boys' Own* flying and he was in his element. He had never really grown up: the air force was responsible for that. But he had found a near-perfect wife, and eventually, what was for him, a near-perfect life. Jennifer envied him. It was sad for her mother that this new family was so far away, but every year she travelled to Australia and spent two months with them. Mrs Stone had made six visits now. She was a veteran, and Jennifer always paid for the tickets, first-class, an arm and a leg job, but the least she could do. One year, not long after her father had died, she had taken a month's holiday and travelled with her mother down under. That had been the best trip ever for Mrs Stone. All her family together again.

Jennifer decided to hint that she might not be going back to the *Globe*. Mrs Stone was unmoved.

'Huh, I knew there was something up,' she said.

Jennifer smiled. She never had been able to pull the wool over her mother's eyes as much as she thought she could. She might as well confess the rest of it.

'Actually I'm thinking of buying a cottage by the sea here in North Devon and giving up London and newspapers for good,' Jennifer announced.

Her mother did not have to say how much that would please her, but she knew her daughter well.

'Are you sure you can do that, maid?' she asked.

'No, I'm not sure – but I think I may be soon,' replied Jennifer honestly. 'There's something I have to do before I can finally make any big decisions.'

'Nothing to do with that old man and they murders?' Mrs Stone queried.

Once again Jennifer was surprised by her astuteness. She shouldn't be, but there it was. She knew her mother would worry herself sick if she thought Jenny was getting mixed up in it all again, so she decided to lie.

'No, of course not,' she said coolly.

But she wasn't quite sure how convincing she was being. She changed the subject.

'I tell you what, how about if we go to Oz together again to see Steve and the family?'

Mrs Stone's face lit up. She'd love that. Jenny didn't need to ask, did she?

'In the autumn,' said Jennifer. 'Their spring. Stay three months if you like – and I'll stay three months with you. Why the hell not?'

'Don't swear,' said her mother. In some ways nothing changed.

And so, chatting comfortably with her mother, the time passed more quickly than Jennifer had expected, and suddenly it was nine-thirty and she set off to drive to the operations centre in Pelham Bay. She arrived fifteen minutes early. But Todd was already prepared for her, as she had guessed he would be. A

238

young constable showed her into the private office he had set up in a small storeroom. It was an airless little room with one tiny high-up window, but at least it gave him some privacy. A temporary phone line had been installed. The furniture comprised a desk covered in papers and two straight-backed chairs.

The constable closed the door, and Jennifer sat down opposite Todd across the desk. She was aware of his face softening as he looked at her, then, with a slight shrug of his burly shoulders, he became the police chief again.

He took several clear plastic bags from the box by his feet, cleared a space on his cluttered desk and spread them out. Each bag contained a piece of the evidence found in Bill's cottage.

'Can I look at the notebook, can I take it out of the bag?' Jennifer asked.

'No,' said Todd. 'But we've copied it. Hang on.'

He got up and headed for the operations room set up in the main body of the village hall. While he was gone, Jennifer studied the items of jewellery laid out before her. Irene's cheap little silver-plated watch stood out like a sore thumb – well, she assumed it was Irene's. It had indeed tarnished badly.

When Todd returned, she asked him if the body had now definitely been identified as Irene. He replied that it had. The dental records checked out, and his next job was to tell Irene's parents. The police had already warned them of the possibility before the news had been announced that a long-dead body had been found. Todd hadn't wanted them to put two and two together from a news bulletin.

239

Jennifer shuddered. She sympathised with Todd on the rotten job he was about to do.

'I've done worse,' he replied flatly. 'They always believed Irene was dead anyway. Said there was no way she would have gone anywhere without telling them.'

Jennifer reached out a hand for the copies of the notebook. There were jottings on several pages. Groups of numbers and letters, disjointed words, nothing that made any sense. Yet she had seen something like it before. She knew she had.

'Are these what you think are codes?' she asked.

'Yes,' Todd replied. 'But so far they are not a lot of good to us. As I told you, Bill Turpin had this super-advanced computer system but no software. If there was anything already on the hard disc, we have yet to break into it. God knows what he was planning to use the thing for, but it seems as if it had been programmed by somebody else and Bill had barely handled it. He was obviously a lot more sophisticated than anybody would have guessed, and pretty clever on the stock market, so maybe he aimed to use the computer to play the market. Who knows? When we checked the keyboard for his finger prints there were hardly any, so he may have tried to move into the computer age and not quite made it.

'At the Penny Parade there is a basic Amstrad that they use for their accounts and stock taking and so on, but, according to Johnny Cooke who does all that sort of stuff, Bill rarely even went near that.'

Todd paused. He was watching Jennifer's face. He didn't know quite what to make of her.

'If you know anything, Jenny, suspect anything, have the slightest clue about anything,' he said quietly, 'why don't you tell me – and then let me do my job?'

'I'm just interested,' she replied.

'That's one word for it.'

'Yes. Maybe I'll write a book.'

'Maybe you will,' he said. 'But that's not it, either, is it?'

She put the copy of the notebook in her pocket and took one last look at the forlorn collection of jewellery.

'Thanks Todd,' she said.

She left her car parked outside the village hall and walked along Old Bay Road to the amusement arcade which she knew was now run by Johnny Cooke. Pelham Bay was something of a time warp. There were video games in the Penny Parade now instead of table football machines, yet surprisingly little else had changed. The resort was perhaps a bit more fish and chippy, but maybe her memory played tricks on her. It always had been a ropy place, the tattiest side of the seaside industry. The deckchairs were still for hire from the same stand, and a new breed of indolent young men had succeeded Johnny Cooke and all the others since. They were clones – immaculately tanned, shirtless in faded jeans, arrogant in the certainty of their youth. Only their hair was different. These lads had short back and sides haircuts, the pudding basin shaven-around-the-edges look that was once again in fashion. Twenty-five years ago Johnny's hair had been long and luxuriant, spreading onto his shoulders in true sixties and early seventies style.

The same local company was still selling its ever-excellent ice cream from a van parked by the slipway, and in the same spot too. She bought a large cornet and paid fifty pence for a deckchair. The price had gone up but the manners of the deckchair boys remained the same. The short swarthy young man handing the chairs out that day watched uncaring as she struggled to assemble the deckchair with one hand while balancing her melting cornet in the other. The blob of ice cream eventually gave up and fell with a resounding splat onto the cobbled promenade. Damn, she thought. Why hadn't she performed this operation the other way around and bought the ice cream after hiring the chair? Maybe the deckchair boys and the ice-cream man were tied together in some unholy money-making alliance. Resignedly she approached the van again and bought a second cornet. The seller was stony-faced. Couldn't she remember from her youth a red-cheeked, smiling sort of beardless Father Christmas of a man who wooed the children with his affectionate charm as much as with his splendid ice cream? She was reminded of how much things do change with the years. It only appears that they remain the same. This fella sold her a second large cornet within just a couple of minutes and his eyes expressed no recognition. No nothing. Stony, all right, icy, even, to match his wares. So much for the warmth of human contact.

She returned to her chair and settled herself down. It was still fairly warm for May but, sitting right by the sea, she pulled her thick woollen jacket close around her. The wind was whistling up the slipway and along the promenade as usual. She pushed her chair into a more sheltered spot by the wall and sat watching the comings and goings at the Penny Parade. Nobody had ever changed its name.

After a while her patience was rewarded. A tall rangy man walked out of the main door and strolled across the path to the deckchair stand. He spoke briefly to the swarthy boy who handed him what she assumed were that day's takings. The man counted the cash and put it into the leather bag he was carrying over his shoulder. He was strongly built and his body appeared more youthful than the age she knew he must be, somewhere in his early forties. But when he turned towards her his face showed every minute of the torment that he had been through. She was shocked. He was tanned by the wind but there was a greyness about him. His hair was grey. His eyes were quite lifeless. She registered all this in a second. Even though she knew he must have been shaken rigid by the events of the last couple of days, she had not expected his appearance to betray his protracted ordeal quite as blatantly as it did. But in spite of the premature ageing in his face, she recognised him right away. She had never met him before, strangely enough, never spoken to him. But she had kept in her mind always, however much she had tried to forget it, the bewildered broken face peering at her from the dock at Exeter Crown Court all those years ago. This was Johnny Cooke, and no wonder he looked the way he did. This was a man who had spent most of his adulthood in prison for a crime he might not have committed.

She knew he was running old Bill's empire, Todd had told her that, told her that Bill had appeared to be Johnny's saviour, helping him rebuild his life from the moment he was released from jail. Johnny would be aware now, of course, of the new police suspicions. The duplicity, the double-take of it all, that must have been the final blow, she thought. If the hand you thought was keeping you afloat turned out to be the one pushing you into the sea to drown, that was hardest of all to take, surely.

She watched Johnny stroll on from the deckchair stand and lean against the sea wall just a few feet from where she was sitting. His powerful shoulders were bowed. His physique looked as if it was probably sensational beneath his big fisherman's sweater. He had always been well built, and she supposed he had further developed his body in prison. That was what strong healthy young prisoners did to keep themselves sane, wasn't it?

He was peering out to sea, behaving much the way she had seen Bill Turpin behave when she was a girl. Ironic really. He looked so tired. She wanted to comfort him. She felt terribly guilty. She asked herself why, but she was just kidding herself. She knew well the reasons for her guilt. She was one of a handful of people in the world who had always had doubts about Johnny's conviction. Severe doubts. And because of the nature of those doubts, she had deliberately made herself forget them, pretend they did not exist.

As she watched him now, as she saw the weariness and the sadness in him, the guilt overwhelmed her. She felt close to tears.

Then Johnny Cooke turned. Suddenly he was directly facing her and a miracle happened. The tiredness went entirely from his eyes. His mouth stretched into a beaming welcoming smile. Joy radiated from every pore of him. He crouched to the ground and stretched out his arms. His eyes were shining, no longer lifeless. Far from that. Every inch of him was bursting with life and love. She could hear a child's voice and, looking over her shoulder, saw a toddler running along the promenade towards Johnny. The little boy was unsteady on his feet, wobbling a bit, but he knew exactly where he was going. Squealing with happiness, he flung himself into Johnny Cooke's extended arms, falling onto his body with the total, as yet unspoiled, trust of little children in their parents. The big man clasped the boy in his arms and, standing up, hoisted the child triumphantly in the air above his head. The boy kicked his legs with delight, his yells of pleasure clear above the roar of the sea. And Johnny Cooke was laughing. A great bellow of a laugh that came from deep inside and poured out in a bubbly torrent like a rushing cliffside waterfall.

On the heels of the child came a pretty dark woman, much younger than Johnny, wheeling a pushchair. She was slightly plump, but that kind of youthful plumpness which made her in some ways even more attractive. It was a cliché, Jennifer knew, and probably nothing to do with her plumpness but more to some inner thing shining out from her, but you were sure that she must have a sunny nature. She was smiling too, although not like Johnny. Hers was a small contended half smile. As she reached the big man, he shifted the little boy into one arm, rested the other casually across the shoulders of the young woman and, bending, kissed her briefly, and with pleasurable familiarity, on the top of the head. The woman was chattering to him. Jennifer could just catch snatches . . .

'He said two more words this morning. Cornflakes and natcha.'

'. . . natcha?' queried the big man.

'Goodness knows,' she replied, giggling.

He roared his appreciation. That great laugh again. And the little family retreated into the amusement arcade, heads close together, forming a secure triangle of love.

Jennifer felt the tears pricking the backs of her eyelids once more, as she blinked quickly in a desperate attempt to stop them flowing. They were a different kind of tears now. So Johnny Cooke had a family which obviously gave him great happiness. Thank God for that, she thought. She sat in the deckchair for another thirty minutes or so. The sun was not so bright now and the wind was quite sharp. She was uncomfortably cold by the time the young woman left the amusement arcade and set off along the promenade. This time the toddler sat in the push-chair, swathed in a fleecy blanket.

Jennifer waited another couple of minutes and then left her chair and walked across to the Penny Parade. She made her way past the fruit machines and the video games to the back of the arcade where, she remembered, the office was tucked in one corner. It was still in the same place. Johnny Cooke was sitting at a desk, head down, studying some papers. She knocked on the open glass door, standing hesitant in the doorway. He looked up.

'Yes?' he inquired.

He didn't recognise her. Why should he, when he had only seen her once, really, in the witness box at Exeter, and her evidence had not even been important to his case.

'Hello. I'm Jennifer Stone,' she said.

The name obviously meant nothing either. He gazed at her inquiringly.

'I wonder if I could talk to you for a minute,' she said.

'Yes?' he said again in the same questioning tone.

'I . . . I . . . found the body,' she began hesitantly.

Realisation spread across his face. The joyful happiness of a moment ago with his young child was instant history. The haunted look returned, and with it the greyness and the emptiness in his eyes.

'And you married Mark Piddle,' he said, using the old, never-to-be-mentioned, name.

'Yes,' she said simply. Her eyes spoke a legend more.

He half smiled. He had always seen humour in so much of it.

'You'd best sit down,' he said.

At first he was not forthcoming. She was aware that she was using her interviewing technique on him to get him going. But he was not a stupid man.

'You're a journalist, aren't you?' he asked.

'Was,' she said firmly.

'I've already had the vultures here, several of them are up the road in the pub, waiting,' he said. 'A long wait they're going to have.'

He passed her a scribbled note. It offered Johnny a great deal of money if he would exclusively sell his story to a certain mass-circulation Sunday newspaper.

She raised her eyebrows. He knew exactly what her look was asking. Strange that there seemed this easy understanding between them under such strained circumstances, especially as he was clearly quite aware of her involvement with Mark.

'No way,' he said. 'It looks like everything I have could be some kind of blood money. I want no more of it.'

He paused, as if deciding whether to trust her or not. 'Is that what you are here for?'

'No,' she said.

His expression did not change. His eyes were boring into her head.

'I promise you.'

He nodded, satisfied. 'They found a will. Apparently the old bastard has left me everything. Millions maybe. How's that for blood money?'

He got up from the desk, walked round and stood looking straight down at her.

'Mark Piddle's missus, eh?' he said. To himself really.

'Ex-missus,' she repeated.

'Oh, aye. I never understood it you know. Never understood why he lied.'

'I know,' she said.

He didn't really hear, just went on talking.

'I said I killed her because I felt I hadn't looked after her properly. He knew what I meant, the bugger.'

He paused, realising at last what she had said.

'And you knew too?'

'Yes,' she admitted.

Her shame was out in the open now.

'You always knew?'

'I am not sure.' She was being absolutely truthful. 'For years I allowed myself to believe that I had misunderstood him. I suppose it was the only way I could live with myself and with Mark. But now, I know. Yes.'

'So that's why you are here.' The eyes were boring into her skull again. 'Guilty conscience, aye?'

'Oh yes,' she said. 'Definitely that.'

'And what do you want?'

'I want to find out the truth. I can't deal with suspicions; and I have so many.'

He made her a mug of tea and sat down next to her and began to talk. He said this would be the one and only time he would discuss it with her; whatever happened next he wanted to get on with his own life.

'Nobody can give me back the lost years, but I'm damned if I'm going to lose any more,' he told Jennifer.

Again and again she went over with him both their memories of that night when he had visited Mark after he learned that Marjorie Benson was dead. His memory of it was still hazy in places; that was partly what had sunk him all those years ago. He had been so vague and frightened and unsure of himself, and Mark so confident and articulate and correctly sorrowful.

Johnny was talking about Marjorie Benson now. She glanced at him. There was no self pity in the man when he talked about his own plight. He had accepted the years lost in jail, and he could take honest joy in his new happiness. He seemed to have so little bitterness. But when he spoke of Marjorie his voice had a catch in it. Even after all these years he looked as if he was about to break down when he talked about his devastation at her death. He had loved her so much he had just gone to pieces. He had been unable to think straight and his complete emotional collapse had not helped his case. In a way he hadn't cared about himself until it was too late. He had been so much in love with her. He paused and put his head in his hands. He was quite a man, this Johnny Cooke, Jennifer thought to herself.

'I'm so very sorry,' she said, and felt what an inadequate, pathetic phrase that must sound coming from her lips, to this man who had suffered so much. She thanked him for his time and rose to leave.

When she reached the door he stopped her.

'Are you sure you really want to know the truth?'

She nodded. 'Don't you?' she asked.

'No. It is over for me. Already it's all coming back. I don't even know why I talked to you. Maybe I thought it would help.

'All that would really help me is for this to end now.' He paused. 'What I dread is another court case.'

She didn't speak.

'Don't take this personal, like.' He paused again. 'But I never want to see you again as long as I live.'

She opened her mouth to speak, but there were no more words. She was standing in the doorway holding the handle of the glass door. Quickly she shut the door behind her and half ran through the amusement arcade. The tears were pouring down her face. A group of youngsters playing video games looked at her curiously. Outside she made straight for the beach and found herself one of those holes dug in the pebble ridge and she curled up in it and cried her heart out. For a half-lost life, for all that sadness, for two young women who died violently long before their time, and for herself. Oh yes, for herself.

When the tears stopped she made for the public lavatory to splash cold water on her face and repair the damage as much as possible with make-up. Eventually she felt suitably recovered to carry on to the next stage. She walked quickly back to the Porsche and drove to Durraton where she sought out Irene Nichols' parent's home. They still lived in the same house on that council estate in the roughest part of town, and they were not difficult to find. Several reporters had set up camp outside. She did not feel able to knock on the door with its peeling white paint. Instead, while being vague about her own identity, she engaged the reporters in conversation and learned that a family friend had indicated that Mr and Mrs Nichols did wish to make a statement and would be coming outside soon. They knew now that the body found in Bill Turpin's garden was their daughter.

A regional TV team had just arrived and was busily setting up its equipment. After a wait of less than half an hour the Nichols came out of the house. They were drawn-looking, faces gaunt and tear-stained. They spoke of their great sorrow and also their relief that their daughter's remains had at last been found. At least they could give her a Christian burial now and mourn her properly.

They were halting and inarticulate and incredibly moving. They went back indoors and the reporters and photographers disappeared swiftly to file their stories and wire their pictures and catch the next TV news bulletin.

Jennifer gathered what was left of her failing courage, and, alone now in the street, knocked on the door. The family friend answered, face tight with hostility.

'Can't you leave them alone?' she snapped.

Jennifer swiftly explained that she was not a reporter.

She gave her name and, then, haltingly, added: 'Tell them I married Mark Piddle.'

Almost at once, Irene Nichols' father came to the door. He was dark with anger.

'You've got a bloody cheek comin' yer,' he said. 'Wife of that murdering bastard.'

Jennifer did not explain that she was his ex-wife. She homed in on the last chilling words.

'Why do you say that, Mr Nichols?' she asked mildly. She could see the hatred in his eyes.

'Because 'e did for her, and I'll never 'ear different,' the man said.

'The police are sure it was Bill Turpin.'

'Yeah,' said Irene's father. 'It wouldn't be Sir Marcus bloody butter-wouldn't-melt-in– 'is-mouth Piddell, MP, would it?'

He looked at her. He hated her too. And he had the right.

'I remember you, you little bitch. In 'is bed before my Irene was cold in 'er heathen grave.'

His voice rose to a hysterical scream.

'Get off my property,' he shouted.

Involuntarily she stepped backwards. He moved forwards and spat in her face. Nothing like that had ever happened to her before, not in all her years of professional intrusion into other people's lives. She just stood there, unable to move.

'Bugger off,' he said. 'And you tell 'im, that evil bastard, I hope he rots in hell.'

252

The friend came through the door and hustled Mr Nichols away. Jennifer wiped the saliva from her face with the back of her hand. She deserved that, she thought. Guilty, by default, of the most extraordinary self-deception.

Oh Marcus, Marcus. She stumbled back up the garden path to the Porsche parked in the road outside and climbed in. There was a box of paper hankies in the glove compartment. She gave her face a more careful clean-up, gunned the motor and drove back to her mother's, more determined than ever to get to the bottom of the whole dreadful business.

Seventeen

In London Marcus was anxiously keeping in touch with the news coming out of Pelham Bay. When he heard on late-night radio that a body had been found in Bill Turpin's garden, he knew he needed help. Things could so easily get out of hand now.

He reached for the telephone and dialled a number. After two rings he was connected to an answering machine. His message was the only one he ever left. Two words. 'Call me.' He knew that the machine was checked every hour, day and night. Now all he had to do was wait. He had once enlisted the help of a friend at British Telecom to get the number traced. Then it had turned out to be a bedsit in London's Clapham – completely empty except for the answerphone. The room was rented and the telephone line listed in the name of a North London motor car tyre company. Their address turned out to be merely an accommodation address.

Since then the contact number he was given, sent to him anonymously by post, had changed many times, around every six months. On one more occasion he had traced it back – this time to an empty room in Hammersmith listed in the name of a property company. Once again the company had only an accommodation address.

Fortunately that night he had not long to wait for the return call. It came just twelve minutes after he had left his message. He picked up the receiver quickly and it was with relief that he recognised the familiar sound of the caller he was hoping for. The voice was high-pitched and metallic. Computerised. It came to him through a piece of equipment known as a squawk box which distorted it and made it unidentifiable. He flicked a switch on the phone. There was no security problem. There would be no Marcusgate tapes. His phone could be scrambled, and by state-of-the-art equipment, naturally. Desperately gathering the wits that had never yet let him down, he explained swiftly and concisely what had happened. The voice at the other end listened carefully and gave him the most difficult advice of all to follow. Do nothing. Let them come to you. Wait for developments.

He replaced the receiver in its cradle, went to bed, and tried to sleep. It was a waste of time.

In the morning he knew he must stick to his usual routine and do what he had been told – nothing. But he so badly wanted to find out exactly what was going on in North Devon. He considered getting in touch with his own local paper editors there, to ensure both that they passed on information concerning the body to him straight away, and that he could control the papers' interpretation of the story.

Several times he picked up a telephone to do just that. But Marcus's brain continued to work smoothly even under the greatest stress. He knew that would only raise questions which at the moment did not exist and would be a mistake – certainly before the body was formally identified. He knew the advice he had been given was correct. All he could do was wait until that identification was made – and wait he must.

It was the police who told him the body of Irene Nichols had been found – and they gave him the news before it was released to the press.

'You're not strictly family, of course, sir, but we thought you'd like to know,' said a voice on the telephone. A London policeman. He was glad of that. He would rather deal with someone anonymous than people from the West Country who might know him.

'Thank you, thank you,' Marcus said haltingly. 'I suppose I had suspected from the moment I knew there was a body . . . but it's always a shock.

'Can I do anything to help?'

'Yes sir, you can,' came the reply. 'We'll need to take a full statement from you.'

'Of course, of course,' Marcus responded. He had expected that – none the less he did not relish the prospect. And he was quite relieved when he was asked if he would be available for interview straight away – at least it would get the ordeal over with.

When Jennifer reached 16 Seaview Road after her traumatic confrontation with Irene Nichols's father, she went straight to the drinks cabinet in the front room and poured herself a stiff Scotch. Her mother heard the front door slam and followed her silently into the room.

'I didn't think you drank whisky,' she said.

'I don't,' replied Jennifer.

Mrs Stone shrugged. 'There's Clovelly herrings for tea,' she said.

'I'm not hungry.'

Jennifer knew she was trembling. She tried hard to appear normal, but she certainly couldn't face eating anything. Herrings were about the last thing she could force down. The very thought made her feel sick.

'You're always hungry,' persisted her mother. 'And you like herrings.'

'I think I've got an upset tummy,' she lied.

Or maybe it wasn't a lie any more. She wasn't quite sure.

'Well, put that bottle away then,' said her mother unsympathetically, as Jennifer poured a second stiff measure into a tumbler.

Jennifer switched on the television and watched the news. The talk with the grief stricken Mr and Mrs Nichols made the local and the national bulletins. It was harrowing stuff. And there was a few seconds' snatched footage of Johnny Cooke going into the Penny Parade. He looked neither to left nor right, ignoring the questions thrown at him by the gathered media.

Mr and Mrs Nichols had said nothing publicly about their suspicions. Their views had been checked out by the police twenty-five years earlier and summarily dismissed. They were resigned to not being listened to properly – and they were just relieved now to have their daughter's remains returned to them. Like Johnny Cooke they did not want to relive it all.

There was no evidence involving Marcus. Irene Nichols had lived with him. So what? In the event of any murder, Jennifer knew, the police always looked first at those closest to the victim. But Marcus had emerged from the beginning smelling of roses and would continue to do so. Marcus was so convincing, and always had been, in his reasoned sorrow. All the evidence of responsibility for Irene's murder now pointed to Bill Turpin. Nobody knew *who* had murdered Marjorie Benson.

The only way Jennifer could find out if what she suspected was indeed the truth, was for her to make all the moves. Only she, with her special knowledge and memories, could point the finger at Marcus; only she could discover what was behind it all. She was certain of that, and she desperately needed to find the truth – although she was not very sure of what she would do with it when she ultimately had it.

She switched off the television and plugged her lap-top computer into the mains. It was her habit to write things down, to clarify her thoughts by arranging them in proper sentences. Her jottings were interrupted by the shrill tones of the telephone ringing in the hall.

'Anna,' she said to herself.

She almost ran into the hallway. Her mother appeared at the kitchen door.

'Don't worry mum, I think it's for me,' she called.

'And whoever else could it possibly be for when you're in the house, my girl?' muttered Mrs Stone as her daughter picked up the phone.

Jennifer was not disappointed. It was Anna.

'Plug in the toy box, your dispatches await,' said the voice she had been hoping to hear.

'You're wonderful, did I ever tell you that Anna?' she asked.

'Not nearly often enough,' came the reply. 'And by the way, your inquiries do not have anything to do with murder and mayhem and bodies in the garden of a certain North Devon cottage, do they?'

Jennifer carried on as if she had not heard the

question. 'I'm going to hang up now and fetch the machine,' she said.

She carried the laptop from the living room into the hall and prepared to insert its jack into the telephone socket.

'Anna, are you ready?'

'Jen, I know something's very wrong. Can't you tell me?'

'Not yet, I just can't. And not on the phone. I'll be back in town soon. OK?'

'I suppose. Just take care.'

'See you very soon. Honest. And thanks . . .'

She plugged in her computer with its built-in fax modem. The newspaper cuttings would be sent down the phone line directly into the lap-top's hard drive and she would be able to study them at her leisure on the screen.

Anna had done a good job. Late into the night Jennifer read and reread the information her friend had sent her. The often only half-expressed queries about Marcus's business dealings were endless. The financial pundits variously praised and wondered at his knowledge of the money market. Eventually she switched off the computer, but she remained thoughtful and unable to sleep properly throughout the night.

In the morning, Jennifer knew exactly what she must do. She was up early again and on the phone. Eventually she tracked down Marcus on his mobile. It was a Sunday morning. She could not try to contact him through his office, which was no great loss because they rarely knew where he was anyway, something of which she had an appreciation born of bitter experience. He was a maverick, Marcus, murder to work with. Thank God he still had the same personal mobile phone number.

He sounded surprised and a little alarmed to hear her voice. The surprise was understandable; she had not contacted him except through solicitors since that dreadful night when she had interrupted his sordid pursuits in their own home. But why should he be alarmed? Nervous even? Rare indeed.

She proceeded to give a performance worthy of an Oscar nomination.

'I've quit the paper,' she announced.

'Have you indeed?' he responded neutrally.

'Look, the reason I'm calling has nothing to do with all the personal stuff between us – I'd still rather not think about that. I want your advice on the job. I want to talk to you – can we meet?'

Marcus believed her at once. What she was saying made sense because he had always been something of a mentor to her, and he knew that. She had seen Marcus operate at full steam, and was quite aware that in both the world of newspapers and later as a businessman and politician he was the most sure-footed of careerists.

'Professionally I have greater respect for you than for anybody else in our world,' she heard herself say. She sounded honest, and indeed she was speaking the truth – as far as it went.

She could feel him relax at the other end of the phone. She had deliberately not mentioned that she was in Pelham Bay, nor the reopening of the murder inquiry and the discovery of the body in Bill Turpin's garden.

He did – as she had expected him to. He knew, of course, that she would have read of it in the papers.

It would have been unthinkable that she hadn't. The whole thing was public knowledge by now, and the identity of the newly-discovered body had been reported in the national as well as the regional press.

'Of course I'll meet you, darling, delighted to give you any help I can,' he almost gushed. How dare he call her darling like that, she thought angrily. But she said nothing. His self assurance positively bristled down the phone line.

Then, perhaps a little too casually, he broached the subject which was actually weighing heavily on both their minds.

'Heard about Irene and the Bill Turpin business, have you?' he asked.

She replied, with what she hoped was equal casualness and without comment.

'Yes, I have.'

'Thought you would have done. The police have been in touch with me already, you know, right after they identified the body.'

He paused, waiting for her to say something. Once again she had no comment to make.

'Poor little cow,' he eventually remarked quite cheerily, and volunteered a brief account of his police interview.

A London-based detective, unfamiliar with the case, had gone over much of the old ground and had apparently left quite satisfied that Marcus could help them no further.

'You know, it's all so long ago I can only just remember her really, and I told the police all I knew at the time,' he said.

By God, she thought, if her gravest suspicions were true, what a performer Marcus was. Any earlier hint

261

of alarm had completely gone now – had she in fact imagined it? He sounded so in control, so unconcerned; but then he always did.

They arranged to meet that night.

'Come to my place for a drink,' said Marcus.

He never lets up, she thought. But she had expected that too, indeed counted on it, and she agreed readily enough. He reminded her of his address in the luxurious Chelsea riverside block which she had never visited.

'Your solicitor knows it well enough, but you probably don't,' he said. There was a smile in his voice.

'Ha, ha,' she responded lamely.

She told her mother she had to return to London for a couple of days, and within an hour was back behind the wheel of the Porsche and on her way. She drove straight to Anna's house. She wanted to see Dominic. She didn't like him particularly, but she had a great deal of respect for his brilliance.

It was early afternoon when she arrived, and Anna was out in the park with Pandora. For about the only time in her life, Jennifer was quite pleased that her friend was not there. Anna would ask too many questions and Jennifer remained both unable and unwilling to try to answer them. Dominic greeted her without great enthusiasm, as usual. She was never sure if he really did dislike her, or if it was all a game. To her it was a game; with him, who could tell? They were chalk and cheese. Rather grudgingly he made her tea, but he came to life when she showed him the copies of Bill Turpin's notebook.

'Definitely computer codes and sign-ons,' he said. 'Ways in to other people's computer systems.'

'Can you do anything with them?' she asked.

'Even you aren't as ignorant as that, Jennifer,' he replied. 'Not without the relevant discs and programmes, of course I can't.'

'You wouldn't have any way of knowing what computer systems they hack into.'

He looked at her as if he thought she had an IQ of 12. Compared with him she supposed she did.

'Not without the discs,' he said.

'And if I could get hold of the discs?'

'Maybe. What's all this about?'

'Oh, just a story.'

He gave a little sniff.

'Whose life are you destroying this time?' he asked.

'What I like about you is that you always think the best of me,' she replied.

She took the sheets of paper from him and headed for the door.

'Aren't you waiting for Anna?'

'Tell her I'll see her tomorrow, not sure when, I'll call,' she said.

She drove to her own house then. There was already a For Sale board outside. Estate agents didn't hang about nowadays, she thought. Once inside she had a bath, washed and dried her hair carefully, and dressed in tight faded blue Levi jeans and a heavy white cotton shirt open at the neck. She knew she looked good. She sprayed a little perfume around and applied make-up lightly. She looked just the way Marcus liked her best. As she was about to leave, the phone rang. She eavesdropped the caller via the speaker of her answering machine. It was Anna. She did not pick up the receiver because she really couldn't talk to Anna yet.

She had arranged to meet Marcus at six o'clock. She arrived early – very unusual for her – and waited in the car for several minutes. At five past six she locked up the Porsche, which she left on a single yellow line, and walked into the foyer of Marcus's block of flats. It was all marbled opulence. It would be. She spoke to the uniformed porter, who called up to Marcus's apartment. After a brief conversation with Marcus, the porter summoned the lift for her and pumped in the special code that would take her up to penthouse level. Without the code, the lift stopped at the floor below.

When she stepped out of the lift, Marcus was waiting in the hallway. He stood and looked at her. His smile was wide, his teeth still perfect. She knew he travelled twice a year to a Hollywood dentist whose clientele were almost exclusively film stars. He was dressed entirely in black. Black Saint Laurent polo shirt. Beautifully cut black trousers and black Gucci shoes. She had a bet with herself that they were Gucci. A racing cert. He looked as fit and handsome as ever, and still disconcertingly baby-faced, his white-blonde curls as bright and shiny as they were twenty-five years ago. Remarkable. She said nothing. His pale blue eyes travelled up and down her appreciatively.

'You look marvellous,' he said quietly. 'Can I kiss you hello?'

Trust Marcus to get the tone just right. Affectionate but polite; interested yet deferential.

She nodded. What was she doing letting him kiss her already? He put a hand on each shoulder, very lightly, leaned forward and kissed her swiftly and gently on the lips. Then he stepped back and looked at her again.

He led her into the apartment. It was magnificent. Very modern; all black and white and shiny, steel and glass and huge windows giving a panoramic view of the river. On the big glass coffee table stood a bottle of Krug in a heavy silver ice bucket and two exquisite crystal glasses. Bloody typical, she thought.

He gestured her to a chair, opened the bottle and poured her a glass. He did not ask her if she wanted champagne. She thanked him and took the drink. His taste remained impeccable. His sense of style had always been devastating.

He sat opposite and asked how he could help her. She told him that she had walked out of the paper and why, and for more than half an hour they discussed her job and the implications of the action she had taken. His advice was good and sensible as ever.

'Maybe what you really need is a new challenge,' he said. 'But you must make absolutely sure that you don't let a tantrum govern the course of the rest of your life.'

She actually had no doubts about what she had done, and her job, or lack of it, was the least of her worries. But talking newspapers and careers to Marcus put her on easy ground.

It was when he stood over her and poured the last drop of champagne into her glass that he made the inevitable move. It was inevitable because for him it was just normal behaviour. He never felt shame. In spite of everything that he had tried to say to her after she had interrupted him with the two young girls, she knew that all he had really regretted was

265

being found out. He was incapable of feeling shame at his own actions.

He put down the bottle, sank to his knees beside her low armchair, wrapped his arms around her and, before she realised what was happening, kissed her long and slow and deep on the lips. She made herself respond – just a bit.

'I've missed you,' he said.

'You should have thought of that before,' she replied.

'I must have been crazy.'

'I've always thought so.'

'Jennifer, Jennifer.'

His lips were against her cheek. He was just breathing the words.

'Nothing's changed. Whenever I see you I want you, and as soon as I touch you I start to ache for you.'

His nerve was staggering, but he knew well the power he had always had over her. She supposed that was why she had refused to see him after the breakup, after finding him with those two girls. The thought made her shudder. So much about Marcus made her shudder, yet when he touched her he was totally confident that he would still hit the spot. It was ridiculous.

His hands were starting to caress her breasts. He slipped one inside her shirt and let out a little gasp of pleasure and satisfaction as he discovered she was wearing no bra. With his other hand he undid the buttons of her shirt. She did not stop him. He sank his face in her breasts and with his tongue he eagerly lapped up the essence of her, tasted again the sweetness of her skin. She did not stop him.

266

After a while he raised his head. He was panting. His eyes were bright.

'Are you going to let me make love to you?' he asked huskily.

The question was rhetorical. He was so sure of himself, the bastard. She nodded. She did not trust herself to speak.

'Stand up then,' he said.

She did as she was told.

'Take off your shirt,' he commanded.

She did so.

He reached up and undid her belt and unbuttoned the flies of her Levis and pulled them down. She was wearing light brogues. He slipped them off each foot and removed her jeans a leg at a time so that she was standing naked above him. He made her stand with her legs apart and then he reached up and buried his head in her. The strength of his animal desire was overwhelming, in spite of her mental revulsion against him.

He pulled her on to the thick carpeted floor alongside him. Somehow he had managed to remove his own clothes without her even noticing. He had always been able to do that. With the last vestige of her control, she made him draw back.

'You must put something on.' She reached for her handbag.

He threw back his head and roared with laughter at her.

I thought you didn't like plastic bags,' he said.

'That was pre-AIDS,' she said. 'And before I knew some of your tastes.'

He was amazed.

'Oh, you don't have to worry – I always get the girlies first. No danger at all,' he said.

He did not even realise what he was saying. She wanted to tell him how much he disgusted her, and then it was too late. He opened her legs and took her for the first time on the floor in the middle of the living room. He was very excited and it was over quite soon.

'Remember how long the second time lasts,' he said. She remembered.

He led her into the bedroom, spread a big white towel over the bed and massaged every inch of her body. Just like in the beginning, except that now Marcus used expensive scented oils instead of baby lotion. She tried not to think about who else he might have used them on. They made love for half the night – in every possible way, it seemed to Jennifer. After a while her brain ceased to have control of her body. Eventually they fell into an exhausted sleep. His deep and satisfied as ever, hers fitful and anxious, her very soul filled with self-disgust.

'Oh shit,' she thought to herself.

In the morning he woke her with his whistling, as usual. It was soon after seven. He was in the bathroom showering. He sounded wide awake and full of himself, as always. He emerged close-shaven, hair washed and brushed, teeth gleaming, but not yet dressed.

'Come on lazy bones,' he teased.

She had not even let him see she was awake. She lay on her side, just peeping out of the corner of one eye as he came through the bathroom door. She feigned a sluggish awakening.

'What time is it?' she muttered.

When he told her she groaned.

'You don't alter, do you?' he chuckled.

'Are you going already?' she asked.

'Breakfast meeting,' he said. 'Come on, out of bed.'

'Can't I stay here for a bit?' she inquired.

She saw the doubt in his eyes. She made herself look as kittenish as possible.

'Why don't we meet for lunch, here?'

He hesitated.

'Well I don't know . . .' he began.

He was standing by the bedside in a black silk dressing gown. She reached out and pulled it apart. He was half erect. She leaned forward and took him in her mouth. All night she had deliberately not done that, she had been saving it up. He reacted at once. She felt him double in size inside her mouth, opened her throat the way she had learned so long ago, and swallowed in the whole of him.

Then as quickly as she had begun, she withdrew.

'Don't stop,' he pleaded.

'You have to go and I'm not going to hurry this,' she said. 'Lunchtime?'

This time she had hooked him.

'How can I resist you?' he asked. 'OK. Stay here and I will be back as soon as I can make it.'

She smiled her appreciation.

'I must go home for an hour, I need some clean clothes,' she said. 'Can I have a key?'

She saw the doubt again. He did not say anything.

'Marcus, if I go out I shall need a key to get back in,' she said.

'Why don't we meet for champagne and sandwiches

269

at the Waldorf and then we'll come back here,' he said smoothly.

She frowned at him. 'Marcus, why on earth should I want to trek into the Waldorf when all that both of us want is here? What is the matter? Do you think I'm going to run off with the silver?'

He laughed what for him was a slightly nervous laugh.

'No, of course not, don't be daft. Of course you can have a key.'

Ten minutes later, the entry phone rang. It was Marcus's chauffeur. His days of tube trains and black cabs were ancient history; even the editor's Daimler was a thing of the past. His Bentley now awaited him. He fastened his silk tie and made for the door.

Just in time she called after him: 'Don't forget to square it with the porter.'

She waited five minutes, then jumped out of bed, hastily pulling on her jeans and shirt. The jeans felt uncomfortably tight now. She was out of practice with Marcus-style sex and she was quite sore. She shook herself angrily. She didn't have time to think about any of that. In the kitchen she quickly made herself a cup of tea with a tea bag in a mug. At the best of times she couldn't function without tea in the mornings. Then she made her way into Marcus's study.

From the time she had first known Marcus, he had always had a place at home to work. In the beginning in the rented flat in Pelham Bay it was just an old desk dominating half the living room. Later, as he grew more affluent and was able to buy space, there was always a room set aside to be his office. And these working places inevitably had one thing in common – they were quite immaculate. Everything in its place and a place for everything.

Jennifer knew the way Marcus worked. She was quite sure that if there was a link between him and Bill Turpin, the secret of it would somehow be stored in his computer system. Marcus was good with computers, not a professional expert like Dominic, but certainly way beyond the level of your average journalist or businessman. She realised that the odds were against her finding what she was looking for. From when she had first known him, Marcus had always kept his desk locked, as he did all filing cabinets and any other office furniture. She was actually quite relieved to find that the door to his study was not locked.

Inside, everything was indeed in perfect order, as she had expected. Marcus had always been not only a very unusual man but an unusual journalist. Journalists are not known for keeping tidy desks or having tidy lives. Marcus could never bear disorder. His clothes and grooming were always impeccable, and so was his home. Even in the days when everyone she knew of their age was living in varying degrees of squalor, Marcus kept perfect house. In Pelham Bay he had cleaned his own flat, of course, yet she could rarely remember seeing him do it. His early rising was the secret. When he used to visit her in her Dorset bedsit, she would often be woken at six in the morning by the sound of her own vacuum cleaner – Marcus having decided that the level of cleanliness fell way below his own high standards. When he cooked, and he cooked very well, he somehow managed to leave no mess at all. He would contrive to leave a kitchen cleaner than when he started – apparently with little or no effort – and he never dropped or broke anything. His coordination and timing were perfect. The thought obscurely occurred to her that it was quite likely he had lived his entire life without spilling a drop of milk.

Jennifer looked around her. The office was the ultimate in high tech, all glass and chrome again. There were two computers, one of them was an Apple Mac linked to the main frame of the *Recorder* group. With that Marcus could oversee the entire content and layout of any of his newspapers without moving from his black leather swivel chair. The second machine was a state-of-the-art IBM 486 equipped with a high-speed modem for communicating swiftly and efficiently with other systems throughout the world. Both sat on specially constructed tables lined up along the wall, with a fax and telephone-answering machine, a laser printer, and a sophisticated photocopier. There was a cabinet which she guessed housed television and stereo equipment. Along a second wall stood a row of filing cabinets, finished in black ash. The top of the huge desk running almost the length of the wall below the window, also made of beautiful black ash, was completely clear, apart from a marble paperweight, a Mont Blanc fountain pen and one framed photograph. The picture was of her and Marcus honeymooning after their wedding in the Caribbean. They both looked deliriously happy. He was tanned and handsome as ever. They were wearing tee-shirts and beach shorts. She peered closely at the picture and, yes, she was sure of it, Marcus's multi-coloured Bermuda-style shorts definitely had ironed creases in them. Typical. She looked comfortably crumpled, which was also fairly typical. She studied the picture further. His white tee-shirt could have featured in a commercial for soap powder. Obliquely she wondered if Marcus ever sweated except in bed. It suddenly occurred to her that she had never seen him do so, however hot the climate they were in. The original Joe Cool. But had he gone just too far? Jennifer's mind snapped back to the present. She needed to know the truth and she had to move fast.

She tried the drawers in the desk first. Locked, and although it was academic because no way was she going to try and bust locks, she could see at a glance these were no ordinary desk locks. They were complex specialist jobs. All the filing cabinets were also locked and had similar locking devices fitted. She looked around the room again. There was not a single sheet of paper lying around anywhere, and more importantly, not a single computer disc. The man was abnormal, but then, that was what she had probably always been afraid of. She allowed herself a dark chuckle.

In one corner between the filing cabinets and the computer table was a forbidding-looking safe set both into the wall and the floor. She noticed it had a combination lock and spent a fruitless few minutes seeing if she could second-guess the number Marcus had fed it. She tried his birthday and her birthday and several other fairly obvious choices, but quickly concluded that she was just wasting her time.

Then she sat down at the two computers. As she had expected, she could not break into the hard drive of either of them. They were each user-protected and

273

it was hopeless. Maybe Dominic could do it, she thought, but she couldn't bring him here. That would be too risky at this stage, and in any case he wouldn't come.

Damn, she thought. Damn bloody Marcus and his perfection. Didn't he ever do anything sloppy? Didn't he ever make mistakes? Wasn't there just one little computer disc sitting somewhere unnoticed that she could get her eager hands on? Carefully she went over every inch of the room again, looking for something she might have missed. There was nothing at all. One last thought occurred to her. With not a lot of hope she checked the floppy disc compartment of the Apple Mac. Empty. Well, what did she expect? As if Marcus would forget to remove and file away a disc. Resigned to finding nothing again, she none the less checked the IBM.

Eureka! She couldn't believe it – he had left a disc in the machine. He had forgotten it. He could make mistakes. She studied the disc. It was labelled, but the label simply bore a number written in letters: seven. Well, it was something, but the disc could be anything – his constituency records, his household accounts, even his blessed shopping list – because she knew very well he kept everything on computer, meticulously. On the other hand it could tell her something. And it was all she had.

She switched on the computer again and changed to disc-drive mode. The result was much the same as before; the floppy disc was coded and she could not get into it. Disappointing, but encouraging at the same time, even Marcus would not code his household accounts, would he?

She glanced at her watch. It was still only eight-thirty. She picked up the disc, her bag, and Marcus's key, and took off at a trot. Outside she gunned the Porsche and headed for the city.

Eighteen

She arrived at Dominic's office at five to nine. It was Monday morning. The dealers had been at their screens for hours, none the less the city gave the impression of reluctant awakening after the weekend.

'He's not here yet,' the receptionist told her.

So she walked outside the front door and waited. At nine o'clock prompt there was Dominic, looking clever and cross as usual. He looked even crosser when he saw her.

'Good God, what on earth do you want?' he asked.

'Dominic, will you look at this disc for me?'

'I suppose so, when I've time,' he said.

'It has to be now, Dominic, it's vital.'

'Jennifer, I am off on a two-day seminar this afternoon and I have a full morning. Are you mad?'

'I'm desperate,' she said.

There was something in her voice that stopped him in his tracks. He hadn't really looked at her. When he did so he was astonished. Jennifer was trembling, her face pale and drawn.

'Please, Dominic, please,' she said.

Good God, the woman was begging him.

'Don't be disgusting,' he said.

She did not respond. Where was the usual banter, he asked himself silently. She bowed her head so that she was staring at the ground. She looked vulnerable, which was more than a little disturbing, because underneath the crossness and the impatience, Dominic was a kind man as well as a clever one. He also loved his wife deeply, and Jennifer Stone, for all her faults, was his wife's best friend.

'Oh, come on then,' he said, turning towards the door.

Gratefully she followed him into the big mirror-panelled hallway, and up in the lift to his third-floor office. The room was full of computers, mostly silent and still, awaiting their master. There was just one in the corner, on a modem to somewhere, buzzing and whirring away like some futuristic robot which was probably more or less what it was.

Dominic took off his jacket and half threw it on to the hat-stand by the door. It missed and fell to the floor in a crumpled heap. He didn't even notice. He was probably the complete genetic opposite to Marcus, she thought vaguely. On auto-pilot she picked his coat up, draped it over a bent wire coat hanger she also found on the floor, and carefully looped the hanger on to the hat stand. He didn't notice that either. He was already at work, hunched over a favourite monster. The computer was going through its warming-up mode. Expertly Dominic punched in the information it needed to get started. Even the way he touched the keyboard was special, almost as if he was playing a musical instrument. He didn't hit the keys like a simple typist, he caressed them. She thought of her grandmother, a pianist of whom they used the old cliché 'she could make a piano talk'. Dominic was like that with a computer keyboard. He knew he could do with it what others had no hope of doing, he was a maestro in his field.

She watched him insert the floppy disc and

attempt to switch to disc drive. He began to play with the keyboard, coaxing the computer to do his will. After a few minutes he shook his head and turned to Jennifer.

'It's user-protected,' he said. 'I can't do a thing without a password.'

Jennifer reached in her bag and came up with the copies of Bill Turpin's notebook with its lines of computer codes.

'Any good?' she asked.

He shook his head again.

'No, this looks like God's gift to hackers. That's different. These are codes which provide information to allow an operator to break into other people's computer systems through a modem. You need the codes and access to the software, one without the other is no good. Catch 22.'

He paused, and with a flash of his usual irritability added: 'I told you that.'

'Sorry,' she said.

Good God, he thought, the woman's apologising to *me*. 'What is this all about Jennifer?'

'Trust me Dom, I can't tell you, not yet. You wouldn't even want to know. All I can tell you is how much I need your help.'

Dom? She called him Dom? Something was very wrong, that was for sure.

'OK,' he said. 'But I still can't help without the password. There's no way I can get into the disc without it. Look, do you know the person who pro-grammed this disc?'

She nodded.

'OK,' he said again. 'Have you any idea what he

may have used for the password. Is it worth having a few guesses?'

She looked at him blankly.

'Well?' he said.

She thought frantically. What on earth would Marcus have used?

'It has to be a word, yeah, not numbers?' she asked.

'Yes, a word of not more than eight letters. It can be just a meaningless jumble of letters, of course, but most people use a word.'

'Yes,' said Jennifer. She became aware that she was biting her nails.

'Try Recorder,' she said. And as she spoke she realised it was stupid. Marcus would not have used the name of his paper, and he hadn't.

She tried some more. KRUG, his favourite champagne; EASTON, the street he had lived in when he first came to London; MARTHA, his mother's name; JAMES, his father's name. Then all of those backwards, GURK, NOTSAE, AHTRAM, SEMAJ. Nothing. It was hopeless. She had to get inside Marcus's head. Suddenly she had a brain-wave, or at least she hoped it was, because it was so simple, so obvious. What was the one constant factor in Marcus's life apart from his driving ambition? The answer was a touch arrogant but also the truth – it was her, Jennifer Stone.

'Try JENNIFER,' she cried.

Dominic glanced at her curiously, but made no comment as he punched her name into the computer. It did not work. Neither did REFINNEJ or STONE or JSTONE or JENSTONE, or any of those backwards.

279

She felt defeated. Dominic was continuing without success to try variations of her name and the other words she had suggested to him. She must think back over all the years she had known Marcus. She had to believe that he had used a word with some significance to him. Almost everybody who ever chose a computer password did that, surely even Marcus. So what else was there?

'It's usually something really obvious, surprisingly enough,' she heard Dominic say in the distance.

She was concentrating hard, trying to be methodical. When had she first had doubts about Mark, vague, indefinable doubts? It had been after the trial when she had half suspected he had lied about Johnny Cooke. He had convinced her that she had been confused, and allowing herself to be convinced had been the easy way out at the time. So it all went back to the very beginning in Pelham Bay. Everything that happened seem to stem from there . . .

'Try PELHAM,' she said suddenly. Dominic did so. Nothing.

'Backwards?' he asked.

She nodded. She felt it was hopeless. She would have to go in cold, but she needed more ammunition. She did not have enough to convince him, or maybe even totally to convince herself, and the stakes were so high. She was lost in despairing thoughts, not even watching Dominic or the computer.

Then she heard him say quietly: 'I think you've cracked it, old girl.'

He was in. He was working the disc. She knew better than to speak.

After a few minutes he said: 'Give me those codes.'

He studied the copies of the pages from Bill Turpin's notebook.

'What I can't understand is why anyone should write codes like this down. They should be in the computer for the user to call up.'

'What if the person who wrote them down never really trusted computers?'

He looked at her as if she were crazy.

'It is possible, you know,' she said with a smile.

It was the first time she had smiled at him that morning, and he realised how pleased he was to see it. Maybe he didn't really dislike the old bat as much as he thought he did.

He turned back to the keyboard. She watched him for about ten minutes more, and ultimately could contain herself no more.

'Any joy?' she asked.

He swung around to face her, brows knitted in a deep frown.

'I am a genius, not a magician,' he said.

She laughed. He found that pleased him too.

'Look, this is going to take time,' he said. 'I reckon that this disc is programmed to plug in through a modem with a particular computer system elsewhere. What exactly and where exactly is another bigger question.

She breathed a sigh of relief: at least it wasn't Marcus's blessed laundry list. It looked as if she had had some luck and stumbled across a disc that might at least give her a clue or two. But could Dominic put it all together?

Her eyes were a question mark.

'The disc can only be put into operation with the right codes. Maybe one of these is it, maybe not.' He held the copied notebook in his hand. 'All I can do is try all the possible codes with all the possible combinations on the disc and give it a whirl.

'I have to interrogate the disc, and if it is that important it will almost certainly be programmed to wipe itself clean if I ask the wrong question or feed it wrong information. It's not a five-minute job.'

She just carried on looking at him, expectant. He sighed.

'OK,' he said. 'I'll work better on my own. I can't stand being watched. Go away and come back in a couple of hours.

She looked at her watch. It was already ten o'clock. Two hours would be cutting it very fine indeed. She wanted to get it all over with quickly, before Marcus had time to do too much thinking – and the man thought fast.

'Two hours?' she queried. Her expression was stricken.

He sighed. 'OK. An hour and a half – but don't build up too many hopes.'

She kissed him on the top of his head.

'You are a genius,' she said. 'I know that because you've told me often enough.'

'That's better,' he replied.

She knew what he meant, and indeed she was feeling just a little better as she left him to it. If anyone could succeed it would be Dominic McDonald, that she believed absolutely.

An hour and a half. She looked down at herself. She was a mess, her shirt was crumpled and her hair greasy and lank. She had not even waited to shower and shampoo, and she was aware that she smelt, which was not surprising after the night she had spent with Marcus. She tried not to think about it. She just hoped Dominic hadn't noticed how she smelt, and in fact doubted that he had. Dominic was unlikely to notice anything like that. She desperately needed clean clothes and a bath, but she didn't have time to go home to Richmond as she had told Marcus was her intention. She walked the streets until she found a branch of Marks & Spencer where she bought fresh underwear, a couple of cotton tee-shirts and a plain black sweat shirt. It was cooler today and she could not stop shivering, but she was unsure whether it was the cold or what she was doing which was the cause of that. Outside in the street again, she slipped the black sweatshirt over her crumpled white shirt. It made her look fractionally more presentable – certainly she felt warmer and more comfortable – and with a bit of luck it might trap her smelliness within its thick cotton. There was a chemist's shop across the road, where she bought toothpaste, toothbrush, shampoo and a jar of her favourite moisturiser.

Little more than half an hour had passed. She began to walk as slowly as she could make herself back to Dominic's office, and stopped on the way at an Italian coffee bar. She ordered a double expresso and found to her slight surprise that she was hungry. She and Marcus had not eaten properly the night before and she had skipped lunch as well. Of course when he was on a sexual roll, Marcus never needed to eat at all, or to sleep – she did. She ordered croissants and bacon and egg and fresh orange juice. The croissants were fresh and warm and mouth-melting, the bacon and egg tasted almost as good as it smelt, and the orange juice had definitely been in the form of several round fruits minutes earlier. There weren't too many cafes in London that served a breakfast like this. She complimented herself on her luck and hoped fervently that it was an omen and that Dominic was also having good fortune and that her plans for the rest of the day would prove lucky too. After another double expresso, the hands of her watch had moved painfully forward to reach eleven-twenty. She paid her bill and headed for Dominic. She was stopped by the receptionist in the hall of his office, and had to wait impatiently while the man called upstairs before clearing a visitor for entry. It was eleven-twenty-seven when Dominic picked up the phone and confirmed that Jennifer was expected. This time with a yellow 'Visitor' tag stuck to her black sweat shirt, Jennifer rode to the third floor in the lift. As she opened the door to his office, the minute hand of the big electric clock on the wall clunked once and settled on the half-hour position. It was exactly eleven-thirty.

'How prompt you are,' said Dominic. He was beaming at her, looking positively smug.

'You've done it, haven't you?' she said.

It was not really a question, because his face had already given her the answer. He was flushed with excitement. Obliquely she wondered if anything else excited Dominic as much as a computer. What about sex? Funny, she'd never asked Anna. They had talked often about sex. When she was much much younger, Jennifer had given the men in her life points out of ten – much to Anna's amusement. Marcus had always scored at least ten and sometimes 11 – also much to Anna's amusement – but Jennifer never gave anything else away about him, and Dominic's sexual prowess or lack of it had somehow not been mentioned. Jennifer had never even tried to imagine him in bed, and could not understand why her mind had jumped to such thoughts now. Perhaps it was tension. She made herself concentrate on the matter in hand.

Dominic had turned back to the computer and was beginning to explain.

'With this disc, these codes and the right modem, I can now plug directly into the G7 computer system,' he said.

Jennifer was no financial whizz kid.

'What's G7?' she asked.

Dominic looked amazed. 'I thought you were supposed to be a journalist, for Christ's sake.

'The Group of Seven. The seven biggest money markets in the world. The seven countries that control the world's finances.

'Naturally they use computers to collate, store and communicate their business. Changes in our Bank Rate would all be communicated within G7 first. They have much more power than most people, including some financiers, think. If an exchange rate is about to be altered, a currency devalued, international loans given or called in – all are done through G7. For a private dealer to be able to plug into their computer is a bit like being fed a fortune on an intravenous drip.'

'Bingo,' said Jennifer. She had picked that up from Todd.

Dominic was fair bristling.

'Rather more profitable than that,' he said. 'If you were fast enough you could always be ahead of the game. Making money is all about information, and you'd never get better information than from G7. You could make billions.

'Amazing. Leaves you wondering how many people throughout the world have access to this.'

'Is it legal?' she asked, feeling stupid as soon as she said the words.

'You're kidding. This could blow the world money market sky high. Who did you get it from?'

'An old friend,' she replied.

He wasn't really listening. He was busy on the keyboard.

'I thought so, algorithms.'

'What?' she asked.

'Algorithms. An obvious protection. Means you can't copy it. I'm afraid of going any further in case I wipe it.'

He paused. 'I suppose you want this disc back.'

She held out her hand.

'No chance of making a quick million quid first?'

'Dominic,' she said. There was a warning in her voice.

'You're right of course. I'd get found out. I'm not designed to be a master criminal.'

'No you're not, and thank God for it.'

There was feeling in her voice. When he offered the disc to her, she took it with one hand and brushed his cheek with her other.

'Thank you Dominic,' she said quietly.

Briefly he took her hand in his. 'Whatever it is you're doing, be careful Jen,' he said.

She felt the tears pricking again. Pull yourself together, she ordered herself, and tried her best to do so. Banter, that was the answer. She flashed a smile at him.

'I never knew you cared,' she said.

'Don't kid yourself,' he told her. 'My only concern for your welfare is that I have a crazy wife who does care, the silly cow.'

She left the room laughing. Dominic would probably never know how wonderfully reassuring she had found him.

Nineteen

She retrieved the Porsche from its parking meter and headed back to Chelsea. She locked the copy of Bill Turpin's notebook and the computer disc in the car. There was little risk of Marcus discovering it missing before she had completed her plans; she would make sure he had no time to go into his study. As she walked in to the entrance hall of Marcus's block of flats, carrier bags containing her purchases under her right arm, she checked her wrist watch. It was twelve-fifteen, and she was almost sure Marcus would not be back before one. The porter recognised her immediately and called the lift for her, as instructed by Marcus, pumping in the appropriate code to dispatch her to the penthouse floor. She wondered fleetingly what selection of women he had ushered up to the penthouse over the years, and decided this was not the time to dwell on that.

As she shut Marcus's front door, the phone rang, and she picked up the receiver in the hall. It was him, as she had guessed it would be.

'Have you just got up?' he asked. He sounded very good-humoured. He always did when he had got his own way.

'Certainly not,' she replied.

'I called earlier, you must have heard the phone?' he went on.

'I told you, I needed to go back home to get some clean things.'

'You sound tense.'

She must be careful, Marcus was no pushover.

'Just knackered, I'm out of practice.'

'Stand by. What you need is one of my knock your socks off Bloody Marys. I'll be there as soon as I can.'

He had gone before she could ask him how long that would be.

She piled her purchases on the bed in the main bedroom and went into the study. Just in case he did look in there, she decided to check it out carefully. It looked fine, nothing seemed to be out of place. In fact there was very little that could have been put out of place, but she knew that if the Mont Blanc fountain pen were to be moved an inch away from where it normally lay, Marcus would notice at once.

Quickly she returned to the bedroom, removed all her clothes, and gratefully stepped under the pressurised shower in the ensuite bathroom. It wasn't over yet, not nearly over, she thought, as she thoroughly shampooed her hair. Then, standing naked on the thick towelling mat, she rubbed herself all over with the newly purchased moisturising cream. She wrapped herself in one of Marcus's big luxurious towels, and scrubbed her teeth energetically. She put moisturiser on her face and then applied a little mascara and lipstick, gave herself a quick spray of the Cartier perfume she always carried in her handbag, and dressed in the clean underwear beneath her new baggy tee-shirt. She deliberately did not put her jeans back on, because Marcus never had been able to resist her legs. She was still brushing the tangles out of her hair when she heard him turn his key in the lock, and she did not go to meet him. He came looking for her in the bedroom and stood in the doorway clutching a huge bunch of Lily of the Valley in one hand and a big plastic bag of limes, for the Bloody Marys, in the other.

'You look good enough to eat,' he growled at her.

She turned away from the mirror smiling. 'Yes please,' she said.

He threw the bunch of flowers at her and she caught them easily. He put down the bag of limes on the dressing table, strode across the room until he was standing behind her, and buried his face in her neck.

'You smell so clean, so sweet,' he said.

She swung around to face him and offered him her lips. He kissed her long and slow and deep. As ever he pushed himself against her and she could feel that he was already aroused. Typical Marcus.

'When do you want your Bloody Marys, before or after?' he asked.

She put a hand lightly over his crotch. 'That's what I want,' she replied, which was, of course, what he had expected her to say.

'You're as randy as ever, you sexy bitch,' he muttered approvingly. 'Why did you ever leave me? I always told you we were two of a kind.'

'Maybe we are – but I left you because you are a monster,' she told him.

'True enough, I expect,' he replied.

'You humiliated and degraded me – but none of that, apparently, seems to stop me fancying you to distraction.'

'That's because I give you what you want.'

His voice was a low growl and he wasn't smiling now. He brushed a hand between her legs, raised his fingers to his face and breathed in the scent of her.

'I know what you need.'

It had been true for so long.

She stepped back, deciding to take control, which she knew he liked.

'Undo your flies,' she commanded.

He did so. He was wearing his customary cotton jockey shorts beneath, which did not do a lot of good. His erect penis jumped out at her, as usual.

She did not touch him.

'You know what I promised you,' she said softly.

His whole body stirred. 'Can I undress first?' he asked.

'No,' she replied.

And she sank to her knees and took him in her mouth as he stood before her fully clothed in his beautifully-cut pin-striped Italian suit. His silk tie was still elegantly knotted around the neck of his Jermyn St shirt, his feet clad in the inevitable Gucci brogues, shined to mirror finish. For a few brief seconds he felt a bit of a fool, then the magic of her tongue cast its spell over him. She was expert and it didn't take long. When his moans of pleasure grew louder and she felt his whole body tense, she withdrew her mouth – there was a limit to what she was prepared to do. He came all down his immaculately pressed trousers and the spunk dripped onto his perfectly polished shoes. Obscurely, she thought with some satisfaction that, although it did not matter to him now, he would later be most annoyed at the state of his clothing. He was that kind of man.

She looked up at him, standing there panting, eyes glazed over, immersed in his own sexuality.

'Now it's my turn,' she said.

'Now can we get undressed?' he asked.

She nodded, and pulled off her tee-shirt, revealing only the briefest black panties and lacy bra fresh from Marks & Sparks. He reached out and touched her first on her breasts and then between the legs through the silky material.

'Leave those on for a bit,' he said.

He led her to the bed where she settled as comfortably as she could while she watched him take his clothes off. As always he folded everything neatly, and she rather hoped his trousers were ruined. He lay down on the bed beside her and played with her through her panties. He was quickly hard again. He wanted to be inside her and took it for granted that she wanted it too. He rolled over on top of her and did it to her around the side of the panties. It felt as if her every nerve end was raw. The material rubbed into her, giving extra friction, and he enjoyed seeing her breasts strain against the silly bra as she writhed in orgasm. It did not occur to him that her climaxing could be anything other than genuine.

When he thought that she had finished, he pulled out of her and removed the bra and pants. Now for the serious business. He had her from behind over the side of the bed, then he laid her on her back and piled pillows beneath her, so that her pelvis was lifted and she was wide open for him – just like the first time he had made her come twenty-five years earlier. He turned her on her side and went in from the back; always he was in control. Finally he made her kneel, and with great, heaving strokes he brought himself to climax.

Afterwards they lay breathing heavily in each other's arms. He had returned home just before one o'clock. It was now three-thirty, and they had barely stopped for two and a half hours. She was exhausted. His stamina remained daunting. He was, as ever, totally confident of his power over her, and he must have been satisfied at last, because he suddenly remembered that he was hungry.

'Good God, when did we last eat?' he asked.

She lied that she did not remember. She could hardly tell him about her Italian cafe breakfast.

'Come on,' he said. 'Bloody Marys and bacon sandwiches.'

He went into the bathroom and returned with his black silk dressing gown and a luxurious cream towelling robe which he threw to her. She followed him into the kitchen and watched him put good smoked bacon on the grill and half-baked French baguettes into the microwave. While the bacon was cooking, he made a lethal-looking Bloody Mary in a huge jug: a generous slosh of Polish vodka, the juice of three or four limes, Tabasco, Worcestershire sauce, celery salt, black pepper, cayenne pepper, a spoonful of mustard and a slurp of tomato sauce for thickness; all well stirred, topped up with chilled tomato juice and poured over crackling ice cubes. He gave her a glassful in a crystal tumbler and she gratefully took a deep drink. He did make great Bloody Marys. She watched him slice open the baguettes, apply a thin scraping of butter and a generous layer of English mustard, and pile them full of bacon. He passed her one.

She was too nervous to eat much, and anyway had already eaten that huge breakfast, but he devoured his baguette hungrily. When he had finished and he had poured them each a third Bloody Mary, he leaned back in his pine kitchen chair and gazed at her appreciatively.

'I do love you,' he said.

She was startled.

'I am not sure you have ever told me that before,' she replied. 'Except in bed.'

' 'Course I have,' he insisted. 'And I miss you to distraction.'

'Hmph,' she said. 'You don't like having your style cramped.'

'I was a fool,' he said. 'If I ever got another chance I wouldn't mess it up.'

'I wish I could believe you,' she said.

'Do you?' he asked.

'Do I what?'

'Do you really wish you could believe me?'

'I suppose I do, yes.'

'Well, you can.' His eyes were inside her head again.

She wriggled uncomfortably in her chair.

'Why does it matter if I believe you or not, anyway?' she asked.

'Because you won't come back to me unless you do,' he said.

He was ablaze with sincerity.

'And, I want you,' he went on. 'I want you more than anything else in the world.'

'I've always known that Marcus,' she said. 'That has never been the problem.'

He laughed, then stopped abruptly.

'I want you to be my wife again. I don't know why I let it go wrong. Would you ever consider giving me another chance?'

'I don't know,' she said.

'Is there anything I can do to make you consider it?' he asked.

She let the silence stretch, as if she were giving his question serious thought. He did not take his eyes from hers.

'There might be,' she said.

'Anything,' he replied.

She took another deep breath.

'There are two things I would absolutely demand were I ever to become your wife again. The first is that somehow or other you would have to gain control of your more unpleasant urges. No more other women – but most of all no more children.'

He looked shocked. 'They weren't children, for Christ's sake.'

'As near as dammit as far as I'm concerned,' she replied. 'Anyway, I don't think you're capable of giving up that side of your life.'

'Of course I am,' he told her, and, as always, he meant it – at the time of speaking.

She sighed. 'If I ever found you with young kids again . . . I would kill you.'

She was very convincing. He blinked at her.

'You will never have cause, I promise you, my darling,' he said.

She sighed again. 'Let's say I believe you . . . and go on to the second condition. No more secrets.'

He raised one eyebrow.

'I mean it, Marcus.'

'He gave in. 'What secrets?'

'The kind of secrets that would put you in jail for the rest of your life.'

'Don't be ridiculous,' he said.

She put down her glass. 'OK Marcus. The game is over. I know more about what you have done than you can possibly imagine. I know more about why than you could ever guess. I know where you have been and where you are heading.'

Marcus's expression darkened. He downed the remains of his third Bloody Mary in one.

'Stop talking in riddles,' he commanded.

'That's another thing. Don't ever again tell me what and what not to do,' she said.

He sneered at her. She was pleased to see that she was getting through at last, cracking the veneer. That had to be a hopeful sign.

'You don't say that in bed,' he remarked crassly.

'That was cheap and unworthy of you,' she fired back.

'Yes, maybe.' He was half apologetic, looking down at his empty glass.

She did not put him out of his misery.

'Look, what are you saying?' he asked eventually.

'I'm saying that I know,' she replied simply.

Her gaze was direct. He found that it was unnerving and opted for bravado. Typical.

'What do you know?' he asked. His smile was a toothpaste commercial.

'For a start I know that you killed Irene Nichols,' she said.

The smile froze on his face. Like a trapped fox he smelt danger, and like the wily old dog fox that he was, all his senses were suddenly alert. He was going to give nothing away, keep his options open, seek out the extent of the danger. He was at his best in tight corners. His eyes were blank as he stared back at her, meeting her gaze. All she could see was emptiness. The ultimate solution: shut it all out, feel nothing. She waited for him to speak.

'I think you've gone crazy,' he said.

'Maybe,' she replied.

She made her own eyes go blank too. He could see nothing at all in their deep greenness, and he sensed a ruthlessness in her that he had never before realised was there – but then, he had always said they were two of a kind.

She began to talk, keeping her voice low and deliberate, and choosing her words with care. She knew exactly what she was going to do now. She had been over it all again and again in her mind.

Her voice sounded as cold as she had intended.

'Maybe I'm crazy to want to go on. But I do. I want my share of you, I want all that you have. I'll go along with you, but only if it's a true partnership this time.'

He shrugged his shoulders.

'I don't know what on earth you are talking about,' he said.

'Oh yes you do, Marcus.'

She paused. The silence was long. Eventually she spoke again.

'Bill Turpin told me,' she said.

'Bill Turpin?' That really put him on red alert. 'Told you what?'

'Pretty damn near everything, I'd say.'

He studied her face. When he laughed it sounded dry and hollow, like wind through a rusty drain pipe.

'Bill Turpin would not talk to you or anybody else,' he said finally.

'Maybe, maybe not. But he did tell me.'

'You're speaking in riddles again.'

He had walked over to the sink and was rinsing his Bloody Mary glass under the tap. It was something to do, and it meant he could turn his back on her. She could no longer see his face, and he was no longer looking at her. That was a relief to her too. She bit her bottom lip, concentrating hard. One false step now and it was all over.

'Bill Turpin called me at the paper,' she went on. 'He said he wanted to talk to me about you. I was busy and I didn't take a lot of notice. We always used to think he was half-mad, remember? Then I had the fight at the office. I just walked out, got in the car and drove – West, naturally.

'On the way I started thinking about Bill, and you, and how it all began, and instead of driving to mother's as I had intended, I went straight to the cliffs and to Bill's cottage. I knocked on the front door and there was no reply. I walked round the back and I could see Bill slumped over the kitchen table. The back door was on the latch. I went in. He had fallen across the tin box of goodies the police found. What they didn't find was Bill Turpin's diary. I have that.'

'What diary?' Mark swung round. It was nice to see him looking pale and shaken.

'Bill Turpin kept a diary. he wrote down everything. I don't know why he kept it, but he did. Like I don't know why he wanted to see me. I never knew him, our only link was you. I don't know if he wanted to confess, or if he wanted to hook me too. Both unlikely, I should have thought, but he did call me, and I do have the diary.'

Marcus was desperately trying to recover.

'What do you mean, hook you?'

Jennifer took a deep breath.

'It was all in the diary. How you went out of control and killed Irene Nichols, how you turned to Bill Turpin for help, how the body was disposed of. And how you have belonged to Bill and his people ever since . . .'

'What rubbish,' he said.

She decided it was time to play her trump. She threw the copies of the Bill Turpin notebook onto the table. The computer codes jumped up at him.

'I also have his master disc,' she said. 'I know about the direct access into G7, and I know the way it works. I know that you have used the *Recorder* to make an unbelievable fortune. I know there is a driving force behind you.

'I know that the level of manipulation and corruption you are involved in is staggering, and that you could never get out of it even if you wanted to because of the weaknesses in you that have put you in the position you are in . . .'

She stopped and looked at him. He didn't say anything. He was leaning against the sink. She noticed that his hands were trembling, which was encouraging, but he had not broken yet.

She had no choice. It was a risk, but she was going to have to go for the ultimate bluff.

'And I know you have murdered more than once,' she blurted out.

His eyes were very bright. He still didn't say anything.

'That's the précised version,' she went on. 'I can give you more detail if you wish. It's all in the diary.'

'What are you going to do with the diary?' he asked as casually as he could.

'That depends on you.'

He just looked at her questioningly.

'If you do what I want I shall burn it.'

'And if not?'

It was her turn to shrug.

'Can I see it?'

'Do you think I would bring it here? You are a killer after all.'

He turned away. 'You know I would never hurt you,' he said softly.

She said nothing.

'What do you want?' he asked at last.

'I want to know everything and I want to be part of everything,' she said.

'OK,' he said.

She smiled. 'You have to trust me as much as I will have to trust you. I understand your weaknesses and I also know your strengths. I want to be part of it all with you. You have always said we are two of a kind.

'I want to get to the top at your side. But I have to know everything first, the whole truth, the dangers and rewards we would face together.'

'So?'

'So, if you want me on your side . . . get talking,' she ordered.

He seemed to have dropped his pretence of not knowing what she was talking about. He walked back to the table and sat down opposite her, trying to stare inside her head, the way he always had. Every-

thing that she was saying, everything about her indicated that she was as full of ambition and lust and
as empty of principle as he was. He had indeed
always said they were two of a kind. He had not
recognised how much further that went than just
their sexual appetites. As he tried to read the deepest
recesses of her mind, he began to realise how much
he wanted to believe that she really would go all
the way with him. Together they could take over the
world, she and he. He supposed he had always known
that, wanted that more than anything.

'There are things I have never told anybody.' He
stopped.

She felt no need to speak.

'I'm not sure that I can, not sure that I dare.' He
looked tired suddenly.

'Two of a kind, Marcus . . .' She said it again.
Barely a murmur.

He nodded.

'Hasn't the burden been lonely?'

He nodded again.

'Well, then,' she encouraged. 'We can fight all the
battles together. Together our future could be
glorious.'

Oh, how he wanted to share it with her. What a
relief it would be. His eyes were locked onto hers.
She waited for him to speak.

'I'm not sure you know what you are asking. There
are things I try not even to think about. I am not an
evil man, Jennifer, but I have done evil things.'

'I have told you,' she said. 'I know a lot already,
from the diary. So far I know nothing I cannot live
with. You have killed, but I don't think you ever
meant to.'

301

She never failed to surprise him. He grasped the straw.

'Of course I didn't. They were accidents, all of them.'

All of them? So she was right – there had been more. She must not allow herself to flinch.

'Begin at the beginning,' she instructed calmly. 'Begin with Irene. That was the beginning, wasn't it?'

'Oh yes,' he said. 'That was the beginning.'

She had known it. Maybe always known that so much of what had happened to both of them in their lives stemmed from that time so long ago in Pelham Bay.

'Go on, tell me about Irene.' She was coaxing him.

He reached for the vodka bottle and the ice bucket. This time he poured a hefty neat slug of the clear spirit into a tumbler with just a couple of lumps of ice. He gestured with the bottle at her. She shook her head. He took a deep drink and briefly put his head in his hands. Jennifer had never lied to him, he was quite sure of that. He was certain she was being honest with him now, about her own aims and ambitions. He had always been able to trust her, hadn't he? How much better it would be if there were two of them to share the good and the bad, two of a kind. Anyway, it seemed he may not have a lot of choice.

He leaned back in his chair, and then he began.

He began with the day he killed Irene.

Jennifer had known it, she really had, but hearing him say it was quite extraordinary. Now it was her turn to get up from the table and walk away because she did not want him to be able to see her face while he talked.

He told how he had gone home to his flat the second night she had refused to sleep with him and how he had been feeling quite desperate for sex. 'You know, the way I get,' he said. Jennifer knew, all right.

He told her how Irene had been asleep on the living-room couch, wearing one of his shirts with just a couple of buttons done up, and had woken as he entered the flat, slamming the front door behind him. He had been unable to wait. Within minutes he had his clothes off and was inside her. He came very quickly – but it seemed to bring him no satisfaction, no relief, so he took Irene into the bedroom and had her in every way he could think of. Nothing seemed to do him any good. The second time he couldn't make himself come at all, whatever he did, and he did almost everything. He knew he was hurting her but he couldn't stop. Eventually he pushed Irene back over the bed and she ended up with her head and shoulders crushed against the floor while he carried on pumping into her with all his might. She began to cry out for him to stop but he ignored her in his desperation to climax.

At some stage he heard something crack, he couldn't be sure when. Eventually he made it. When he rolled off her she slumped in a heap on to the floor. To his horror he realised that her neck was broken and she was quite dead.

There was a catch in his voice. Was he crying? Jennifer did not dare to look round. So he had some feelings left, did he? She doubted it, but yes, he was definitely sobbing.

'I have never been able to tell anyone, so I have

never even thought about it, not since it happened,' he said. 'Blocked it out. You were right, you see, I am a monster.'

She did not react. He looked at her imploringly, seeking reassurance. He was gabbling a bit, talking too much, and that was just what she had been hoping for.

'Look,' he continued. 'My first thought when I realised Irene was dead was to dial 999 – of course it was. Then I asked myself what good it would do, nobody was going to bring her back to life.

'So I just concentrated on getting myself out of the whole dreadful mess . . .'

And Irene? Did he spare one fleeting thought for poor little Irene, Jennifer wanted to inquire, but she didn't.

'Why did you go to Bill Turpin?' she asked instead.

He let out a big breath. 'I've never known really – I had to get rid of the body. I just sensed he would know what to do. I'd been checking him out, you knew I did that. We all wanted to be investigative reporters in those days. I was just one of a long line of would-be Carl Bernsteins to probe into the past of our local mystery man.'

'So you did have something on him?'

'No, but I tried to con him that I did, bloody fool that I was . . .'

'He went along with it though, didn't he?' she responded. 'He helped you . . .'

'Yes. I didn't know why at first, of course. But it suited him – in more ways than one.'

Marcus told her how he had run across the fields to old Bill's cottage, and hammered on the door.

'I was in a right state, but I tried to be Joe Cool

all the same – true to form, I suppose. I told Bill I needed help right away with something very serious – that I'd put together an exposé of his criminal past, and in return for his help I'd destroy it.'

Marcus managed a high-pitched giggle. 'He just smiled at me. Then he said: "You'm not trying to blackmail me, be 'ee boy?" He looked amused, not angry. It all seemed so unreal.

'I didn't know what to say. I was frightened out of my mind. I thought I had blown it altogether.

'But, quite abruptly, he asked me what I had done. I told him. Then he made me tell him everything that had happened in the last few days which in any way concerned Irene, anything that could be connected to her death and exactly how she had died.

'I gave him every detail. All about Johnny coming to us after Marjorie Benson was found, everything. He had that sort of effect, you know, you obeyed him. Of course I didn't realise I was manna from Heaven for him, really. I provided a second murder and even a suspect for the first one. Poor Johnny, asking for it.

'Eventually Turpin put down that blessed pipe of his and said he would sort everything out. He told me to stay where I was, so I did – while he went off in his car. It was some hours before he came back, it seemed like days. He just walked into the cottage, sat down at the kitchen table, got that old pipe working again and then he said: "You can go home now, it's all clean." '

Marcus's voice sounded distant. He'd gone back in time now, remembering. He explained how the old man had instructed him on exactly what to say to the police: Irene had left home for work and never returned, simple as that. Keep it simple and stick to it.

'Oh, and a word of advice,' Bill had said, 'if you ever want to blackmail anyone again, you'm going to have to be a bit more convincing . . . you young puppy. Go on – get off 'ome now.'

But as Marcus had reached the cottage door, Bill had called him back. It was the old man's last words which held the sting in their tail.

'You'll hear from me – I may want something from you in return.'

What he had wanted from Marcus was custody of his life.

From that moment on, Marcus was never again to be entirely his own man.

'Why did Bill Turpin want you under his control?' she asked.

Marcus shrugged. 'He told me he thought I was very clever, didn't have any morals, and had a weakness that would always be with me. The combination made me valuable to him, I suppose. I would have all the help in the world to raise me to positions of great power. All I had to do in return was to be absolutely loyal and always do exactly what I was told. Then I would remain infallible . . . whatever I did . . .'

Jennifer appeared totally shocked.

'Bill Turpin was certainly not what he seemed, was he?' she remarked mildly.

'In a way he was,' Marcus replied.

And he told her what he knew of Bill's history, his time in the services, the death of his wife and children. Bill had told Marcus that during the war he had met a group of men who were as disillusioned with their country as he was. They shared his bitterness and despair, his anger at the hell they had been thrust into, and felt the world owed them something special after all they had been through. At the time Bill saw himself almost as a kind of Robin Hood, making up for society's various injustices and inequalities and cruelties. There were real villains among them, Marcus was sure, but they came from all walks of life and it was only their aim which united them – to be free and powerful, and that had to mean rich as well. Bill's involvement had initially been political in a way, although he would never have understood that, but had he been a more educated man, he would have channelled his rage against society differently; he might well have joined the communist party, as so many did in the reaction days of the fifties . . .

Jennifer interrupted him at that point. Marcus was warming to his theme, arguing around it in the way he was so good at, sounding quite smooth. She was not going to let him prevaricate.

'So what actually was Bill Turpin?' she asked.

Marcus shrugged again. 'Not a man to cross,' he said. 'In the early days he was top muscle. The old Pelham gossip wasn't the half of it.

'He was involved in the Lord Lynmouth burglary, at least two other major art robberies, and God knows what else. Arms dealing – one of the great markets of our time. It seemed crazy, a joke when people talked about it back in Pelham, but Bill and his lot knew all about the international arms market from the beginning, from the war. Arms to Korea. To Suez – by fancy routes, of course. And to every African banana state invented. If it still seems far-fetched, think about what is public knowledge now – British firms, legitimate British firms, supplying weapons to the enemy during the Gulf War. Bill and his mates knew what they were about. They knew how to use the stuff they were flogging, for God's sake – they'd lived through all that.'

Marcus was sweating. He wiped a silken arm across his forehead. She had been aware that he had been sniffing profusely. He took a handkerchief from his pocket and blew his nose. He still didn't stop sniffing. Strange that it had not ever occurred to her until this day that Marcus's extraordinary energy could sometimes have been chemically encouraged. Maybe he read her mind, she'd often felt he'd done that before – within seconds he had the sniffing under control.

She tried not to look at him. 'Go on,' she commanded.

He did so, quite intently. 'Bill Turpin once told me that he learned during the war that he had one great talent – it was for killing people. Then he laughed as if that was a joke.'

Jennifer remembered what Todd had told her about the unsolved murder of the Earl of Lynmouth, about the string of fine-art robberies just after the war, and even about illegal arms deals out of Bristol. She had a vision of a small gang of highly trained soldiers, breaking and entering into big houses and galleries, using their army skills, and one of them with a special job for which he had a special talent – to listen, to watch, to wipe out anybody who got in the way. Swiftly. Cleanly. Silently. Bill Turpin. She had not believed what she was saying when she had asked Todd if he thought old Bill was some kind of hit man. It seemed that was more or less what he had been. The puzzle was starting to fit together finally. Marcus was still talking, and all she had to do now was listen.

Once Marcus began to tell the story, he could not stop, it was as if the floodgates had been opened. He tried to explain his mixed feelings of revulsion and gratitude towards Bill. When Marcus ran to the cottage he wasn't even sure what he was asking for, he said. It was Bill who had immediately begun an elaborate cover-up operation with a calm efficiency which suggested it was not the first time.

Bill had always said they were kindred spirits, the two of them, which in the early days had sent shivers down Marcus's spine. Bill unnerved him because Marcus never understood what he had got out of it all. He had always known Bill was a very wealthy man, but he never lived as if he was. He lived exactly the way you would have expected without the other secret side to him. For Bill Turpin the game had all been in the playing. He had talked to Marcus about the perfect murder, enjoying the conversation.

'And Marjorie Benson – it was Turpin who killed her, wasn't it?'

Marcus nodded. 'Not that he ever put it into words. He wouldn't, the bugger.'

'And Johnny Cooke?'

'Yes, poor Johnny,' said Marcus, in a voice which held no sympathy at all. 'Wrong place, wrong time. Probably his destiny. Suited Turpin though. I had my instructions, all I had to do was give a more or less verbatim account of Johnny Cooke's midnight visit the day after the murder. It certainly sounded like a confession – and what could make a murderer feel safer than to have another man convicted of his crime?'

Jennifer kept looking away. With difficulty she kept her voice neutral, pleasant even.

'So why did Bill Turpin kill Marjorie Benson? Who was she, for goodness' sake?'

Marcus shook his head. 'Didn't the diary tell you?' he asked.

Jennifer answered him quickly.

'Only that Marjorie had to die because she knew too much, because she could destroy everything.'

Marcus nodded. 'Yes,' he said. 'She was always the real mystery – not Bill. I never had a clue who she was – but she really did have something on the old man, him and his buddies.

'That's all I ever knew really. I had nothing and he helped me – she had everything and he killed her.'

'So did she try to blackmail him too?'

Marcus shook his head. 'I don't know, doesn't seem likely the way Johnny described her. Bill was in no doubt that she had come to Pelham Bay to get him though, in some way or other.'

'I wonder why he put her body in the sea,' Jennifer said suddenly.

'How the hell do I know?' Marcus replied with a question. 'I don't suppose he did. I would imagine he rolled her into the river, there where it cuts through the dunes, and she was swept into the estuary.'

Of course, that would make sense. Out of sight, out of mind, until the tide carried her back the next day. Bill Turpin might have expected it to be longer before she was found. If Jennifer had not swum out so far, the tide would probably have taken the body out to sea again without anyone noticing, it could have been several days before she was discovered. But in the end that turned to Bill Turpin's advantage. He had something tangible with which to frame poor Johnny Cooke . . .

Marcus was carrying on with his story. Jennifer listened carefully. Nobody had troubled him much for some time after Irene's death; he had been instructed to join the Freemasons, which he did.

Bill Turpin's friends were always referred to as just that – The Friends. At first Marcus had taken the innocent-sounding name for what it was, and not realised the extent of the formal structure involved. Only gradually had he learned just how big and influential The Friends were. They had considerable powers. With his move to London came a phone number, and he told her about his abortive attempts to trace it, always ending with an empty room rented to a non-existent company with an accommodation address. Apart from Bill, he only ever talked to disembodied voices, for many years to a voice that came to him through a voice box, so it sounded like a machine – he couldn't even tell if it was a man or a woman.

But he had learned that almost everything he wanted he could have, all he had to do was ask.

'And in return you gave them the power of the *Recorder*, and the influence of your whole business empire, and now your position as a junior minister,' she said.

She felt his eyes on her back.

'It's easy to moralise,' he said.

'I am not moralising,' she replied. 'I am stating the facts.

'I have no doubts at all that the way in which you have behaved is quite usual in the circles in which you move, and that there are always casualties. I don't have a problem with that. High finance, big business, politics – all spell corruption to me. I've come to believe that if you can't beat them, you may as well join them.

'I want my slice now.'

She had swung around to face him again as she spoke. She looked slightly flushed, the way she did when she was having sex. She was excited. What a woman, he thought.

How could he ever have let her go?

He smiled his appreciation.

'You are absolutely right,' he said. 'Every Government has a hidden agenda. Almost everyone in the Government in this country has an ulterior motive for everything that they do.

'Think of what we pay our politicians and the way most of them live. Doesn't often add up, does it? They nearly all have a lifestyle way above their income.

'And think about the great political coups nowadays. The overthrow of Communism in Russia, for example. All about money, wasn't it? Do you think Gorbachev did it on his own? Do you think he wasn't backed? And who keeps that man Yeltsin in power – he's so far up the Western backside it's embarrassing.

'Look at the Gulf war. All about money. All about oil. The most powerful governments in the world sent their armed forces into action on the orders of their money men. Everybody knows that – and why Saddam was quite deliberately let off the hook. If he had been wiped out, Iran would have ended up with a virtual oil monopoly. Bad economics, that's all.

'Even Bosnia is not what it seems. Europe's money market has been stood on its head by the disruption there – and that suits certain people very well.

'There is always a hidden agenda. Always. And I am just a tiny part of it, of course I am, part of the real motivation behind what happens in the corridors of power.'

Jennifer found what he was saying frightening yet impressive, and totally convincing. He was telling the truth. She had no doubts about that.

'Did you know that twelve per cent of the world's revenue is now generated by so-called criminal activity? If you pulled the plug, the economy would really collapse.

'The Friends are simply a group of people, many in very influential positions, all with something to give, who ensure each other's wealth and futures by securing information and power.'

Jennifer shivered.

'Surely the Masons wouldn't go as far as murder, would they?' she asked.

'Not as an organisation, of course not,' Marcus said. 'The Friends recruit the bad eggs from the Masons and con the good ones.

'I remember asking Bill how he had got rid of Irene's body, and how he was so sure my flat was clean. He touched the side of his nose and said not every PC Plod wanted to stay that way. I always assumed that he had called in a couple of tame policemen – and it made sense that they would be Masons.'

Jennifer imagined Todd's reaction to that little

theory. Good, decent Todd, why couldn't she have stuck with him?

She sat down again at the kitchen table. 'Do you know who runs The Friends, do you know other people involved?' she asked.

'No,' he replied. 'I've never known. That's the way it is . . . Sometimes I have suspected people, but never got any further. The only Friend I have ever definitely known was Bill Turpin.

'Other than that, they have always just contacted me over the phone.'

She turned to face him, keeping any expression out of her eyes. 'And they funded you from the start? Made it possible for you to make even more money?'

'Of course.'

'Tell me about the other murders,' she said.

'I thought you knew?'

He was unwilling to relive it all. He looked at her appealingly. She was still smiling, quite relaxed, sexy, cool, in control. Her lips were very full and red from the sex. He could smell her. Now that they were talking like this, he found that he wanted her even more than before. He had to make himself listen to her.

He stared at her, fascinated by the change in her.

'I want you to tell me,' she said. 'If we are to be a team from now on, you must tell me how they happened. I need to know the worst as well as the best.'

He took another deep drink of vodka. It had been after the first time she left him, he said, the time she had walked out when he hired the young stud for her. He had been distraught. Devastated. And in those days he really couldn't live without her sexually.

He was desperate for the kind of sexual satisfaction only she could give him. It got out of control.

She kept smiling. He was amazing. He was shifting the blame on to her again. If she had been there to fulfil his sexual needs, whatever it was he was about to tell her would never have happened. That seemed to be the theme.

She knew he liked Oriental women, he went on. There were two of them, just like the night she had interrupted him when he thought she was in Paris. This awful night, these two girls were delivered to his flat. They had both been virgins, and he had sex with each one of them again and again, but he could not satisfy himself. His body craved for Jennifer. These were just substitutes on whom he took out his frustration. And eventually it had gone too far.

He began to wallow in his own self pity. He broke down and began to cry in earnest. She went to his side and put her arms around him and comforted him.

'It will be all right now there are two of us standing together, sharing the guilt,' she said.

When he had calmed down she turned away from him once more.

'Go on,' she commanded. 'Tell me what happened.'

It was a re-enactment of the death of poor Irene. He had hammered so harshly into one of the girls that her neck had broken. He only realised it when her sister started screaming at him and pummelling his back with her little fists. Eventually he had rolled off the girl, who was stone dead, her head at an impossible angle. Her sister became hysterical. He had tried to quieten her, that was all.

'I didn't mean to hurt her as well, really I didn't.'
He was appealing to Jennifer now.

'When I put my hands around her neck it was just
to quieten her, that was all. But I closed my fingers
too much.

'I was over-excited – in a panic. Suddenly I felt
her go limp in my hands. They were both dead – but
I didn't mean to kill either of them. Really I didn't.'

He was bleating. She thought he sounded pathetic
as well as disgusting. But what he was telling her
now was so appalling she could barely take it in. It
was worse than she had expected. She had lived with
this man, married him after he had done all this,
been prepared to have his children. And she had
suspected so much and done nothing.

She heard herself say quite coolly: 'What did you
do next?'

'I called The Friends, called my contact. I was told
to check into a hotel for a couple of days and then
carry on as usual.

'When I went back to the flat it was as if nothing
had happened. The bodies were gone, the place as
it had been before. I knew there would be nothing
to link me with the murders. The Friends only use
professionals. Sometimes I cannot believe any of it
ever happened.'

How convenient, she thought. Vaguely she remembered newspaper stories about the mutilated bodies
of two Thai girls found tied together somewhere in
Dockland. Another sex murder, the killer never
found.

'Is that all?' she asked.

'What do you mean, is that all?'

'Any more bodies in the closet I should know about?' She made her voice light.

'Of course not. What do you take me for?'

'I don't know Marcus, not any more.'

Now her voice was flat. The tone in it startled him. She sounded different again.

'I think I'd like to put some clothes on,' she said.

He followed her into the bedroom and watched her take off the towelling robe and put it carefully on the bed. He was waiting for her to say something else, to make the next move. She had her back to him. Beneath the robe she was wearing the panties she had bought that day. She said nothing until she was dressed. She did not bother with a shower. She pulled on her old Levis and new sweat shirt, and then reached into the pocket of the dressing gown.

She drew out a small tape-recorder and held it up to him.

'Thanks Marcus, I have everything I need to make sure you rot in jail now,' she said.

His face disintegrated before her eyes. It took him ten seconds to grasp it all – no more. Even at a time like this, Marcus remained quick.

He reached for the bedside table lamp, wrenched it from its socket and lunged at her. She ducked and avoided the attack easily. Had she misjudged him? Was he going to try to kill her after all?

He took a step backwards. He looked pathetic. No, she had not misjudged him. He was a dangerous man, but still her power over him remained. That hadn't changed. Curious. He was trembling. He began to scream at her.

'It was all a trick, wasn't it? The whole damn thing. The sex – everything!

'You conned me, you bitch. You conned me.'

He leaned forward and caught hold of her arm, shaking her.

'Dreadful thing the collapse of morality, isn't it, Marcus?' she said. Even under the stress of the moment, Marcus remembered her saying that to him once before, when she had blackmailed him into divorcing her. Why did he continue to underestimate her?

She wriggled out of his grasp. He half fell across the bed, yelling incomprehensible obscenities at her. She was astonished by how calm she felt.

'Careful Marcus. Your true nature is showing.'

She thrust the tape-recorder into her handbag and headed for the front door. He was following her.

'What are you going to do?' he wailed.

'What do you think? I'm going straight to the police.'

'Huh.' For a brief moment he attempted to look as if he was in control.

'That'll do you no good. Half the top men in the Met are Friends.'

'I am glad you are so confident,' she said, reaching for the door handle.

He lunged at her again, one hand over hers, preventing her from opening the door. He was leering.

'Aren't you afraid of me?' he asked.

'No,' she said.

She never had been, which was probably the reason for her power over him.

'I could kill you, he said.

'No, you couldn't,' she replied.

Even now, with what she had done and what she had against him, she was sure it was the truth.

'Let go of me,' she ordered.

Slowly he removed his hand and stepped back. He looked beaten. She sincerely hoped he was. His face was dark with rage and despair and fear. She felt only revulsion for this twisted shadow of the man she had married. He was evil, and she was going to get him. She had done what she should have done years ago. She had used her power over him to nail him. She was glad.

It had been part of her plan to destroy him, and the atonement of her own guilt, that he should know she had deliberately set out to do so. That is why she had shown him the tape-recorder.

As she walked towards the door, she looked back over her shoulder at him.

'By the way, there never was a diary,' she said. That admission put her most at risk of all, but not to have told him, she was sure, would have been even more dangerous, because while she remained remarkably unafraid of Marcus, she was becoming quite terrified of his Friends.

As soon as she spoke she saw the panic lift and Marcus's brain start to work again.

'Then the only evidence is your tape, isn't it?' he said quietly. His eyes were ice, biting into her head.

He lurched forward for the final time and pulled her handbag from her with such force that the strap broke. He opened it and shook out the contents, catching the recorder as it fell. He tossed it forcefully into the room behind him so that it smashed apart as it hit the wall.

When he looked at her again his eyes were like death. It was time to run. Hastily she reached for the things which had fallen from her bag – all her keys were among them. As she bent down he kicked her in the kidneys with all his might. She fell to the floor, retching and clutching her side. The pain was intense, and so, at last, was the fear.

He stepped astride her, looking down, his face just a contorted mask. With his left hand he caught her by a shoulder, pulling her slightly upright towards him. He swung his right arm back, fist clenched. He was aiming for her face. She knew the full extent of his physical power. She cowered at his feet, too winded to speak, and waited for the blow, certain now that she had indeed made a fatal misjudgement. She was suddenly quite sure that he was going to kill her after all.

Abruptly he let her drop.

'Just get out, you bitch,' he hissed. The voice was barely human.

Something had stopped him. She had got it right, but only just. She made a desperate grab for her keys, abandoning money, credit cards, and all else that had been in her bag. Still clutching her side, she stumbled into the lift and made her escape.

Twenty

She half ran to the carpark where she had left the Porsche. She wanted to get away. The sun was still shining, it was not yet five o'clock, and that seemed wrong. It should be the middle of the night. As she began to pull the car out of the carpark, she hit the accelerator with such fury that she stalled the engine, something she never did. She was in more of a state than she realised. What Marcus had told her was so appalling she could barely take it in.

When she had put what she considered to be a safe distance between herself and Marcus, she slowed the Porsche to a halt. She leaned back in her seat and unzipped her jeans. Tucked into her pants was a micro tape-recorder, a masterpiece of modern engineering. She wound the tape back a little and checked that it had recorded. Incredible quality for such a small and concealed instrument. She had deliberately let Marcus believe that he had removed the only evidence from her – she still felt that he would find it impossible to hurt her seriously himself, but was sure his friends would have no reservations.

She sat for a moment looking at the small tape-recorder. She had achieved all that she had set out to achieve. But she felt quite sick.

She must calm down, be careful. She mustn't blow it now. She had the tape and the computer disc. She certainly had him. She turned the car east and headed for Scotland Yard. After a couple of minutes, she pulled into the side of the road, remembering what Marcus had said.

'Half the top men in the Met were Friends.'

The ramblings of a desperate man, or the truth? Probably a bit of both, she thought – a gross exaggeration for certain, but one friend in the Met could be enough to scupper her. And anyway, how could she be sure of getting to somebody who would take her seriously if she went in cold. She had not thought beyond conning and confronting Marcus, she realised. That had been a daunting enough task. So, now how should she handle it? Todd Mallett. She trusted him totally. She would call him and seek his advice. Damn. She had left her mobile phone at home in Richmond. Unlike her, but then it was an unlikely time in her life.

And so she decided to drive home. The traffic would be terrible at that time of day, and it would probably take her the best part of forty-five minutes to get there from Chelsea. None the less it was a good idea. She needed the comfort of her own familiar surroundings around her. She would phone Todd as soon as she got there.

The journey took forty minutes. She pulled the Porsche into the driveway and opened the electronic door to the garage with the flick of a switch inside the car. The garage door shut behind her. There was a connecting door from within the garage to the house. She opened the glove compartment at the front of the Porsche and took out the computer disc. Clutching her car keys, the computer disc, and the micro tape in her left hand, she used her right to unlock the house door, ran up the steps to the living room, flung herself full length on the big squashy sofa, and burst into a fit of painful, body-racking sobs.

It was a luxury she could not allow herself for long. It was no good falling apart now. She hoisted herself up to a sitting position, reached for the telephone on the coffee table, and asked directory inquiries for the number of Durraton Police station. She dialled it. Todd was not in and was not expected back that evening. Damn. And damn again.

She called directory inquiries once more, and got Todd's home number. Then she looked at her watch. Still not six o'clock. There was no way he would be home by now, not Todd. He must be off somewhere working. She would leave it at least half an hour. She did not particularly wish to speak to his wife Angela, she was not sure if she could deal with that right now.

She was also not sure that she could cope with being on her own and keeping all of this to herself for much longer. It might be time for Anna. She thought about it. Yes, it definitely was. She needed another brain, and Anna was the one person she could trust one hundred per cent.

She dialled the Barnes number. Anna picked up the phone, which was a relief. Then she remembered that Dominic had told her he was off on a seminar. Would that be a problem? She hoped not.

Anna was furious with her.

'What on earth is going in?' she stormed. 'You put the fear of God into Dominic this morning. He actually seemed concerned about you, said you weren't yourself at all – which would usually have delighted him . . .'

Jennifer did not have the energy to respond. Her voice was quiet and distant. It stopped Anna short.

'If you can come over this evening I will tell you everything,' Jennifer said. 'I need your help.'

'Can't you come over here?' asked Anna.

'No. I have some calls to make and I may have to leave messages and I need to use the computer and it would all be too complicated.'

'Don't babble,' said Anna, in an attempt at normality. 'Dominic's away and I was just about to give Pandora her tea and put her to bed.'

Jennifer was ready for her. 'Give her her tea, put her to bed, and when she's asleep carry her out to the car and bring her over here. You've done it before, the last time she never stirred.'

'Oh God,' said Anna. 'OK. I should be able to make it by eight.'

She paused. 'And Jennifer . . . this had better be good.'

Then Jennifer did manage a wry laugh.

'I don't think "good" is quite the word for it,' she said.

She put the receiver down with, in spite of everything, just the merest flash of the sense of well-being that she almost always experienced after talking to Anna. She went to the bathroom and peeled off her clothes. She put them in a plastic bag for the dustbin. Even the much-loved old Levis. A bit extreme, perhaps, but when it was all over she wanted nothing that would ever remind her of Marcus again.

She kept thinking about the sex with him. She had made a conscious decision to go to bed with him again, because she knew no other way that she could have convinced him to trust her and talk to her like he had, no other way to use her power over him. Jennifer had never lied to him before, she didn't think, and never pretended either – certainly not in bed. That had given her all the advantages in the final confrontation, but it had been obscene, and with what he had told her afterwards, the obscenity was overwhelming.

Suddenly she felt nauseous again. It happened quickly. She fell to her knees in front of the lavatory pan and just managed to lift the lid before being heartily and extensively sick.

Afterwards she felt very slightly better. She clambered under the power shower and let a steaming hot jet of water drench her in its powerful stream. She stood there for a couple of minutes and then energetically shampooed her hair and soaped every half inch of her body, as if she was washing the last vestiges of Marcus away. By the time she had let the water pour over her for several minutes more, she really did feel better.

She dressed in tee-shirt and leggings, wrapped a towel around her hair, and then tried Todd at home. Angela answered. He was not there. She really was not having much luck.

'Do you know when he'll be back?' she asked.

'Haven't a clue.'

The voice at the other end was cold and unhelpful. Angela had never forgiven Jennifer for not only escaping from North Devon, but also, in every practical appearance at least, being highly successful in London. Jennifer had conquered worlds Angela could only dream about, and it made the policeman's wife resentful. Little did she know how much at that very moment Jennifer envied her her rural family existence with Todd and their children. 'Is there any-where I can contact him?' she asked.

'Nope. He's off playing cricket in a field somewhere.'

Cricket? Jennifer couldn't believe it. It was absurd. Her ex-husband had just confessed mass murder to her, and the only man she knew who could help her and whom she could trust, a policeman re-investigating one of the murders, was playing cricket.

'Please,' she said. 'It's vital that I contact him.' She was pleading, but the voice did not become any more friendly.

'He's playing cricket,' Angela repeated. 'And then it'll be the pub afterwards. You know Todd.'

'You know Todd,' repeated Jennifer to herself in her head. Oh God, did Angela know about her and Todd? Or did she just suspect? It all seemed so unimportant now . . . to her. But she had to speak to him, she had to.

'Look,' she said. 'It's about the murders in the Bay. I have new evidence. I must talk to him, hasn't he got a mobile phone?'

She sensed Angela relenting slightly. Maybe she recognised the desperation in her voice. Not that she would be much moved by that. Come to think of it, Angela had always given every sign of disliking her, even when they were at school together, even when they were supposed to be friends.

'It's not working, I just tried it, it might be the batteries, they don't seem to hold charge, he's been meaning to get new ones,' said Angela. 'As soon as he gets in I'll tell him to call you. That's all I can do. Give me your number.'

Jennifer did so. It was the best she was going to

get. Anyway, she supposed another few hours wouldn't make a difference. She was probably being hysterical.

In North Devon, Angela replaced the receiver and reached for the message pad kept on the little shelf by the phone. It was where the whole family jotted messages and everyone checked it religiously. That way Todd would get his message as soon as he walked through the door, even if Angela had already gone to bed – which was quite likely knowing his cricket nights. Blast. The notebook wasn't there. She roundly cursed her boys, one of whom had doubtless not replaced the book where it should be kept. Her endeavour to extract an admission from any of them proved fruitless. They barely paused in their extermination of innocent planets featured on the latest computer game which they had jacked into the living-room TV. The noise was deafening. And the baby was crying again – that child never seemed to stop.

Angela swiftly abandoned her rather half-hearted search for the notepad, and began a futile attempt to quieten her now screaming daughter.

'To hell with Jennifer Stone,' she muttered to herself.

When Todd Mallet came home there was no written note waiting for him, and his wife was, indeed, already in bed and asleep.

While she waited for Anna, Jennifer towel-dried her hair and then set herself up in her study with laptop computer and tape-recorder. She jotted one or two thoughts into the laptop, just as she had done every day since the whole business had begun.

Then she braced herself for an unpleasant task, but something she none the less wanted to do. She wound back the tape in her voice-activated recorder and listened to her conversation with Marcus. It had only lasted around half an hour, she realised, but it had been the longest and most terrible half hour of her life.

She began to transcribe the tape methodically into her computer. By the time the doorbell rang she had almost completed the transcript. It made chilling reading.

At the front door she paused. She wanted to be quite sure who was outside. She peered through the peep-hole, and there stood Anna, comforting, wonderful Anna, clutching a woollen-wrapped bundle which presumably contained Pandora. She opened the door laughing.

'Shush,' commanded Anna.

Jennifer dropped her voice to a whisper. 'Do you want to put her to bed?' she mouthed.

Anna nodded. She followed Jennifer upstairs to a bedroom. Jennifer pulled back the duvet on one of the twin beds, and Anna carefully unwrapped her bundle and revealed a deeply sleeping Pandora. The child barely stirred as her mother laid her gently in the bed. Jennifer pulled the cover around her neck. Pandora snuggled down. A wonderful expression that, and when you watched a child settling into deep sleep you really knew what 'snuggling down' was, Jennifer thought.

She realised she was just standing there appreciating the peacefulness of the little girl while Anna tugged impatiently at her arm.

Together they left the room.

'Come on,' said Anna, taking charge. 'Let's sit down with a stiff drink, you look absolutely diabolical.'

'Thanks,' replied Jennifer.

But she caught a glimpse of herself in one of the mirrors on the landing, and it was indeed the truth. She had not dried her hair properly, or combed it through. It was damp and tangled. There were dark bags under her eyes which were still red and swollen from the tears she kept being unable to prevent, and her skin was blotchy and raw-looking for the same reason.

Downstairs she headed for the kitchen to make drinks. Anna steered her to an armchair in the sitting room.

'Sit down, for Chrissake,' she commanded.

Jennifer did so, obediently like a child. Anna disappeared into the kitchen and returned with a bottle of Scotch, an ice bucket, a big bottle of fizzy mineral water and two glasses.

'I don't drink whisky,' remarked Jennifer mildly.

'Exactly,' said her friend.

And Jennifer was reminded of the uncannily similar incident with her mother two days earlier. Two days? Was it only two days? She could not believe all that had happened.

Anna handed Jennifer a tumbler filled almost to the brim with whisky and ice and water, then poured a much smaller one for herself. She had to drive Pandora home, after all.

She watched Jennifer take a deep drink and slump back in her chair.

'Shoot,' she ordered.

Jennifer just looked at her. She didn't know where

to begin. She said 'Umm.' No more words came. As ever, Anna seemed able to almost read her mind.

'Begin at the beginning,' she coaxed.

And so Jennifer did. She began with how she had found the body of Marjorie Benson in the sea at Pelham Bay, how Mark Piddle had come to interview her and they had embarked on an all-powerful relationship that had lasted most of their adult lives.

This much Anna knew. Then Jennifer told her about the disappearance of Irene Nichols, Mark's former girlfriend, which Anna also knew about because she had read about it in the papers – all of which had mentioned the Piddell connection – but Anna was amazed that Jennifer had never told her about it in all their years of friendship. Surely it wasn't the kind of thing you forgot. And Anna, who did not mean to interrupt, heard herself say exactly that.

'In a way I did forget,' said Jennifer in a very small voice. 'I made myself forget, which is just part of my guilt.'

She went on then, becoming more and more fluent, taking Anna through it all in chronological order, how the old nightmare had returned from the moment of her return to Pelham Bay; and how, with every new little piece of information she gained, her terrible suspicions about the man that she married became a growing certainty.

She told Anna of the half-mad plot she had hatched. Her determination to trap Marcus. How she had decided to sleep with him again, to convince him that she was indeed his kindred spirit in more ways than just sexually. She had been sure she could do it if she kept her head. And she had been sure she was the only person in the world who could trap Marcus: that was why she had felt compelled to go through with it.

She told Anna almost every detail of the night she spent with Marcus, and how she tricked him in the morning so she could search his flat and how she took the computer tape to Dominic.

Then she stopped.

'But you still don't know for certain, do you?' Anna queried.

'Oh yes I do,' said Jennifer. 'I went back. Then I played my trump card. You haven't followed it, have you?'

'Not entirely, obviously,' admitted Anna.

'I convinced him that we were a true pair, that I only wanted to be his equal, to share every secret with him. He always said we were two of a kind. I convinced him that was so. That way I knew I could trap him.'

She stood up.

'This afternoon I spent three hours in bed with Marcus, during which we drove each other to the heights of physical excitement that we could only ever reach together. At least, as far as he was concerned we reached them.'

Her words were quite clinical. She sounded robotic. It was the only way she could do this.

'Sexual power is an extraordinary thing,' she went on. 'Marcus knows he has always had complete sexual power over me. That is why each time I have left him I have never dared see him again. In spite of whatever I might be feeling about him, I could never trust myself.

'I was banking on him overlooking the sexual

331

power I have always had over him, or at least, in his usual arrogant way, totally ignoring the possibility that I might ever use it against him.'

Anna was just staring at her, mesmerised.

'Stay there,' said Jennifer.

She was in charge again now, even if only briefly. Jennifer left the room and returned with her little tape-recorder. She put it on the coffee table.

'When we had finished in bed this afternoon, I called Marcus's bluff,' she announced in a matter of fact manner. 'It worked. And this is the result.'

She pushed the recorder's play button and went back to her armchair opposite Anna. As the tape played she drank whisky steadily and watched her friend's face. Anna appeared to be in a state of complete shock. The conversation ended before the tape. Jennifer rose to turn the machine off. After she had done so, there was complete silence in the room. Anna leaned forwards and poured herself another whisky.

She looked at her friend. Jennifer's face was blank, expressionless.

'God, you took a risk,' said Anna at last.

Jennifer seemed startled. 'What do you mean?' she said.

'He could have killed you,' replied her friend in a hoarse whisper.

'No,' said Jennifer, gingerly fingering her side which was beginning to display fairly substantial bruising. 'A kick in the kidneys was as far as he could go. Marcus could never quite kill me. In any case, in the end he didn't think he had a reason to.'

And she told Anna how she had tricked Marcus with her second tape-recorder.

Anna took a swig of whisky.

'I have never been so shocked in all my life,' she managed to say.

Then: 'Why haven't you taken this straight to the police?'

'After I turned off the tape, his last words to me were: "Half the top cops in the Met are Friends." '

'Oh come on, Jennifer, he's bluffing you with that. It's too far-fetched.'

'Really. I'm sure he was bluffing when he said half – but I wouldn't like to call his bluff that they don't have anybody high up in the Met. Anyway, can you think of anything much more far-fetched than this entire story?'

Anna admitted that no, she couldn't, not off-hand. But in that case she wanted to know exactly what Jennifer was planning to do. It seemed to her that she was sitting on dynamite.

Jennifer explained about Todd, the one policeman she could trust. She was waiting for him to call. Either in London or back in North Devon, she would make sure she saw him in the morning. That would be the beginning of the end of it all. What else could she do?

Anna had no fast answer to that, but still some questions to put.

'So who are these murky Friends, do you know?'

Jennifer shook her head. 'I'm not even sure how much Marcus knows about who they are.

'After I've talked to Todd tomorrow, that will be for the police and I suppose the Government to find out, won't it? All I do know is that they are devious enough and powerful enough to have enabled Marcus literally to get away with murder.

'He really has turned into a monster.'

Anna put her now empty glass on the table at her side. 'Have you considered the danger you are still in?' she asked.

'I don't think I am actually. I told you. Marcus does not think I have any evidence.'

'Maybe not, but his friends may want to play safe.'

'He thinks he has dealt with it, he probably won't even tell them.'

'Maybe not,' said Anna again.

'Are the doors and windows locked?' she asked.

'Anna, the place is like Fort Knox. Look, folding bars, all shut and locked. Marcus always insisted on incredible security . . .'

She paused, realising what she had said.

'Ironic really,' remarked Anna, pouring herself yet another Scotch.

Jennifer experienced a brief flash of normality. 'Anna, you're driving. You mustn't drink any more.'

'Coming from you that's rich – but you are right,' said her friend. She thought for a moment.

When she spoke again she sounded decisive. 'You shouldn't be here on your own. Look, let's get a taxi back to Barnes, and you stay the night with me.'

'I told you, I'm waiting for Todd to call,' said Jennifer stubbornly.

'All right, then I'll just have to stay here,' said Anna. 'No reason to go home with Dom away in any case. Just remind me to phone him before we go to bed. He'll go frantic if he rings home and only gets the answering machine.'

'I love you, missus,' said Jennifer.

'I should think so,' her friend replied. She added that she was starving. As usual she had fed her daughter and forgotten herself. What about getting a pizza delivered? Jennifer agreed readily enough, although she was not a bit hungry. The thought of food made her feel sick again, in fact.

But she dialled the number of the local Pizza Express and let Anna do the ordering. As she did so she reflected that she was glad Anna was staying for more reasons than one. It had not occurred to her before that she might be putting her friend in danger by confiding in her, and it was typical of Anna that she did not think of it that way either. None the less, it was reassuring that Anna would be with her now until the whole business was dealt with – because her security really was first-class. She was sure nobody could get to either of them as long as they were locked in the Richmond Hill house.

When the pizza arrived, Jennifer was surprised to find that she was hungry after all. The smell of it seemed to revive her battered senses. She opened a bottle of red Italian wine, and the two women settled down to eat and drink. While they did so they went over and over again the implications of the last few days.

'It sends shivers down my spine,' remarked Anna. 'I just can't understand how a man like Marcus could go mad like that. The first murder of Irene is just too awful on its own, but then to go on and kill two more in the same way. And don't forget that's just what he has told you about.'

'Don't,' said Jennifer.

Anna repeated that she didn't understand how Marcus could have allowed himself to be taken over by the same sexual behaviour again and again, when he knew how dangerous it could be.

'There is nothing more compelling than the sex urge,' said Jennifer, who knew what she was talking about.

'Look at the way men in the public eye go again and again to massage parlours and knocking shops. They know they are going to get found out, and yet they can't stop themselves.

'Look at the way men in powerful positions come to believe that they can literally get away with anything, that the laws of the land aren't for them, that they can get away with murder if they choose. Right back through history there are examples of men in high places believing they are above and beyond the law.'

Anna sighed. 'The sex urge and the power complex,' she said. 'There is also the survival urge – and that is probably the greatest of all, whatever you say.'

'While we are citing examples of such things, did you read about that couple in America who were involved in the Mafia and killed their own daughter because she presented a threat to them?' Jennifer shook her head. 'Well, maybe you should look it up in cuttings . . . if you get the chance,' said Anna.

'Don't be melodramatic' replied Jennifer.

'Melo-bloody-dramatic? My best friend tells me that her ex-husband is a mass murderer under the control of some secret effin' criminal organisation, and then she says I am melo-bloody-dramatic?'

She was beginning to get a bit drunk. They both were.

'Shall I open another bottle?' Jennifer asked.

'Are you sure you wouldn't rather call a cab and be bundled off to Barnes?'

'Quite sure.' Jennifer didn't think that was a good idea at all.

'Oh . . . get another bloody bottle then.' Anna gave in.

An hour or so later she called Dominic.

'Don't say anything on the phone,' instructed Jennifer.

'Do you think I'm effin' daft?' asked Anna in reply.

She had every intention of saying as little as possible to Dominic anyway. He would know she had drunk far too much as soon as she spoke, he always did.

When the two women had finished the second bottle, they prepared for bed.

'Are you sure this blessed house is safe?' asked Anna one last time.

'Nobody could get in here, I promise you,' said Jennifer.

'And before I come up I shall put the alarm on down here. If a mouse stirs we will be wakened by the biggest racket you have ever heard – and it's connected to the cop shop.'

'Ah, to Marcus's friends,' murmured Anna.

She was slightly drunker than Jennifer, but then, she didn't usually drink as much any more.

'Go to bed,' said Jennifer. 'New toothbrushes, towels etc. in the bathroom for you.'

Anna obediently hoisted herself up the stairs. Jennifer watched her with affection. At the top of the stairs, her friend turned. She stood above her holding the banister and swaying gently.

'Have you got mice then?' she asked.

'Go to bed,' said Jennifer once more, giggling in spite of everything.

Anna focused with difficulty, and all that whisky and red wine was starting to cause problems with her diction.

'D'you remember when I told you Pelham Bay wasn't Hollywood? Place ish more like bleedin' Chicago! It'sh like a gangster movie, thish ... The Pelham Connection ...'

She threw her arms above her head in an extravagant theatrical gesture and nearly fell over.

'Go to bed, Anna,' said Jennifer yet again, this time as sternly as she could manage. But she was grinning broadly.

Dear Anna, what a good friend she was. Uncertainly Anna began to make her way along the landing to the bedroom she always used when she stayed with Jennifer. But she turned for one final time. She wagged a finger at Jennifer in what was supposed to be an imposing manner.

'Jusht don't unlock your bedroom windows,' she ordered.

'I won't,' promised Jennifer. 'Good night.'

As she turned away, Anna called out: 'Aren't you coming up?'

'I'll be right behind you,' said Jennifer. 'Just something I want to do.'

She headed for the study where her laptop computer was still set up on the desk. She switched it on again and went to work. When she left the room fifteen minutes later, she was carrying a back-up floppy disc of all the material she had pumped into the machine over the last few days, as well as Marcus's G7 disc. She entered the living room briefly to remove the micro tape from its recorder and then climbed the stairs. She could not resist peeping in at

338

Pandora and then at Anna. Both were soundly asleep. Anna lying flat on her back. The booze had knocked her out. She was snoring. Jennifer smiled. It was reassuring to have them there with her, she had to admit. She went into her room and put the floppy discs and the tape on the bed, then she paused. It was no good – Anna had got her at it.

She left the room and toured the house, checking all the window locks, the bars downstairs, and that she had indeed part-set the burglar alarm. It would go off if anything moved downstairs, or if any of the locked or barred external doors and windows were tampered with. Everything was fine. The place really was totally secure. She had known that – but paranoia was obviously setting in. Back in her bedroom, she took the tape and the computer discs and put them both under her pillow.

'Just in case,' she said to herself, feeling faintly ridiculous.

Then she went into the connecting bathroom and brushed her teeth and cleaned her face. Old habits, she thought, even at a time like this. Finally she undressed and climbed gratefully beneath the goose-down filled duvet. Bliss. She was exhausted and she knew she could do no more that day, so she may as well give in to sleep. If Todd did call during the night, there was a bedside extension and she would wake up when the phone rang. If not she would deal with it in the morning.

She could not even think about Marcus any more. She had to have sleep. Even as she was falling exhausted into her bed, she had wondered whether sleep would be possible. Amazingly it was. A combination of the relief of having shared her burden, of the close proximity of her best friend sleeping peacefully in the next room, and the soporific effect of two bottles of red wine preceded by rather a lot of whisky overwhelmed her.

She fell quickly into a deep and dreamless sleep. Her first proper sleep since the nightmare had begun.

Twenty One

Marcus removed the incriminating tape from the smashed recorder he had taken from Jennifer, extracted it from its plastic casing, cut it into several pieces with sharp scissors and fed the remains to the waste disposal unit in his kitchen sink. He stood by it until the grinding finished, only then satisfied that the tape had been effectively destroyed. He was still stunned by what had happened. What a crazy fool he had been, ruled by his cock yet again. If she had not told him about the tape, she could have broken him. Brought down by her own self-indulgence, he supposed.

Then a thought struck him – Jennifer should have remembered how streetwise he was. Even with The Friends behind you, men did not achieve what Marcus had achieved without a quick and brilliant brain which continued to operate under extremes of pressure.

Christ, he thought suddenly, what do photographers and reporters do if they think someone might try to stop them getting a picture or a story? They have two cameras, two tape-recorders; the old double bluff. He had done it himself when he was on the road. So had Jennifer used that trick on him? He did not know, he must think this through.

There really was no other evidence, was there? The copy of Bill Turpin's notebook was still on the kitchen table. The original was presumably already with the police, but it meant nothing without the appropriate software. Software. He decided to be methodical. He went into his study to check that nothing had been touched. It all looked in order, but suddenly, and with dazzling clarity, he became quite frighteningly sure that he had left the G7 floppy disc in the drive of the IBM computer the last time he used it. He remembered the phone ringing just as he finished editing a document, and when he returned to the computer to close it down he had been preoccupied. He checked the drive. Nothing. A little shakily he unlocked one of his big filing cabinets and began checking through his store of floppy discs. The G7 disc was missing.

He relocked the cabinet, sat down at his desk and went over and over what had happened and what it could mean. The computer disc alone would not be enough to incriminate him, would it? It would not necessarily lead back to him at all, but it would have his finger prints on it. Still, that could probably be dealt with. It wouldn't put him in the dock for murder, anyway. But if she still did have a tape? The more he considered it, the more he became convinced that the bitch really had outsmarted him. Two of a kind, he thought.

It was not the first time he had underestimated Jennifer. It would definitely be the last. He realised he was sweating, although it was quite cool in the flat. Jennifer would have been interested to see that he could sweat out of bed. He was also shaking quite badly now.

He had to make sure that there was no second tape. Would she have gone straight to the police?

He would have to confess to his Friends, like he always did, and he would just tell them they needed to get the disc off Jennifer and search for a tape. That was all. They had always done what he asked, hadn't they? They had always given him everything he wanted, they would do so again, wouldn't they?

And so he picked up the phone and dialled. It was still only just after five o'clock.

By five-fifteen a specialist team was on the case. Two men in a British Telecom van arrived to check out Jennifer Stone's Richmond home at just past six o'clock, only minutes after she arrived there herself.

They could see there was someone inside the house. And by using powerful binoculars were able to identify Jennifer – from photographs biked to them en route from a source in the *Globe* office – through the big picture window on the landing. So far so good, at least they knew where she was. Swiftly they located the position of the distribution point governing the phone lines into the house. In built up areas like Richmond Hill, these are concealed either beneath concrete pillars on the inner side of the pavements or behind green-painted iron cabinets set into walls. The distribution point for Jennifer's house was beneath a concrete pillar which, with the right key, simply unlocks and is easily removed, revealing up to 1000 pairs of wire, connecting subscribers to the exchange. To sort out which wires lead where, a copy of British Telecom's records for the area is essential.

These men had such access, just as they had access to a British Telecom van, although they were not employed by BT at all.

By the time Jennifer made her second phone call

to Todd Mallet – and spoken to Angela, the two bogus telephone engineers had successfully fitted a tap, with a radio transmitter allowing them to monitor Jennifer's line from a distance.

They listened in to that call and reasoned, taking into account the time by which Jennifer had arrived in Richmond and her apparent desperation to reach the Devon policeman, that it was an acceptable risk to assume that Jennifer Stone had yet to take her evidence to the police. It seemed there was still time to act.

An hour or so later, the BT van pulled away. Anna, driving her Golf GTI without a great deal of skill as usual and noticing frighteningly little, had not even been aware of the departing van as she swung into Jennifer's driveway. Jennifer herself hadn't looked out of the window since arriving home, but to have remained in the street outside could have aroused suspicion, if only from a nosy neighbour. Because of its radio transmitter, the tap could be monitored from any place at all where the receiver was able to pick up an adequate signal. There was no sign of a surveillance operation in Jennifer Stone's tree-lined street that night, yet her home was being watched every second, and when the downstairs and then the upstairs lights in the big imposing house were eventually switched off, at about midnight, figures started moving silently in the street again. Two dark-clad men slipped through the gate and disappeared into the shadows of the garden.

The explosion happened at just after five in the morning. Its roar could be heard right across the river in Chiswick and Brentford and in the other direction as far away as Kingston. It was a huge and devastating thing. The house which took the main force of the blast was almost completely flattened. Daylight was to show that barely more than a few isolated bricks remained intact. Such was the power of the blast that, although detached and separated by trees and high walls, the two houses on either side were both almost completely demolished too. One was empty – its inhabitants thankfully away on holiday. The elderly couple in the second house were killed. Neighbours in other badly damaged houses, particularly the one directly opposite, also suffered appalling injuries. A pregnant woman was not expected to last the day in intensive care. A child was blinded, and one man lost both his legs.

Jennifer Stone, Anna McDonald, and her daughter Pandora were in the house at the heart of the explosion.

All three of them died at once. They were blown to pieces.

Twenty Two

Dominic was on his way into breakfast when the police called at his seminar hotel to break the news to him. They only knew Anna and Pandora were in the Richmond house because Anna had called a neighbour to ask her to feed her cat. The neighbour, an early riser and a worrier, had heard of the Richmond explosion on a radio news flash soon after it happened and immediately called the police. Two officers from the Yorkshire force took Dominic, who never listened to the radio in the mornings, into the hotel's conservatory overlooking the Yorkshire Moors and told him as gently as possible what had happened.

There was no gentle way to tell Dominic McDonald that his wife and only daughter were both dead.

Dominic did not seem able to register it. Eventually the police left. Shocked colleagues, also informed by the police, tried to comfort him. Dominic told them he would rather be alone and that he wanted to go home. He seemed calm and composed in spite of his distress. He went to his room to pack and then he disappeared.

They found him late that night shivering on a rock escarpment. It was raining and he was soaked to the skin and shivering violently. He was wearing only light trousers and a shirt. His feet were bleeding and bruised because he had forgotten to put shoes on.

When he saw the rescue party clambering towards him he was not sure if he felt relief or disappointment. He was well aware of how easy it could be to die of exposure in open moorland at night, even in late May. But he was not at all sure he wanted to live without Anna and Pandora.

They took him home to Barnes and as he stepped through the door of the comfortable, reassuring town house he burst into tears. The sobs racked his whole body. He could not stop crying for two days.

Todd Mallett was phoned at home while he was drinking his morning tea. The shock was terrible. He had vaguely heard on the radio of an explosion in the London area, but he didn't even know where Jennifer Stone lived. No warning bells had sounded. Why should they? Mrs Stone was listed as Jennifer's next of kin. She had to be told, and when the news came through to Durraton police station the desk sergeant, an alert and ambitious man, remembered seeing an entry in the log left by the duty officer the previous evening. Jennifer Stone had been trying to contact Detective Inspector Mallett.

Todd said very little, except that he would go to see Mrs Stone himself, and he wanted a policewoman to go with him.

After he put the receiver down he was overcome at first with a great sense of sorrow and loss, and then, when his brain cleared a little, his head was filled with crazy thoughts and suspicions. No. It was all too far-fetched. There couldn't be that kind of connection. And he couldn't work it out yet, but there were many questions to be asked. Frightening questions.

His wife came into the kitchen, fresh from the bathroom shower, and he told her about Jennifer. She went white.

'Oh my god, Todd,' she said.

And then she confessed how Jennifer had called the previous night and she had somehow failed to pass the message on to him.

'She sounded a bit desperate, I suppose . . . but I didn't know . . .' Angela Mallett's voice tailed away.

Todd could think of nothing to say to her. Not for the first time since their marriage, he only narrowly stopped himself lashing out with his fists. Certainly he couldn't be bothered to hide his own personal grieving.

The unanswered questions were whirling around his head, including the most obvious one of all which he had forgotten to ask the station sergeant and which had not been volunteered.

He called back.

'What caused the explosion?' he asked.

'Gas,' replied the desk sergeant. 'Apparently it was one of those great gas explosions, like Ronan Point, and like that one that flattened God knows how many apartment blocks in America last year. Some fault which had caused a dangerous build-up for weeks . . .'

Todd interrupted. 'Are they sure?'

'I suppose so, sir.'

Todd replaced the receiver. Gas. And yes, if his suspicions were right they would be sure, like they had been sure all those years ago of Johnny Cooke's guilt and Mark Piddle's innocence.

Mrs Stone's face turned grey when she opened the

door to Todd and a uniformed woman police sergeant.

She had been in a trance since hearing, a few minutes earlier on the radio news, about the explosion on Richmond Hill. She had immediately called Jennifer's phone number. It had been unobtainable. She had been just about to call the police, but something kept holding her back. She could not quite bring herself to make the call. Now they were with her.

Todd did not need to say anything.

'Jennifer?'

And the word was more than a sentence. It was the final chapter of a life story.

He nodded. He felt so inadequate.

He should have been prepared for the next words, but he wasn't.

'Could you drink a cup of tea?' asked the old lady.

On an impulse he reached out and took her in his arms. She clung to him, her whole body shaking, and he realised he was weeping.

Marcus also heard the news on the radio. He listened to the six a.m. bulletin as usual. The victims were not named and neither was the street in that first report. Richmond Hill was quite enough. He knew at once, and he cried out in anguish and despair, self-disgust and frustration, and of course, self-pity.

He phoned his contact number at once. The line had been disconnected. He was still in his bedroom. He climbed back into bed, pulled the covers over his head, and lay there whimpering. He just wanted to hide away from the whole world for ever.

When the doorbell rang, his first instinct was to stay there under the covers in the warm darkness.

But the ringing was insistent, and then he thought, perhaps it's them.

Half hysterical, his eyes wild and red-rimmed, he ran to the door. It was the police, a uniformed inspector and constable, let in by a surprised porter – he wasn't used to police calls in his smart Chelsea building. The police were there simply because Marcus was, after all, Jennifer's ex-husband, and he was a government minister. They had come to tell him – but it was apparent that he already knew.

They expressed condolences and shock. Marcus could not communicate. He was incoherent. Eventually the two men said they would call back later.

'He was in a state, wasn't he?' said the new-to-the-job young constable on the way down in the lift from Marcus's apartment.

'He must still have loved her, even if they were divorced.'

'Hmph,' snorted the inspector, who didn't like politicians very much. 'His sort only love themselves.'

Jennifer Stone's funeral in Durraton Parish Church was a grim affair.

Todd Mallett sat in the back of the church. He was convinced her death was not an accident, but in spite of his requests that the cause of the explosion be checked and double checked, the same answers always came up. The blast had been caused by a massive build-up of gas over a period of time. A leak which had gone unnoticed. It had happened before. It was just a tragic accident.

Todd watched Mrs Stone walk into the church. She looked broken, suddenly a very very old lady, grief etched in her face. She was being comforted by her son. The funeral had been delayed a week to allow him time to return from Australia and help with the arrangements.

They both looked to be in total shock. Todd Mallett was still in shock.

Just along the aisle he noticed a man of an acutely intelligent appearance who could not stop crying. He was every bit as distraught as Mrs Stone. Such was the degree of his distress that Todd made inquiries about him. The man was Dominic McDonald, the husband of Jennifer Stone's friend who had died with her. No wonder he was in such distress. He had lost wife and daughter in one foul instant. Todd did not really know why, but after the service he felt moved to approach the man.

'It was good of you to come,' he said.

Dominic did not even focus. 'She was my wife's best friend,' he said simply.

On an impulse Todd asked him if he knew if Jennifer was working on anything before she died, if she had confided in her best friend. The other man looked at him – just for an instant – as if he was mad. It had not occurred to Dominic McDonald to put anything together, to consider a link between Jennifer's extraordinary computer disc and her disturbing behaviour and her death. Dominic did not have that sort of brain. His entire family had been wiped out in a freak accident – and that was that. He shook his head in anguish and walked away. Nothing could get through to him.

Marcus Piddell sat at the front of the church. There was no way that he was going to blow all he had ever gained, no way he was going to make a sacrifice of himself with one emotional outburst. He was on autopilot, he was a nervous wreck, but he continued to operate, to do what he had to do.

His statement about his ex-wife's death, expressing his shock and distress, had been properly prepared and issued to the press. Now he was at her funeral. He was immaculately dressed in a black three-piece suit. He looked grief-stricken, his face the perfect mixture of pain and sorrow. After the service he had gone to Mrs Stone and bent over her so that his immense height seemed to form a protective comforting shield. His whole body language screamed out how much he cared. The photographers waiting in the churchyard leapt into action. They were mostly there because Jennifer Stone was Marcus Piddell's ex. In the end she was better known for that than for anything, and how she would have hated it, Todd thought. The cameras flashed. High-profile tycoon and government minister comforts the mother of his tragic former wife. That would be tomorrow's newspaper picture.

'Nice performance, Mark,' said Todd to himself cynically.

Outside the church, a figure stood apart from the rest of the mourners, alone and very still over by the lychgate, half concealed by rhododendron bushes. Was it? Todd was almost sure, yes, it was Johnny Cooke.

A touch uncertainly, the detective inspector walked over to him. Johnny looked as if he was about to turn away, but he didn't. It was Todd who had kept him informed about everything concerning Bill Turpin, Todd who had so far been able to say so little to Johnny, but whose whole being had expressed concern and maybe even regret. Todd whose father had been the only one who seemed to care even a jot about the real truth all those years ago.

The two men nodded a somewhat awkward greeting.

'I didn't even know you knew her,' said the policeman.

'She came to see me.'

Had she indeed? Todd studied Johnny carefully.

'And?' he said.

'And nothing much. She said she wanted to discover the truth . . . there's not a lot of it about.'

Todd looked down at his feet. Johnny continued, unwittingly using almost the same words as his mother at the funeral of Jennifer's father.

'I just wanted to pay my respects . . .'

Todd met the other man's steady gaze. 'Look, I'm sure she did discover something, something important. If you know anything that could help, I mean, do you have any idea what she was after?'

Johnny shrugged and shook his head, he didn't even seem interested.

'I have a feeling it could be something that might clear your name, once and for all,' encouraged Todd.

Johnny laughed. It was a hollow sound.

'Do you know anything that can give me back half a lifetime?' he asked. And then he did turn away.

Todd watched him stride down the lane outside the church, and like Jennifer Stone such a short time ago he was struck by his dignity. He knew he could never help Johnny Cooke, and Jennifer, always so full of the joys of living, was dead. But he owed them a debt, he felt, and his father too, and he wasn't going to stop until he had done his best to settle that debt.

353

* * *

Marcus got his driver to take him straight to his London apartment. He had indeed done all that he should do, but he was genuinely severely shaken. He had loved Jennifer after all, hadn't he? In as much as he could ever love anyone, yes he had. Now what was he going to do? He felt alone and desperate.

As he walked through the front door, the phone was ringing, and when he picked it up the scrambler light blinked. The computerised scrambling mechanism could be operated by an incoming caller using the correct codes, as well as by the recipient of a call. The Friends took no chances.

An educated voice introduced itself as John Fitzsimmon. Marcus was astonished. John Fitzsimmon was a senior civil servant, well known throughout Whitehall. He was powerful and much respected, a pillar of the establishment, a man with a flawless reputation, tipped to be the next head of the civil service.

'Good evening,' said the caller, his cut-glass public school voice echoing from the receiver. 'I understand we are members of the same club.'

'I am a member of a lot of clubs,' replied Marcus.

'Waste of time,' said John Fitzsimmon. 'There is only one that matters.'

He then suggested that they go for a walk together in St James's Park and have a chat. They should meet at the bandstand. Surprised but curious and, oddly, already heartened, Marcus had quickly agreed.

He and John Fitzsimmon had never met, but each recognised the other.

'Understand you've had a spot of bother, old boy,' said Fitzsimmon by way of greeting. He held out his hand. Marcus took it. The Masons' handshake –

well, that was no great surprise. Fitzsimmon's public-school drawl held all the confidence of generations of power and wealth, but family history and the right education were not quite enough to guarantee either of those any more.

'Not to worry,' continued the drawling voice. 'Not your fault. These things happen. Got to be sorted out, nobody likes it. But we can't let anything interfere with the main game plan, can we?

'Been sent by some mutual Friends . . .' There was an almost imperceptible pause, and the lightest of emphasis on the word Friends. '. . . to give you a helping hand, old boy.'

Fitzsimmon seemed to know everything – he made that abundantly clear – which Marcus at first found disconcerting. But this man referred to the murder of six people and the maiming of several others as if to the correction of an accounting error. He treated it like a routine business operation. And maybe, thought Marcus, to these people he was mixing with that was exactly what it was. So much that happened involving so many people at the top in the world was undoubtedly hidden-agenda stuff. He knew that. He had told Jennifer that. Things were rarely as they seemed. To the men and women who were really in charge of the world's politics and finances, a few deaths in a suburb of London would be just a hiccup along the way to completing whatever plans were in progress. He began to feel not quite so alone.

In a straightforward businesslike manner, Fitzsimmon explained to him more than ever before how The Friends worked in protecting and cultivating their own. There were casualties along the way, only to be expected, couldn't be helped.

'You're the important one. After all, you're going to be Prime Minister, eh old boy? eh? Can't let you down, can we?'

From now on, John Fitzsimmon would be at his right hand.

'And we'll find you one of ours to be your PPS when you're the PM eh, old boy? Eh?'

Marcus was in something of a daze. But when he returned to his Chelsea apartment he began to feel much better. He had started to convince himself that John Fitzsimmon was right. He was too important to be put at risk. Sacrifices had to be made, and the death of Jennifer Stone was a sacrifice. A terrible sacrifice, but a necessary one.

Over the next week he met Fitzsimmon every day. They dined together, drank together, and talked endlessly. At last Marcus had someone who seemed to know everything, in whom he could confide. Fitzsimmon had that air of infallibility about him exuded only by his kind, and Marcus found it infectious. The Whitehall wizard had instructions to give Marcus all the help and support he needed, to rebuild him, to steer him forwards, and to do everything he could to keep Marcus happy.

John Fitzsimmon had also been given detailed instructions about exactly what kept Marcus happy.

On the seventh day after Jennifer's funeral, Fitzsimmon took Marcus to a safe house in Ealing.

'I have a surprise for you, present from The Friends,' he said.

In an upstairs room furnished with a big double bed and a settee, two Oriental girls stood nervously by the window. They were twins and they were wearing matching silk kimonos. They were breathtakingly pretty.

'There you are, old boy, they should take your mind off things,' drawled Fitzsimmon.

Marcus wasn't sure that he was quite ready yet. It was this that had got him into the mess he was in, after all.

'I . . . I'm not sure I can,' he heard himself stammer.

'Oh, from what I've heard you'll manage,' said Fitzsimmon unconcernedly. 'They're yours for the night, very young – the way you like 'em, eh old boy? – but they know what to do, I'm told. Take care, won't you?'

And he left Marcus to it.

Together the two girls undressed him. He did not protest or help, moving only enough to make it possible for them to remove his clothes. When he was standing naked, they slipped off their kimonos. Underneath, both were wearing silk teddies trimmed with lace. Their bodies were exquisite, pale and perfect in every detail.

Still Marcus did not have an erection. He stood limp and unsure of himself before them. Then first one and then the other of the two girls knelt before him and began to play with him and take him in her small soft mouth. It was like transmitting an electric current to a dormant robot. Marcus could feel his appetites being returned to him by tongue and touch. His sexuality was so much his driving force that it frequently overwhelmed him without his knowledge, sometimes almost against his will. He had reason to hate this lack of control – he who in every other way was such a controlled man. But his sex drive was a thing apart, and it could, as Jennifer Stone had found out – turn him into a monster.

Soon he was big and hard and all he could think about was sex. Everything else was dismissed from his mind and body by the urgency of his desires, which had indeed been the intention. He let rip. He went for it. Just like always.

In the next room, two men were watching Marcus Piddell's sexual antics through a two-way mirror. They had been told he could do almost anything he liked, that it didn't matter if he hurt the girls, that he probably would hurt them, but there was to be no permanent damage. Not again.

The fat man turned away in disgust. He had a daughter about the age of the twins in the other room, and if any man did to her what that bastard was doing to those two poor kids, he would kill him, he thought.

'What are we now?' he asked in a broad Cockney accent. 'Fucking pimps?'

'We're just doing our job,' said his partner calmly. He was a little weasel of a man who, in better days, had once been a jockey.

'Why have they laid all this on for that bastard anyway?' The fat man was looking through the mirror again.

He felt sick. Not for the first time he wished to God he had never become involved with The Friends. He had landed himself in trouble with the bookies. They had bailed him out . . . in return for certain services. And that was it, no escape after that, sucked in for ever, like it or not. There were a lot of racing people in the same situation.

'Because "that bastard" is going to be Prime Minister one day,' he heard the ex-jockey say.

Marcus had forgotten that anything in the world except his cock existed. He was now in his favourite situation. He had the two girls bent over the sofa and was hammering into them relentlessly from behind. The twins had not been prepared for this, nor for his size. First he plunged into one, holding the other one down with a strong arm, then he would change. Great powerful strokes. He was doing exactly what Jennifer had seen him do all those years before when she had returned unexpectedly to their apartment. The girls were looking in the direction of the two-way mirror, their faces registering pain and fear. Their little bodies were trembling, one of them was crying. Marcus's face showed only the violence of his lust. His eyes were wild. He looked quite mad.

'Gawd help us all,' said the fat man.

Todd Mallett felt angry and frustrated. He had spent the week since Jennifer's funeral going over and over the events that had followed the death of Bill Turpin. His chance meeting with Johnny had somehow made him even more determined to get to the bottom of it all. And his father, still racked with guilt and uncertainty over Johnny's conviction, had begged him to find the truth at last, but Todd could not seem to get near it.

Jennifer had been trying to contact him to tell him something important about the murders of Marjorie Benson and Irene Nichols. He had known the night they had drunk together in the Old Ship that she had suspicions and maybe knowledge she wasn't yet prepared to share. Now it was too late. Whatever she knew about Bill Turpin and Marcus Piddell had died with her.

Todd was convinced that she had been murdered too, quite convinced of it. But if she had been, then her killers were so skilled that they managed to rig a gas explosion that had fooled the greatest explosive experts alive. Todd had asked for more and more investigation. His superiors, the London Fire Brigade, and even British Gas who would have loved nothing more than to have been able to blame foul play, were beginning to be bored with him.

The Richmond Hill Explosion was to go down in history as a terrible accident, like so many other gas explosions when whole buildings had been destroyed. The experts reminded him again of the precedents: Ronan Point, the London tower block which collapsed like a pack of cards after a gas explosion in 1968, killing five people; the explosion in Motta Visconti, Northern Italy, in July 1994, when twenty-seven elderly people died in an old people's home; the Coventry house flattened killing three when the priest who lived there lit his pipe – an IRA bomb had at first been suspected, and it was some days before the truth was uncovered; and, most spectacular of all, the explosion of an underground gas main in America's New Jersey in August 1994, which vaporised eight blocks of flats leaving a one hundred and fifty-foot crater and killing more than fifty. These things happened, and this latest explosion was yet another accidental tragedy. Todd must accept that.

He didn't – but there seemed to be nothing he could do about it.

He had followed every possible lead, painstakingly checking back over old material, looking into those fine-art burglaries again, following all the other rumours about Bill Turpin, even the off-the-wall stuff, like the arms dealing out of Bristol. He just came to the same dead ends. Nobody had ever got anywhere with that burglary network after the war, that had been some well organised operation. There was certainly nothing concrete to link anything criminal with Bill Turpin – apart from the murder of poor Irene Nichols. Much of the evidence he had compiled even now against Bill was purely circumstantial, like the horde of crime cuttings the old man had collected, and the discovery of the extent of Bill's wealth and his dealings on the stock market and the Swiss bank accounts. But how did a man like Bill Turpin get into all that kind of stuff, and what was he doing with some of the most elaborate and sophisticated computer equipment in existence?

Todd had taken to staying at the Pelham Bay operation centre – where investigations into the deaths of Irene Nichols and Marjorie Benson were continuing, although probably not for much longer – virtually all day and all night, desperately trying to make sense of it all. His gut instinct told him that the Marjorie Benson murder must be a vital part of the riddle. He meticulously studied the court records, the statements taken, and even dug out Marjorie's few pathetic personal effects. He had found them still stashed away in an almost forgotten corner of the Devon and Exeter Constabulary stores – after all, nobody had claimed them: there was, it appeared, no one to do so.

And so Todd sat at the desk in his temporary office, staring at piles of neatly folded clothes, a few books, a bunch of keys, so little, all so uninspiring.

He touched things, picked objects up, as if hoping for inspiration. There were four keys. One he knew had been the key of Marjorie's room at the golf club. There was a car key to a Ford of some kind – the records showed that attempts to trace it had proved futile, and there were two small suitcase keys. Nothing. Bugger all.

Todd was still fingering the keys, tossing the bunch up and down in his hand, when his sergeant rushed into the room.

'Still here?' asked Todd without a deal of interest. 'Thought you left ages ago.'

'Yeah – I've been down the road to the sports centre – got a game of squash booked. I left the key to my locker here somewhere . . .'

The man had started to rummage in his desk. Todd continued to throw Marjorie Benson's keys monotonously up and down.

'Shit,' he said suddenly. With surprising speed for a big man, he lurched to his feet and half dragged the bemused sergeant out of the door with him.

'Never mind your blessed squash – come with me!' he ordered.

And he instructed the man to drive as fast as he could to the Royal Western Golf Club in Pelham Bay.

The lockers at the RWG were a law unto themselves.

It seemed there was only one man who knew anything at all about the system, such as it was, and he had been working there for a million years. Todd's sergeant was despatched to bring him to the Club at once.

The elderly man who arrived looked as if he should

have been retired years ago. But Bert Cousins was part of the institution at the Royal Western. He peered short-sightedly at the two little keys Todd handed to him, and pointed to the slightly larger one.

'Oh yes, that was one of ours,' he said. Bingo, thought Todd. He looked around the ranks of lockers. Could one possibly have remained locked and abandoned for all this time? From the disorganised state of the place it seemed just possible . . .

'What number, can you tell me?' Todd asked.

Bert shook his head. 'No way of telling. Long time ago though – we had a clear out a while back. Sorted out a lot of forgotten stuff, changed the locks and all, we did, got different keys now.'

Todd felt his heart sink.

'What happened to the old stuff you found in the abandoned lockers?' he asked desperately.

'You should have seen it,' muttered Bert. 'Rotting sports gear mostly, 'ad to chuck that.'

Damn, thought Todd. But Bert was still talking.

'Anything that looked as if anybody might claim it we put in the storeroom.'

Todd stood very still. 'Is it still there?'

'I should imagine so,' replied the old man. ''Aven't looked for donkey's years meself.'

Todd and his sergeant took the storeroom apart. Todd didn't even know what he was looking for, but he was quietly certain that if he found it he would recognise it.

There were a number of ancient sports bags in varying degrees of decay. The fourth one Todd opened contained reams of paper, most of it covered with what seemed to be poetry, meticulously handwritten. There were also some letters. At the bottom of the bag was a sealed envelope. It contained a Canadian passport in the name of Claire Pearson. The photograph was of a young woman, probably in her early thirties.

Todd found that his hands were trembling.

'You must have been here with Marjorie Benson, do you remember her?' he asked Bert.

The old man nodded.

'Can you remember what she looked like?'

Bert nodded again. 'Not likely to forget after what happened to that poor maid.'

Todd showed him the picture in the passport. 'Is that her?' he asked.

'Could be,' mused Bert. ''Er hair's the wrong colour, but I reckon that's 'er right enough. Yep, I'm sure of it.'

Todd was on his way back to his office before the old man had finished speaking.

It was an extraordinary night. Todd spent much of it communicating with the Canadian authorities by fax, phone and computer link. He and his sergeant sorted through and read the poems and the letters.

'This is incredible, you wouldn't think anybody would put stuff like this in a tatty old locker,' said the sergeant at one point.

'Presumably she thought it was a safe hiding place – and as it's taken us twenty-five years to find it, she was probably right,' replied Todd wryly.

By dawn a fairly clear picture had emerged. Marjorie Benson was really Claire Pearson, all right.

Several of the letters were from Claire Pearson's mother, badly spelt, in places difficult to follow, painstakingly handprinted on lined paper torn from an exercise book. The one which shook Todd and his sergeant rigid was at the bottom of the pile.

'It's your 21st birthday, my dear Claire, and I want you to know the whole truth about your past, about who you are,' it began.

'I should've told you a long time ago, I couldn't find the words to your face . . .'

The story the woman told was a horrifying one: it was like something from the darker side of Dickens. She had been a housemaid to Lord Lynmouth. And when Todd checked his records, he found that the housemaid who had claimed Bill Turpin had killed Lynmouth was a woman named Audrey Pearson.

Audrey had indeed always been slow and of below-average intelligence, always used by others. When she was just a teenager she became pregnant by Lynmouth, who was already an old man. An old man who should have behaved better.

Her mother sent Audrey away to have the baby.

'That's what they did in them days. Me mam went to school with Bill Turpin's missus. When I began to show, they sent me to stay with the Turpins. They took me at night and I wasn't allowed out of the cottage, because of the shame. When the baby was born they took the little mite away – I never even knew if it was a boy or a girl . . .'

'They didn't tell His Lordship until it was all over, and he was proper angry. He was never a cruel man. Still didn't leave me alone, though, and I fell pregnant again – but I was allowed to keep you when you were born just at the start of the war. It was easy then, you see, they called me Mrs Pearson, said I'd wed a soldier killed in action . . .

'So you had a proper name, respectable like.'

The letter went on to explain that the Earl of Lynmouth's wife had been unable to give him children, and the Earl doted on his illegitimate daughter. But appearances had to be kept up at all costs. The wife accepted the situation as long as the truth was never told. Audrey's parents were the fourth generation of their family to be in service to the Lynmouths. It was feudal. They did what they were told.

'Then came the night when I saw His Lordship killed and I saw the man who did it and I knew him to be Bill Turpin. I was that frightened – I knew he did me wrong, but His Lordship was the only person ever to show me kindness. I wanted them to catch the man who killed him so I told the police – but they didn't believe I even knew Bill Turpin and I couldn't tell them how I did. I couldn't tell them that . . .'

The Earl's widow did not trust Audrey to keep quiet, and feared the whole scandal might break. She had a distant relative, a farmer in Canada who needed help on his land. Audrey and little Claire, then six years old, were shipped out to Canada. The old woman and Audrey's parents died soon afterwards.

'I wanted you to know the blood you have in your veins,' wrote Claire Pearson's mother. 'Your father wasn't some unknown soldier, he was an Earl.

'He'd always have looked after us, he would never have let the bad things happen. If he hadn't been killed it would all have been different . . .'

After Todd and his sergeant had both finished reading the letter, there was a moment of total silence in the ops room, shattered only by the shrill ringing

of the fax phone. It was the first response from
Canada to Todd's inquiries concerning Audrey and
Claire Pearson.

The farmer Audrey Pearson had been sent to work
for had married her, but there were no further
children. Both of them were now dead. The farmer,
Jethro March, had been stabbed to death.

And Claire Pearson had been convicted of his
manslaughter.

Todd could not believe what he was reading.

Immediately he reached for the phone and called
Canada. Eventually he tracked down the by then
retired detective inspector who had worked on the
case.

'One of the saddest cases I ever had,' said the
Canadian DI. 'He was a vicious bastard, was Jethro
March.

'He used that poor woman he married like a slave,
worked her half to death and knocked her about
when he felt like it. But the daughter he put on a
pedestal. She had a good education, went to college,
the lot.

'She'd flown the nest too, off doing a degree in
Toronto. Then when she was twenty-one, suddenly,
she went home to the farm, maybe because she
wanted to protect her mother. Not long afterwards
she stuck old Jethro in the gut with a bread knife.
And once she'd started she couldn't stop. Carved
him to pieces, she did.

'She might have got away with it altogether but for
that – he'd been laying into her mother again and
young Claire couldn't take it any more. As it was she
served four years – and a lot of people thought
she shouldn't have done a day.

'The mother, who'd always been slow-witted, was damn near a vegetable at the end – Jethro'd knocked her about so bad. She died not long after Claire was released and then the girl just disappeared. She was half off her head by then, folk said . . .'

Todd was stunned.

He shuffled through the poems again. Yes. Here it was, the one he was looking for.

> You have hidden in the night
> Thinking you are out of sight
> But I shall find you.
>
> She was such a gentle soul
> And life took a wicked toll
> Because of you.
>
> Her hopes destroyed
> My future crushed
> Because of you.
>
> You have only death to give
> And so you don't deserve to live.

Straightforward little number, although not much of a peom, Todd thought. He didn't know a lot about poetry, but he suspected some of Claire Pearson's poems were quite good. Others like this one were just blurted out emotion in rhyme. The message certainly seemed clear enough, though.

Marjorie Benson, or Claire Pearson, her mind disturbed by her horrific experiences, blamed Bill Turpin for the plight which befell her and her mother. If he had not killed Lord Lynmouth, everything would have been all right – that was what her mother had believed. And Bill Turpin was in fact the only one left to blame.

Marjorie Benson had come to Pelham Bay to get revenge, with some idea that she was going to kill Bill Turpin, Todd was sure of it. Trouble was, she might have been seriously unhinged, but she wasn't a cold-blooded murderess. By nature, by all accounts, she was a gentle romantic – a gentle romantic who had stabbed a man to death . . .

So what had happened that night twenty-five years ago on the sand dunes? Todd suspected that they had all been looking at it the wrong way around. Nobody set out to kill Marjorie. More likely she had simply seen Bill Turpin walking over the dunes after Johnny Cooke had left her and had been unable to contain herself any longer. She confronted him, told him what she knew about him, maybe threatened him, the silly bitch.

And Bill Turpin was a cold-blooded killer. He knew exactly what to do. He knew how to get rid of a problem like Marjorie Benson, and was well capable of framing an innocent man – poor muddled Johnny had been a gift on a plate.

What a story! Todd shook his head in disbelief. He felt a kind of elation. For several hours he had almost forgotten his own personal involvement. He was just a policeman unravelling a mystery, making discoveries which had lain dormant for a quarter of a century – and that was a very exciting thing to do.

Only gradually did he begin to drift back towards the present. So his father had been right all these years, and learning that was going to destroy him. Johnny Cooke had been wrongly convicted. Todd was quite sure of it. Poor bastard . . .

Todd Mallett's sudden sense of euphoria evaporated as swiftly as it had arrived. The more he thought about things, the worse they seemed.

He might have solved one half of the mystery, but what about the rest of it? What about little Irene Nichols? What about Marcus Piddell?

Damn it, thought Todd. None of the night's revelations had helped with any of that. In his mind, Bill Turpin was sown up as the murderer of Marjorie Benson – but he was sure so much more lay behind it all. He was even more convinced than ever that Jennifer Stone had known that it did – and that is why she had died.

He had learned nothing to shed any new light on Jennifer's death. And he had learned nothing to link Marcus with any of it. In fact just the opposite.

He clenched both his fists in exasperation and smashed them down on his desk.

His sergeant, who had fallen asleep exhausted in his chair, jerked awake.

'What's up guv?' he asked groggily.

'The real villains have got away with it yet again – that's what's up,' said Todd Mallett.

Twenty Three

Dominic McDonald was a broken man. He decided not to go home after Jennifer's funeral. He couldn't face the empty Barnes house. Instead he went to stay with his sister, a painter who lived alone in a cottage in the Lake District. For a week he walked and wept alone, striding endlessly over the hills, and at night his sister cooked him big nourishing vegetarian meals. She didn't eat meat and didn't think her guests should either. Dominic didn't mind, he probably didn't even notice. He didn't notice either how carefully she gave him space. She barely spoke to him unless he spoke to her first. He didn't really want to talk and she sensed that. All day he walked. At first she feared the repetition of the Yorkshire Moors episode, but Dominic had moved on from the early craziness of his shock. He was not self-destructive any more. He just needed time and space to work out if he could rebuild his life, if he even wanted to.

At the end of the week he felt surprisingly healed. He would never get over the death of the wife and child he adored. It would be a very long time indeed before he would again lead a normal life – if that ever happened. He felt only half a man – because his relationship with Anna had been a complete one, which had made them both whole – but he knew

371

he could function, and he decided that was what he must do, start functioning again.

And so he set off for London on the very day that The Friends provided the Oriental twins for Marcus, and that Todd Mallett sat glumly at his desk still trying in vain to read the mind of a dead woman.

Dominic forced himself to shut out the tide of grief which swept over him as soon as he stepped into the empty Barnes house. Quiet as the grave, he thought to himself. He shuddered.

Resolutely, he unpacked his small bag and went into the kitchen and cooked himself some supper. He made toast and scrambled egg. He didn't really want the meal, but he needed to start a routine. After he had eaten, he did what he had so often done when Anna and Pandora were alive. He went to his study and switched on his computers. It was the first time had even been in the room since the dreadful night when they had both been killed. The gentle hum of the machines was familiar. In one way that was comforting, and in another it hurt even more. The last time he had sat there, contentedly working, everything in the room had been more or less the same. But the familiar little world, the cocoon of private love in which he had existed, had now been shattered for ever.

He checked the big desk-top computer, routine, something he always did. This was the IBM machine he kept permanently attached to his modem, able to receive messages automatically from other computers. Several documents had been sent to him. That was not surprising. He cast an eye down the files, nothing he could be bothered with. Then he stopped in his tracks.

Jennifer Stone had sent him a computer message. He checked the date and time. May 28th at three minutes past midnight. A file had been fed from her computer to his around five hours before her death. His brain was starting to work again now – for the first time since it all happened. Before going to bed that dreadful night she had decided to send him a document. Why? And what was it?

He quickly checked its length. 44K. That was nearly 7000 words. Quite a document.

In trepidation he called it up and began to read.

It was a detailed account of the last five days of Jennifer Stone's life. And it included the transcript of a tape.

ELLEN FELDMAN

Too Close for Comfort

Isobel is a stylish, streetwise New Yorker. Smart and sophisticated, she knows how to take care of herself.

Or did, until she decided to marry Pete, her psychiatrist lover, and move into his East side apartment where their hall is the waiting-room for his patients.

Suddenly it all gets a little too close for comfort. She starts receiving anonymous telephone calls and crazed threatening letters from one of Pete's female patients. A patient who seems to be on far more intimate terms with him than Isobel herself . . .

As disturbing as *Fatal Attraction*, *Too Close for Comfort* is a seat-gripping psychological thriller that will have you wondering about every person you thought you knew.

THOMAS HARRIS

The Silence of the Lambs

THE MOST FRIGHTENING BOOK YOU'LL EVER READ

There's a killer on the loose who knows that beauty is only skin deep, and a trainee investigator who's trying to save her own hide.

The only man that can help is locked in an asylum. But he's willing to put a brave face on – if it will help him escape.

'Thrillers don't come any better than this . . . razor sharp entertainment, beautifully constructed and brilliantly written. It takes us to places in the mind where few writers have the talent or sheer nerve to venture'

Clive Barker

'The best book I've read for a very long time . . . subtle, horrific and splendid'

Roald Dahl

LIONEL DAVIDSON

Kolymsky Heights

Kolymsky Heights. A Siberian permafrost hell lost
in endless night, the perfect setting for an
underground Russian research station. One so
secret it doesn't officially exist. Once there,
scientists cannot leave. But someone has got a
message out to the West – a message summoning
the only man alive capable of achieving the
impossible.

'A fabulous thriller . . . a red-hot adventure with a
stunningly different hero'
Today

'Spectacular . . . a breathless story of fear and
courage'
Daily Telegraph

'A tremendous thriller . . . warmth, love, heart-
stopping action'
Observer

'A sustained cliffhanger – brilliantly imagined,
thrilling, painfully plausible'
Literary Review

'The book is a triumph'
Sunday Times

A Selected List of Thrillers available from Mandarin

While every effort is made to keep prices low, it is sometimes necessary to increase prices at short notice. Mandarin Paperbacks reserves the right to show new retail prices on covers which may differ from those previously advertised in the text or elsewhere.

The prices shown below were correct at the time of going to press.

ALL MANDARIN BOOKS ARE AVAILABLE THROUGH MAIL ORDER OR FROM YOUR LOCAL BOOKSHOP AND NEWSAGENT.

PLEASE SEND CHEQUE/EUROCHEQUE/POSTAL ORDER (STERLING ONLY) ACCESS, VISA, DINERS CARD, SWITCH, AMEX OR MASTERCARD.

EXPIRY DATE .... SIGNATURE ....

PLEASE ALLOW 75 PENCE PER BOOK FOR POST AND PACKING U.K.

OVERSEAS CUSTOMERS PLEASE ALLOW £1.00 PER COPY FOR POST AND PACKING.

ALL ORDERS TO:

MANDARIN BOOKS, BOOKS BY POST, TBS LIMITED, THE BOOK SERVICE, COLCHESTER ROAD, FRATING GREEN, COLCHESTER, ESSEX CO7 7DW.

NAME ....

ADDRESS ....

....

Please allow 28 days for delivery. Please tick box if you do not wish to receive any additional information ☐

Prices and availability subject to change without notice.